D1606289

The Forerunners

By Reed M Holmes, Ph,D.

The courageous story of 156 Americans led from Jonesport, Maine, to Jaffa in 1866 by charismatic G.J. Adams to plant the seeds of modern Israel.

Introduction by Dr. Carney Gavin

Epilog 2003: A Dream in the Making
By Jean L.Holmes, M.A.

Reed and Jean Holmes
Auerbach Street 10, Tel Aviv-Yafo 68119 Israel / POB 680, Pepperell, MA 01463 USA
jeanreed2@springmail.com
globalpeacerainbow.com

Library of Congress Cataloging in Publication Data

Holmes, Reed M.
The forerunners.

1. Adams, G. J. (George Jones), 1813-1880.
2. Mormons—United States—Biography. 3. Church of the Messiah—History. 4. Palestine Emigration Association—History. I. Title.
BX8695.A3H64 289.3'3 [B] 81-2673
ISBN 0-8309-0315-1 AACR2

First paperback edition 1981
Second edition Israel, 2003

CONTENTS

FOREWORD

I love Maine, and especially this axehead-shaped peninsula, bordered on the west by the inlet of Indian River and on the east by Chandler Bay. Jonesport runs the length of the sharpened edge. A flurry of large and small islands fans out from the blade of the axe like so many chips flung into the sea. The nearest, just across Moosabec Reach, is Beal's Island, named for Manwarren Beal, the forerunner of today's multitude of Beals, Alleys, and Nortons.

From the vantage of the flag pole on Dobbins Knob I can see Jonesport stretch out eastward along the Reach. I can look past Norton and East Sheep Islands to Western Bay out back of Beals. In imagination, I can see a three-masted bark, with sailors casting off lines at the old steamboat wharf. The date is August 11, 1866. It is 10:30 a.m. Brand new, with not a barnacle on her, the *Nellie Chapin* is putting out to sea. The tug boat, *Delta*, strains away under a controlled head of steam a few yards forward and to port. Three shouts from the combined voices of 157 passengers are echoed by three more from the chorus of several hundred voices along the wharf and the shore. The Palestine Emigration Society is on its way to Jaffa, and G. J. Adams is soon to secure a reputation as prophet—or charlatan.

George Jones Adams led that colony to ruin—or glory, whichever it may prove eventually to be, and I've come back to Maine to satisfy a curiosity which was stimulated more than thirty-five years ago and won't be quieted. In fact, it has grown considerably as I have prowled around Jaffa and Jerusalem off and on during the last few years. So, here I am on Dobbins Knob remembering a day in early spring, 1943. I was a young man and had a date with a real lady, age 88. Her name was Theresa (that's pronounced Thressa) Rogers Kelley. She was twelve when the associates pulled away from that wharf on the *Nellie Chapin* and she was saying good-bye forever. . .or so she thought. It was no excursion or pilgrimage. It was an emigration. It was for keeps.

She spun a story that day which I've learned since has inspired many feature writers to exercise their powers of expansive narration, only to fill untold column inches with a few grains of fact embellished into fable. Writers who came close to telling it the way it was were Peter Amann and Clarence Day. Both of them did their research well. They both came close, but something was missing. I think it has to do with motivation.

The story of G. J. Adams and the Jaffa Colony has occasioned a lot of wry comment, with the mood being set by none other than Mark Twain: "The colony was a complete fiasco." With that offhand dismissal, he prompted the debunking air of nearly every report made of the astonishing venture. The mood has been sustained by the recollections of one who experienced the Jaffa Colony as a lad, less than ten years of age. Anger increased through years of recounting the story until some of the facts changed to fiction, and much that was fiction became undeniable fact. The smoke-screening of the truth by so many has made it difficult for three generations to see anything redeeming about the ill-fated journey of their forebears to assist in the return of the Jews.

The other side of the story was hinted at by Ralph Leighton-Floyd of Independence, Missouri, who said recently, "There probably was no one more excited than my father when the modern State of Israel was founded in May 1948. This had been the dream of his forefathers, and he had a share in it. In his opinion the Jaffa Colony wasn't a failure. He had seen the Jews return, first by tens, then by hundreds and then thousands. Just as God had promised they were gathered from their long dispersement to their homeland."

Ralph's grandmother was Mary Jane Clark—later Leighton and then Floyd—good friend of my own grandmother, and a child of five when she went with her family from Jonesport to Jaffa. Through a family of my own relatives, the Wentworths who also shared the venture, I have a vested interest in the story. It has spurred research along a faintly marked path in Maine, Massachusetts, Washington, D.C., Israel, Salt Lake City, Independence, Missouri, and eventually to Nauvoo, Illinois.

Charles Forbush, editor of the Machias (Maine) *Republican* back in 1866, voiced a significant clue: "It is impossible to understand this venture without knowing something about the way these people believe." Theresa Kelley and Clarence Day, baffled, said, "What drove G. J. Adams on is a mystery locked in his own mind." If we can find the answer to that mystery I think we will also understand why 156 men, women, and children cast their lot with Adams' great obsession. And, if my surmise is right, the offspring of those who went need no longer carry the humiliation of their ancestors having been duped by a charlatan.

We must, then, visit the people who lived and laughed, loved and cried through adventure and privation as they followed G. J. Adams from Jonesport to Jaffa to plant a dream.

Peace Valley Farm
Peppeell, Massachusetts

Jonesport Center, Me. Theresa (Thressa) Rogers Kelley in front of her home with friends

INTRODUCTION

In some ways this is the strangest story I know.

As a Yankee yarn, *The Forerunners* spins a seldom-told tale of stalwart venturing despite human frailties during those decades when regions more exotic than the Palestinian coast were traversed by New England vessels laden with whale oil, rum, pepper, porcelain—and far grimmer cargoes. Yet among all the stirring sagas of the last century's seas, the Nellie Chapin brought along with her 157 passengers from the Gulf of Maine that most precious—or most sinister—of cargoes: dreams of destiny. . . .

Reed Holmes has told this story well.

Discoveries from a worldwide quest for clues are shared with fairness, sympathy, and—whenever possible—in the words of those actually caught up in what Mark Twain had simplistically dismissed as "a complete fiasco." Sailors, farmers' wives, and officials, believers, skeptics, and visionaries recount: the predictions and hopes which inspired this mystical exodus as well as the "downeast" practicality which prepared prefabricated houses, pine shutters, and *diligences* for life across the sea; adversity encountered among dubious diplomats as well as warm hospitality received from Arab farmers among the flourishing citrus groves nearby; homesickness growing among the disillusioned faithful and paranoia in their increasingly more frustrated leader; visitors ranging from U.S. Grant to Kaiser Wilhelm; reflections upon the meaning of history and their own part in it among the colony's survivors decades after leaving Jaffa.

Is this story finished?

Some mysteries may remain about the complex personality of the colony's leader and the reasons why things went so wrong. Puzzles surface about dangers of charismatic leadership as our world ponders the lesson of the Jonestown Colony. Deepest of all, the Jonesport colonists' fate raises questions about the fate of the land of their dream and its peoples today . . .

The Forerunners presents us with more than an eccentric nineteenth century "folly." In this all-too-human attempt at divinely inspired settlement, do we discern an unsettlingly eschatological microcosm? The colonists were convinced that they were accomplishing that which had been foreordained to come to pass. Were they wrong?

Other better known and more ambitious efforts to settle in Palestine have been carefully studied. Unlike the feudal orderliness of the Barons d'Outremer or the meticulous agronomy of the Templar Society, the Jonesporters' attempted settlement was brief, small in scale, and unthreatened—or unbuttressed—by external military threats close by or shock waves from empires clashing far away. The simplicity of *The Forerunners*' attempt permits us to observe the tragic process of internal disintegration within an alien organism transplanted to the Promised Land.

Scripture in hand and sacred soil underfoot, many have been led to interpret the Promise of that Land for themselves—in ways which have brought disaster upon themselves. Today such miscalculations promise disaster for all—unless we learn from history.

In this case, history's lessons come as an extraordinary tale of Yankee Saints abroad.

CARNEY GAVIN
CURATOR, HARVARD SEMITIC MUSEUM

Chapter 1

THE GENESIS

With the last flurry of shouts and vigorous waving of hands and kerchiefs, the master of the *Nellie Chapin*, Captain Warren Wass, spoke to the chief mate, "Set your sails, Mr. Hinkley." James Hinkley was an old hand with sailing ships, fully qualified at twenty-eight years to take the captain's wishes and transform them into action. A Jonesporter himself, he knew many of the passengers. Now he called out the command which would change the gently rolling vessel into a thing of beauty before the wind.

The young people on board, savoring the adventure, turned eyes aloft to watch the orderly haste of seamen up the rigging on the weather side so as to be pressed into the ropes instead of away from them. Reuben Hall, seventeen-year-old seaman, went quickly aloft and gave a last wave to the *Delta*. Then, in their places and laid out on the yards, the sailors responded to the mate's orders. True to the custom of the years they sang out the ropes and sails into position. Land swells put the ship into a pitching motion as the great sails filled and backed against the masts with a noise like thunder. The decks yielded their horizontal position to the wind. The sea began beating against the bows. A wake pointed back toward home and gradually became indistinct, merging with a surface no longer glazed by calm. The *Nellie Chapin* plunged her head into the sea as if restless for the voyage. Then, as her stern settled down, her bows rose to show new and still bright copper.

G. J. Adams, the man responsible for the voyage of the *Nellie Chapin* to Palestine, moved from the farewells at the stern to the bow's uncertain future he wanted desperately to make certain. At last, after a quarter century of dreaming, he was on his way to fulfill the most persistent longing of his life.

A strong sense of destiny burgeoned in Adams' heart. Back in 1840 it was more of an intimation than something he could articulate, even with all his eloquence. He felt the winds of change more than most, and the time of his perceptive youth and early adulthood coincided with the youth of a nation that was "in heat" with a fertility of ideas. The United States of America was incubating a new age which would bless and curse the world. At the time of George Adams the earth which had known simple ways for thousands of years was beginning to feel extended fingers probing and gouging. Great engines would shortly crawl on the earth and plow her waters at increasing speed. Frontiers to the West were beckoning. Manifest destiny was thumping in many hearts.

Born in 1811 in New Jersey—a black-haired scion of that Adams family so prominent in the development of the United States—George was an offshoot of an obscure root. In an era of large families he grew in moderate circumstances with a widowed mother. Little is known of his early life, but it is reasonably certain that he was indulged by a doting mother who fed his ego as she struggled to feed his body. He had one sister, Mercy, and another who became a Mrs. Stephens of Newark, New Jersey. In his growing years he grew less than others his age and made up for it by being testy and quick to anger. He was a volatile youth, with sharp dark eyes, who learned early that an adversary could be subdued by words aptly chosen as well as by fists. He stored up from quiet fantasies of battle ways to parry and thrust with a tongue honed by a quick and eager mind enriched by the words of bards and prophets. Through words, others' minds became his and their power of thought and suasion swelled his own. He was a bright star rising, always threatened by eclipse. Insatiable thirsts both equipped and threatened him—thirst for fame . . . appropriate to an Adams; thirst for liquid fire. . . to still the ache of injured pride. He was self-assured, unless his own integrity was under attack; then he became a small child again, fighting with sarcasm and invective.

Soon after he had completed his apprenticeship as a tailor in Boston he responded to the lively evangelism of a Wesleyan revivalist. In no time he was charming the multitudes as a Methodist preacher. He spoke in rented halls and theaters, filling them to capacity.

During the years of his apprenticeship he spent his spare time in dramatics and was an enthusiastic member of an amateur association of players. He preferred the openly dramatic roles which called for full range of vocal expression with appropriate action. Contemplative, subdued roles he disdained.

Dramatics served him well and as a preacher it gave him additional self-confidence, with which he was already well-endowed. His preaching was noted for eloquence. He could hold attention, and his delivery suggested deep commitment.

A theatrical producer named Purdy, planning to use the same public meeting house and checking it out for adequacy of appointments, stayed on one evening to hear Adams preach. He was impressed by the obvious ability the man had to hold listeners in rapt attention, taking them from smiles to tears and back again.

Needing a drawing card and lacking a big name actor for *Richard III*, Purdy approached Adams, assuring him that anyone who could quote scripture by the yard would surely master lines from Shakespeare. Besides, they could be mutually helpful to one another—the play would draw crowds to see their favorite preacher perform on the stage, then appropriate announcements could be made for his preaching. Adams, still with unfulfilled ambitions for the stage, was flattered by Purdy's confidence and said yes.

He was a smashing success. . . at first. The public was curious to see what the preacher could do. He did well until he gave in to the invitation and chiding of the cast to celebrate. They went to a public house and, against his better judgment, George Adams downed a drink. There are those who can hold their liquor without much seeming effect but George Jones Adams was not one of them, especially when he drank on an empty stomach. He not only became inebriated, but also developed an insatiable thirst for alcohol.

He turned abusive, his mind quickening with insults. His sensitivity to derogatory remarks of others spurred him on. At the same time, his facility for memorized lines of scripture or drama was impeded. The next few performances were a disaster. One night the pitiable creature was taken outside, doused with cold water, then brought back in and dosed with salt water—to get him through the play.

At the end of nine nights as Richard III, Adams was fired. His theatrical and preaching careers died simultaneously. One editor called him a "nine-day wonder" which infuriated him. When the two of them met on the street Adams demanded an apology. When it proved slow in coming he gathered all his strength and dropped the editor with a blow to the face. The editor retaliated in print, scathing Adams with ridicule.

Later, quite penitent (having been brought back to sobriety by his wife), Adams returned to tailoring. Slowly his confidence came back as he abided by firm resolutions to avoid what he could not handle.

Then the "Mormons" came. More out of curiosity than anything else he went to hear what they had to say and was spellbound. They spoke of the Christ with great assurance and embellished their preaching with accounts of a God who continued to reveal himself, and of a youthful prophet who had been called by the Almighty to usher in a great and marvelous work which was as new as tomorrow yet old as the ancient prophets of Israel.

From all that Adams had heard and read, the Mormons

had been driven from one state to another because of their wild claims of present day revelation and for upsetting the status quo wherever they went. It seemed unlikely they could have endured the abuse meted to them in Missouri—yet here they were, lively and confident as ever.

Heber Kimball, one of the apostles—now that took some cheek, prophets and apostles!—was speaking on the restoration of the primitive Christianity of the New Testament and how a restored priesthood was not only necessary but already an accomplished fact.

Kimball was in New York on his way from the church's new headquarters in Nauvoo, Illinois, to England to assist in the harvest of souls and to help prepare converts for gathering to America—the land of promise where Zion, the Kingdom of God on earth, was soon to be established.

New enthusiasm stirred in the breast of George Adams. This was a new beginning. He was ready to believe, and eight days after hearing the first Kimball sermon, he was baptized. "Eight days after that," he wrote to a friend later, "I was called by the spirit of prophecy through Elder Kimball, and ordained by Elder P. P. Pratt just previous to the time they sailed for England. Since that time I have tried to preach from three to five times each week, and worked with my own hands to support my wife and son besides."

That was in February, 1840, and within weeks he had "held three public discussions with the great men of this generation, one with the very celebrated Origen Batchelor, which lasted twelve nights. . . in Brooklyn. . . . It took the chairman three hours to sum up the testimony and gave the decision in favor of the fulness of the gospel." George Jones Adams was back in the harness. It was a foregone conclusion that he would be at the church conference in Nauvoo.

"Brother Adams"—the prophet's recognition of him told him that others had carried news of his zealous endeavors—"Welcome to Nauvoo, and to the Conference."

"Thank you, sir, it's an honor to be here, and especially to meet you." Adams was looking into the silver blue eyes of a taller than ordinary man, young in appearance in spite of struggle and abuse. A high forehead shadowed the deepset eyes. An aquiline nose and high cheekbones accompanied expressive lips which could be firmed into a straight line of determination. The eyes were what impressed him most, friendly but piercing. Under their steady gaze, George Adams remembered himself and looked away. A moment ago he was self-assured. Now he was no less certain of his superlative powers of persuasion but he was acutely aware of his mercurial disposition and his weaknesses.

He felt a large hand on his shoulder as Joseph said, "Let's go to meeting."

There wasn't a building in town large enough to hold the crowd. Some day soon, if Joseph had his way, there would be a Temple—larger and grander than the one in Kirtland, adequate for conferences, and for greeting the curious visitors who were already coming to inquire what was going on. For now, a platform had been built at the corner of Water and Main, across from the Homestead where Joseph lived with Emma and the children—the oldest of them the eight-year-old namesake of his father. Little Joseph ran toward them and flung himself at his father who caught him under the shoulders, swinging him up and around in a complete circle. George Adams felt drawn to this dark-haired, bright-eyed child.

"What is coming before the Conference, President Smith?"

"Three of us have recently returned from Washington where we sought redress from the wrongs done our people in Missouri. We found some members of Congress, especially those from Iowa and Illinois, who were both knowledgeable and friendly to our cause. But there were others, some of them members of the Judiciary Committee charged with making recommendations, who dodged the constitutional issue and made it a matter of state's rights. We feel that the Constitution was violated in denying essential rights presumably secured for all by the federal government. Martin Van Buren was insolent—a disgraceful opportunist. We were surprised at his candor, though. He said bluntly, 'Gentlemen, your cause is just, but . . . if I take up for you, I shall lose the vote of Missouri.' It was a shocking display of cynicism and self-aggrandizement. We feel that our people deserve a report, and that they may wish to instruct us in some further action."

Joseph paused, then went on. "That item of business, as you might expect, Brother Adams, is on the minds of everybody here. We're not far removed from tragedy . . . but there is another item we'll consider first. Orson Hyde, one of our most able ministers, will bring a matter before the body which may be more important in the long run than redressing our grievances. The nation of Israel will be reborn—soon. The Jews are going home, and the children of Ephraim will push them toward Jerusalem from the corners of the earth as the Bible says."

When they arrived at the platform Joseph Smith dismissed his son with an affectionate pat on the head and went directly to the stand, leaving George Adams tantalized by a half-spoken prophecy. Surveying the crowd, he was understandably proud that the people had seen him walking with the prophet.

NAUVOO

Joseph Smith was in full vigor in April of 1840. He was thirty-four years of age and six feet three inches tall. He knew the heft and swing of an adze, and he had piled stone upon stone in helping to build the beautiful Temple at Kirtland. Like the ancient Joseph for whom he was named, he combined the visionary and the physical into one. "Spirit and element is the soul of man," he said, and meant it. He was equally at home in prayer and in competing with sturdy youths who tried but couldn't outdo him in pulling driven stakes from hard ground.

As with that ancient son of Jacob, heaven had laid a hand on Joseph. So had the sons of earth. He had known tar and feathers, and the thudding ache of fists and stones. More than once he had been shoved into jail on trumped-up charges. For twenty years he had known the jeers of those who were "righteously" indignant at his pretensions of a speaking nearness to the Creator.

With a heartsickness unmatched, he remembered two years before in late 1838 when he heard the infamous order of Missouri Governor Lilburn W. Boggs: "The Mormons must be treated as enemies, and must be exterminated or driven from the state." One direct result of the extermination order of October 27 was the massacre at Haun's Mill. The tiny Mormon village consisted of Jacob Haun's mill, a blacksmith shop, and a few houses. A dozen Mormon families living nearby, frightened by the order and news of Missouri troops on the move, had set up tents and other temporary shelters in the village. On the evening of the twenty-ninth, four more Mormon immigrant families had arrived in wagons.

Haun had ridden the day before to Far West to get advice from Joseph Smith. He was counseled to get to Far West to save their lives. When he replied that the mob would burn their property, Joseph said, "Better to lose your property than your lives." But Haun insisted that they were willing to defend themselves and that others at the mill opposed retreat.

About eight miles northeast of Haun's Mill, two hundred men were organized for an attack on the Mill. Captain Nehemiah Comstock was in command of the "company." As the column approached the little hamlet, word was passed along, "Shoot at everything wearing breeches, and shoot to kill."

The villagers, quieted by a "truce" with Captain Comstock, had relaxed their vigil. They had agreed to a pact of mutual nonaggression. Children were at play along Shoal Creek, women were caring for domestic duties, and newly-arrived immigrants were enjoying the beauty of a Missouri autumn.

At four o'clock in the afternoon of the thirtieth the air was filled with shouts and shots. The Mormons were taken completely by surprise. The women, screaming to the children in terror, grabbed them and ran across the mill dam, seeking safety in the woods and bushes of a hill.

The men ran for the blacksmith shop. It was a mistake. They were too closely packed in the small log building, and there were large cracks between the logs. Shot after shot from the attackers found its mark inside the building. Then the wide door was thrown open and a voice shouted "Run for your lives." They tried to reach the woods but few made it.

The mob turned immediately to carnage. Coming upon three of the wounded, the "militia" hacked them to death with corn knives. William Reynolds of Livingston County entered the blacksmith shop and found a ten-year-old boy, Sardius Smith, hiding under the bellows. Reynolds drew up his rifle and shot the child. Charlie Merrick, nine years old and also under the bellows, ran for the woods only to be downed by a load of buckshot and a rifle ball. Thomas McBride, seventy-eight years old and a veteran under Washington's command, was shot in the chest as he ran by a ferry keeper named Rodgers who then mangled McBride's body with his corn knife.

All that night the survivors remained alone with their dead and wounded, with no physician to tend to injuries. The next morning the grieving villagers buried the seventeen victims in a large unfinished well not far from the mill.

The day after the massacre Captain Comstock's company returned to Haun's Mill "to help bury the dead" and to inform the survivors that they must obey the governor's order to leave the state or they, too, would be killed.

Joseph and other leaders were seized at nearby Far West under another "flag of truce," hastily court-martialed (although they were not military), and sentenced to be shot. Brigadier General Alexander Doniphan was commanded by Major General Samuel D. Lucas to carry out the order. He answered, "It is cold-blooded murder. I will not obey your order! My brigade shall march for Liberty, Missouri, tomorrow morning at eight o'clock; and if you execute those men, I will hold you responsible before an earthly tribunal, so help me God!" Under this pressure, at the last minute, Lucas countermanded his order.

Joseph's wife, Emma, with two small children in her arms and two more at her side, escaped across the February ice of the Mississippi. Driven from Missouri, she and other refugees were welcomed in Quincy, Illinois, where the editor of *The Argus* expressed the sentiments of many: "We are prompted to ask ourselves if it be really true that we are living in an enlightened, humane and civilized age. . . . We have no language sufficiently strong for the expression of our indignation and shame at . . . Missouri . . . a state of which we had long been proud . . . but now so fallen that we could wish her star stricken out from the bright constellation of the Union."

While being transported under guard to Boone County in a change of venue, Joseph, his brother Hyrum, and three others took advantage of their guards' intoxication and disappeared into the night. They made their way to Quincy and thence, with their families, to Commerce, an Illinois village of a few shanties and log huts on the big bend of the Mississippi between Keokuk and Ft. Madison.

On June 11, 1839, he wrote: "The place was literally a

wilderness...so unhealthful very few could live there; but believing it might become a healthful place by the blessing of heaven to the Saints, and no more eligible place presenting itself, I considered it wisdom to make an attempt to build up a city."

The Mormon movement, initiated by Joseph in 1830, had caught the imagination and zeal of thousands in the United States and Canada, and more recently in England. Others dismissed it, while still others considered it blatant and presumptuous. It may have been the shock of innovation that caused many to be scandalized. Belief in prophecy, revelation, and an open canon of scripture was not new, but it had been some time since such had been considered as contemporary experience. When the Latter Day Saints went further and dismissed the popular notion of original sin, thinking more in terms of original gift, it made wide-ranging changes in Christian thought and practice. They claimed that infant baptism was no longer necessary, atonement had to be reassessed, and even hell had to be modified!

When Joseph Smith proposed a restoration of primitive Christianity he was not far different from the Wesleys and Alexander Campbell, but when he declared he was God's instrument for doing it his pretensions seemed ridiculous to many, especially to the clergy of his day. With the story of the Book of Mormon as an inspired translation of additional scriptures from plates of gold, the heresy seemed complete regardless of the book's message—"believe in God" and "seek Christ."

With other religious movements of early nineteenth century beginnings, the Mormons believed in the imminent return of the Christ. They did not fall into Miller's trap of naming the day and the hour, but they read the portentous events and felt the time was right for the coming of the Messiah. That belief carried an inevitable corollary, the reestablishment of the Jews to Palestine—inevitable corollary because the same biblical prophecies foretelling one also foretold the other. Christadelphians and many within mainline Protestant traditions believed it, too. It was a tradition calling for the reign of right for a thousand years under Christ, with swords beaten into ploughshares, with the lion and the lamb at peace.

Joseph's doctrine required the building of a community, specifically an approximation of the biblical ideal, Zion, the tangible expression of the Kingdom of God, a community fit to receive the Messiah. Joseph's converts were under a divine mandate to establish that ideal city as "an ensign to the nations." Joseph had felt the impulsion of the Spirit and voiced it to his attentive followers: "Seek to bring forth and establish the cause of Zion."

It was a cause calling for the best one could muster, and it had roots in the prophetic traditions of Israel. Joseph was also convinced that he and the church had been called to participate in the process of restoring Israel and to provide a companion community to the Holy City yet to be realized in Jerusalem. His followers called themselves not only Latter Day Saints but also Latter Day Israel—without feeling it to be presumption.

Joseph had outlined a plan for the "New Jerusalem." Intended for Independence, Missouri, the plan was adapted wherever the Saints had settled, only to have their labors aborted by the violence of intolerant neighbors who felt them to be inexcusably peculiar and a threat to the way things were.

Joseph recalled a word from his study of Hebrew and renamed Commerce, Nauvoo (beauty and serenity). That was better. Here, the planned city would be a beautiful place instead of an ugly, sprawling settlement on the shores of the river.

The Nauvoo version of the city plan would be as close to a mile square as could be designed on a bend in the river. It was a simple grid, dividing the land into four-acre blocks subdivided into four square and equal lots of one acre each. There would be space for a garden, a small orchard, and some domestic animals on each lot.

Mormon communities were to be based soundly on agriculture—a garden near at hand for fresh vegetables, with farms outside the city, not unlike the cluster of family houses and barns in many a German community with farmlands reaching out to touch those of the next village. Each family was to hold title to its own land, and from the surplus—voluntarily given—the common weal would be secured. Joseph invited: "Come into the cities to live, and carry on [your] farms out of the cities, according to the order of God."

As other people came and the natural increase expanded the census, either the borders could be enlarged or satellite cities would be established—the "stakes" of Zion. The streets were to be wide thoroughfares for safe traffic, ample for walking, and ready for the future. Main Street would be eighty-seven feet wide, complete with a canal in the middle running the length of it.

Scarcely more than a year away from Boggs, who was still seeking by extradition or kidnapping to "bring him to justice," Joseph looked upon Nauvoo with a measure of satisfaction and hope.

It was into this setting that young George Jones Adams came from New England and, with the spontaneous enthusiasm which was to win him both fame and notoriety, idolized the prophet and shared the dream.

THE REVIVAL OF ISRAEL

In the fall of 1839 when Joseph Smith had dispatched most of his apostles to the fruitful field of the British Isles, he held back Orson Hyde. He had other things in mind for Orson which rose out of his own deep conviction concerning the return of scattered Judah to its homeland. Joseph felt "led" to assign Orson to go to Jerusalem and to dedicate the Holy Land as the gathering place of the dispersed Jews. He was convinced from his study of the Bible that the prophecies of the Old and New Testament would shortly be fulfilled. Indeed, he frequently mentioned a vision in 1823 in which he was told that the time was near at hand. Then, at the dedication of Kirtland Temple on March 27, 1836, he prayed: "We therefore ask thee to have mercy upon the children of Jacob, that Jerusalem, from this hour, may begin to be redeemed, and the yoke of bondage may begin to be broken off from the house of David, and the children of Judah may begin to return to the lands which thou didst give to Abraham, their father. . . ."

Hyde spent the winter months contemplating the mission and by spring was ready to speak to the Conference. No one could do it better. With great persuasion, he recounted the prophecies and added the hopes of the living oracle before them. He spoke of his own vision, received from heaven in anticipation of his mission.

The people, so recently subjected to all manner of abuse, identified with the oft-persecuted Jews who were always strangers in the lands of others yet maintained through the generations their identity as the chosen of God. They, too, had been driven to one land after another. Now both the Jews and the Saints, intent on the same goal of Zion, could look with a trace of hope to the future. Joseph forthwith made the assignment.

On the weekend of October 17-18, 1840, Orson Hyde was in New York for a church conference. His expected traveling companion, John E. Page, had not arrived yet. Page was a good man, though petulant, and sometimes he wasn't where he was expected to be. This was one of those times.

In the meantime Hyde was in George J. Adams' territory.

Though new to the church, Adams was very much in evidence as he preached the truth "beyond the power of successful contradiction." And Hyde preached with his "usual energy, simplicity, and eloquence." Each was impressed by the other. Hyde, restive because of the absence of Page, saw in Adams potential for the English mission and possibly Palestine. Able to draw large crowds, preaching with finesse, and a genius at recall of appropriate scriptures, Adams prompted admiration in Hyde, the "Restoration's polished shaft." It could be a blessing if John Page didn't make it in time.

By the time of the next church conference, held in the Adams house on December 4, Hyde knew what must be done. He waited until January 1, 1841, and then counseled Adams to make ready to sail. They booked passage for two on the packet ship, *United States* due out of New York on February 13, bound for England.

"I commenced to set my house in order," Adams wrote later, "to leave my native land and go to the nations of the earth to assist in declaring the fulness of the gospel of Jesus Christ to a dark and benighted world. . . . I left my friends and the companion of my early days. . . . In company with and under the direction of (Orson Hyde) . . . I arrived (in England) after a short passage of eighteen days."

It was indeed a short passage. They talked their way across the Atlantic, fully expecting to go on to Palestine together. When they had settled in, fully clear of the mainland, and had mastered pitch and roll through the first meal, George and Orson sat together in the small salon. "Orson, I remember the first words you declared at Nauvoo last April. You stood and spoke as if the centuries had waited for that moment: 'The children of Israel wait to go home. Their generations have cried, "Next year, Jerusalem!" and I say to you now, this is the time they shall go home!' My heart leaped! You were speaking, not just out of your heart but out of the Book. It was more than oratory. You were one with the ancient prophets."

"You minister to my soul by sharing my dream," replied Orson. "My dream, indeed. It is the dream of the chosen people of God for centuries, and it is now time for that dream to be fulfilled."

"I sense your certainty and feel right about it, Orson, but what makes you so sure that the time has come?"

"Because the Almighty is beginning to stir the pot!" Orson laughed.

"What do you mean?"

"The ancient prophecies are coming true, you've said so yourself in a dozen sermons that I've heard since arriving in New York."

"That's true, Orson, but you have a grasp of this I don't yet possess, and you sense an urgency about the Jews which I haven't felt until now."

"Well, George, you know that the Lord Jesus himself gave prophetic testimony that in the last days—our days, George—heaven shall move upon the nations and especially upon the children of Israel to gather them, his elect, from the four quarters of the earth."

"Indeed he did."

"And Isaiah said: ...the ransomed of the Lord shall return, and come to Zion with songs and everlasting joy upon their heads; they shall obtain joy and gladness, and sorrow and sighing shall flee away.'"

"They could use a bit of joy. No one has suffered more," remarked Adams.

"The one that clinches the issue for me is the testimony of Ezekiel as contained in his thirty-sixth chapter. In it he prophesies concerning the barrenness of the land, and about gathering the people into their own land. It's unfair to brief it. Let's read it. Wait here while I fetch my Bible."

As he walked rather awkwardly on a deck that wouldn't

hold still, Orson thought about his strange, complex traveling partner who was both lovable and a "pain in the neck." More than any other, G. J. Adams seemed to feel along with him and yet he was not a warm companion—too much his own man, both sure and unsure of himself.

It was not far from salon to stateroom and back again on the small packet. Orson returned very soon. The Bible he carried showed signs of wear and fit his hand as he turned to familiar words. "Here it is—and this is the heart of it:

> Ye mountains of Israel, hear the word of the Lord God. . . .
>
> Ye shall shoot forth your branches, and yield your fruit to my people of Israel. . . ye shall be tilled and sown;
>
> And I will multiply men upon you, all the house of Israel; even all of it; and the cities shall be inhabited, and the wastes shall be builded. . . I will cause men to walk upon you, even my people Israel; and they shall possess thee, and thou shalt be their inheritance, and thou shalt no more henceforth bereave them of men. . .
>
> Therefore say unto the house of Israel. . . I will take you from among the heathen, and gather you out of all countries, and will bring you into your own land. . . and ye shall dwell in the land that I gave to your fathers; and ye shall be my people, and I will be your God. . .
>
> And the desolate land shall be tilled, whereas it lay desolate in the sight of all that passed by.
>
> And they shall say, This land that was desolate is become like the garden of Eden; and the waste and desolate and ruined cities are become fenced, and are inhabited. . . I the Lord have spoken it, and I will do it.

"He will, too—and soon!" added Orson.

George was visibly moved by the prophecy and did not speak immediately. As Orson had read it was as if he shared the spirit and confident hope of the one who had written the words.

"You said soon. Why now?"

"I feel it in my bones, in my head, and in my heart. I can give you a rationale but the real testimony is the 'burning in the bosom' that accompanies thinking it out in my mind. That's putting warmth of discernment with the light of intelligence."

"There's ample evidence," Orson continued. "Isaiah, in the twenty-ninth chapter, speaks of these days and the coming forth of a book, and a little later, the transformation of Lebanon into a fruitful field. The book has come forth already. Now comes the fruitful field. For the first time in 1900 years the Jews are stirring toward return."

"If Lebanon begins to flower then it is a foregone conclusion that the Jews will begin to take a new lease on life," George interjected.

"Of course what Ezekiel is talking about is the resurrection of Israel and the rising of the Jews into newness of life. Ezekiel was graphic, as always.

> Therefore prophesy and say unto them, Thus saith the Lord God; Behold, O my people, I will open your graves, and cause you to come up out of your graves, and bring you into the land of Israel. . . and shall put my Spirit in you, and ye shall live, and I shall place you in your own land; then shall ye know that I the Lord have spoken it, and performed it, saith the Lord.

"There's the promise, George; now note the timing—at least as far as sequence is concerned. If it says what I'm sure it does, we are on a highly significant mission:

> Behold I will take the stick of Joseph, which is in the hand of Ephraim, and the tribes of Israel his fellows, and will put them with him, even with the stick of Judah, and make them one stick, and they shall be one in mine hand. And the stick whereon thou writest shall be in thine hand before their eyes.

"Now listen closely to what Ezekiel says next:

> And say unto them, *Thus saith the Lord God; Behold, I will take the children of Israel from among the heathen, whither they be gone, and will gather them on every side, and bring them into their own land; and I will make them one nation in the land upon the mountains of Israel.*—Ezekiel 37:21, 22.

"And Orson," George said, excitedly, "if our Book of Mormon is that book, that stick of Joseph, to go with the stick of Judah, as we claim, then the very next thing to happen is that the children of Israel shall be drawn from every side into their own land! How it will happen, whether by more hatred than they have already known or by responding to some call, who can tell?"

Both men were silent. It was almost more than they could grasp. They were to live to witness the fulfillment of the prophecy which had been the hope of the Jews through their centuries of despair. "Next year, Jerusalem" was a delayed hope soon to come alive, but with what suffering still? They were so often tormented by those who, in ghastly error, justified their acts of terror in the name of the Jew, Jesus.

"Orson, you know that I have a deep affection for the Bible, and will probably always depend on it first and foremost in my preaching. So, let me ask you if the Book of Mormon speaks as certainly of the Restoration of the Jews to the land of their fathers."

"It does indeed," said Orson. "As a matter of fact, it is even more specifically comforting. Here, read it yourself in First Nephi 4:31-33." George read from the Book of Mormon:

> Yea, I spake unto them concerning the restoration of the Jews, in the latter days; and I did rehearse unto them the words of Isaiah, who spoke concerning the restoration of the Jews, or of the house of Israel; and after they were restored, they should no more be confounded, *neither should they be scattered again.*

They'd been talking about it, realizing it, but all of a sudden it hit them both with startling impact, the time had come.

"It's one thing to discern the signs. It is quite something else to convince the Jews and Gentiles!"

"I, for one, will try," said George Adams.

For the two ministers time passed quickly. The days of February were short anyway, and they talked late into each night. George Adams had much to learn from this man who was so steeped in the ancient doctrines of the Bible and in the embryonic traditions of a church established less than eleven years before by Joseph Smith.

ADAMS IN ENGLAND

Orson Hyde and his traveling companion landed at Liverpool on March 3 and were met by John Taylor. Two days later they went to Preston where Hyde had ministered formerly. Here they were joined by Heber Kimball. "This made my joy complete. . . as it was from this brother that I first heard the fullness of the gospel," Adams later wrote.

After preaching in the area of Preston, Farington, and Southport, Adams attended the church conference in Manchester in April. At dinner after the Conference, the ministers shared a large cake, loaded with fruit, zesty and well-preserved with sherry. It was prepared especially for the conference and sent by Mrs. Adams all the way from New York.

During the 1840's England was the prime mission field. Joseph Smith had sent most of his twelve apostles there. Hundreds were being baptized and sent off to swell Nauvoo, which was passing Chicago as the largest city in Illinois. The apostles were agents of emigration as well as missionaries.

Brigham Young and his council of apostles provided for the ordination of Adams to the office of high priest, and then because opportunities were so abundant they assigned him to Bedford, England. On the ninth of April he left for Birmingham. Here he preached eleven times in eight days, then proceeded to Bedford where a congregation of less than fifty members and friends met in cramped quarters.

Adams was pleased to be working under the supervision of Parley P. Pratt who had baptized and ordained him. After two months of enthusiastic endeavor, he reported to Pratt that the hall was too small and that they had moved to Castle Hill which would seat 1000. In the report he also spelled out his first major confrontation with the incensed clergy of England.

Halfway through his second lecture (admission twelve pence, ha'p'ny) the "sectarians" had interrupted the proceedings. A Mr. Mallows was the first to speak. "Mr. Adams, I put a question to you. Who are the two witnesses spoken of in the revelation given to John on the Isle of Patmos?"

"Sir," Adams replied, "that question is completely irrelevant to the subject at hand. . . "

"Answer. . .answer. . .answer that question!" These shouts came from every quarter. This well-planned interruption led to confusion, during which an independent preacher, Reverend White, arose. Then the sectarians chanted, "Hear, hear, hear Mr. White!"

White raised a newspaper aloft, "I have here a history of Mormonism and propose to read it."

Adams was incensed. "I object to having the cause of truth tried by lying newspapers!"

The crowd began yelling, "The newspaper story—give us the newspaper story!"

White commenced reading the "Athenaeum" concerning money diggers, fortune telling, the gold bible, etc. When he had finished reading, White declared that he was prepared to prove the precepts of the Latter Day Saints all false.

George Adams grasped the opportunity and offered to meet White in debate with an unbiased adjudicator, using the Bible as the standard of evidence. It was agreed.

The sectarians held a strategy session the next day, the upshot of it being that White would gather all the newspaper accounts they could muster and use them as the basis of an appeal to the audience and he would conclude by demanding a sign.

It happened just that way. White closed with "Show us a sign. Give us a miracle. Raise a dead man and we'll believe. A new religion needs a miracle to confirm it!"

"Mr. White, you had better search the scriptures. You'll find that signs are to follow those that believe, not go before to convince men! What is more, the Lord never promised miracles to those who say they are done away and are no longer needed. His satanic majesty once desired a miracle or two of our Lord, likewise Herod wanted a sign. . . . What a pity you were not there to have instructed our Lord how to act on that occasion. But the words of Jesus will suffice. He said that it is a 'wicked and adulterous generation which seeks after a sign.'"

It may have been a telling reply, but it only infuriated the sectarian crowd who began to cry for blood. "Shoot him! Hang him! Stone him out of the place!"

Then, the non-Christians who had come to see the contest, rose to the occasion and prevailed on the "Christians" to hold their peace.

Adams strengthened his hand by going to the London Conference to bring back Orson Hyde who addressed the next meeting "entirely freeing the Saints of the charges and leaving our enemies writhing in shame, confusion, and disgrace." It was a slight over-statement, but the Mormons had met a crucial test.

By June 6 George Adams could testify, "We came here not knowing a single individual in the place; the Lord has been with us, and opened our way in a wonderful manner; we have obtained a chapel to preach in that will hold more than 500 people. It is in a respectable part of the town. Then, we had about 50 members; now we have more than 100, and the members are increasing almost daily. We had two or three preaching places. Now we have preaching places open in Bedford, Crawley, Kempston, Malden, Gravely, Honeydon, Thorncutt, Wibrison, Whaden, Wellinbro, and Northhampton." He was doing so well in England that the apostles decided to keep him there into the autumn. It was with a heavy heart that he said goodbye to Orson Hyde who went on to Palestine alone.

Arriving at Liverpool on his way home to New York, October 28, he discovered that large placards had been posted through the town announcing that he would preach on the following Sunday, giving his reasons for renouncing Methodism to embrace the doctrine of the Latter Day Saints. The Music Hall was filled to overflowing. More than 2000 persons were present. Adams preached on the Book of Mormon as "the book spoken of by Isaiah, twenty-ninth chapter, and also that it was a record of Joseph in the hands of Ephraim, to be brought forth in the last days, just previous to the gathering of Israel."

To the delight of Adams and to most of the audience, it was a sensation but the Protestant clergymen were dismayed and angry. One of them, J. B. Phillips, pulled out a glass of poison, inviting Adams to drink it to prove that he was in fact a true disciple of Christ. "If you succeed in downing it without harm to yourself we will all be Latter Day Saints, even if I did say that all your doctrines and principles came from hell."

It was a mistake. He played into Adams' hands. "I have always understood," said George, "that the Bible, not poison, was to be the rule of evidence, but if you will point out one single place in the New Testament where a servant of God ever drank poison to convince a set of ungodly infidels of the truth of the religion of the blessed Jesus, I will drink your poison."

Phillips failed the point and lost the day. On a show of hands more than half the congregation voted in favor of George Adams.

On Sunday evening, December 5, he delivered his farewell address to the people of Liverpool on the subject of restoration—of the gospel and of Israel. Twenty-five hundred crowded into the hall for the occasion. He left in a glow of victory. He had done well.

His own words describe the eventful journey on the ship, *Mersey:*

Owing to contrary winds and stormy weather we did not sail until the 31st of December. We had 200 souls on board, and among them a clergyman of the Church of England; the first eight days we had fair wind and good weather, but after that time we had gale after gale for five weeks with head winds, which finally ended in a tempest that commenced on Sunday the 6th of February, 1842, and lasted with unabated fury for seven days, during which time we were driven back towards England seven hundred miles; our helm broken, our round house washed away, our main-mast sprung, our bulwarks stove in, and our provisions almost exhausted; so much that it was deemed advisable to return to England.

They returned to Liverpool on February 25, and before he left again, this time on the *Sheridan*, a letter from Alexandria, Egypt, was shared with him by Parley Pratt. It was from Orson Hyde. He had been to Jerusalem.

ORSON HYDE IN JERUSALEM

When the decision was made to leave G. J. Adams in England to work at Bedford, it was expected that John E. Page would finally catch up with Orson Hyde en route to Jerusalem. He never did. Orson went on by himself, leaving England in July, but not before he had talked with Jewish rabbis there. They were sufficiently impressed by his concern and his diligence that they raised money to support him on his journey.

On July 17, 1841, Orson wrote to Joseph Smith. He reported conversations in Bavaria about the Jews:

There is an increasing anxiety in Europe for the restoration of that people; and this anxiety is not confined to the pale of any religious community, but it has found its way to the courts of kings. Special ambassadors have been sent, and consuls and consular agents have been appointed. The rigorous policy which has hitherto characterized the course of other nations towards them now begins to be softened by the air of friendship, and modified by the balm of humanity. The sufferings and privations under which they have groaned for so many centuries have at length touched the main springs of Gentile power and sympathy; and may the God of their fathers, Abraham, Isaac and Jacob, fan the flame by celestial breezes, until Israel's banner, sanctified by the Savior's blood, shall float on the walls of Old Jerusalem.

What he wrote was probably more than he heard, but he did sense keenly the stirring of a new spirit that would soon prompt action. One of the Bavarian rabbis told him, "We believe that many Jews will return to Jerusalem. . . the capital of our nation, the standard and ensign of our national existence. In fact, they are now gathering there almost continuously." Orson's heart leaped within him. Here was proof of the vision and the timing. Prophecy's fulfillment was in process. The rabbis lent further encouragement by additional financial support. More convinced than ever, Orson made his way to Beirut, Jaffa, and then up to Jerusalem.

Jerusalem! His whole body responded involuntarily at first sight of that great walled city. Roughly in the shape of a square, a bit lopsided and unevenly drawn, the city was surrounded by an ancient wall which, if stretched out, would reach halfway to Bethlehem, five miles away. It was generally about ten feet thick but occasionally narrowed to five where the descent outside was steep as on the Kidron side.

Hyde entered through the Jaffa Gate at the middle of the city's western wall. He made his way through narrow stone streets to a gate leading onto the great tabletop known as the Temple Platform atop Mt. Moriah. Here Abraham had led young Isaac to a place of sacrifice. Here Solomon had built his magnificent temple only to have it destroyed by command of Nebuchadnezzar. This was where Jesus walked into the later temple built by Herod.

Walking past the great Muslim shrine, the Dome of the Rock, built in 691 A.D., Orson went to the Eastern Wall, climbed it, and looked across the Kidron Valley to the Mount of Olives. It was covered on its lower slopes by olive trees as it had been for centuries. A few patches of wheat and millet were at midheight. The crest was green with mishmish (apricot) trees. To that hill destiny was calling him. There, according to the prophets, the Messiah would come and the world would know the judgment of God, the glories of the resurrection, and the beginning of peace.

He was not yet ready to go, however. It was still the Sabbath of the Jews. He would go to the place that had drawn them and focused their longings for centuries—the Wailing Wall, the supporting wall of the Platform or esplanade, part of the defense perimeter of the Temple. He went back through the gate and into the Street of the Chain, working his way around to the left and down into the Old Tyropean or Central Valley, so filled with debris of conquered buildings that it was no longer a deep ravine. Then he walked back toward the Temple Platform but at a much lower level. Before him, partly obscured by hovels, was the wall of tears, the Wailing Wall.

His heart ached. There was scarcely any access to the wall, and what the Jews cherished in memory and hope as the nearest proximity to the Holy of Holies was a place of excrement. Yet here they were, this persistent people, leaning into the wall until flesh and stone seemed to merge as one. The stones absorbed the sound of weeping. How could hope ever prevail over the generations of abuse and inhumanity?

When access had been denied them, they had climbed the hills or descended into the valleys in order to peer at the Temple Mount through cracks in the walls. The Divine Presence might minister to them fleetingly elsewhere but never, never would desert the Wall which kept calling them home.

Armed with their confidence, and with the assurance that he was there on a divinely appointed mission in their behalf, Orson Hyde rose the next morning, "a good while before day. . . and went out of the city as soon as the gates were opened, crossed the Brook Kidron, and went upon the Mount of Olives."

From that vantage point on the crest of the sacred hill he looked to the east toward the Moabite hills that still held the sun in their grasp. In their shadow he could just make out the Dead Sea beyond the desolate Judean wilderness. Turning from his climb he looked down into the city. Thoroughly knowledgeable of the scriptures, he found his mind assailed by a flood of them, each signaling some sacred recollection. Now he was to pray for the elusive peace of Jerusalem.

His strong hope, heightened by a keen sense of history, prompted Hyde to record the auspicious occasion. It falls to few to know their time of destiny. Orson was sure of this moment and came with pen and paper. Prayerfully, and almost ecstatically, he wrote:

O Lord, thy servant has been obedient to the heavenly vision which thou gavest him in his native land; and under the shadow of thine outstretched arm he has safely arrived in this place to dedicate and consecrate this land unto thee, for the gathering together of Judah's scattered remnants, according to the predictions of the holy prophets—for the building up of Jerusalem again after it had been trodden down by the Gentiles so long, and for rearing a temple in honor of thy name. . . .

O thou who didst covenant with Abraham thy friend, and who didst renew that covenant with Isaac, and confirm the same with Jacob with an oath, that thou wouldst not only give them this land for an everlasting inheritance, but that thou wouldst also remember their seed forever! Abraham, Isaac, and Jacob, have long since closed their eyes in death, and made the grave their mansion. Their children are scattered and dispersed abroad among the nations of the Gentiles like sheep that have no shepherd, and are still looking forward for the fulfillment of those promises which thou didst make concerning them;. . .

Grant therefore, O Lord, in the name of thy well-beloved Son, Jesus Christ, to remove the barrenness and sterility of this land, and let springs of living water break forth to water its thirsty soil. Let the vine and the olive produce in their strength, and the fig tree bloom and flourish. Let the land become abundantly fruitful when possessed by its rightful heirs; let it again flow with plenty to feed the returning prodigals who come home with a spirit of grace and supplication; upon it let the clouds distill virtue and richness, and let the fields smile with plenty. Let the flocks and the herds greatly increase and multiply upon the mountains and the hills; and let thy great kindness conquer and subdue the unbelief of the people. Do thou take from them their stony heart, and give them a heart of flesh; and may the Sun of thy favor dispel the cold mists of darkness which have beclouded their atmosphere. Incline them to gather in upon this land according to thy word. Let them come like clouds and like doves to their windows. Let the large ships of the nations bring them from the distant isles; and let kings become their nursing fathers, and queens with motherly fondness wipe the tear of sorrow from their eye.

Thou, O Lord, did once move upon the heart of Cyrus to show favor unto Jerusalem and her children. Do thou now also be pleased to inspire the hearts of kings and the powers of the earth to look with a friendly eye towards this place, and with a desire to see thy righteous purposes executed in relation thereto. Let them know that it is thy good pleasure to restore the kingdom unto Israel, raise up Jerusalem as its capital, and constitute her people a distinct nation and government . . .

It was prayer, and it was prophecy after the manner of the ancient prophets. In that moment he felt he was one with them, only more fortunate because it was the beginning of the day of fulfillment. There were tears in his eyes as he searched out stones— twelve of them in token of the tribes of Israel—and piled them together as an altar, after the manner of the patriarchs of old. It was a tangible witness of a sacred act, a symbol of the eternal longing of a people, and a confirmation of prophetic hope.

Proceeding down the steep hill and climbing Moriah, he went around the south wall, past Dung Gate onto Mount Zion. There he built another altar of stones in honor of the Zion that was yet to be, the tangible city of God, an ensign to the nations. Jeru -salem, -salaam, -shalom would yet become the city of peace.

He wrote his report to Parley Pratt from Alexandria. Before closing his letter he wrote, "My best respects to yourself and family, to Brothers Adams and Snow, and to all the Saints in England."

Because he had returned to Liverpool on that storm-wracked vessel, George Adams got the message, and it was one he would remember.

Jaffa Beach, looking south

Entrance to Jerusalem by Jaffa Gate c. 1870
Courtesy Harvard Semitic Museum

The Western (Wailing Wall - late 19th century
Courtesy Harvard Semitic Museum

Chapter 2

RETURN TO NAUVOO

When George Jones Adams finally arrived in New York City, plans had already been laid for him to strengthen the work in Boston. His fame as orator and debater had preceded his return to America. Lorenzo Snow, impressed by what he had seen in Bedford and grateful for results during his absence from London, sent glowing reports across the Atlantic. But already Young, Kimball and others had borne their testimony before a New York conference, and then carried the message on to Nauvoo. Word was getting around that there was a valiant and brilliant defender of the faith in the person of G. J. Adams.

Before the May conference in New York City, Young and Kimball took up lodging at the Adams home. They were joined by the prophet Joseph Smith himself. Even with these prominent men at hand, it was G. J. Adams who was the featured speaker. Not only was the Boston assignment agreed upon, but Joseph invited George to come to Nauvoo as soon as he had finished his speaking engagement in Boston.

With scarcely enough time for his family after an absence of more than a year, Adams was on the road again. . . to environs he knew well and where people might remember him too well. It was, for him, a calculated risk. But it had been several years since he, under the influence, had belted the editor. Besides, he had been dry ever since. As long as he personally was not under attack and besmirched, and was in good company where the expectations were high, he had no need for liquid stimulation or solace. Now he had things under control, including himself.

The conquest of Boston was carried in detail in the *Weekly Bostonian.* This time a correspondent covered events regarding the Latter Day Saints without prejudice. His eye was open to the possibility that they might be onto something of significance. Even the editor was kind: "Joe Smith and his followers are creating as great a revolution in the morals of our country as our fathers in '76 did in its political destinies."

The first lecture on Wednesday, June 1, 1842, in Boylston Hall, was predictable as to subject matter, the difference being that this was the locale where he had espoused the Methodism he was now renouncing, and it was here that he had been one of its most vocal advocates. He got a crowd. The Bostonian correspondent said, "His reasoning was unanswerable."

On the next night Adams took on the Millerites who were even then preparing for the advent of Christ during the next year. The correspondent reported that "he fully showed the ignorance and folly of Millerism, clearly proving by the scriptures that the Jews must be gathered home from their long dispersion, and rebuild their city on its own heap of ruins, even Jerusalem itself, before Christ should come." As always, he bolstered his arguments with quotations from the Bible, recited by heart . . . dramatically.

There it was again, the persistent theme of Adams' preaching, lending reason to all else he had to say—the Jews were to be gathered home! It was all part of the same fabric, each thread woven into the dominant theme and design which this tailor had in mind. For him it carried all the weight and authority of the scriptures. Nothing was more real.

The *Bostonian* correspondent temporarily broke off his reports when the inevitable wrath of the "sectarians" came down on Adams. He finally wrote:

> The reason of my so long delaying. . . is not that there was nothing worthy of notice in the lectures; but about the time I should have written, Mr. Adams and his society were charged with blasphemy, lying, fraud, treason, and murder; and I thought if they were guilty of these heavy

charges, they were unworthy of anything but the halter and hangman; however, since that time Mr. Adams has nobly met the man that made the heavy charges. . . and entirely freed himself and the society to which he belongs, of every vestige of said charges; and the opposers of the Mormons, are left in shame, confusion, and disgrace. . . and the general cry among sectarians is, "how shall we put them down. . . some of our best and most devoted members are leaving us and joining them."

The scene of battle moved to Marlboro Chapel where Adams voiced what is now a familiar sequence—the validity of the Book of Mormon and the building of Zion at Jerusalem. Then he added a rousing lecture on "the pouring out of the vials of the wrath of God in the last days."

Once again the feisty orator had to be answered, and a preacher of some renown, Dr. West, was called on to do the job. West was a robust Englishman, about fifty years old (Adams was 31). He had been a Methodist, later Episcopalian, and at the time of this encounter, an independent—"one of God's volunteers" as he called himself.

Dr. West made the same error as his predecessors in battle with Adams. Once again the stipulation was that the Bible should be the standard of evidence. West resorted to vitriolic outburst on the credibility and character of the Mormons. His words were predictable: "Mormonism is a humbug and all pretensions to revelation or miracles in this age, blasphemy! This is sufficient to fix upon you the charges of lying, fraud and blasphemy."

Whenever West would introduce items from Mormon literature, Adams would thank him for bringing it to the attention of the audience and proceed to elaborate on it, paralleling with abundant scriptural references. Adams was not only making points but having fun as well. After one exchange in which Adams outwitted the doctor, the audience burst into applause.

Then, as a last resort, West fell into the trap of demanding a sign: "If you will work a miracle I shall forthwith kneel and receive a blessing at your hands."

The *Bostonian* correspondent wrote:

> Adams quoted scriptures in such torrents as sometimes astonished the people, and made his antagonist writhe under it.... Being unwilling to follow West in his wanderings, Adams took up his time in briefly wiping off [West's] sarcasms, and proving his doctrines from the Bible, which he seemed to have all on the end of his tongue. In the midst of clamor he was as calm as a summer evening.

Again, with scant attention to his family, and flushed with the excitement of Boston, Adams joined with an Elder Rogers to make the long journey to Nauvoo. They stopped to visit John E. Page in Pittsburgh, the man who hadn't made the journey to Palestine. Page was so impressed with Adams that he wrote a letter of hearty recommendation to Joseph Smith about "one of the best and most able of God's servants."

On September 12 Adams and Rogers were guests of the prophet in Nauvoo. They were received with uncommon eagerness. With no delay, Joseph Smith said: "I have received a letter from Apostle Page." If Adams knew anything about the letter he had no opportunity to dwell on it because the prophet moved on to concern about newspaper coverage in the Eastern states affecting himself and one of his primary aides, John C. Bennett.

Bennett had been Quartermaster General of the state of Illinois in 1840 and a military man of some repute. He was one of several prominent men in Illinois courted and converted by Joseph Smith in an attempt to secure relationships so badly lacking in Missouri. Bennett, a man of polish and great public presence, could sway audiences with his command of language, embellishing his speeches and his correspondence with facile use of Latin phrases. He was an opportunist, too, and saw in the young settlement at Nauvoo a chance to make a name for himself.

Joseph Smith, though brilliant in his perception of abstract truth, tended too often toward emotion and intuition in his estimate of men. At least, this was the case after the first years. Burdened by an abundance of practical necessities, he was desperate for help and John C. Bennett knew it.

Joseph's most competent staff members—the real organizers like Brigham Young and Heber Kimball—were in England. Sidney Rigdon, who had proved so helpful in the first decade of challenge and trouble, was not equal to the demands of building "the Kingdom of God" on the shores of the Mississippi. He settled for appointment as postmaster, and hardly kept pace as a counselor to Smith in the church presidency. Anxious to hold to yesterday's values, he was beginning to seem like an obstructionist to the prophet, the more so as Joseph began to explore paths of doctrine which were inconsistent, according to Rigdon, with the golden days of Kirtland.

Smith and Bennett wrote the Nauvoo Charter, basing it sufficiently on the Springfield Charter to have a familiar ring but investing it with a three-fold stroke of genius: providing for unlimited annexation of adjacent territory, an army of its own to guarantee protection against any repetition of the Missouri disaster, and a habeas corpus provision protecting anyone (Joseph in particular) from being subject to extradition.

The proposal was taken post haste to the state legislature by Bennett, no stranger to Springfield. There, with the assistance of a young going-places Secretary of State, Stephen A. Douglas, the charter was walked through. The legislators, preoccupied with a fiscal crisis, were deluged with forty-seven articles of incorporation and eight charters.

Bennett returned to Nauvoo a hero in February 1841, less than five months after his arrival in Nauvoo. He was not only elected mayor but he was at the prophet's right hand in a situation where the line between church and state was so thin as to be invisible.

Bennett designed, organized, and commanded the Nauvoo Legion, leaving to Joseph the ceremonial generalship. With his imperious way and grandiloquent speech he began to effect changes in the demeanor and public speech of the prophet. The extraordinary demands of running a church, a city, a store, a steamship, etc., were enough to put any man on edge, even a prophet, and he became strident and demanding.

To top it off, his missionary force in England was too successful, not only converting people to the gospel but sending recruits by the hundreds to Nauvoo—most of them poor. The situation was getting out of hand. Then, Sidney Rigdon seemed to put barriers in the path of progress, cautioning, and apparently conniving with others to slow things down, if not upset them. Joseph released him as counselor only to have the people put him back against Joseph's wishes. The prophet smarted under the rebuke.

When Bennett, an attractive and eligible bachelor, began philandering and using his position with the prophet as both cover and rationale, Joseph denounced him but kept him on. Shortly after, Bennett was caught in a plot to have Joseph assassinated. He was expelled from the church and threatened with public exposure. Bennett left Nauvoo abruptly, swearing vengeance. He made a career of exposing "the holy and immaculate Joe Smith."

When Adams and Rogers finished their report on Bennett's exposures in the Eastern press, Joseph said, "Brethren, it's hard to build the city beautiful, but it must be done. Well, to the work at hand. Brother Rogers, you've come to paint my portrait. We'll start tomorrow. Brother Adams, you have a well-deserved reputation for persuasive language. My beloved Emma has tackled the governor, trying to protect me from Boggs. He wants to either extradite or kidnap me into Missouri. The habeas corpus provision of our charter is our best hope of security—plus eternal vigilance. But the charter is threatened. Talk with Emma. She has just received a letter from Governor Carlin."

During the next week the painting went well, as did the writing of a well-thought-through letter to Governor Carlin. Then Emma became seriously ill, running a high fever. Joseph chose to care for her himself. Little Joseph, at ten years, could look after the chores, bring water from the well outside the door, and care for the horse (Major) and the milk cow that grazed in the acre of land between the house, the store, and the river.

Neighbors brought in food for the family and hot broth for Emma. Snatching moments whenever he could, Joseph would go to the store and his office above it, or—as happened frequently—the people needing to see the busiest man in town came to his door. This included a growing multitude of the curious, including editors, politicians, and visitors from abroad.

George Adams didn't stay in Nauvoo long. He was troubled after stopping in to visit with the wife of his good friend, Orson Hyde, who had not yet returned from Palestine. Adams seemed to be the only person embarrassed when he found one of the prominent church officers, Willard Richards, living with Nancy Hyde. Richards' wife Jennetta was in Massachusetts.

Residents of the city beautiful were becoming very human and earthy. All of a sudden George Adams was lonely. Returning to his home in New York, he found it more drab than he had realized and less of a comfort than he had hoped.

FEET OF CLAY

In the dead of winter George Adams headed for Boston, only partially warmed by the anticipation of getting back into the excitement of lectures and debates. His impassioned appeal on behalf of Mormonism on January 19, 1843, may not have brought the same glow of satisfaction as before. At least there is reason to believe that his mood of despondency had not ended.

What happened is conjecture—but conjecture that is very close to the truth in light of a letter written to Adams on order of Joseph Smith by Brigham Young and Willard Richards, in which he was instructed to come to Nauvoo and answer to a charge of adultery. He also was told not to preach anymore until he got to Nauvoo.

In light of the battles yet to ensue between Adams and Elder John Hardy, president of the church in Boston, it is safe to assume that the charge was leveled by Hardy.

George Adams buried his sins of the flesh in the waters of baptism in February, 1840, and he had kept them under complete control for nearly three years. A flurry of creative and exciting activity had removed temptation. There was no need. He was busy, admired, and fulfilled. Even the disappointment of not going to Jerusalem had not really gotten to him. But since the journey to Nauvoo he had been a man with a troubled heart. In that condition Adams was vulnerable.

After preaching at Boylston Hall, Adams walked past a downtown pub called Park Hall. He walked past it because he was on his way to New Bedford. There was preaching to do and he had not mixed the pulpit and alcohol for a long time, but he recorded the location in his mind.

In New Bedford he went to the home of Mrs. White, a widowed member of the church. He and the other elders had taken board and room there before, and being so filled with their venture of faith G. J. had never discovered how much of a comfort Sister White could be. She understood his despondency, and to cheer him seated him at table next to a Miss Susan Clark.

They found themselves talking with increasing confidence into the late evening until all the others had gone to bed. Susan would have been attractive in any circumstance, but to lonely George Adams she was breathtakingly beautiful . . . and so young. He was unable to escape the recollection of a choice phrase from King Richard's beguiling of the widowed Anne, "So I might live one hour in your sweet bosom." The thought was betrayed in his eyes. She took his fingers and touched them lightly with lips that were slightly open. Satisfied by his spontaneous and involuntary response she pulled him to his feet and walked him gently but insistently to her room and closed the door.

Later, when George went ever so quietly to his own room (shared by another elder because they always went two by two for mutual strength and protection) he found that gentleman restless and stirring to wakefulness. When a sleepy voice asked where he'd been, George softly said, "Heaven," and went to sleep. If atmosphere and that brief word had not betrayed him, his mixture of preoccupation and bravado the next morning did.

George Adams got himself away from New Bedford in haste, but not without carrying a troublesome mix of remorse and longing. He entered into a frenzy of ministerial activity, mending fences, and preaching as if he were doing battle with the devil in person, or remembering the Ghost of Buckingham who taunted the guilty King Richard with ". . . and Richard falls in height of all his pride."

On March 10, 1843, the day he received the letter sent by Young and Richards, Adams wrote a feverish reply promising his immediate removal to Nauvoo, with his family as ordered. He made no reference to the stipulation that he was "not to preach any more" until his arrival in Nauvoo. He signed the letter "Your repenting and sorrowful brother in the New Covenant."

The reason for not stating agreement to the order on preaching was that he was already booked for an important appointment. On Thursday evening, March 23, according to the *Boston Bee:*

Agreeable to appointment, Elder Adams addressed a large concourse of people on the character and mission of Joseph Smith, the prophet. In speaking of him he bears a positive and direct testimony to the divinity of his mission. He does this without hesitating just as if he meant what he said and said what he meant. He does not say he hopes Joseph Smith is a true prophet, but says that he is positive that such is the fact. . . . The Boston Hall was a perfect jam during the day and evening. On Tuesday evening he gave his farewell lecture. That was a rich treat indeed embodying the outline of the faith and doctrine of Latter Day Saints. But on Wednesday evening at the great Tea Party was the time it was clearly manifested that kindest feelings existed in this city towards the Mormons . . . three hundred and fifty sat down at the first table. After supper Elder Adams delivered a very appropriate and eloquent address. It was listened to with profound attention during which time we saw the tears start in many an eye.

The correspondent signed his report, "Yours truly, not a Mormon, but one of the many friends to that much abused people. DWR"

Even though Adams was supposed to be heard by the High Council in Nauvoo, Joseph Smith said he would handle the matter himself. Writing to Peter Hess in Philadelphia some time later (July 7), George said,

My beloved Brother, I this day set down to address a few lines to you. . . as to myself, there are many reports afloat. Some say that my license was taken from me. That is a lie. Some say I was tried before the Twelve—that is also a lie . . . and let me say to you that I never was brought before the authorities of the church for there was no one to lay charges against me . . . some say that I confessed to Joseph that the reports in circulation about me were true—that is another wilful lie.

What really happened in that interview may never be known. Joseph's report of it to his council on May 27, 1843, was very brief. The secretary recorded:

Brother Joseph further remarked, concerning Elder Adams, that he had given satisfaction to him concerning the thing whereof he was accused. He had confessed all wherein he had done wrong, and had asked for mercy, and he had taken the right course to save himself; he would now begin anew in the church.

During the months of May, June, and July, 1843, George was very close to the prophet. They spent many hours in conversation, with Joseph teaching his protegé. It was a dangerous time for Joseph. Governor Lilburn Boggs of

Missouri had redoubled his efforts toward extradition. Others, knowing how much Joseph was wanted, laid plans to kidnap him late in June.

Also in June, Joseph and the Council of Twelve Apostles appointed Orson Hyde and George Adams to undertake a mission to Russia. In consequence of this extraordinary assignment, the two men were to deliver addresses on the Fourth of July. Orson, reconciled to Nancy and striving to get a house built for the family before leaving, preached in the morning and Adams in the afternoon. Adams' new prominence occasioned some dismay among the established leaders as evidenced by charges brought against him by Austin Cowles, a prominent Mormon leader in Nauvoo. The High Council, however, decided in favor of Adams, and Joseph saw fit to have a notice published in the *Times and Seasons* indicating that George J. Adams had been "honorably acquitted. . .from all charges heretofore preferred against him from any and all sources; and is hereby recommended as a faithful laborer. . .and a servant of the Lord that is entitled to the gratitude, confidence, liberality and clemency of the Saints and honorable men in all the world."

ASSASSINATION

After a foray into New York and Boston, Adams went back to Nauvoo in time for the church conference in early April, 1844, where he was to be a featured speaker. On April 8, at 9:45 a.m., Joseph Smith presided. He was handicapped by laryngitis from an open-air funeral oration the day before, so Brigham Young read the scripture—I Corinthians 15. Then, obviously very serious, Joseph arose and said:

> Saints and friends, in regard to the Temple [we are building here] and that magnificent baptismal font supported by great oxen. . . .There must be a particular spot for the salvation of our dead. [Now] God made Aaron to be the mouth piece for the children of Israel, and he will make the elders to be mouth for me. . . I have been giving Elder Adams instruction in some

principles to speak to you, and if he makes a mistake, I will get up and correct him.

George preached for three hours and "it could be heard at a great distance." There is no evidence of interruption by the prophet. Adams' rationale for baptism for the dead has remained classic ever since, neither more nor less plausible than ever. It was, however, his first excursion into the unorthodoxy which was causing Sidney Rigdon and others to be alarmed.

Joseph Smith was becoming a strange mixture of patience and frenzy, courage and fear. This prompted some deliberate and some desperate actions. There was mounting alarm at the possibilities of his own death, triggered by the increased tempo of attempts to bring him to trial. He had enemies within and without, and even the hidden closet in his bedroom could prove inadequate to save him.

One day, after a special meeting of the church's High Council in Joseph's second floor office above his red brick store, George Adams ran to the Smith apartment in the new Mansion built for the entertaining of guests. He was, according to the testimony of Emma Smith, almost overcome with joy. He said, excitedly, "The matter is now settled, and we know who Joseph's successor will be—it's 'little Joseph'—we have just seen him ordained by his father." To add to his joy, Adams received the horn of oil from Joseph's hand to hold during the blessing which designated young Joseph.

In January, 1844, Joseph had prepared a document stating that his son, Joseph III, would "be my successor in the Presidency of the High Priesthood and a Seer, and a Revelator and a prophet unto the church which appointment belongeth to him by blessing and also by right." Thomas Bullock had been the scribe and now, in April, what had been perceived and written down was confirmed by the laying on of hands in prophetic blessing.

Troubled, Joseph was taking steps to provide continuity of

leadership. What if his fears were well-founded? His son was too young—a mere twelve years—but time was running out.

Just before the April Conference Joseph Smith decided to bring all his basic leaders—fifty of them—into a cadre of trust, bound together by strong personal allegiance to himself. Among this council of fifty was George Jones Adams.

They concerned themselves with heady matters, even drafting a treaty with the Republic of Texas. A memorial was also drafted, (probably by Adams, with his reputation for golden prose) to the President and to the Congress, relative to settling west of the Rockies. With the help of Stephen A. Douglas this very nearly became reality in Oregon.

The most immediately dramatic proposal was to run Joseph Smith for President of the United States. They were serious, not only in protest to shoddy treatment by both Whigs and Democrats but because they believed that Joseph was better fitted than any other to serve in the office.

Most of the Council of Fifty left for campaign missions throughout the land. For some reason, perhaps because he was a trusted assistant to Joseph. Adams remained in Nauvoo.

With most of the prominent Mormons out of town, a group of former church leaders decided to take action. One was William Law, who had been Joseph's counselor for three years. With his brother, Wilson, William had been ousted from the church by a council including G. J. Adams. They were not so angry at Adams as they were incensed by the beliefs they saw creeping in—particularly the plurality of wives and plurality of gods. They published their views in an opposition newspaper named *The Nauvoo Expositor*. The only issue was published on June 7, 1844.

With extreme personal sensitivity to newspaper attacks Joseph Smith acted summarily. First he met with his brother Hyrum, Willard Richards, and G. J. Adams. Then he called for the city council to declare the *Expositor* a public nuisance. Within three days the press was destroyed, including confiscation of all copies of the paper on hand. The editors fled to Carthage and swore out a warrant for the arrest of Joseph on a charge of riot.

There was a ferment of angry voices. Normally nonviolent men conversed with malcontents and bullies. Newspaper editors, spoiling for verbal combat, joined the battle. What Joseph had done was to strike fire to tinder all too ready for burning. The convulsive malaise that tore the Saints out of Missouri was surfacing again in Illinois. It was the beginning of the end of Nauvoo as Joseph's City Beautiful.

Thomas Ford, successor to Governor Carlin, already advised of the unrest between the people of Nauvoo and the rest of the countryside, was alerted that a time of crisis had come. Anger of the "Gentiles" focused on Joseph Smith who, to them, had rigged a sanctuary for himself in Nauvoo. They were intent on jarring him loose for what they deemed to be justifiable punishment. One of them, speaking to Dan Jones, captain of the *Maid of Iowa*, pointing to his pistols, bragged, "The balls are in there that will decide the case!"

On June 12, 1844, the Sheriff of Hancock County confronted Joseph with a writ to appear before a magistrate in Carthage; he was charged with destroying the press of the *Nauvoo Expositor.* There were delays, charges, and counter charges for the next few days but on the twenty-third, Joseph was again demanded to appear at Carthage, and this time there was a guarantee of safety by Governor Ford himself.

On the morning of June 24 Joseph mounted his horse and said good-bye to his wife and children and several hundred who had gathered early in dreaded anticipation of what that day would bring. Dan Jones, who rode along, reported the prophet's words on leaving: "My friends, I love the City of Nauvoo too well to save my life at your expense. . . . If I go not to them they will come and act out the horrid Missouri scenes in Nauvoo:. . . I may prevent it, I fear not death, my work is well nigh done, keep the faith. . . . I am going like a lamb to the slaughter."

On the morning of the twenty-fifth Joseph and the others surrendered voluntarily in answer to the writ charging them with riot against the *Nauvoo Expositor*. Then they were arrested on charge of treason against the state of Illinois. The judge, however, asked only for an answer to the charge of riot and thus freed them on bail and their own recognizance. They returned to Hamilton's Hotel only to be required by the constable, Bettisworth, to go to jail. Joseph's counsel appealed to the governor, who refused to intervene.

By June 27, at the height of tension, the governor incredibly disbanded one detachment of troops and ordered a company of cavalry to proceed with him to Nauvoo. Only eight of the Carthage Greys were left to guard the jail from threatened attack. Ford was early in Nauvoo and, apparently at the request of Joseph Smith, George Jones Adams sought an audience with the governor. Whether his considerable powers of persuasion, added to the testimony of others in Nauvoo, had any modifying effect on Ford may never be determined. Violence took over at Carthage.

In the governor's absence, mobbers with painted faces stormed the jail, encountering little or no resistance from the Greys. Both Joseph and Hyrum were shot, Joseph falling to the ground from the second story room in which they were held. The prophet, and candidate for the Presidency of the United States, was dead.

For George Jones Adams it was the end of the world, the devastation of a dream, and a defeat of his own power to persuade. Stunned, he offered his sympathies to the bereaved families and dully heard himself commissioned to carry the message of tragedy to church officials in the East.

He left Nauvoo but never delivered the message. That was left to another, while George Adams fell victim to despair and drowned his sorrow.

Adams was next heard from in a letter to Brigham Young in August. By that time Young had taken over leadership of the church, denying all others, including one who was still too young to act—"Little Joseph." In the letter, Adams protested his public acceptance almost too much, and his protestations suggested that he had been feeling the fire of ridicule:

> In the first place I will say that I never was so well received in the East as I have been in this time. Thousands turn out to hear me, many are believing and many baptized. . . . I never slander or backbite or envy my brethren in their success. I thank God that I am not a crow. I don't love stinking meat as well as some do. About the continuation of the Russian mission, it is for you to decide. . . Brethren, remember me in your councils, the head loved me and confided in me. Won't you, for their sake? If you see my beloved wife give my love to her and tell her to be wise and faithful.

In a conference of the church in New York City in early September of 1844 George Adams made "his usual bold, pointed and forcible" remarks. As a matter of fact, the conference was regularly interrupted by his insistence that he had been slandered. He said, "It is hard enough for a man during the prime of life to suffer while he might be engaged at a large salary without being slandered." The self-assurance of George Adams was eroding away. As long as he was defending constancy within the organization he carried it off very well, but when it came to defending the inconstancy of his own personality he had a penchant for stumbling. He was marked with, as he had declaimed so frequently in the person of King Richard III, "a . . . condition that cannot brook the accent of reproof."

KING JAMES STRANG

Adams associated himself with William Smith, brother of the dead prophet and Sam Brannan, for a round of the branches of the church. Their purpose was identical—fund-raising—but for different reasons. Smith was raising money for the Temple in Nauvoo, begun by Joseph Smith but still uncompleted. Brannan was to fulfill the Council of Fifty's plan to colonize in the West, specifically San Francisco, which he later did. Adams was still raising money for a mission to Russia, proposed by Joseph Smith prior to his assassination.

Leaders of the local Mormon churches were up in arms. To them this was a looting venture, bleeding off their limited finances. The three were living off the local congregations, acting imperiously, and preaching celestial marriage which by now had become spiritual wifery and—according to the Boston Branch president, John Hardy—an out and out excuse for illicit behavior.

Wilford Woodruff, visiting his relatives in Maine, was instructed by Brigham Young to investigate the whole situation and bring back recommendations. Young demanded strict and unquestioning obedience, but he was having trouble keeping some of his top leaders in line. Lyman Wight had proceeded to Texas against Brigham's wishes and was cut off from the church (besides, Wight was in favor of Little Joseph). Sidney Rigdon had proposed a temporary guardianship and was axed for his trouble. William Smith had put his claim in as the prophet's brother. Brigham would have none of that. Emma Smith who opposed the intrusion of the doctrine of plurality of gods and wives and knew of her son's rights to leadership, was put under surveillance by Brigham Young.

G. J. Adams, who also had convictions about Little Joseph but was being discreet about them, was stirring up trouble in the East. There were rumors that he was frequenting Park Hall in Boston and bedding down in a home in New Bedford. Woodruff, at first hopeful, finally reported on the "injudicious course of George J. Adams."

In the *Times and Seasons* for April 10, 1845, one year after Adams arrived at the pinnacle of his career in Nauvoo, a notice of expulsion was aimed at cutting that career short:

> This may certify that Elder George J. Adams had been disfellowshipped and cut off from the church of Jesus Christ of Latter-day Saints. His conduct has been such as to disgrace him in the eyes of justice and virtue. . .; we have for some time been unwilling to believe the foul statements made concerning him; but the nature of the testimony now adduced, compels us to believe that the statements are but too true, and that under the sacred garb of religion, he has been practising the most disgraceful and diabolical conduct. . . .
>
> BRIGHAM YOUNG, Pres.

Embarrassed and antagonized, Adams became a thorn in the side of Brigham Young as attested by further notices aimed at stopping "his mad course" and commenting on his "hellish conduct and unvirtuous practices." By December 1, 1845, he seemed whipped into submission and was discovered at his old secondary interest, playing in a theater.

Nearly two months before the murder of Joseph Smith, with most of the leaders away campaigning, the prophet had encouraged Thomas A. (Tom) Lyne, a tragedian player from New York and Philadelphia to give Nauvoo a lift. Cultural events were all too rare on the frontier. Lyne teamed up with his brother-in-law, George Jones Adams. Adams had not only given his sister in marriage to Lyne but had been on stage with him, playing Richmond to Lyne's Richard III. He had also converted Lyne to the church and encouraged him to go to Nauvoo to meet the prophet. Lyne did, and stayed on.

Together the two of them determined a repertoire of plays for the month of May. They would do the *Orphan of Geneva*, *The Idiot Witness*, *Damon and Pythias*, and perhaps others. Actors were chosen to support the principal stars, Lyne and Adams. The lower room of the new Masonic Hall "was fitted up with very tasteful scenery," and George was in his glory. The performances were "marked with success," the hall being well-attended each evening. "The audience expressed their entire satisfaction and approbation" according to the diary of the prophet.

Now, in late 1845 and finished with preaching, Adams gathered to himself a troupe of players and capitalized on lines so recently learned. He could make a living. He took his family with him and found temporary housing in Cincinnati.

News of his starring role came to the attention of John C. Bennett, himself in Cincinnati and, with the prophet dead, no longer so venomous. Indeed, he had been in touch with a late convert to Mormonism, James J. Strang, who was contesting Young and the twelve apostles for leadership. Claiming a letter of appointment from Joseph Smith and a vision of divine approbation at the very moment of the Martyr's death, Strang was bidding fair to claim a large segment of the church members, especially those in the East who were far enough away from the dynamic personal presence of Young.

Learning of Adams' disenchantment with Young, Bennett encouraged him to write to Strang offering his several abilities. Bennett was already one of Strang's leading disciples and prevailed on Strang to allow Adams to join them with his former "place, standing, and appointments."

In view of Adams' remarkable ability with language, his letter betrayed not lack of learning, as some have supposed, but a weakness he displayed in times of disenchantment:

> . . . I now feel to make a few adional remarks. . . I am aware that I have many enymies among the Twelveites and Rigdonites, whose jealosey will lead them to say and infer many things at me. They have reported that i was a Drinker of Liquor it is a base Phalsehood, put afloat to destroy me and my influence, but they have failed for I draw crowds whereaver and wheneaver I lift up my voice. They have reported that I was fond of womin it is a Base lie I never for according Fowlers chart of my head it is the smallest development in my head I mean Amativeness is only No. 2 in the scale of 7—I don't mention these things because I care for them—partickulary. . . .

Whether the letter was written in some variation of his normally bold handwriting, or by another at his dictation is uncertain. It is the same person, George Jones Adams, but in a mode completely unfamiliar to Boylston Hall and Nauvoo. It seems to have been written through a liquid haze.

Acceptance by Strang bolstered Adams, and by the time he arrived at Strang's home in Wisconsin he was dry and filled with hope.

They made quite a trio—Strang, Bennett, and Adams. It was a combination of ego-bumps predestined to run into strife, but they had a church to save from Brigham Young, and eventually a kingdom to build, a very real kingdom, complete with a ruler—King James.

Their first sortie was into Kirtland, Ohio, where they rallied the church to their banner—then back to Boston and New Bedford. It was a dangerous journey, but Adams had buckled on the armor of righteousness and pulled off another victory. Even John Hardy, just months earlier dead set against Adams, joined the Strang fold. Adams was often down but never completely out, bouncing back with further evidence of his charisma. Like King Richard III he could win the most unlikely arguments, artfully turning enmity to unexpected support. Unlike King Richard, he did not victimize others by intent or design.

When Bennett quarreled with Strang, Adams became second in command. When they moved from Voree, Wisconsin, to Beaver Island in Lake Michigan and established the Kingdom of God on Earth, Adams pulled a royal red robe from his theatrical trunk and draped it ceremoniously over the shoulders of Strang. He also placed a kingly crown on the prophet's brow.

With such preeminence, Strang no longer denied to himself two of the doctrines that Brigham Young had espoused, and he did it with as much enthusiasm as if he had conceived the notions himself. He instituted baptism for the dead. George Adams was one of the first into the water, being baptized for Napoleon Bonaparte, Samuel Adams, John Adams, and John

Quincy Adams. Then he baptized Strang for the salvation of Oliver Cromwell and Lord Byron.

When Strang proclaimed polygamy as a divine principle he sent George Adams to offer the hand of King James to Elvira Field of Charlotte, Michigan, just turned nineteen. Elvira was handsome but not yet conspicuously endowed. Already a convert, she proved willing. To avoid the inevitable misunderstandings attaching to a newly promulgated doctrine, she submitted to a short masculine haircut, probably at the hands of Adams, and then traveled with Strang as his secretary under the name of Charles J. Douglass. Imagination is staggered by the deception, but it was so successful that when George Adams the following spring brought a young widow to Beaver Island from his journey to the East, Strang—still protecting himself—threatened to run the both of them out of town, the lady "on a black-horned buck, with her face backwards and the boys to hoot at her!"

The subjects of King James were righteously indignant and incensed. They knew that Adams was a family man, though often far removed from them. He had often spoken of his wife and especially a young namesake, George Oscar. Unaware of Strang's own deceit, they would not tolerate lasciviousness—and George Adams had to go. The wife of his youth apparently went to New Jersey where she was reported in 1850, probably living in Newark near the mother of Adams, and his sisters. Divorce was likely, for she had had enough before the young widow ever came on the scene.

George Adams had come to another end, his world crashing down around him once again, but not until after he had joined with James Strang and William Marks (formerly stake president at Nauvoo and also dismissed by Brigham Young) in a "Memorial to the President and Congress of the United States and to all the People of the Nation." It was written on April 6, 1850, twenty years after Joseph Smith had founded the church. The language reflected George Adams at his b st, reminding the nation of the horrors of persecu ion suffere by the Saints, the martyrdom of the innocent Josep and the inability of the government to redress the wrongs committed. The memorial closed with a plea to be able to occupy "all the uninhabited lands of the islands in Lake Michigan."

After a spate of publicly condemning Strang and his followers, Adams resorted once again to drama. He pulled together a traveling troupe of players and, according to legend, drew interested persons on a trial basis for a period of thirty days. If they proved to be promising actors they would be on the payroll. According to the story, they seldom were approved.

Adams was wandering again but this time it was with a new and considerably more ambitious partner, the very amply endowed widow, known as L.I.L., born in Maine in 1825. Whatever her background, she was very much a "take charge" person, and when he was with her if he drank at all it was in small quantities, taken with meals, and sipped instead of quaffed. For the time being, she kept him on the wagon except in moments of lonely remembrance when he was away from the house and his feet obeyed the magnetic pull of the Park Hall saloon.

Jaffa, looking south. c. 1840

Bazaar at Jaffa. c. 1850

George Jones Adams

CHAPTER 3

INTERLUDE

Back in New England George and L.I.L. settled in the vicinity of Vermont sometime after the birth of Clarence Augustine (probably near Lebanon, Maine) in 1855. He was named for that valiant Augustine who added England to the fold of Christ, and for Clarence, brother, coconspirator, and victim of King Richard III. "Noble Clarence" he would be.

Following the murder of Strang in 1856, Adams no doubt wondered about "Little Joseph" who by that time was twenty-four years old. He may not have known that forces were gathering the faithful who remained aloof from Young and the aberrations of both Young and Strang. It would be another four years before they would be gathered together under the moderate leadership of "Young Joseph," as he would be called until the day of his death in 1914.

By 1860 Adams was launched on a new career. He found once again that he could work profitably seven days a week by acting during the week and then announcing that on Sunday he would preach at such and such a church on a certain text. He was even drafted to fill a vacant pulpit for a while. Mrs. Adams joined the lecture team, her topic being "Temperance." It was a subject about which she was highly motivated, and at least one sinner kept getting her message.

In October 1860 Adams and his family moved to Boston, Massachusetts. A second child had been born which was not to survive long. It was a bad fall and winter for L.I.L., and she was frequently ill. George was as hearty as ever, moving about among the prominent people of town, introducing himself as a Christian minister of some experience, now connected with the Church of the Messiah which, although he did not mention it, was in gestation in his fertile mind.

Although his church was yet to be organized, the very name signaled the revival of Adams' strong emphasis on the coming of the Messiah in the last days. Under the persuasion of many who wished to hear him, Adams leased Goodrich's Hall in Springfield, Massachusetts, and held several meetings. Large audiences responded, and among those electrified by his strong emphasis on the redemption of Israel and the near coming of the Messiah was a congregation of Adventists needing a minister. Disappointed but not totally dismayed by the lack of fulfillment of Miller's prophecy of the coming of Messiah in 1843, the Adventists responded avidly to the new preacher.

Adams accepted their invitation to preside over them and, to their delight, filled the local Music Hall. It was finally necessary for them to lease a large room in Rice's new hall on State Street. During this time Adams preached the funeral sermon of the last survivor of Bunker Hill, Ralph Farnum. The crowd was so large that he had to preach the sermon twice, a tribute to his incredible appeal.

A Mark Allen (apparently one of the young actors released after the thirty-day trial) recognized him from former times. An investigation was begun by some of the Adventists and brought to light on February 10 in public meeting. Under the leadership of one of their most trustworthy members, Randolph Ladd, they discovered to their dismay that the Reverend G. J. Adams had been popular in "dramatical and Mormon circles." What was even more to be condemned, he "also resembles very much a person branded as an imposter and drunkard." Adams pleaded for time so that he might be prepared to meet the charges and a time was agreed upon—the evening of February 18, 1861.

The spacious hall in Rice's building was jammed. Adams presented a sworn affidavit denying that he was ever a Mormon preacher, thus removing himself from the church he had once loved but which was now dominated by leaders and doctrines which were soundly condemned in the popular press. Then a George T. Adams of Boston, an Advent preacher, was introduced as a witness against George J. Adams. Recognizing G. J. in his Boston store as one he had seen in Springfield, he had greeted G. J. by name and said that he "had denied ever being in Springfield, [asserting] that he was aware of a Reverend Adams that was in Springfield and having trouble with his flock but he was not that Mr. Adams. Later that same day they had followed G. J. to a drinking saloon, and later still to Redding & Company's store, No. 8 State Street and found him in a state of beastly intoxication."

When George J. was accused of being a Mormon preacher by George T. Adams he replied that that was really a G. G. Adams who had been dead for several years and that he had been mistaken for that Mormon hero before. Did he imbibe spiritous liquors in Springfield? "The nearest was at Mr. Ladd's house where I partook of a glass of cider," replied G. J. Adams. Someone in the audience called out, "two glasses and a half." G. J. acknowledged it.

He also denied any acquaintance with Mark Allen. Erastus Inman, a friend of G. J. Adams, supported him with a statement regarding his character. Then Adams appealed touchingly to the audience to decide the case in his behalf, and in consideration of a sick wife at home with two small children, he asked that the mantle of charity be thrown over the whole affair, and that the press would deal kindly with him.

It looked like all would go well. Then, Erastus Inman got the floor and said that Adams had instructed him how to testify and that he, Inman, knew for a fact that Adams was a theatrical actor and manager, that he had preached on Sundays, acted during the week, and did neither very well because he was too drunk. Then S. F. Otis stood to relate that Mr. Gibbs, the railroad baggage master, had told him that

Adams got on the train in Boston drunk and had no money to pay his fare.

The matter was put to a vote and a majority of the audience decided that Mr. Adams was guilty as charged. It had been a trial of sorts, one commonly called "kangaroo."

The editor of the *Springfield Republican* added his own cutting remark in his typically sarcastic reporting of town events:

> Altogether the investigation has developed the most consummate, bold and plausible deceiver that ever went unjailed, and the facts are conclusive evidence that broadcloth and white neck-ties are not always sure garbs of decency and devotion.

Afterwards the staunch supporters of George Jones Adams came to his support and he agreed to stay and fight it out. On February 21 the editor of the *Republican* reported that Adams would continue in another hall and that his "party will rally around and sustain him," relying on the moral support of the Masons to which order he belonged. "We hope," said the editor, "to be able to publish in a day or two a pretty full and accurate history of the clerical imposter."

True to his word, the editor blistered George Jones Adams on February 23, giving an "Authentic History of Adams' Fall." Pegging him as a Mormon preacher in Boston in 1843, he detailed Adams as an intoxicated actor at the Howard Atheneum in 1844-45, and then at West Pawlet, Vermont, in 1856, at a "one-horse theater at Whitehall, New York in the Winter of 1859-60" and then filling a Baptist pulpit wearing a white cravat, and drinking whiskey in the pulpit. Then the "trial" of the preceding week was rehearsed, and to cap the article the editor spoke of those who regret that "they had not applied a sticking plaster to him from his head to his foot, and softened it on the outside with down."

From then on, announcements in "City Items" carried barbs. On March 9:

> George Jones Adams, the independent preacher of the Church of the

Messiah, and the exposed hypocrite, will deliver three discourses in Union Hall tomorrow. An attempt to prove a good character is expected.

The article covering the address concluded:

Curiosity to hear Mr. Adams will soon be satiated, and unless, ere that happens, he should be justly forced to leave the city, the community will then be rid of one of the most accomplished and plausible hypocrites that ever breathed a New England atmosphere.

One of the last comments before the departure of Adams to other parts seems hardly matter of fact and of questionable merit for the editor of a newspaper:

That he is a hypocrite, drunkard, ex-stage actor, and every way qualified for a suit of plumage, fastened by other and more secure means than buttons, none conversant with his past history and present course can consistently dispute.

On the night that George Pauncefort, the renowned actor, was producing a stage play to the "lyrical delight" of the *Republican's* editor, George Adams tried in vain to establish his credibility. The editor of the *Republican*, in the same column in which he was lauding Pauncefort, lowered the axe on his favorite whipping boy, Adams. "He said last night was his final attempt to refute the charges against him; and upon that assurance the respectable community leave him to kick his clerical bucket."

Which of the two, Adams or Sam Bowles, the editor, prostituted his profession more is debatable. Adams might have been more candid as to his identity and placed himself on the mercy of his hearers, but it was a bad time to be a Mormon. . . and a time when play-acting and pulpits hardly seemed compatible. On top of that George Jones Adams had been to Park Hall in Boston too often and, one might surmise, some other rum shops as well.

As for the editor, he seemed to be gaming, his thinly veiled references to tar and feathers scarcely being appropriate to the accountability of the fourth estate. Feelings were running high in 1861 and beyond that some of the people of the press seemed to feel under necessity to come up with dramatic trivia, nonsense, and even exploitation, to sell the "news." Where was the search for substance, where responsibility?

At this point Adams was trying desperately to make something of his life. His cause célébre was the redemption of Israel, and with the Church of the Messiah he had found a way to haul from the dust the dream buried in a martyr's grave in Nauvoo. It was buried, too, in the turn of Orson Hyde from his magnificent obsession to preoccupation with rationale for plurality of gods and wives.

Adams felt that he was the only one who could lay hold on the dream couched in a hundred prophecies and even then sweeping toward the time of fulfillment. Israel needed those strangers from afar mentioned in prophecy, those lost sons of Ephraim, to pave the way and start pushing the children of Israel home to the land of their fathers.

Deprived of his heroes, however, he was no longer a hero to himself. Abased by his own sense of guilt, he was unable to resist the very demon which deepened the abasement. He was driven by the need of acclaim and devastated by its absence. He rejoiced when he was the focus of attention and in despair during solitude. He was moved to devastation when maligned. He was unable to handle ridicule aimed at him.

It was a time to get steaming drunk, and he did. He got the name, and played the game, with the boys of Springfield jeering him as he stumbled through the streets of a city that despised him.

There was no Alcoholics Anonymous to help, no concept of alcoholism as disease. There was only L.I.L.—sick of body and sick of George Jones Adams, as she waited for him to come home and prepared choice words to drive him deeper into his private hell. The redemption of Israel would have to wait until tomorrow.

OTTOMAN PALESTINE

When the Crusaders took Jerusalem in the eleventh century, those defenders of the Cross gathered the remaining Jews into a synagogue and burned them. Crusader horses were stained red to above the knee joint from sloshing through Arab, Turk, and Jewish blood running deep in the stone streets of the city. There was nothing new about it—the only variation being motive. For the crusaders, like the Byzantines before them, it was justifiable slaughter of those who had slain the Son of God. It was policy. Christian theology declared that loss of Jewish national independence was an act of God designed to punish the Jewish people. To help in the punishment was cause for reward and rejoicing. That it was a bloody denial of the gentle Galilean's offer of forgiveness mattered not at all.

Before the Byzantines the Roman Empire had scourged the land and the people, sacking Jerusalem in A.D. 70, destroying the Temple, and dumping its remains over a broken wall into the Tyropean Valley. When the Jews rose in rebellion again, under Bar Kochba in A.D. 132, to all intents the Romans finished the task. How could anyone be more thorough? Roughly 580,000 Jewish soldiers died in battle; 985 villages were destroyed; and Jerusalem was leveled until it yielded to the plow. Hadrian, the man responsible for it, renamed the scar on the land Aelia Capitolina, and the country of Judea he renamed Syria Palestina.

How the people of Judea, subjected to abuse in their homeland, dispersed into the world, hunted and slain in pogroms and inquisitions, could endure staggers thought. But they did. Never, even in greatest persecution, did they renounce their faith or stop circumcising their sons in visible testament of identity. Always, in every century and in every ghetto, in privation, ridicule, and torment, they were in exile. Exile in strange lands to hold tenaciously to a sense of home. Never quite assimilated. The land of their hearts, neglected and under torment of constant invasion, was always the object of hoped-for return. "Next year, Jerusalem!" More to the point: "Next year, Jerusalem—rebuilt!"

Not all were scattered abroad. Some were scattered in their own land, especially in the Galilee. The "absent" people were present always, here and there, waiting for the others to come home. It was a persistent belief in a restoration to materialize, and always they turned back to Jerusalem until in 1267—under Moses ben Nachman, the renowned RaMbaN—they settled into the old city and remained until temporarily driven out in the mid-twentieth century. Other communities of Palestine contained Jewish people through the centuries: Gaza, Ramleh, Shechem, Safed, Acre, Sidon, Tyre-Sidon, Haifa, Caesarea, and El Arish. But by the end of the eighteenth century the desolation of the land, political uncertainties, and marauding bands of Bedouins reduced the Jewish population until there were no more than 10,000 to 15,000 (there had been over five million in A.D. 70). Those who were left were the guardians of the Walls of Zion until they could be joined by their brethren in God's own due time.

The wall most sacred was the Western or Wailing Wall. In earlier years it had provided support and defense for the Temple Platform. It was part of the great perimeter wall, or box, filled in to provide the esplanade for the Temple. It was part of Herod's extraordinary building program. The Romans pushed its top down, piling debris into the Tyropean Valley. In so doing they inadvertently spared much of the lower portions of the wall. Inconsistent stonework brought it up to level to protect the Muslim shrines, the Dome of the Rock, and El Aqsa. The Dome of the Rock was built over the topmost stones of Mt. Moriah where Abraham brought Isaac for sacrifice and from which Muslim belief declares Muhammed ascended to heaven.

The platform is therefore sacred to Muslims, but no more than to the Jews, who refused to walk on it for fear of unknowingly stepping on the spot of the Holy of Holies, reserved for the high priest only. They prayed and wept below, clustering as near to the site of the destroyed temple as possible. Following their prayers and reading of the scriptures they left small notes of petition in the crevices of the stones.

Here they were mocked and harassed. Here they had to wade through garbage and human urine and feces deliberately placed to inconvenience and affront them. Pierre Loti, French author of Tahiti fame, stopped by Jerusalem and wrote:

> In the alleys leading to the Wall, blocked up with dead dogs, dead cats, filth of all kinds, I encounter a crowd heading the same way for the purpose of mocking—a whole Neapolitan pilgrimage escorted by monks, men and women wearing the red cross, like those noisy hordes back home heading for Lourdes.
>
> Along with this profane flood, I arrive at the foot of the Wall. Old velvet robes, gray old forelocks, old hands raised to curse (sic!), they are there as expected, the elders of Israel, who soon will be nourishing the grass in the valley of Jehosaphat;. . . There before us. . . is a band of Arab children, there to torment them: little ones disguised as animals, as dogs, under burlap sacks, coming up on all fours with wild laughs to bark at their feet. On that occasion these Jews did rouse me to profound pity, in spite of everything. . .

Regarding another visit to the wall Loti made a comment that revealed both his sensibilities and the prevailing prejudice: "One could almost cry with them—if they weren't *Jews*. . ."

Increasing interest in the Holy Land by France and England in the midnineteenth century brought an action by the Ottoman government which was intended to favor the Christians but, by association, brought hope to the Jews. The Turkish decree in 1856, following the Crimean War, affirmed the equal rights of "the Christian Communities and other non-Muslim subjects."

This meant eventual hope, but at the first it meant

enduring Muslim anger. Fortunately for the Jews it was directed primarily toward the Christians. Thousands of them were killed in Lebanon and Syria. Countless women were raped. Property damage was extensive, including European consulates. European naval vessels appeared on the scene, and a French expeditionary force landed, freeing Lebanon for special semiautonomous status where many Christians lived.

The Jews, impoverished and ill-equipped for resistance, threw themselves on the mercy of all and continued timid and abused, awaiting the day of deliverance. Whether they would have ever been able on their own to provide resistance to their tormentors is a question. But they did not have to do it on their own. They had kinsmen afar off who were mindful of them, and who themselves had a combined reason for Aliyah, "going up" to Jerusalem. Persecution and the sense of exile—of being away from home—these were finally to prove sufficient motivation.

What of the land? It echoed the suffering of its tenants. Centuries of warfare devastated cultivated plains and valleys. The strategic site of Hill Megiddo (Har Megeddon or Armegeddon) had reeled under 700 battles, leaving the soil well fertilized but dormant generation upon generation. Year after year Bedouin flocks had denuded the land.

Slaughter of persons and desolation of the land were not only intermittent with major invasions by visitors but constant with the marauding of local Bedouin tribes. They filled wells with stones, destroyed reservoirs and cisterns, cut down fruit and olive trees, and generally harassed villagers and farmers by destroying their crops.

In the first forty years of the nineteenth century the country was invaded by Napoleon, then the Egyptians, and finally retaken by the Turks.

Midcentury travelers into the Holy Land made dreary notes on what they saw:

. . . a complete eternal silence reigns in the town, on the highways, in the country . . . the tomb of a whole people.—Alphonse de Lamartine in 1835.

. . . both in the north and south [of the Sharon plain], land is going out of cultivation, and whole villages are rapidly disappearing from the face of the earth. Since the year 1838, no less than 20 villages have been thus erased from the map [by the Bedouin] and the stationary population extirpated.—H. B. Tristram in 1865.

Desolate country whose soil is rich enough but is given over wholly to weeds—a silent mournful expanse— We reached Tabor safely. . . . We never saw a human being on the whole route.—Mark Twain in 1867.

There is not a solitary village throughout its [the Jezreel Valley's] whole extent—not for thirty miles in either direction. There are two or three small clusters of Bedouin tents but not a single permanent habitation. One may ride ten miles, hereabouts, and not see ten human beings.

Of all the lands there are for dismal scenery, I think Palestine must be the prince. The hills are barren. . . . The valleys are unsightly deserts. . . . It is a hopeless, dreary, heartbroken land. . . . Palestine is desolate and unlovely. . . . Palestine is no more of this workday world. It is sacred to poetry and tradition—it is dreamland.—Mark Twain

A little later in the century, Pierre Loti summed it up as "This melancholy of abandonment, which weighs on all the Holy Land."

* * *

Jaffa was renowned in legend as the place of the chained Andromeda, and sacred to the memory of Jews and Christians. It was the port of entry for Cedars of Lebanon intended for the Temple. Peter beheld a vision on the rooftop of Simon the Tanner, opening the way to conversion of the Gentiles. By 1850 Jaffa had become a filthy hole, a disease-ridden combination of windowless hovels, picturesque only when viewed in anticipation from ships anchored a mile or more offshore—anchored offshore because of the shallows near the town, and because there was no wall or harbor protecting against the stormy Mediterranean.

Palestine had known a siege of locusts in 1864 and was in the midst of weathering the cholera epidemic which destroyed nearly 10 percent of the population from Constantinople to Alexandria with an agonizing feverish death. At Jaffa hundreds were dumped into a common grave dug into the beach on the north side of the town. Decomposition reeked up through the sand.

In spite of all adverse circumstance, pilgrims continued to come to the holy sites, and Jewish immigrants came, eyes shut to the squalor. In 1810 Avraham Yaari, one of the disciples of the Vilna Goan, wrote:

> Truly, how marvelous it is to live in the good country. Truly how wonderful it is to love our country. . . . Even in her ruin there is none to compare with her, even in her desolation she is unequaled, in her silence there is none like her. Good are her ashes and her stones.

No stronger sense of identity has there been in history than the affinity of the Jewish people for Palestine. Exile meant absence from home, but to that home they would be restored by Providence.

The inconceivable tragedy regarding this wasteland is that it was seen by prejudiced Christians as justifiable punishment for "a crime without parallel, one that no chastisement can expiate."

In spite of all adverse circumstance, there was a stirring in the midnineteenth century. In Britain Sir Moses Montefiore struggled with practical plans to resettle the Jews in their homeland. He believed in the restoration of Israel. So did another, a little man of incredible gifts, driven by a dream of Zion and tortured by forces he could not manage. Each of these, one notable and the other in spite of himself, would prompt and foster Aliyah. One knew he was of the tribe of Judah. The other was convinced he was of the tribe of Ephraim.

Ships had to anchor offshore at Jaffa

Street in Old Jaffa

Chapter 4

CHURCH OF THE MESSIAH

In Springfield, Massachusetts, just before editor Sam Bowles heated up his personal vendetta, George Adams struggled with the dream he had shared with Orson Hyde. The prophet Joseph was long since dead. Strang, although he had started strong, had become too absorbed by one folly after another; now he too was dead. Sidney Rigdon, William Smith, and others who had made their bid for leadership had largely failed. Brigham Young was brooking no questions regarding leadership, and he had gone full tilt to the logical conclusion of the doctrine of plurality and temple ordinances speculated on at Nauvoo. Even if Young Joseph were available, what was there left to lead? Even Orson Hyde had been seduced away from the regeneration of Israel. George Jones Adams knew that he was the only one knowledgeable enough to pull things together. Put down, he had again survived crisis. Once more revived and resurrected, his convictions regarding the return of the Jews and the coming of Messiah prevailed.

So just before sundown on January 1, 1861, G. J. Adams wrote a covenant to be signed by all who would join with him in a venture of faith:

CHURCH COVENANT

We, whose names are hereunto affixed, for the mutual benefit of each other, and that we may be the better prepared to build up and establish the church of the living God, in truth and righteousness, upon the earth; and, that we may be prepared to meet our Lord, the Messiah, in peace at his appearing and kingdom; and, for the purpose of watching over each other for good, according to the law of God, laid down in the teachings of Jesus; and, that we may the more fully confess the Lord Jesus, the Annointed One, before men and angels; and, that we may openly confess ourselves pilgrims and strangers on earth, seeking a city out of sight, a city that hath foundations whose maker and builder is the Living God:

We do therefore most solemnly covenant and agree to form ourselves in to a church of the everliving, and only true God; to be called the CHURCH OF THE MESSIAH; to be governed by the commandments, precepts, and teachings of the Lord Jesus, the Messiah, and his apostles, and to contend earnestly for the faith once delivered to the saints, and to seek after and embrace all truth past, all truth present, and all truth to come.

By the end of January forty-three persons had signed the covenant. One of the signers was that same Randolph Ladd who had earlier joined with Sam Bowles to destroy Adams' credibility, now testifying to the drawing power of Adams' dream as well as his charisma. The new church barely survived a storm of protest in the community. Innuendo had so far destroyed Adams' reputation that he had to go looking for greener pastures. For a year and a half he preached on a self-determined circuit with primary emphasis in Maine and New Hampshire. The people of Lebanon, near the New Hampshire line in Southern Maine, responded more enthusiastically than any others and in larger numbers. There, where his son Clarence had been born, he made his headquarters.

At Lebanon, Adams began a small monthly religious magazine. He had long since established his ability as a writer and under Strang had even tried his hand at editing. His *Star in the East*, begun in November, 1846, was in his hand in September, 1862, as he put together *The Sword of Truth and Harbinger of Peace*, Volume 1, Number 1. Each prospectus carried similar and, in some instances, identical phrases, for instance:

The Star in the East will stand aloof from the common, political, and commercial news of the times. Its pages will be devoted to the spread of the pure doctrine of Christ, and all the light and truth that can be obtained which stands connected with the work of God in the last days.—*Star in the East*, page 3.

The Sword of Truth. . . will stand aloof from all the popular theological "isms" of the day and contain the pure, plain, simple truth.—*Sword of Truth*, September 15.

As to temperance, we shall contend earnestly for men to be temperate in all things; and particularly to beware of drunkenness and all its train of evils and abominations.—*Star in the East*, page 3.

Temperance, we shall contend for temperance in all things, especially that men should touch not, taste not and handle not that strong drink which has made a hell of many a home and rolled the fiery flood of ruin over the peace and affections of many a once happy family.—*Sword of Truth.*

As to slavery, we shall contend boldly and fearlessly for the universal emancipation, liberty and equality of the whole human family. And we pray God to interpose and reveal an eternal law of Brotherhood. . . . —*Star in the East.*

Slavery. We shall contend for the universal emancipation and freedom of our race. Freedom from tyranny and oppression of every kind and description . . . and we pray God to hasten the time when an eternal law of brotherhood and humanity shall be introduced and established. . . . —*Sword of Truth.*

Each prospectus signaled the imminent return of the Jews to the land of their fathers, the establishment of Zion, and the coming of the Messiah. In the *Sword of Truth* Adams specified that the Jews should return "as Jews, not as Christians," providing a rationale for his later nonproselyting approach to Palestine.

It was in the statement on temperance that Adams became poignantly candid as a man seeking to establish his own soul:

. . . men should not handle—that strong drink which has destroyed heroes, sages, patriots and orators of every age and country. That strong drink which has often entered the house of God and sometimes invaded the sacred desk and hushed in death the voice that could plead like an angel the cause of God and man. [underlining mine—RMH].

He also commented on a "once happy family" providing a clue to what had happened to his original family. Apparently the first Mrs. Adams, weary of his drunken vacillation, divorced him. Given his sense of pride, he would not admit to this, preferring to take abuse in regard to his acquisition of L.I.L., the second Mrs. Adams.

His frank statement that "strong drink . . . [which had]

invaded the sacred desk and hushed in death the voice that could plead like an angel the cause of God and man" was confession from an aching heart, the realization that he had allowed himself to spoil or could not keep himself from spoiling his remarkable gifts. Perhaps writing it, getting it said, was what he needed, because he then and there began his longest dry spell and his most productive period.

Adams drank for the classical reason—to escape. His drinking added guilt which led to more drinking which heightened his insecurity which led to more drinking. He was an alcoholic, and once he gave in to drink, his thirst was uncontrollable. He became tense, irritable, and abusive.

He was curious enough, and studious enough, that if he could have had available information about what was happening in his body he might never have had to write that personal indictment. But there was no way for him to know that the alcohol he craved went straight to the frontal lobes, the seat of reasoning, judgment, conscience, and self-control. Dulling those higher centers, ethyl alcohol dimmed their functions and finally impaired them. All the while the drinker felt more relaxed because he had "released his tensions."

The only hope for him was abstinence, and that required the motivation of a strong sense of calling plus the support of strong family and social ties. As long as he had these going for him, he was in control, especially if he could be driven beyond shame to humility. But if somebody got to him—especially an editor who could make him the butt of ridicule, publicizing his weaknesses and recalling his failures—the magnetism of alcohol was too strong for him to resist. Beyond that, if the ever more demanding Mrs. Adams nagged at him, searing him with the tongue of Xantippe, he simply "escaped" all the more.

The religious journal, *Sword of Truth*, offered help in two ways. He could promote his cause and he could answer charges through a public medium. The first edition included, besides the prospectus, a statement of beliefs of the Church of the Messiah and the first of a series on "The Jews, Jerusalem, and the Holy Land." It was also an exposure of "Falsehoods and Slanders," specifically those of his old Springfield enemy, Randolph Ladd, plus Harvey Brewer of South Lebanon, a Freewill Baptist preacher, "one of that class of men who always love a lie after it is made. After becoming its step-father, will tell twenty more to prop up the first. Such men put me in mind of crows and buzzards, they love to wallow in filth." Adams also put the record straight on the misrepresentations about himself by one Hiram Manser. He then apologized to his reader "for taking up so much room. . . but sometimes we must 'answer a fool according to his folly.' And now," he continued, "let me say once for all, hereafter, when men publish falsehoods about me, I will find out as much truth about them as I can, and publish it far and near, no matter how hard it hits." Adams was ready to fight fire with fire, not realizing that by doing so he was kindling new fires where there was no call for flame.

Definitely pro-Church of the Messiah, his masthead was nevertheless surprisingly liberal and reflective of his insistence on the slogan "all truth," which was a direct inheritance from Joseph Smith.

> The *Sword of Truth* will be devoted to the propagation and spread of free, independent truth on any and every subject, connected with the great moral, political and ecclesiastical revolutions of the present age. We shall pay not the slightest attention to old creeds, old dogmas, or old musty theology, any further than they contain truth. We shall seek for truth and contend for it, wherever we find it; whether in the Catholic Church—the Greek Church—the Armenian Church—the Mohammedan Church—the Swedenborgian Church—the Spiritual Church—the Advent Church—the Mormon Church, or any of the long array of Protestant Churches; we shall oppose error, false doctrine, tyranny and priestcraft, wherever and whenever we encounter it. We shall fearlessly expose the wrong, and vindicate the right, on any and everything that comes under our notice.

> We shall be independent in everything and neutral in nothing. We shall open our columns freely to the oppressed and downtrodden, without asking their nation, country or religion, and we cordially invite progressive men or women to contribute to our columns. Write short, write vigorous, write plain and send in your contributions.

The journal featured, in later issues, the history of the Church of the Messiah, editorial journeyings (a detailed account of places and people visited, ministerial activity, and editorial comments). Nearly every issue contained at least one article about the history and destiny of the Jews.

In spite of every untoward circumstance and defeat, George Adams was coming into his own. He had overcome vilification, and with the *Sword of Truth* had his own means of clarification and retaliation. He would strive for the truth and a new sense of editorial accountability. He was fed up with editors who answered to no one and who created their own news at the expense of others. But, if called to do it, he would best them by using their own weapon. The battle would be joined, and he knew that his verbal arsenal was the equal of any opponent.

Beyond that he could multiply the effectiveness of his oratory, document his hopes, and buttress his own persuasion with appropriate scriptures and anything else that would bolster his cause. It was a new day for George Jones Adams and—please God—for the scattered seed of Israel as well.

INDIAN RIVER

Apparently it was impossible to have no opinion at all about G. J. Adams. People were enthusiastically for him or violently opposed to him. John Chamberlain, one of his converts, "accused Adams of preaching doctrines contrary to scripture." With the matter being aired in a conference session, and with Adams' incredible ability with the scriptures it was a foregone conclusion that Chamberlain would lose. The conference sustained Adams and excommunicated Chamberlain. Other members of his family withdrew with him. Adams won, but his volatile personality—which triggered opposition in Boston, Beaver Island, and Springfield—was already threatening his new venture toward peace and brotherhood.

Until late 1861 he had done his best and sometimes his worst in large cities—Boston and New York City. To return to these would have been disastrous. He avoided them and went to the country towns of Maine. His "editorial journeyings" show him preaching still in the most prominent halls, but in places like Vassalboro and St. George, small towns in the Kennebec Valley and fronting on Penobscot Bay.

Struggling to build a new identity and to forestall further unfavorable publicity, "G. J." was avoiding all references to his Latter Day Saint connections. There is never a reference to the halcyon days of Boston, New York, and Nauvoo. No reference to successful ventures in Bedford and London. No crediting of the source of doctrinal viewpoints. No tracing of ministerial authority back to ordination. A new thing had burst upon the scene at the most propitious time in history.

He had to move circumspectly because he was working in an area covered in earlier days by fellow ministers from Nauvoo. While he was establishing the church in New York in 1840, William Hyde and John Herrett were doing the same thing in Vinal Haven, St. George, Hope, and Vassalboro. He was laboring among their converts, like the Seaveys at St. George and the Wentworths at Surry. Others, like the Pendletons, had gone west with Brigham Young, while the Holmes family went to Illinois to wait for Young Joseph.

Generally he pulled it off without reference or recognition; however, in Machias, Washington County, the *Machias Republican* carried this comment.

We observe by the Portland papers that one Reverend G. J. Adams is edifying and instructing the good people of that region in relation to their religious duties. We had supposed that the redoubtable "Elder" was played out long ago, as the last we heard of him he was connected with a company of strolling actors, and "doing" Richard III nightly to a crowd of verdant individuals at a shilling a head. We believe he was at one time a disseminator of Mormonism.

If G. J. had known of that notice in Machias he might not have come so soon to Washington County but, in company with Vinal Dyer, he did come, stopping at Addison Point where the two of them were entertained by Mr. and Mrs. S. L. Wass. Mrs. Shadrach Wass was Dyer's daughter. Her husband had already become a prominent citizen of Addison, a beautiful town of fresh-built Maine style houses. They were square, well-constructed frame buildings with six-over-six windows of poured glass. They were substantial, large enough to accommodate families with six to twelve children. Leander Knowles had a shipyard at the Point which could handle the construction of ships up to 600 tons. The Masons were well-established with a hall on the main street.

Adams, a loyal Mason, attended a meeting at the Lodge. The Universalists offered the use of their meeting house, and Adams delivered a lecture on "Jews, Jerusalem, and the Holy Land." The response was excellent. A series of meetings followed, and at the conclusion Vinal Dyer, Shadrach Wass, and others went down into the waters of baptism. No matter the temperature of the water, baptisms were conducted at the time of decision. Salt water in Maine in March calls for conviction.

In April, Adams returned to the Rockland-St. George area, but in May he was back to Addison and Indian River, about four miles away and half the distance to Jonesport. Abraham K. McKenzie received him with a warm welcome, and the Calvinist meeting house was offered free of charge. Abe McKenzie thought things over while Adams went to Machias to speak in the old town meeting house and also in the new courthouse.

When he returned to Indian River, Abe McKenzie had made up his mind to be baptized as had Captain Warren Wass. McKenzie was the leading businessman in Indian River—postmaster, justice of the peace, owner of the general store, and involved with shipbuilding and coastal traffic. Adams was getting substantial citizens, none better or more capable.

He was gaining converts and building churches up and down the coast. Members of the Church of the Messiah were in Rochester, New Hampshire, York, Rockland, Thomaston, Vassalboro, Orrington, Surry, Sullivan, and Lebanon, Maine, and there was a thriving congregation in Springfield in spite of Sam Bowles and his *Springfield Republican.*

It was at Indian River that the Church of the Messiah thrived more than any other place. Adams was not long in deciding that the work would center there. He and his wife and son Clarence were given a hearty welcome by the Abe McKenzies in a typical Maine house stretching out into shed and barn, with no need to go outside in the bitter weather of a Maine winter. The McKenzies and the Adams family were to live together for "a short season" at the foot of Hall's Hill. Adams was delighted.

> As our paper will hail from this place in the future, many no doubt will feel an interest in relation to its locality and situation, as to health and business. It is located in the county of Washington, state of Maine, part in the town of Addison, and part in the town of Jonesport, the largest part being situated in the town of Addison. Indian River (from which the village receives its name) runs through the village from north to south, and is a stream quite sufficient for mill purposes and privileges. It is situated four miles from Jonesport—six miles from Addison Point—seven miles from Columbia—nine miles from Jonesboro,—and sixteen miles from Machias. There are two meeting houses in the place, and a small society of Baptists, and also a very small society of Methodists. The Church of the Messiah numbers more than all other societies put together, and is constantly increasing in numbers and influence. The principal business of the place is lumbering, shipbuilding, fishing and boatbuilding. One of the finest boatbuilding establishments in the state, is carried on in the village,

by Mr. E. B. McKenzie. The people, with few exceptions, are progressive, liberal, intelligent, and a thinking people. Such is a brief outline of our new and future home, which is to continue upon this continent for but a short season only.

Adams had always appealed to people across the spectrum of poverty and wealth, occupations and professions, young and old. It was so now. And he had arrived at the time when he could plan seriously to implement the fondest dream of his heart. He began in earnest to move from generalities about the redemption of Israel to specifics as to who was to be involved—the children of Ephraim, those strangers from afar who were to initiate the great prophecy-fulfilling move of the children of Israel to the land of their forefathers. Any who responded to his call would recognize themselves to be, by blood or adoption, of the tribe of Israel's Ephraim. His great sense of urgency—which would drive him, and hence his followers, to immediate action—was a conviction that the gathering of the Jews, their establishment as a nation, and the coming of Messiah, would "take place before the generation now living shall pass away."

If he previously had been a man always in motion, he was even more so at this point. Everything was crucial. There was a sense of obsession about him, yet his very seriousness added to the impression of earnestness. He *was* in earnest. His cause was great—the greatest—and as things had turned out, in spite of his weakness, he was the right man in the right place at the right time.

Traveling with a horse and buggy and accompanied by one of the elders, or by his wife and eight-year-old son, he covered his field. He was on the move. He was expected, supported, and coming close to being loved by an expanding group of followers.

The great seriousness of G. J. Adams and his constant activity might have led to an impression of his being a humorless boor. During this season of successful endeavor, however, when he was with people in homes and small meeting places, he seemed "downright human." The first son of his first marriage, George Oscar Adams, was happily received on his return from Civil War service. Adams enjoyed a fishing expedition with friends in New Hampshire. He was utterly delighted with his association in a marathon of visits to homes across the state of Maine. In his "journeyings," he spoke with much warmth regarding brothers and sisters who shared a real bond of affection. Generally complimentary in his remarks, and inviting others to stay where he had enjoyed accommodation, he even wrote with wry humor about some hotels he would not recommend:

> Our horse was tired out from the long drive and constant travel and we were compelled to stop at Derry Hotel. We don't know the landlord's name, and have no desire to learn it; cold meat for supper, and raw at that, only think, raw veal, and blood running out of it. Now we can stand raw beef, but not raw veal; well, we had cold meat for breakfast, and coffee; did I say coffee?. . . Well let me say the Derry Hotel was remarkable for just three things. Setting a poor table, charging a high price, and having a Yankee quiz for a landlord.

By contrast the American Hotel in Ellsworth was a favorite resting place because "the gentlemanly landlord always treats his guests with kindness and hospitality."

Traveling in a small open buggy was a delightful experience in good weather when all was going well, but in his diary he mentioned the Maine snowstorms which subdued even the glee of children, "large drifts between Ellsworth and Cherryfield" and sudden storms which made them put in unexpectedly at homes of strangers. Invariably the reception was warm, the conversation lively, and the down-east food excellent. Once in a while a wheel would break down. Passersby would take L.I.L. on to the next town while George remained for repairs while "preserving my soul in patience." That in itself is a tribute to the new George Jones Adams.

Frequently he used a phrase in introducing a sermon topic. It was "by particular desire" that he gave an address. When

Mrs. Adams, apparently without prior announcement, was the speaker of the evening it was usually "by particular desire." It was a way of saying that there was a special need, discerned by the Spirit and therefore "led by the Spirit."

While Adams preached on a broad range of gospel themes, he interspersed them with reflections on contemporary affairs, especially the Civil War, and the problem of slavery. Quite often he would insert an address on elocution and oratory. In Indian River the former actor started a drama society and even had Abe McKenzie playing roles. Abe's way of learning lines was different from George's. During a play Abe, slightly deaf and forgetful, would move nearer to the prompter, sometimes having to ask for a line the second time and then go on his way. It all added to the fun. It was great having the town's leading citizen willing to risk embarrassment to the amusement of all.

Then the Shakespearian himself responded to their pleading to do something from the stage. It was pure magic. After a few moments the man they knew became another—a slightly mishapen, malevolent, would-be king. To draw the character of King Richard III in their minds, Adams began with the closing scenes of King Henry VI. Richard has just slain the king:

> I have often heard my mother say
> I came into the world with my legs forward:
> Had I not reason, think ye, to make haste,
> And seek their ruin that usurp'd our right:
> The midwife wonder'd; and the women cried,
> "O, Jesus bless us, he is born with teeth!"
> And so I was, which plainly signified
> That I should snarl, and bite, and play the dog.
> Then, since the heavens have shap'd my body so,
> Let hell make crook'd my mind to answer it.
> I have no brother, I am like no brother;. . .
> I am myself alone.

From there he launched directly into Richard III, warming

to the opportunity to transport his hearers and to prove himself the artist:

> I, that am rudely stamp'd, and want love's majesty
> To strut before a wanton ambling nymph;
> I, that am curtail'd of this fair proportion,
> Cheated of feature by dissembling nature,
> Deform'd, unfinish'd, sent before my time
> Into this breathing world scarce half made up,
> And that so lamely and unfashionable
> That dogs bark at me as I halt by them;—
> Why, I, in this weak piping time of peace,
> Have no delight to pass away the time,
> Unless to spy my shadow in the sun,
> And descant on mine own deformity:
> And therefore,—since I cannot prove a lover,
> To entertain these fair well-spoken days,—
> I am determined to prove a villain,
> And hate the idle pleasures of these days.
> Plots have I laid, inductions dangerous,
> By drunken prophecies, libels, and dreams . . .

So eloquent was he that his listeners were, indeed, transported. Their rude unpropped stage was Boston and New York, and Adams was a scheming dissembler from another time and place. The applause was spontaneous and loud. Not only did they accept him, most of them came close to loving him. Their hearts were opening to make him one of them.

Everybody was family—or seemed to be—as had always been part of the genius of small town life in Maine—nearness with its inevitable impact for good or ill. Personal behavior was subject to the immediate social control of reaction by family and neighbors. Persuasion might be aided or thwarted by the intermeshing of lives. Humor might become barbed by the very proximity and familiarity. Secrets were not easily kept, especially if they were illicit. But let tragedy strike, and the whole community responded to personal and family need. When the essential sense of community was threatened, or presumed to be threatened, let the intruder beware. To become part of the community was easy, if by birth. To become part of the community by moving in was something else. It helped to have roots or a precondition of shared relatives or faith.

Rapid acceptance of the Adams family, and especially of G. J. throughout Maine—but especially in Addison, Indian River, and Jonesport—was a tribute to his persuasive powers, but more, his ability to relate to people on a personal basis. It was a warmth noted especially in the frequency of his returning to the table of many families. It was marked by the sincerity of prominent D. J. Sawyer's offering a resolution in public meeting inviting Adams to return soon to Jonesport.

Given the background of Springfield's vilification and his own need of approval, G. J. Adams' heart was melted by the action of a conference of the Church of the Messiah in Indian River:

> Whereas, Brother G. J. Adams has labored with us in word and doctrine from time to time . . . and faithfully preached unto us the gospel of our Lord Jesus the Messiah, as contained in the scriptures of truth, and
>
> Whereas, God has blessed his labors, and made him a means of turning many to righteousness and led them to embrace and obey the truth in all its fullness, therefore
>
> *Resolved*, that we receive, confirm, and will sustain Brother G. J. Adams, by our prayers, our faith, and our sympathy in the Church of the Messiah with all the gifts, callings and authority, that the Lord has confirmed upon him.
>
> *Resolved*, that we, as a church and conference, deeply sympathize with our worthy brother for the almost unparalleled persecution, that he has been called to pass through in establishing the Church of the Messiah in this age . . .
>
> *Resolved*, that we have unwavering confidence in his integrity, honesty, and purity of purpose and we believe that he is a man called, and sent of God, to lay the foundation of a great work in the last days, and as such we cheerfully recommend him to the kindness, consideration and sympathy of Christians and good men, throughout the world.

It was in the friendly climate of Indian River that Adams

gained sufficient confidence to risk sharing a little of the George Jones Adams others knew so long before. One night, "by particular desire, we gave our experiences in the early part of our life, and related a wonderful shipwreck, together with some visions that we had received in our early days, and gave many incidents of our early life and travels."

A mellow, more confident and accepted George Adams sensed the support with which to move confidently toward fulfilling the vision shared by Orson Hyde over twenty years before. If their surmise was right about timing, the children of Ephraim would soon act in behalf of the children of Judah.

The time had come, and Adams could not resist the irony of proposing the Mission to Palestine in the midst of his enemies. He called a church conference on May 19, 1864, in Springfield, Massachusetts. One of his most ardent supporters, Helen Hazelwood from Riverside, New York City, phrased the resolution, including a flowery declamation regarding the lively church in Springfield which was thriving in spite of opposition. She offered an avowal of "confidence, respect, and affection" for G. J. Adams.

The heart of the resolution came next:

> That this church approve of the contemplated mission to the Holy Land, and of the object of it, and that we will cheerfully assist the brethren entrusted with it by all means in our power, and we do hereby most cordially tender to them, our prayers, our good wishes, and our blessing; and have faith that they will be prospered in it, and return to us in safety.

Ten days later at Lebanon, Maine, Adams convened a supplementary conference for the purpose of further completing the priestly organization of the church. He spoke at length "on church organization, and the duties and callings of the various officers of the church." With no reference to his Mormon background, he added apostles to his bishops and elders. Andrew Jackson Tibbetts was then called "to the office of an apostle in this church, to bear witness to all nations, of the Dispensation of the Fullness of Times." The church with a united vote confirmed the call. It was right out of Latter Day Saint procedure, including provision for "common consent." Adams was leaning heavily but covertly on his Nauvoo heritage.

From then on the frequency of sermons and articles on the redemption of Israel increased. The *Sword of Truth* carried additional information regarding the current status of affairs in Palestine. Headlines reflected the feeling of increased tempo: "Number of Jews," "Signs in the Holy Land," "The Jerusalem Mission Once More," "The Jews and Their Future," "Improvements in Jerusalem" "Ancient Telegraphing."

Like Caleb and Joshua sent by Moses to spy out the Land of Promise, two were designated to search Palestine for signs of promise. G. J. Adams was to be accompanied by Joseph Bennett of Springfield. Funds were raised by public appeals from the pulpit and the pages of the *Sword of Truth*. But when the time came to go there was severe illness in the Bennett family. The alternate was easy to choose—Abraham McKenzie of Indian River. Besides, Adams felt "led by the spirit" to select him.

Adams said two were required to go, but there was another who decided to accompany them, and George would not or could not say no. Circumstances decided against her going, however. They were unable to find passage from New York without a long delay, so Abe McKenzie went back to Boston to arrange passage on the "Jehu." Accommodations for two only were available.

George and his wife stopped in Newark to visit with his older sister, Mrs. Stephens. After arrival in Boston he wrote for the *Sword of Truth:*

> It is well for me to state, that owing to a combination of unforeseen circumstances, Mrs. Adams has now made up her mind not to accompany us, although she had made her arrangements so to do. The deepest interest is everywhere manifested in our mission. Thousands are waiting to hear

our report from the goodly land, the "Heavenly Country," the place of gathering in the last days. . . The vessel, the *Jehu* in which we purpose to sail to Malta, is now loaded, and sails tomorrow morning, June 20th. So now dear friends and brethren, farewell for the present. I remain most truly and sincerely yours in hope of a new and glorious age of peace on earth and good will to men.

Looking down Hall's Hill, Indian River, Maine

Abe McKenzie home, Indian River, Maine
(where G. J. Adams lived)

Chapter 5

JOSHUA AND CALEB

After a delay of twenty-four years George Jones Adams was on his way to Palestine. He was no tourist although he enjoyed historic sites more than most. He was going home as surely as any child of Israel. He was, like Joshua of old, going into Canaan to spy out the land.

Back in Boston a lonely and disappointed Mrs. Adams penned her feelings in prose and poetry. Her facility with words was a portent.

She went, a white winged creature,
A sea gull in her sweep.
Her proud keel kissed the waters,
Her sails salute the deep.

She sped before the breezes,
A thing of life and light,
The waters ope'd before her,
A pathway clear and bright.

Her towering masts were pointed
Towards the smiling sky,
As if she said so hopefully,
"I put my trust on high."

She bears our loved ones from us,
To a far and distant shore;
Heaven bless the hearts that fill her.
And return them home once more.

L.I.L. Adams

Neither George nor Abe was stranger to the sea. While it was the fate of some to "endure 'til death won't come" the retching agony of seasickness, they greeted a heaving, rolling deck with anticipation. If there had been other passengers these two would have been cursed for their good fortune. There would have been no sympathy among the damned for those with rosy cheeks and hearty appetites.

Their vessel—the bark *Jehu*—had three masts, square-rigged, with a fourth rigged fore and aft. Having cast off from the steam tug and under free sail they soon lost sight of their native shore. A fog "shut down" over them as night came on. George and Abe soon found themselves stowed comfortably in their berths. Exhausted from the exertions and excitement of leaving and, submitting readily to the rhythm of a ship on a gentle sea, they slept until midmorning.

Still in fog and rain *Jehu* was moving before an oblique wind varying from south to southwest, bringing about a six-knot breeze. In addition to George and himself, Abe counted eleven other men on board: Captain James E. Smith; Mr. Hurd, first mate; Mr. Adams, second mate; Mr. Anderson, steward; George Smith, captain's boy; and six sailors completed the ship's crew.

When the rain let up in the afternoon he counted the other "passengers:" two fighting cocks which were brought out for a few moments of excitement and wagers; six hens for fresh eggs; and a pig, reserved for a later feast.

On Friday the twenty-third the fog cleared just long enough to allow an observation: they were, at noon, in latitude 42-32, longtitude 64-45. They sighted something else too—the loss of their hoped-for roast. Breaking loose somehow, hooves slipping on the hard deck, the pig slid into the sea. It was probably just as well; since he was already a pet, they would never have been able to raise a knife to him.

The weather continued alternately foggy and bright with a light sea for several days. Sometimes there was a flat calm. George and Abe, having taken on board several newspapers, broke one out each day and called it "The Morning News." They were also reading a travel book to ready them for the

Holy Land. It was the 1859 edition of William Thompson's *The Land and the Book.*

One hen, proving herself to be unproductive in the egg department, became chicken stew on the first clear day, Sunday, June 25. That evening George Adams talked with the crew about the fullness of the gospel.

With the breeze settling to a consistent four to six knots, *Jehu* left a wake of progress across the Atlantic. Abe was impressed with the crew as a "very quiet set of fellows, each attending to his several duties without noise or hustle." It was "a beautiful sail, at no time since we left Boston has it been rough enough to upset a pepper sauce bottle sitting on the table." That night the wind increased to 11 knots, still south-southwest. They had averaged 150 miles per day.

Abe reveled in the action of the bark. "Spent considerable time on deck today looking at the white cap waves and seeing our noble bark lush her long smooth sides through them. So Jehu-like, the sailing qualities of our noble bark prove appropriate [to] her name as far as relates to speed and power and then she has a hull of equal strength to almost any pressure of sail." He added, "Our steward proves to be a splendid cook, makes nice mince pies and sets his table with great variety of dishes."

On July 1 the wind freshened from the northwest corner. They ran directly before it with the sea roughening, "Brother Adams was up part of the night, a little restless as he has never been used to being tumbled about quite so smartly before. The vessels which he crossed the Atlantic in before were vessels from 8 to 1400 tons which did not dance about in a sea quite so lively as our little bark does." Abe had experienced lively tossing as close to home as Western Bay and Moosebec Reach, which turned wild before the wind and a fast running tide.

On July 3 two events loomed larger than would have seemed possible back in Indian River: "At six o'clock this morning a whale ship laying to under close reefer main tops'l and fore stays'l, the first we have seen for a number of days. We considered it a treat to have something to look at besides the vast ocean and blue heavens." Aloneness gave way to eager, pulsing necessity to shout across the water, helloing strangers as if they were long-lost kin. The second event was in anticipation of Independence Day, "The steward has slain two chickens to cook for Fourth July dinner tomorrow."

Abe's journal entry for the day of celebration was first wistful (at being away from home) and then turned to the excitement of festivities that seemed all the more festive for being in the midst of vast isolation. "We commenced to celebrate the day as best we could, being in the waters of Europe and with only a small pistol of which Brother Adams took command. . . .He first ordered a salute of 13 guns, had the stars and stripes hoisted and gave three cheers for the flag, three for the President of the United States, and three for the bark *Jehu* and her captain."

They were four days out from Gibraltar—God willing and the wind holding—and Abe was feeling grateful for their good health, his salt water bath, a warm clime, and the soups Brother Adams was enjoying: "First pea soup, then bean soup, mutton soup, veal soup, beef soup, and potato soup." Clearly there was nothing wrong with their stomachs. Of course they had sea biscuits to absorb the liquid and cut down the internal action.

The captain ordered an awning put up over the poop deck for the travelers. When Adams wearied of preparing the *Sword's* manuscript for mailing at Gibraltar, he and Abe lounged "and smoked some of them nice cigars presented to us by some of our friends in Boston for our enjoyment."

Becalmed and agonizingly close to Gibraltar, they looked at the sand hills of the Cape to port and the African shore to starboard. Having made excellent time, they were only twenty days out of Boston. Now, well in view of the Straits of

Gibraltar, they could do nothing but watch vessels heading north and south with sails more limp than full. At last a breeze took them close enough to Gibraltar to allow Adams to take his letters and manuscript to shore for mailing. A boat was lowered with him, the second mate, and four sailors.

The Machias papers had reported a cholera epidemic in the Middle East but death, even by the thousands, reported days or weeks after the fact from six thousand miles away, was remote and unreal, with a momentary spasm of hurt or alarm. Abe and George were more concerned with wind for sails and whether they could get their letters on some packet bound for New York or Boston. When George was refused permission to go ashore from the lighter and then the mail was lifted from him with a pair of tongs, cholera began to be a fact of life. That really dawned on him later, however, because at the moment he was incensed by the officious manner of the English functionaries. As happened so frequently it was a relatively minor matter which triggered his reaction and because he reacted vocally he probably got worse treatment than if he had remained calm or at least courteous. When outrageous payments were demanded for tonnage dues, quarantine money, and postage, he became furious. The posting of nine items cost him $26.13—and then the recipients washed his money before touching it! Scant attention to the incident was found in Abe's diary, but Adams vented his anger for several paragraphs—none of them complimentary to the British officers at Gibraltar. The memory of the tongs lingered as a reminder that they were approaching a vast area troubled by cholera.

For several days they beat against an east wind or were becalmed. Snow-capped mountains of Spain won their attention. They gazed for hours, wearying only because they were scanning the same vista from the same spot. Abe, so accustomed to the crystal clear atmosphere of Maine, was irritated by the smoke-filled sky which they had experienced "ever since we made this continent."

When becalmed under the hot July sun, both of them stripped down to their underwear and slippers and alternately sun-bathed and lounged under the awning over the poop deck. Having exhausted their "daily" newspapers, they turned to the pages of the *Sword of Truth* to be refreshed on the prophetic background of their mission. They continued reading from *The Land and the Book* and *From Dan to Beersheba.* The first of these was especially helpful in readying them for scenes they would soon be viewing.

"Hey, look," Abe pointed to the rail, and George saw one of the sailors disappear head-first, trailing a yell of gleeful anticipation. The yell and a mighty splash merged. Momentarily forgetting the sharks they had seen from time to time, Adams called for a line to be cast over the side. Over he clambered, hand under hand until he was in the water. At that point some idiot in jest called out, "Shark!" Adams changed directions post haste, trying to hoist his overweight body up the side of the vessel. It was too much to expect of arms unused to hard labor. Abe and the captain answered his frantic cries for help and hauled him in, wet, frightened, and angry until he saw the fun of it all. Then he laughed with the others.

That evening, lounging on a deck that rolled gently, Abe asked George how it all had begun—this obsession for the return of the Jews which had brought the two of them from the restless waters of the Maine coast to this gently rocking cradle on the Mediterranean.

There was nothing strident or preachy in his voice when he replied. He had no need to convince Abe who was here, sharing the mission. George was almost pensive, "It happened a long time ago before William Miller's followers even thought of camping outside Philadelphia to await the Messiah. I heard a man of eloquence and conviction speak of the prophecies of the Return. When he had finished I knew he was right and, as fate or God would have it, I started with him toward the very same destination which claims us.

"When we had gone as far as England and I found it necessary to remain there while he went on, I followed his journey with prayerful hope and conviction and while in England was overjoyed to discern signs of the movement of men towards prophecies fulfillment. Not long since, Napoleon had promised to restore Palestine to the Jews. Lord Shaftsbury, Disraeli and others were pushing for the return. Just before we landed in England the *London Times* printed 'A Memorandum to the Protestant Monarchs' pleading for the restoration of the Jews to Palestine. The time was ripe and now of course it is riper still.

"But before my friend or any of us who felt the call to be our own, could take effective action, our dream was shattered for reasons I have never told you and which are too grievous to relate. But the dream remained and kept on swelling within my soul. God knows I have let it languish from time to time. I have told you enough about me as I have told no other so that you will understand my trials and my shame. But the Lord does not leave us alone and I know he has called and set us apart in these latter days to assist in Zion's cause." Abe felt the magnetism of the man and his dream, and he knew the scriptures well enough to know that the time had come. Whether this man or others succeeded, it was time for "going up to Jerusalem," or Aliyah as the Jews called it. And it was time to lend a hand to a nation in exile. He was glad to be a Caleb to this enigmatic, brilliant, and earthy Joshua.

BETH-EL

"Damn!" George Adams exploded. It was more than an oath, it was a cry of frustration. Here they were, less than two miles offshore from Jaffa, in sight of the ledge of rocks that forced them and any other ship of reasonable draft to drop anchor. The mound of stone buildings with its skirt of citrus groves surrounded by sand and more sand was right there and they were denied a chance to land. Jaffa already had its share of cholera without adding more from Alexandria. They would go on to Beirut, 150 miles north, and then be put in quarantine for ten days.

Cholera! As they sensed its pain and stench, it became more than a mere annoyance to them. Alexandria, Egypt, where they changed from sail to steam, had been largely closed down, shopkeepers and families having headed out of the city. Boats by the hundreds tried desperately to land cargo in custom sheds already chock full. Ahead of them at Beirut 60,000 of the 80,000 population had fled to mountain villages for safety—and no wonder: there were as many as thirty-five deaths per day. Moslem women, especially those who were pregnant, were among those quick to die. Dispatches from the U.S. Consul in Beirut, Augustus Johnson, to Secretary of State W. H. Seward, were indicating deaths in excess of 10 percent of the population along the coast from Turkey to Egypt within a three months period.

Although they could not land, there was nothing to hinder passengers from boarding their vessel. One hundred came aboard the Austrian steamer *Stambul*, adding to the forty deck passengers already spread out with their bedding and provisions. The noise and scramble was beyond belief. At 10:00 p.m. the captain weighed anchor for Beirut.

When daylight came, Abe went on deck to watch the shoreline of Palestine. They were heading north, and the captain had stopped during the night in the bay at Haifa. The long mountain called Carmel was background for the village and reached inland alongside the valley of Jezreel. Then they went past Tyre and Sidon to Beirut and the prison which was to be their place of quarantine.

They had scarcely settled into their miserable quarters

when news came that the quarantine was lifted throughout Palestine. It was good news to be free to go. They were quick to move into the Grand Hotel de la Universe, "well furnished, the table bountifully supplied, not less than six courses served at dinner and four at breakfast and all for about 90 cents each per day." Then they were faced with the necessity of finding passage back to Jaffa. It took five days, but they thoroughly enjoyed the beautiful city, largely deserted. Then on Friday, August 11, 1865, they "landed at Jaffa . . . went and found Mr. Loewenthal, found him to be a gentleman and willing to do everything for us that was in his power to make us comfortable." They had corresponded with Herman Loewenthal, a young converted German Jew and prominent banker and merchant in Jaffa who also ran an enterprising import-export business. It was good to have feelings of confidence about the man who could pave the way for them locally.

They took the Nablus Road which, near the town, ran to the northeast through level ground. Any hurry they felt was offset by their joy at the fertility of the soil and the abundant fruit. The late-blooming, rocky coast of Maine at Jonesport was never like this. Low-bush blueberries were incomparable but hard-won while here one could lean out windows to pluck an orange or pomegranate. Oranges! They were Christmas fare back home, one to each member of the family, peeled with haste and relished slowly to prolong the joy.

They walked slowly, pausing to wonder at the unfamiliar sight of neat rowed citrus bordered by date-palms and interspersed in untended plots by tangled ground cover and prickly-fruited cactus. Scarcely 400 meters from the gate of Jaffa they were drawn to a slight rise in the ground on their right. They turned to walk no more than seventy-five meters to the crest. A stone house was falling apart, trees were sparse and untended. There was a well. The view was unbelievable, offering the Mediterranean to the west and the outlined buildings on Jaffa's hill to the southwest. At their backs orchards and fields of grain gave way to sand and the hills of Ephraim.

Their eyes met and they started simultaneously to speak: "Abe!"—"George!" Each laughed, louder than usual because emotions needed release, each one sensing the other's thoughts. Then George said: "Abe, we may not find a better place than this, but we had better look around to make sure before we talk with Loewenthal."

For a moment they looked westward into the reddening sky of sunset over the Mediterranean, each thinking his own melange of thoughts, on being in the place of sacred memory, on loved ones far away, and on gratitude to the God of Abraham, Isaac, and Jacob.

Abe's journal contained the best portrayal of the next few days of their orientation and search for a place to build their future.

After getting ourselves and our baggage on shore we were very fortunate in getting our quarters for the time we were to stop in Jaffa. At the San franciscan [sic] convent which is Catholic, they received and treated us very kindly. We then took a walk up through the city, which is called one of the oldest cities in the world and I should not doubt it from its appearance. We went out through the gate and took a stroll among the fruit gardens which looked very beautiful, orange trees, lemons, pomegranates and any amount of fruit that I cannot name.

The next morning they took breakfast with Loewenthal and his pleasant family. They have a beautiful stone house and live in good style. He gave us an invitation [to] come on Sunday and hold services in his house. We went at the appointed time [and at] 10 o'clock Brother Adams preached a short discourse on prophecy and some of the objects of our mission. We sang with help at the piano which Mrs. Loewenthal played. Jack Philips a Scotchman and the city physician was also present and took part in the services.

On Monday, we started about sunrise with our guide who could talk English, a Turk by the name of Alla Sulliman, [sic-Ali Solomon] on an exploration to the North and Northeast of Jaffa, on horseback, a distance of some 6 miles over vast tillage lands where there is raised large amounts of wheat and barley until we came to the river Ogee, travelled up the river which is about 8 rods wide, waist deep, on either side of which is large plains of mulberry trees. After travelling some three or four miles up the river we came to a falls on which was erected a stone dam and mills for grinding wheat. There were some 12 run of stones all at work grinding wheat but at a very slow rate, everything stone but the waterwheel, shaft, and hopper, any amount of camels, donkies and mules bringing the wheat in bags and carrying the flour away in the same. We then came back passing some very nice looking fruit and vegetable gardens until we struck the Jerusalem road.

No final determination was made regarding the purchase of land to build a community. They were partial toward the small rise so near town but vexed by the problem of land to till. For that they would have to go farther out, perhaps a mile or more, and that presented problems of access, wasted time in going to and from, and the danger of fields being molested by Bedouins who had a reputation for spoiling the grain by stealthily and quickly cutting it for hay and trampling the rest for meanness. There were problems as well as hopes.

On Tuesday, August 15, they commenced packing and getting ready for the journey to Jerusalem, proposing to start on horseback at four the next morning. Then they

visited the Ancient house of Simon the Tanner, where the Apostle Peter was stopping when Cornelius was ordered by vision or an angel to send men from Caesarea to come there and tell him words whereby he could be saved. It comprises two rooms with a court in which is a well and is located by the Seaside. It has stone steps to go up on the outside, no doubt the same ones which Peter travelled when he went up on the house top to pray as recorded in the Scriptures. This city from a distance on either side presents a very pretty appearance, but when you have to travel through it the inside has more the appearance of a subterranean cavern without order or system.

Wednesday, August 16. After leaving Jaffa last night on our noble steeds with Alla for guide we journeyed on for Jerusalem, the Holy City, through vast plains of the most beautiful soil on earth, the thousands of acres on which the wheat had been taken off were now growing millet. About sunset we reached Ramley 9 miles from Jaffa where we stopt and bated our horses and got a nice supper at the Russian convent, about 10 o'clock. We left Ramley and travelled 4 hours when we reached the foot of the mountains or hills of Judea where we stopt again at a coffee shanty, took some coffee and laid down on some benches until daylight when we again mounted our steeds and proceeded through the mountain an Oh such a road or mountain low path it would be utterly impossible to describe. Must be travelled in order to be realized. Many of the hills side hills and bottom of the vales were under a state of cultivation, mostly olive trees, grape vines which presents a beautiful sight. At 8 o'clock A.M. we reached the quarantine grove and pitched our tent or took one that was already pitched among a great number of others in an olive grove where all travellers and freight carriers have to stop and ride out a quarantine of five days about 4 or 5 miles from Jerusalem. Among the people there is quite a large number of Jews emigrating the city of their fathers.

Thursday, August 17. Our quarantine grounds is at the bottom of a very deep cut in the mountains and therefore very hot in the middle of the day. Our landlord Mr. Shiel about dark last night sent us in our bedding which was ample allso for eatibles bread cooked chicken beef a nice pudding and 3 bottles of the juice of the grape or what they call white wine, therefore we are as comfortable as can be expected under the circumstances, but oh the expenses of travel by steamboat or on the land and our living it is enormous, and our detention makes it doubly so to us, everything is very dear except the products of the land, the means of transportation is very bad and will probably be so as long as it is under Turkish rule, a people that are opposed to all improvements, the most bitter hatred exists even now among the Arabs against the Jews. We saw some of it exhibited yesterday by a dragoman who would not let one of them come near or pass by our tent. The nights are very much cooler here than at Jaffa or Beirut. Our quarantine is rather lonely as there is none on the ground that we can converse with. I am now looking out of our tent on a beautiful young olive grove of about 20 acres.

Friday, August 18. Still in our tent and as patient as we possibly can be waiting our time. The olive grove above spoken of is a work of five years as we learned by Mr. Mordacai our dragoman who is to take us into the city of Jerusalem when our time in the quarantine prison is up. The grape also is cultivated to a very great extent on the sides of these hills, the present crop is just beginning to ripen and they look very beautiful. I took a very bad cold either here or on way up from Jaffa and with rather a poor chance to doctor for it. I wrapt up as warm as I could, set a gallon jar of water longside of me for medicine and drank pretty heartily about every half hour untill I emptied the jar which relieved me very much. All we have had to see or notice here is the different characters in quarantine about two thirds of which are Jews emigrating to Jerusalem and the Arabic officials, and the passing and repassing of camels, horses, mules and donkies, freighting between Jaffa and Jerusalem, all freight was allowed to pass but not the carriers of it.

Saturday, August 19. We feel some relief knowing that we have only today and tonight to stay here. Our landlord has been out here today and is going to send our dragoman early tomorrow morning with his horses to take us to the City. My cold still hangs on to me and I feel everything but comfortable. Quite a number of the party left this morning, their time being up, and others arrived to take their places.

Sunday, August 20. And now comes the tug of war and that is to settle with Arabs for their system of business is all they can get and after that is paid, every one that has looked at you will rush around you poking his hand out for baksheesh. We finally got through with the expense of about $40 from Jaffa to Jerusalem. Bills paid, we mounted our horses and moved on through a deep cut in the hills for about three miles. . . the first object that breaks in view in the vicinity of the Holy City is the Mount of Oives which has quite a number of trees on it. We soon came in sight of the Russian grounds outside of the City on which are erected some beautiful buildings and around which is built an expensive wall about 15 feet high then passed through the Jaffa Gate and soon reached our hotel.

Monday, August 21. Suffering from the effect of my cold and the fatigue of my ride from the quarantine grounds, I did not leave my room until this afternoon. When Brother Adams and I with our guide Abraham Mordacai a Jew and also a gentleman who has a good knowledge of the city and country we went forth to explore around the city. We passed out of the Jaffa Gate, took our way to left on the West Side of the City, passed first the valley of Gehenna which descends toward the South the southern part of which is called the vale of Hinnom. At the southern end of this vale stands Joabs well from which men were drawing and carrying it on donkies into the City. We then took our way up another vale on the south and east of the city first passing Solomon's Gardens then the pool of Siloam opposite of which on the side of a steep hill stands the ancient town of Siloam. A little further to the north and on the same side hill on our right we passed the tomb of Zachariah first then the tomb of St. James and last the tomb of Absolom. We then ascended a very steep hill to the St. Stephens Gate and back to our hotel.

Tuesday, August 22. Kept my room this forenoon as the state of my health will not allow of my travelling around much. Started this afternoon in company with our guide to visit the Mount of Olives, the place where Christ ascended from the earth in his resurrected body in a cloud and also the place where he will set his feet when he comes again the second time without sin unto salvation and sit to judge the world in righteousness. On our way there we entered and examined the Garden of Gethsemane. On arriving at the Summit of the Mount of Olives we felt as we never had before as in casting our eyes about we could look on so many of the familiar Bible scenes, to the East and some three thousand feet below the level of our feet lay the Dead Sea and a portion of the river Jordan. To the West the city of Jerusalem. Between us and the city and coming from the north the Brook Kedron, to the South and left being a continuation of the Brook Kedron is what is called the Valley of Jehosophat. All of which is now more or less under cultivation of fruit trees.

Wednesday, August 23. Today am not able to go outdoors. It is very unpleasant in such a place and at such a time, where there is so much to see that is interesting from its antiquity and its connection with history and teachings of the Old and New Testament. I visited most of the places of interest outside, and around the city but there were many places of interest inside the walls of the city that I was not able to visit being unable to walk about. There is a great deal of building and improvements of a public character beside private residences in process of erection at present although there is a great deal of old ruins and rubbish in many parts of the city to be got out of the way and built up. A short distance from the city north or northwest the Russians have built a large number of very nice buildings and walled them in which they call New Jerusalem. It stands on an elevation considerable higher than the Holy City and presents a most beautiful appearance, being all built of a beautiful light coloured stone and must have cost an immense amount of money.

Thursday, August 24. As sick as I am and have been this morning our dragoman according to arrangement came for us with his horses and tent for our journey to Bethel, some twelve or fifteen miles, and we got ready and left the city about nine o'clock A.M. Our party consisted of Brother Adams, myself, and Abraham Mordacai, our dragoman, an attendant who rode a donkey and led the mule that carried our tent, and three Arab soldiers. The country we rode through was mostly under cultivation of wheat. Although with no appearance of life or vegetation at present with the exception of scattering olive groves and grape vintages. I think the side hills and vales must present a beautiful appearance after being sown and growing with wheat and barley. We arrived at the town of Bethel about 1 or 2 o'clock and pitched our tent alongside of one of Jacob's Wells which supplies the town of Bethel. . .

Leaving Abe to rest from the journey, George went straight to the sacred hill between Bethel and Ai. To this very spot Abraham had come from Haran in response to a voice from heaven, looking for a city "not built with hands," a city that would be more than stone upon stone. At this spot, the voice spoke to Abraham again. Here he had built an altar.

The story persisted in the generations that followed. His grandson Jacob, when distraught at the deserved anger of his brother, Esau, had come to the same place. Here he had seen a ladder extending into heaven. On this mount the promise given to his grandfather was repeated, the promise of a homeland and a mission, and here Jacob received the name Israel, an identity to last through all generations.

It was all written in these jumbled stones. Somewhere among the multitude of them were the very ones Jacob had used to construct an altar of memorial, pouring oil upon them. George pled with his memory to recall the Stone of Scone which he had seen in the Coronation Chair at Westminster Abbey. It was purported to be the pillow stone of Jacob, by legend hefted and hauled from Beth-el to Egypt and eventually to England. Was there resemblance between that dull purple sandstone—that Stone of Destiny and this multitude of rocks? This was no mighty mountain as size is measured in feet or meters, but it was mighty in terms of memory and of hope.

George laboriously hefted stones to clear a small area, while piling twelve stones, one upon the other, in honor of the tribes of Israel. That done, the beating of his heart was not in weariness. It was in aching memory of Orson Hyde, in expiation of his own sins, and now—by the grace of God—in anticipation of the return of the Children of Israel to this rock-filled, desolate, scorpion-infested land which, like Israel itself, was shortly to be redeemed. Not wanting to duplicate the experience of Orson Hyde on the Mount of Olives, but in the same spirit of anticipation and dedication, he had chosen this spot—the place of the Promise to the Children of Israel. There was no better place to pray for the return of the house of Israel. Ready at last, he returned "to the tent for Brother McKenzie, who had remained behind by my advice on account of being unwell. I found him ready to accompany me. At just one hour before the sun went down, we commenced our ascent of the hill of Hope [and] soon reached the altar."

Abe was weary and feverish and could hardly do anything but go along with what George had in mind. He preferred to do that seated, leaning back against the ancient ruin at the crest of the hill. Abe was thrilled to share the moment, especially in a place holy to generations of Jews, Christians, and Moslems, but headache and nausea threatened to engulf him.

Alighting from his horse, he stumbled over some of the million stones which covered the crest of the place which Abraham, and Jacob after him, had called Bethel, the house or place of God. He looked down into the Jordan Valley and beyond in the perpetual haze to the mountains of Moab. Gazing beyond the troublesome rocks underfoot, he visualized the yesterdays when vines were heavy with grapes and fields were green with the year's second crop, millet, following the harvest of winter wheat. Beyond olive groves the hills of Samaria stretched to the north, and the hills of Ephraim fanned out toward the Mediterranean.

The demands of his feverish body subsided before the wonder of a privilege given to few, and most certainly envied by the folks back home. Abe bowed his head and heard the strong voice of George Adams in prayer:

Oh! Lord God of Israel, thou great Jehovah, God of Abraham—of Isaac—of Jacob and of the prophets,—thou great I-AM, who doest thy will in the armies of heaven, and among the children of men—Oh! thou who raised Messiah from the dead, and gave unto him the key of David and named him the Lion of the tribe of Judah,. . . O Lord! thy hand has been heavy upon thy land and people. Now O Lord have mercy upon this land, which thou didst give unto Abraham and his seed, remove the curse Oh Lord from this land, and restore the land for thy people Israel. We praise thy name that thou hast restored the former, and the latter rains in fulfillment of the testimony of the holy prophets. We now O Lord! beseech thee to restore the former dews from heaven, and the showers of rain, in the midst of the seasons; that this land may again produce plenteously and in great abundance for thy people Israel. And now we rebuke the curse which has long hung upon this land and we bless the land,. . .

We have seen the afflictions, witnessed the abuse, and heard the groanings, and seen the oppression of thy covenant people. O Lord have mercy upon them, pity their low estate, and deliver them from oppression and sorrow. O Lord turn all nations in their favor and let the set time to favor Zion speedily come and turn the glory of the Gentiles like a flowing stream to Jerusalem. . . . O Lord we have heard the wailing, and witnessed the sorrow of thy people, have mercy upon them, and deliver them from their low estate. Remember thy oath unto their fathers and deliver them as thou hast sworn unto Abraham and Isaac and Jacob, and also unto David, and O! Lord bless the land as they come in to possess it. O Lord bless all nations and kings and rulers of the earth and all churches, and societies who are friendly to and will help downtrodden and oppressed Israel. But O! Lord those nations, and churches, who oppose and oppress Israel, let confusion, darkness and destruction come upon them; for in thy word, thou hast said that the nation and kingdom which will not help them shall perish; yea, those nations shall be utterly wasted. And now Oh Lord! we pray for thy church, the church of the Messiah . . . And when thy servants the watchmen of Ephraim, go forth to push the people together to the ends of the earth, give them favor with thy people Israel and may they see that thy servants, the watchmen of Ephraim are their true friends. . . . And now O! Lord of hosts have mercy upon thy servants who have come this long journey to perform this work, forgive our sins, and purify our hearts; give us faith and courage to persevere and hold out to the end, and never falter or deny the faith. . . . We now feel to renew our covenant to be faithful, with all we have, and all we are, and all we hope for, God being our helper. . . .

And now, O Father, in thy presence, in the presence of angels, in the presence of the hosts which surround us, we pour this oil upon this altar of twelve stones, to be a witness forever that we have done as thou hast directed us. . . .

George testified in his diary:

Thus closed the most eventful day of my life. The sun had set before we left the hill of Hope. We returned to our tent and partook of a good supper. The tent for that evening was left entirely to ourselves. Thus we had it during the evening as a place of worship. Our dear brother A. K. McKenzie, who had been sick some days, after evening worship, had a good night's rest notwithstanding the day's exertion. I spent much of the night in prayer and other religious devotions. . . .

On Friday morning, Bro. McKenzie being much better, after we had partaken of a good breakfast, we rode out and viewed the country. . . . We then rode on to the holy city, passing through Ramah and other small towns, or villages, having a grand view of Jerusalem and the Mount of Olives from the north. We reached the city in time for a late dinner, after which we visited the wailing place of the Jews.

George was certain that the wall was of such antiquity that it had been built by Solomon. One could tell, he said, "by looking."

Clustering toward the north end of the wall, as close to the site of the ancient and destroyed Temple as they could be and yet not defile it by their footsteps, the Jews, dressed in black, swayed and bent their bodies toward the Wall, or leaned into it and wept. They wept in loneliness, in fear, in frustration, and with a persistent hope that seemed like madness. Most of them had come with one great last exertion of their life, to fulfill at last their annual pledge, "Next year in Jerusalem." They did not come to live but to die in Jerusalem. Yet, even in this fatalism, they were asserting the persistence of their dream. Leaving the Wall, they pressed small scraps of paper folded against the prying wind into the crevices of the weathered rocks.

Some of these were the same persons Abe and George had seen near the Church of the Holy Sepulchre. Newly arrived and unfamiliar with the city and its Christian holy places, they had wandered too close while treading the maze of streets from Damascus Gate to the Wall. "Stop! Stop!" voices of Arab and European Christians screamed at them, "Christ killers!" Angry shouts and brandished sticks drove them away just short of defiling by their presence the sanctuary of

Christ. Had they persisted into the presumed place of his crucifixion they would have joined him in death, so bitter the hatred was, and yet these who might have been slain by the Christians for trespassing in their holy place, did nothing to lift a hand against the Christians who now stood gazing at them in their hour of worship and pain.

How could God make of such despair a kingdom of glory? Others of the children of Israel would have to be called and challenged, a generation that would leave home, not to die in Jerusalem, but to live there, not to wait for providence to act but to act with providence to establish the long cherished dream.

George Adams stood weaving with them without realizing it, sensing that somehow that Wall was his as well as theirs.

From twenty-five years deep inside himself he yearned for the prophet he had known at Nauvoo, whose discernment had propelled him to this place of destiny. He was homesick for Orson Hyde who had stood on this very spot.

He reached out his hand and grasped the arm of Abe McKenzie, "Let's go," he said. Abe, eyes moist, turned with him. The two walked in silence back to the hotel, scarcely aware of small grasping hands begging baksheesh.

THE PLOT

They were restless to get back to Jaffa and to be on their way home to Indian River. As soon as George and Abe arrived at Jaffa they got in touch with Loewenthal. He was ready to sign a contract with them for land and supplies, including some livestock to be ready for their arrival in June or July of the following year.

After a review of the various sites they had previously considered they settled on the very first they had seen, out Nablus Road (now Eilat) at the crest of the small rise, only five minutes of pacing walk to the northeast from the city gate and the market. Due west from them, and only four minutes away was the shore of the Mediterranean. It was handy for those who would find their living on the sea and close enough for youngsters to run off their energy. G. J. reached in his pocket to touch the small seashells he had gathered for his eight-year-old son, Clarence.

Standing on the flat crest of the small rise, George and Abe dreamed and planned. Two streets would intersect at right angles. A one-storied church would be built in the southeast segment of the intersection. Otherwise, two-story houses built to a standard plan but allowing for some variation would grace the streets. It was a pleasant lay of land. The streets would be broad enough to accommodate a line of graceful pools down the center, watered from the well situated on the property.

To facilitate the view of the Mediterranean Sea and of Jaffa itself, a family could modify colonial frame house designs to allow porches above as well as below. New England shutters would provide privacy and protection.

With a flash of insight, one of them came up with a simple suggestion bordering on genius: "Let's build them in sections before we come, and on the way. It will speed the building process. Why not bring everything we can, built to standard size—doors, windows, shutters?"

Standing on the spot, they already had the colony built and were luxuriating in the achievement. Although he said nothing about it, another "City Beautiful" was in the memory of George Adams. There was too much of hurt to speak of it, but this little spot would be an unheralded memorial to a man and a city that had long since set him on the path to Zion.

They did not permit themselves to be troubled by the one fact that should have concerned them a great deal. Conviction of the inevitability of their cause, and belief that God would sweep opposition out of their way as needed, dulled their usually acute perceptions. It was not like Abe, the alert Yankee businessman, to brush aside a potential hazard, but G. J.'s confidence was compelling.

The Supreme Porte, Sultan of Turkey, looked with disfavor upon any colonization or land-holding in Palestine by aliens. Turkey had already suffered from many incursions, and the Sultan was particularly sensitive to threats of overt or subtle invasion from Western powers. He had signed a decree of religious freedom, but he was adamant about land purchase. Loewenthal gave assurance that there were ways to get around the restriction. He could arrange it.

For farming they hoped for an acreage of superlative soil about a mile away. Some of the land had already been under cultivation by the ill-fated colony of Clarinda Minor. Brushing aside any thought of barriers to his mission, Adams paid little attention to the Bedouin raid, rape, and murder of that small colony's members. He would have a large enough colony to discourage raiders. Nearby was land under investigation by Sir Moses Montefiore.

The soil of the Plain of Sharon was fertile enough. Simply add water and it pushed up crops beyond imagination, honoring farmers of enterprise with two, even three diverse crops a year. They could hardly wait to tell the folks at home whose experience with growing seasons was limited to a very short one indeed.

They would secure enough land for crops normal to the area—wheat, barley, millet and cessin (sesame)—and they would need land for experimenting with crops they felt more at home with, which would add dimensions to the life of Palestine. They would try potatoes and cabbage and berries. Eventually they could add to the citrus and apricot trees that already produced so abundantly—and grapes—preserves and jelly for themselves; wine for others. There must be flowers which would remind the settlers of home. . . perhaps hollyhocks.

Five days were scarcely enough to finalize arrangements, but they did their work well. Their understanding with Loewenthal was summed up in a letter which they both signed:

Jaffa 2d Sept 1865

Gentlemen:

We authorize you to buy for our account the part of the property belonging to Haramkin Pourtongast, a Greek Christian at Jaffa, this plot being the deserted biara situated on a hill on the side of the way to Nablus about 7 or 800 steps from the Jaffa gate on which hill there is a well and a house in ruins as also a number of orange trees, dates, pomegranates, figs and others.

We allow you to pay for it the price demanded if not exceeding L450. It is understood that you do your best to get the above named plot of ground as cheap as possible and that you will charge us your direct outlays and all your expenses to have the title deeds drawn up in due lawful form and that you will deliver this letter to our consul against a receipt in duplicate, one to be sent to us, the other to remain with you. To cover your outlays we have withdrawn forty pounds, for which please to hand us receipt in duplicate, and we engage ourselves to remit to you the remaining part of the cash for the Biara as soon as we receive your notice that the sale has been concluded.

(Signed) Yours truly,

G. J. Adams
A. K. McKenzie

There is no doubt expressed in the contract. They left with full conviction of the success of their venture and of the certain victory of the colony. Their association with Loewenthal and his family was congenial. They had no reason to expect anything other than fair treatment and good measure. Even Consul Victor Beauboucher in Jerusalem was to welcome the prospect of additional income for his poorly paid staff in consequence of the forthcoming arrival of the industrious Yankees. In a later report to William Seward he was to confess that there might be difficulties but that he was sure all things could be arranged.

George and Abe met many interesting people. They were particularly impressed by the commitment of the Franciscan monks and by the enterprise of the leaders of the Jewish community. The Jewish rabbi and money changer, Meyer Hamburger, was also serving as correspondent for *Hamagid*, a Hebrew weekly published in Lyk, East Prussia, whose editor was an ardent Zionist. Hamburger's eyes queried their sincerity and conviction, and their ardent disclaimer of proselytizing intent but, once convinced, he warmed to their venture and saw in them an exemplary lever to inspire his own people back in Europe to similar ventures. To the pair from Indian River it was precisely their intent as the "Sons of Ephraim."

Aharon Chelouche was in the forefront of those eager to see a Jewish neighborhood extended north beyond the walls. There would have to be enough people to give reasonable guarantee against marauding Bedouins. The proposed American colony would strengthen that guarantee. Chelouche was looking at the land adjacent to and between the Americans' intended purchase and the sea.

Several people shared the dream of a burgeoning city beyond the walls of Jaffa. It had to be. It would be. Whatever that larger community beyond the walls might come to be called, it would yet become—as George Adams was predicting—the commercial center of Palestine. There would be a small hilltop crowned with a settlement committed to an Israel yet to be reestablished. There was no more strategic location than the one they chose. The Arabs, looking on casually but catching the rumor of what these two Americans were planning, began to talk about the "Amalikans," a name that was to designate the area for a hundred years.

Their groundwork mission done, George and Abe left on the French steamer *Ilyssus* for Alexandria and Marseilles. They oh'd and ah'd their way across Europe and were especially impressed by Paris. In London George took his friend to neighborhoods which kept his own heart pumping with nostalgia. Scarcely a word was said about past history, however. It was the sharing of new experience which bound them together, especially listening to the great preacher, Charles R. Spurgeon, and visiting the sights which draw every tourist—Westminster Abbey, British Museum, Parliament, St. Paul's Cathedral, and the Tower of London. At the Tower, George could not resist a dramatic telling of Richard IV whose villainy had focused there. At the Abbey, Abe was excited about the Coronation Chair, and the Stone of Destiny. "Look at the color of it, and the size. How did it get here?" he wondered.

The long trip home was rough and stormy. George and Abe ate heartily while others took to the rails. One day, with the storm increasing, another minister hastily called a prayer meeting to the amusement of the veteran travelers from Indian River. Abe encountered animosity by pushing his testimony where it was not wanted. George found few to respond to his offer to preach. The voyage was a dead loss except that it accomplished its major purpose—it got them home.

People from Addison, Columbia Falls, and Jonesport poured into the Indian River meeting house to hear the report of "Caleb and Joshua." They were not disappointed as the pair left the details until later and took the congregation straight to Bethel, Jerusalem—and Jaffa!

There was no early curfew that night. Children, at first responding to the thrill, fell asleep one by one, in parents' arms and on the edge of the rostrum. To the youth and adults, until now it had all seemed like a far-fetched dream—real enough as the scriptures were real . . . but for somebody else to sweat through and to realize. All of a sudden they were face to face with two who had been there. These eyes had seen and these feet had walked on holy ground. What was more, George Adams and Abe McKenzie were more convinced than ever. They talked of departure during the next summer and already were speaking of a second contingent a year later!

For carpenters there would be building of houses and hotels. For shipbuilders and captains there would be coastal traffic waiting for Yankee enterprise. Craftsmen of all kinds could work their trades, and they would have a joint venture—to plant and harvest fruit, vegetables, and grains. The land was fertile, the rains were more plenteous than ever—and even the dew was abundant.

They did not dwell on the heat and the surrounding sand and, of course, had no way of gauging the severity of winter storms. Nor could they know that the Sultan of Turkey had heard of their intrusion and would eventually issue the edict intended to sink their dream before it was fairly launched.

Ledges at Jaffa
Ship at anchor in distance

Beth-el, c. 1870
Courtesy Harvard Semitic Museum

Chapter 6

FINAL PREPARATIONS

Tim Drisko was angry, not angry as hell but angry *at* hell which was threatening to engulf his whole peaceful village of Indian River. He was especially angry at what he viewed as the devil himself in the person of George Jones Adams.

Only three people seemed to see through this devil's disguise. He, Tim Drisko, a God-fearing Methodist, merchant, and earnest keeper of the welfare of Indian River. (He was Timothy Driscoll by birth, and Drisko by his own choice among the many Driskos he found in this part of Maine.) Then there was Morey Wass who reckoned, as Tim did, that the silver-tongued orator had beguiled the whole community. And there was that smart anti-Lincoln editor of the *Machias Union*, G. W. Drisko.

There was somebody else, but nobody knew for sure who—the one who had sneaked into the McKenzie barn when everybody else was enraptured by Adams' Bible-quoting palaver in the meeting house and bobbed the tail—right up to the dock—off Adams' high-stepping horse. Besides that, the culprit had slashed the baptizing pantaloons of the sheep-stealing preacher the neighbors were beginning to call a prophet.

Like the editor had said in the *Machias Union*, G. J. Adams' scheme of helping restore the Jews to that God-forsaken land of Palestine was a hoax, the worst ever to be perpetrated in those parts. Nobody could get ahead of the fast-talking preacher—he was clever and always had at tongue's end the right scripture to end the argument and quiet doubt among his glaze-eyed followers.

Just to look at the man was enough! According to editor Drisko:

G. J. Adams is of medium size, black curly hair, sharp dark eyes, intellectual forehead, Roman nose, lips that shut tight as a clam-shell, showing great firmness if not absolute obstinacy. His countenance is Jewish, and he claims to have Israelitish blood in his veins. He has an exceedingly glib tongue, and his quotations from the Holy Writ are always on hand. He appears to be some years older than madam, hale and hearty and ready for any emergency.

The editor credited the observations to a Dr. Bradbury who said of Mrs. L. I. L. Adams (those initials providing her with the nickname Lil):

Mrs. Adams is quite fat, very fair, and has seen some forty-five summers. Her face is oval, her neck is short, bust full as a prima donna's, her eyes dark blue and sharp, her voice pleasing, her tongue exceedingly voluble and her command of language ready. When not excited or angered by opposition, her conversation is intelligent and ladylike and quite agreeable. But oppose her peculiar doctrines and you stir up a hornet's nest at once. Her appearance is not so ladylike and her tongue runs like a pepper mill.

"That's the two of them all right," mused Tim. He had his own way of describing G. J. Adams. He told Morey Wass, "Adams' eyes are set so close together he can look down the neck of a Johnson's liniment bottle without crossing 'em!"

Even a smart fellow like Abe McKenzie had been taken in . . . Gram Burns and her whole tribe . . . the Ben Rogers and the Nortons were supporting the hare-brained scheme of emigrating to that land which was cursed of God 2,000 years ago and had not been "worth a continental" since.

Maybe Ackley Norton, skipper of the *Elvira Conant*, and fresh home from the sea, would help. Tim hadn't had a chance to say hello since Ackley had stepped ashore a couple of days before and was glad to run into him while he was visiting at Lang Leighton's house on top of Hall's Hill.

After greetings and passing the time of day were over, Tim asked, "You been over to Gram Burns, Ackley?"

"Yes. It was some good to see her again."

Tim turned sober and then jumped into what he was

hoping to talk about, expecting at last to have some support.

"You been to any meetin's at the hall down the road?" (He pronounced "road" with two syllables—ro-ud.)

"Sure have!" said Ackley, and waited. Gram and the others had already warned him of a possible tirade.

"Ackley Norton, you've been around and have tucked away a lot of experience. Tell me, what in tarnation possesses these otherwise intelligent friends and 'relatives' of mine to take departure of their wits and listen to—no, *swallow*, what that devil Adams has to say?"

Ackley paused a moment, wanting to avoid an argument and knowing he couldn't.

"Well, it seems to me that what Adams says makes a lot of sense, especially in light of the Old Testament prophets. It even looks like he might be a prophet himself. Tim, to tell the truth, I plan to go along!"

"Sacrilege. . .heresy. . .he's a damned imposter! I warn you, like I've warned everybody around here, your brains have been replaced by a lobster's tomalley. You'll see the day you regret listening to this nonsense."

Tim stalked out, more intent than ever to find some way to bring the village to its senses before the whole lot of them got sucked into Adams' charade. That's what it was—a senseless game, with the devil himself calling the tune.

That night Tim Drisko went to church, not to his own Methodist church but to G. J. Adams' Church of the Messiah. As he strode down the aisle he could hear the sudden hush, followed by a wave of whispering as he took his seat near the front.

After the customary singing and praying—the hymns being familiar ones Drisko had sung himself many times—G. J. stepped to the pulpit. He wasn't a big man, but behind that pulpit he looked big, and the way he took hold of it made him look as if he were piloting a vessel through stormy seas. He was in charge.

"Brothers and sisters . . . and friends," Adams said, looking Tim Drisko squarely in the face. "Many pious people are becoming quite excited in relation to our object in going to Palestine and are extremely anxious to know what we will do when we get there. We answer first that we are going there because the Lord has, by his Spirit, put it into our hearts to go there in fulfillment of many prophecies in the scriptures of the Old and New Testament. Second, we are going there because the set time has come to favor Zion and Jerusalem, as foretold by all the holy prophets. Third, we are going there because 'The times of the Gentiles treading under foot' are now running out and drawing to a close. Fourth . . "

Tim's own faith was pretty solidly based on the "good book." He'd always thought of it as the Word of God. Hearing those Bible references, just for a fleeting instant, his conviction that the Word was being manipulated wavered a trifle, and then his resolution snapped back in control.

"Fourth, we are going there as benefactors to the people and country, and to pay a debt of gratitude which we owe to down-trodden and oppressed Israel. And last, but not least, we are going to prepare a place for the 'Bride, the Lamb's wife [the church] to flee unto at the time the midnight cry is made. . . .'

"As to what we will do when we reach that glorious land, we answer that we will just do what people do in other countries—we will raise wheat, barley, millet, cotton, castor oil, olive oil, wine, hemp, and all kinds of fruit, produce, and vegetables. Some will work as carpenters and boat builders. We'll run boarding houses and a stage line for the 30,000 European pilgrims that go each year. We don't expect to die for lack of employment."

Tim didn't hear much after that. He'd heard about the oranges and pomegranates—and the earthly paradise. So much hogwash. He waited for what he had to do.

Finally, Adams finished with, "Are there any questions?"

Some asked questions that showed they wanted a little more assurance, but most were curious to hear about the goodly land to which they were going, how long it would take to get there, would they get to walk where Jesus walked, and would Mr. Loewenthal have everything ready when they got there.

Young Ellis McKenzie, Jr., already an elder of the church at twenty-two, raised more thought-provoking questions. He wondered about relationships with the natives, and was it true that the Turkish sultan was not too kindly disposed toward Christian or any other colonies, and how was property to be held—as it was here, or in some other way?

They were questions demanding answers and an opportunity to add that credibility which comes with certain knowledge or at least honest facing of the inevitable.

Tim listened to Ellis and became aware of the young man's sincere conviction. These folks really felt that they were on the Lord's side, and that they were going on a mission which could not fail. Most of them were convinced that the Lord would overcome all obstacles. He waited for Adams to answer young McKenzie.

Adams hesitated. It was unlike him. Whether he was hedging or struggling to find ways to give assurance at the crucial points so shrewdly perceived by Ellis was uncertain. His voice rose a pitch or two, more nasal than usual. He delayed precise answers with more of the certain prophetic words of old. That momentary loss of his customary self-control, and what Tim took to be deception and lack of Yankee candor by Adams, prompted Tim to proceed with his errand.

"Reverend Adams!"

"Yes, Mr. Drisko." Adams knew full well that here was a man who had set himself the task of cutting his credibility to shreds. Tim Drisko would like nothing more than to reduce him to laughing stock, discrediting him before his supporters. What Drisko did not know was that Adams believed fully in there mission as divinely inspired and had believed in it for twenty-six years—longer than young McKenzie had been alive. Something else Tim never suspected was that the other Drisko in Machias was succeeding in rubbing old wounds, reminding Adams of what he had labored hard to forget—that he had feet of clay.

Tim began, more quietly than he'd intended, "I've had a vision."

This caught the listeners by surprise. They didn't know whether to laugh at the absurdity or cry with joy that it might be true. They were expecting a harangue or some sarcastic, accusing question. Maybe Tim Drisko *had* seen the light.

"Yes, my friends, I've had a vision. Part way through a restless night, I had what I think you'd call an open vision—in the spirit, so to speak. I was walking on the far side of Hall's Hill when what should I run smack into but the arms of the devil. It was a fearsome experience. He had me, right there, but said he was going to give me three chances to go free. I hadn't thought of the devil as being one to play games, but there it was.

"'Find one thing I can't do,' said the devil, 'and I'll let you go free.'

"I thought of some pretty impossible things and then settled on one.

"'I'd like to see you take Moosepeak Light out there and set her down on Ames Hill back of Jonesport.'

"The devil acted like I'd set a pretty hard task for him but then, quick as wink, Moosepeak Light was sitting on top of Ames Hill.

"He smiled patient-like and then said, 'You've got two more chances.'

"It was going to have to be a sight more difficult than I'd

supposed. Then, I said, 'Remove the water clean out of Moosebec Reach.'

"The devil said, 'That's easy, chum,' and quick as before the water was gone, the boats were down, and the fish were flippin' on dry land.

"The devil was having more fun than I was. He rubbed his hands in anticipation and said, 'Tim Drisko, you've got just one more chance. If you fail this time, I've got you. Name one thing I can't do.'

"Well, I thought for a long moment and then said, 'Devil, you find me a bigger liar than G. J. Adams!'

"'I'm done!' said the Devil."

Tim Drisko had warmed to his story, and when it was over he gave a raucous, triumphant guffaw of victory, slapped his thigh and stalked, head high, out into the night.

There was a moment of awesome silence in the congregation. . . not a whisper. Then everybody started to laugh. It was a good story, but its point was preposterous. Tim had made a fool of himself instead of the preacher. But, with some, the thought did linger.

ON HALL'S HILL

Winter was a bearcat in Washington County, hanging tight until too close to June. Natives grumbled about living on the frozen rim of the world, complaining that there were only two seasons—winter and the Fourth of July. Sometime during the first fortnight of May winter delivered a last desperate blast, burying everything with a foot or more of snow. Then the sun declared, "Enough!" and the miracle of spring began.

Within hours, bleached-bark birch, popple, and gangly spider-limbed hackmatack donned tender green coats. Spruce was flecked with light green growing tips, contrasting sharply with the almost black green of winter's mantle. All of a sudden, the snowy-white blossoms of wild strawberries mingled with violets and the small cup-like flowers of blueberries beneath and around the crest of Hall's Hill. Straggly raspberry bushes hung on to clothes brushing past.

A tiny forest of pines and spruces hugged close to Lang Leighton's cottage perched on the top of the hill. Small garden plots, laboriously shaped and encouraged between rock outcroppings, were tucked here and there. Everywhere, in trees and bushes, small birds, home for the summer, were in a flurry of building and repairing. It was late May, 1866.

Except where massive rocks made it awkward, houses of Leightons, Rogers, and Driskos marched downhill like dominoes. At the bottom, Abe McKenzie's house, between school and Union church, served as anchor—one of those Maine homesteads built to flout bleak winters. Abe could leave the kitchen and never set foot outdoors, while stopping at barn, necessary, and woodshed before turning in for the night.

Lumber for most of the houses had been milled alongside the Indian, the river that gave the town its name and divided it into two parts. Flowing water powered the sawmill. Since 1763 this Washington County area, especially around Machias and Whitneyville, furnished millions of feet of lumber to a growing state and nation. In addition to pine, cedar was found in abundance near Indian River providing lumber for the shipyard of E. B. McKenzie which flourished with the building of tenders and yawl boats.

Fronting on salt water as well as being halved by Indian River, the village was advantaged by numerous inlets and reaches for rowing small pods or scudding up under mutton-chop sails. At the mouth of Indian River on the Jonesport side a small beach beckoned to boys intent on wading or skipping flat stones six to a dozen times across the water.

It was home, a good place to live—neither as prosperous as

Addison with its affluent houses nor as busy as Jonesport with its swelling lobster business and steamboat wharf. There was stability, and one would have to admit that Abe McKenzie was a major factor. He was not alone. His two brothers and Ben Rogers were also pillars. And now, with their families and a husky segment of the three communities, at least two of these were committed to go with G. J. Adams to Jaffa. There were many who wondered if the whole tightly knit area would ever recover.

The most verbal in their skepticism were Tim Drisko and Morey Wass. They felt that they had reason to be alarmed with a host of relatives planning to leave within weeks. Both of them were Methodists and rued the theft of family and friends who had walked into the waters of baptism with the black-pantalooned sheep-stealer Adams. It was a foregone conclusion that Tim and Morey would be aided, if covertly, by the Methodist preacher. What he might conceive and feel impolitic to do himself, Tim and Morey bent into eagerly. Thus it was that during the late months of winter and early spring, 1866, they fired off letters to Sam Bowles, editor of the *Springfield Republican*, and found him happy to cooperate.

On June 5, following an excited visit by a mighty pleased Morey Wass, George W. Drisko, editor of the *Machias Union*, began in earnest to dredge up the past of G. J. Adams. Morey had secured the 1861 articles exposing Adams as a drunken imposter in Springfield. Apparently Morey had written not only to Springfield but also to several townsfolk and editors from Rutland, Vermont, to Newark, New Jersey, pleading for information against Adams to be sent to the *Machias Union*. George Drisko was impressed by the volume of mail, claiming to be swamped by more than fifty letters leveling reliable criticism at George Jones Adams as "an unworthy and extremely wicked man."

The tempo and volume of editorial warning to the residents

of Addison, Indian River, and Jonesport increased. It was 1861 all over again and Adams, so long on the wagon and with his reputation and Palestine venture at stake, increased his efforts. He began to lose his temper, loudly proclaiming his innocence, and taking up the cudgel against George Drisko.

"Lil, the dogs are at my heels again and won't let up. If they destroy my reputation and credibility with these people the whole thing is lost. I've done my level best and now, in sight of our goal that fool—oh, it was him all right, Morey Wass—has conspired with George Drisko to smear me all over Washington County."

In the old days of debate, thrusting and counter thrusting, George could keep his calm, only occasionally flushing with anger. His face was not flushed now, it was white, as if death had touched him too soon. He was afraid, and in the moment of his need he turned hopefully to the one who had known him longest and shared his struggles. But she had never shared the weight of his guilt, only the shame. Now, for the first time in their hectic career in sight of victory and seeing it threatened, she drove him deeper into despair, "You'll be the ruination of this family yet, George Adams, I swear you will!"

There was a time he would have turned easily to drink, but there was too much at stake. Besides, liquor would not be easy to get quietly. So he lashed out at George Drisko, venting his frustration in a torrent no less abusive than the editor's. He first rebuked Drisko for his anti-Lincoln, anti-Union sentiments:

> Have you forgotten your dirty meanness, your treasonable and secession principles. . . your croaking against your country?. . . You, G. W. Drisko! You talk of "wind of doctrine," you never was anything but wind politically or religiously. . . you are a miserable humbug.

He needn't have written thus, nor did he have to make public issue of it, railing against the Driskos and Morey

Wass. He was the revered leader and needed only to live above the abuse, but that was easier to say than to do, especially when memory burned with past failure, disappointment, and guilt.

George entered into a near frenzy of final recruiting and fund-raising with no let-up in preaching and baptizing. A visit to St. George to see a bark being built there made him more determined to firm up arrangements for the *Nellie Chapin* nearing completion at Addison Point. It was being built by Leander Knowles, a master carpenter of excellent reputation and known to them all. A partnership of eight owned the vessel, including a major partner with 4/16 ownership, Nahum Chapin. He had the right to name it. Another was Samuel P. Adams of Boston. A sleek and beautiful bark of 567 tons, 133½ feet long by 30.3 feet beam and 18.8 feet from deck to keel, it was built with square stern and billet head. There were full seven feet 'tween decks to accommodate her unusual cargo of families. Cabin house and galley were enlarged. Overhead were two square-rigged masts plus one rigged fore and aft. From bowsprit to rudder the *Nellie Chapin* would be a master's dream, and Captain Warren Wass, 1/16 owner and long-time member of the Church of the Messiah, would be its master.

If all went well they should be able to embark for Jaffa by the end of July or the fore part of August. The *Sword of Truth* carried the news already shared around Indian River but eagerly awaited in Surry, Lebanon, and Rochester where other families were preparing to go:

> We give notice that we have chartered the new and splendid barque *Nellie Chapin*. . . . The cabin is finished in splendid style. The price of first cabin passage from Jonesport to Jaffa, is one hundred dollars in currency. The price of second cabin passage is sixty-five dollars in currency. Lumber will be carried from Machiasport to Jaffa for $20 per thousand feet. Freight taken twenty per cent lower than the common price up the Mediterranean.
>
> The average price of lumber at Machiasport will be about $13.50 per

thousand, instead of $13... Good panel doors will cost from $1.85 to $2.35, and window sashes will cost from nine to twenty cents per light, according to the size. Four thousand feet of boards will make our smallest size two-story houses. These houses will contain four good-sized rooms, and a cook room. The parlor of this house will be twelve by thirteen feet, the dining room 10 by 13 feet, and the rooms upstairs will be the same size, the cook and wash room 8 by 10 feet. The entire cost of lumber, doors, windows and nails for such a house delivered in Jaffa will be about $175. Brick and cement for chimneys will cost about $15; gutta percha for roof $20, making all together $210—add $15 for butts, screws, and other little items, and it will be about $225. Cheap enough for the substantial part of a neat small two-story house delivered in Palestine, this will build a house that will make any small family comfortable for the time being. Now let it be understood that this will be a house with frame well boarded, a good roof and chimney, doors and windows, good floors, and closets. But this will be an unplastered house, but it can be made comfortable. . . . Children over twelve years of age will be charged full price. Children over three years of age, and under twelve, will be charged half price. Children under three years of age, free.

All preparations for raising houses—in fact, the ability to proceed with the whole venture—were predicated on the availability of the plot of ground they had agreed upon with Loewenthal who, in anticipation of their coming had been appointed to serve as United States vice-consul in Jaffa. Neither Beauboucher, a Belgian, nor Loewenthal, a converted German Jew, were United States citizens which seemed, at first, no more than an interesting anomaly but which would turn to distressing irritant as months wore on. Further to guarantee the arrangements for land, Adams had gone in February in company with Rolla Floyd to Washington, D.C. Armed with a letter of introduction from Senator Lot Myrick Merrill of Maine to Secretary of State William Seward, Adams was ushered into the presence of President Andrew Johnson and then into the office of Secretary Seward. A petition had already been prepared for transmission to the Sultan of Turkey and received the approbation of Seward who agreed to send it along to the Sultan via the United States Embassy in Constantinople.

Highlights included in the petition signed by fifty adult petitioners included:

> . . . being fully convinced of the great fertility and immense resources of that partially desolate land if brought under a proper state of cultivation, and having a strong desire to introduce American agriculture, with all its modern improvements, that we may aid in developing the immense resources of this part of your Majesty's dominions, we do therefore most sincerely and respectfully pray and petition your most Royal Majesty for a firman of protection, and a grant to settle upon and improve the unoccupied lands on the plains of Sharon and Mucknah and other waste and unimproved lands in the vicinity of the above named plains, on the land once known as the land of Ephraim and Samaria. We further pray your Majesty, that in the firman of protection, your Majesty will grant unto us the right to purchase such lands at any time your Majesty may wish to have them sold at such prices as your Majesty receives for other government lands in Palestine. Our object is not to go to Palestine as missionaries, or as politicians. . . . We have no wish or desire to interfere with the religion or laws of your Majesty's government or empire. But we wish to come as peaceful sojourners. . . . We are farmers, mechanics and artisans, and we wish to introduce all the useful improvements of the age which have been made in agriculture, science and mechanism . . . and as our emigration will be attended with much expense, we pray . . . the privilege of landing the building materials for our houses, our household furniture and agricultural implements, and also our mechanical tools at Jaffa, free of duty.

Sent in the first part of March, the petition would require a minimum of eighty days for travel alone and with the delays of processing in Washington, Constantinople, and again in Washington there could be no guarantee of an answer before departure. They lived in hope of a favorable answer but could not imagine refusal for so worthy a cause with a prophetic timetable moving inexorably in their favor.

Word received from Loewenthal in July seemed a portent of the complete success of their petition—the Pasha of Jerusalem was granting them the right to land all items they had mentioned free of duty. Also, Loewenthal said he had been successful in securing several plots of land. He had also purchased for them twenty horses, eight cows, 2000 bushels of seed wheat, 1000 bushels of barley, a large amount of lime, and other things. He indicated that the rains were abundant, as were the crops. "Thus the great work of restitution rolls on and none can hinder," George assured the readers of the July 25 edition of the *Sword of Truth.*

In spite of the opposition of G. W. Drisko and the "raging and foaming" of a few "sectarians" in Indian River, plans were proceeding well.

By this time an idea, oft-mentioned by Adams, detailed at length by him in the *Sword of Truth*, September 15, 1862, and recently reiterated in the pulpit, had been received enthusiastically among the people who were going . . . and cynically by the press. Several nicknames were being tossed at the Jaffa bound members of the Church of the Messiah. Off-beat believers had to have an easy handle, for scorn or affection—Methodists, Mormons, or something-ites depending on the name of their leader, like Millerites. But these folk were not known as Adamsites. That was awkward. They were not Mormons or Saints, although the rumor was making the rounds that the relationship, at least in doctrine, was more than anyone was admitting. They were coming to be known as the "associates" in reference to their new entity for doing business, the Palestine Emigration Association, or "regenerators" because they were going to regenerate the land and people of Israel. Mostly, however, they were calling themselves the "Children of Ephraim."

"Why, Pap?" asked twelve-year-old Theresa Rogers of her father, Ben. "Why all this talk about Ephraim when we're going to the land of the Jews?"

Ben reached out affectionately to his attractive dark-eyed daughter. "Because it says in the scriptures that the descendants of Ephraim, the favored son of Joseph, shall be lost among the Gentiles, and then, at the time God plans to restore the offspring of Judah, who are also scattered but not lost, to the land of their fathers, the sons of Ephraim shall learn of their true lineage and shall gather to the land of their fathers, establishing an ensign to draw the children of Judah to Jerusalem."

"Oh, Pap, you went too fast. Everybody says you've got a knack for scripture, and that you're spiritual, but take it easy for your not-so-spiritual daughter!"

He went through it again, explaining patiently that the seed of Ephraim would be forerunners of the Jews to encourage them, as Jews and not as converted Christians, to get a move on and return to the promised land. For this reason, the Church of the Messiah, called of God through his servant, George Adams, and of the blood and lineage of Ephraim, had a great and marvelous calling. Were they of Ephraim? Adams said so, and Ben Rogers could believe it, whether by lineage of blood or sympathy, it did not matter. The cause was just. Furthermore, as Pastor Adams had said many times, there was a debt owed the Jews, for the heritage of faith they had brought to the world, for the birth of Jesus, and for having taken so much abuse at the hands of Gentile Christians. The heart of Ben Rogers responded to that.

Theresa picked up her baby brother, George, a child she cherished, straddled her hip with his tiny legs, and reached out her other hand to Bradford, age eight. They went off together in search of the mischievous six-year-old Arthur, who was far more interested in playing store than going to Jaffa. "V.P.", at fourteen, was absentmindedly helping her mother, Lucy Drisko Rogers, prepare supper. Her thoughts were really on the girls and boys preparing to emigrate to the land of Turks and Bedouins. Imagine being on board ship for more than a month with the likes of Everett Batson and Orrin McKenzie . . . and who could tell what manner of handsome young men might show up from Lebanon and Rochester.

Lucy Rogers, just beginning to feel the soft, thrusting movements of tiny limbs beneath her heart, wondered how she would get along on a pitching, rolling ship, especially in time of storm. She was, however, thoroughly convinced that they were doing the Lord's will. The prophecies were true and due to be literally fulfilled—soon. George Adams had shown them, beyond doubt, that the signs of the times called for action now. If, by the grace of God, their lot could be improved in a land that was full of promise, where crops were abundant in a climate more mild than on the top of Hall's Hill, that would be extra and accepted with thanks. For the children it could be rough—a different and troubled culture, an area frequented by war, with necessity to provide for them some semblance of education and community. Well, Yankee ingenuity and hardiness had much to recommend it. And they would not be alone. There would be 157 of them in a small community, smaller by far than what she could see between their house and Abe's at the bottom of the hill. Given any kind of breaks at all, they'd manage.

Ben stood, thinking similar thoughts, and gazing past Andrew Tabbutt's house below his own and on toward Western Bay. In a few days . . .

Theresa came back around the house with one more boy in tow. "Come on, Pa," young Arthur said, "Let's get some gut waddin!"

"Arthur!" Theresa scolded, and then turned her head so he could not see her smile.

GRAM BURNS AND COMPANY

"All right, all right!" Gram Burns was weary of the fuss that started somewhere outside the house and then invaded her kitchen. Tim Drisko kept sniping away at her menfolk and she had to keep starting all over again. She was Bible-solid in her faith and had carefully checked every reference President Adams had hurled at the congregation in public meeting and private conversation.

"Look," she said, "you can trust Abe McKenzie. His word's as good as his bond, and he has seen with his own eyes. Ask him."

"No need to; we know what he'd say. He gets blame near poetic when he talks about the Holy Land." James, at twenty-nine, was slow to get married and slow to make up his mind about going.

Charles, strong and handsome at eighteen, tossed in the question that troubled many: "If he's so sold on it, why isn't he going?"

In light of Abe's enthusiasm for others to go, his own decision to stay was raising eyebrows and starting a lot of rumors. Young and brash, the Burns boys hurried down the hill to put the question to Abe. They found him in the combined store and post office, surrounded by customers and the inevitable spit-and-whittle crowd. "How come you're stayin' home, Abe? You feared of goin', or do you know something the rest of us need to know?" They were blunt and impertinent, but the question was in everybody's mind.

"Yeah, Abe, you and G. J. had a fallin' out?"

There was no dodging the issue, and Abe saw no need to. "I'm still planning to go," he said surprisingly. "In twelve months." He then explained to them how right it was for George Adams to be "Joshua," leading the children of Israel over the Atlantic into the Promised Land. Adams knew the lay of the land and had the contacts. Besides, he'd have the help of good men like Bishop Shad Wass, the other McKenzies, Ben Rogers, and Rolla Floyd.

"As for me," Abe continued, "we're thinking that I should stay to run the *Sword of Truth*, contract for building a small schooner for trade between Alexandria and Constantinople—maybe beyond that when the new Suez Canal is completed—and to recruit the next shipload of colonists for Jaffa. We also plan to arrange for some import-export business, including canned lobsters from Jonesport!"

"Well, I'll be damned!" said one irreverent listener.

"Chum, you'll be losin' your britches as well as your shirt unless I miss my guess," said another, while one more was heard to say, "It'll be a good trick to get old G. J. to listen to Shad Wass or anybody else."

To Abe, it seemed inevitable that Adams would lead the first contingent, but knowing G. J. better than all the others, and knowing L.I.L., it was a calculated risk. It *had* to work. After all, George Adams was the Chosen Servant of the Lord. It *would* work, if Adams could keep himself and her highness under control. The closer they came to departure the more she was giving orders and, when everybody else was selling everything including heirlooms to raise money, it was rumored that she was acquiring a few luxuries, including jewelry.

James and Charles walked slowly up Hall's Hill, and by the time they were at home each had strengthened the other's decision to go. "Good on you both, we'll need you. In fact, we'll need all the help we can get." Gram Burns accepted Abe's reasons for staying. "That makes sense, except . . ."

"Except what, ma?"

"It does seem like we'd be better off with his business sense there and G. J.'s persuasion here. . .but God knows best." She was willing to leave it in divine hands.

It was likely that no one besides Adams had recruited more people than Gram Burns. Born Lucy Leighton sixty-five years earlier, she was almost as old as her country. She was young when she married John Drisko, and he was father to most of her children. After his death John Burns became their stepfather and the father of James and Charles, who were to go, and Lucy, who was to stay.

Gram's oldest daughter, Phoebe Drisko, married Abraham Lincoln Norton. Their five children ranged in age from George, sixteen, to Daniel, six. Lucy, John, and Rebecca were in between. It was to be a family affair. Seventy-four of the emigrants were minor children, with the majority of them under fifteen years of age. It was an act of faith.

The next oldest of Gram Burns was Priscilla Ann Drisko Norton, known as Ann. Her husband was Ackley Norton, skipper of the two-masted schooner, *Elvira Conant*. They were enthusiastic about the venture and willing to give up their beautiful home and surroundings in the lower east side of Addison.

George Alvin Drisko, her oldest living son, was a skilled ship and house carpenter. With his wife, Elizabeth, he would be a valuable addition to the company, readying prefab units to be installed as partitions for makeshift cabins 'tween decks, and then, in Palestine, lending his skill to building more than twenty houses, a church, and possibly workshops and stores.

John Drisko and Cassie (Charlotte) were a joy to Gram Burns. He was an elder in the church at Addison and showing signs of leadership. There were twenty-three of Gram's offspring heading for Jaffa, and that didn't count her relations among the Leightons and Rogers. Nearly one-third of the colony belonged to her.

There were also Wasses, Tabbutts, Emersons, Grays, Kelleys, Lynches, Batsons, Alleys, and Watts. From Addison, Indian River, and Jonesport there were approximately one hundred persons. Others came from Lebanon and Orrington, Maine. Large families of Clarks and Corsons came from Rochester, New Hampshire. Wentworths, Withams, and the Higgins family were scheduled on board from Surry. (The Clarks and Wentworths were related through Ellen Wentworth Clark.) C. K. Higgins was to serve as physician for the colony. Four Moultons from York brought the total from the Church of the Messiah to 153. In addition there were four passengers from Boston, including the spiritualist, doctor, and dentist, Mayo G. Smith, and a piano teacher, complete with piano, Miss Jane Flagg. There were several ship captains, including A. H. Wass of San Francisco. Farmers, carpenters, boatbuilders, and masons lent guarantee of ability to build a community soundly based in agriculture but not limited to farming. Rolla Floyd hoped to combine a hotel with a stage venture, Jaffa to Jerusalem, thus taking direct advantage of the swelling tourist trade in the Holy Land.

The colony was not communistic. Farming lands would be purchased or rented and cultivated by families. Their houses would be built on individually owned lots. Each family was to meet its own expenses, and each bread-winner was expected to support his family from earnings. Members entrusted their money to Adams as banker and trustee. It was not given to him or to the Association.

Although Dr. Higgins planned to take an adequate supply of medicines and surgical instruments, each family was to lay in popular remedies for ailments they were accustomed to. They were also cautioned regarding the possible recurrence of the cholera which had cursed the Eastern Mediterranean the previous year. Typically, they took laudanum, spirits of camphor, and tincture of rhubarb to be ready for the nausea and diarrhea of cholera. For severe vomiting they added tincture of capsicum, tincture of ginger, and tincture of cardamon seeds. For colds some took along Dr. Poland's White Pine Compound, while others took Coe's Cough Balsam. Quantities of castor oil were to make the voyage along with Coe's Dyspepsia Cure. The ladies added a supply of Lyon's Periodical Drops. The most popular remedy was Bryan's Life Pills. Their promises staggered belief, and were advertised as curing everything from A to Z:

A gentle and effective purgative
Bilious derangement removed
Cleanser of the blood and system
Debility and Loss of power dispelled
Energy supplied to the Muscles and Nerves
Female irregularities removed
Gloomy disposition banished

Headache entirely cured
Jaundice and Liver complaints cured
Kidney diseases relieved
Loss of appetite and sick stomach removed
Melancholy and ennui disspelled
Neuralgia and Nervousness cured
Opium and other stimulants avoided
Pimples and eruptions removed
Quinsy and Sore throat healed
Rheumatism soon alleviated
Sleep produced Sweet and Sound
Toothache and inflamed gums relieved
Urinary diseases benefited
Vitality produced in the nervous
Worms invariably expelled
Xactly the Medicine wanted for
Young and old can use them
Zeno, Miximus, Capitatis.

It further promised that "tears of anguish are changed to smiles of joy by using them"—and all for twenty-five cents!

Here and there a bottle or two of Speer's Sambuci or Port Grape Wine were tucked away for medicinal purposes, especially for "kidney affections, rheumatism and bladder difficulties." The President of the Association took along an extra supply for the Communion table and for purifying the water in case the well proved troublesome.

While the newspaper controversy raged, and rumors were rife throughout Washington County, Gram Burns and her family took particular delight in the mounting counterattack of Editor Charles Forbush of the *Machias Republican*. He would not allow the townsfolk to forget that George Drisko was still fighting Abe Lincoln out of season. Forbush found much to applaud in the courage and faith of the followers of George Adams. When he did find something to approve of in the *Union*, his comment was backhanded: "It is so seldom that we see a leading article in the *Machias Union* that has anything in it that is commendable in principle; that we take pleasure in especially commending the editorial in this week's issue. . ."

Forbush was disturbed by the wild accusations going back and forth and felt that his competitor was a strong factor in the mounting ill-will and mood of mistrust. He wrote an editorial which was filled with sober hope.

He said it was an error to suppose that the colony was composed of ignorant men.

> Many of these colonists for Palestine are men of intelligence—ordinarily not readily moved by every "wind of doctrine"—farmers, merchants, ship masters, ship owners, and mechanics—men of property and of means—who have sold out all of their possessions and contributed the avails toward the accomplishment of their plans.
>
> What the final results of the undertaking may be we are not prepared to predict. There is however a romantic charm about it which has always attracted our attention. It is not indeed the old crusade of past centuries with all its "portents of war," but on the contrary the organism of peace, by which it is proposed that modern civilization and its concurrent blessings may be introduced, and final abiding peace in a land whose history has ever called up the warmest interest. It may be the initial step to carry out plans yet undeveloped, for restoring the sacred territory of Palestine to the domination and control of Christianity, and in the *Nellie Chapin*, it may be, in after years will be found the companion of the *Mayflower*.

It was indeed a reminder of the *Mayflower*, in religious motivation and commitment and in the determination of families to risk leaving the known for the unknown. These were not hand-picked for strength or wealth. They were not free from family obligations, these pioneers; they were families, with children making up nearly half of the total—and many of them sucklings. They had no financial backers, no reservoirs to turn to in case of a bad turn of events.

Their motivations differed—some going only because others they loved were going, and some under the umbrella of faith but hoping to be in on the ground floor "with corner lots." At least three of the men turned with heavy feet toward the *Nellie Chapin*—Zebediah Alley, Daniel Watts, and Linc Norton. All were married to strong-willed women. Phoebe Norton, not unlike her mother, Gram Burns, said simply and firmly, "If you don't go, you'll stay here alone!"

JULY 4 AT SANDY RIVER BEACH

The Sunday before the Fourth of July the Church of the Messiah was chock full, and two who had intended to worship there—or at least to hear G. J. preach—went across the road to the Union Church. Not realizing that the pews had been purchased by families, they sat down in one paid for by Almenie Leighton and her husband. Those two hurried in late only to find their pew occupied. He looked down at the interlopers with firm intent and said:

If I know myself,
And I think I do,
Almenie and I
Will take our pew.

Who could resist the poetic turn of phrase? The gift for rhyming, even if it did not result in great poetry, was often expressed. With Manwarren Beal it was a means of presenting little homilies to friends and neighbors. With another, looking at the gulls easing down to rest on Moosebec Reach, the rhyming was not quite so sublime:

I'm glad I ain't a seagull
Sittin on the wata -
It'd make me mighty chilly
Right where it hadn't oughta.

Ackley Norton, once he made up his mind to be Jaffa bound, began to pen his observations. In fact, he became the poet laureate of the affair. Of the last few weeks of angry sharpshooting by Drisko, Drisko, and Wass, Ackley declared:

Now Morey Wass and Uncle Tim
To do their worst they did begin;

They scattered lies and did their best
Our noble leader to arrest.

But all did prove a false attempt,
And on themselves they heaped contempt.
They scraped the country far and near
To stop our friend in his career.

Fictitious letters soon were brought;
Said they, "We've got him now, he's caught!"
But God was with him and we're glad
It drove those Methodist demons mad.

The case was tried, and to their shame
Our noble leader's friends did gain.
To their surprise their lies did prove
A blessing to the noble truth.

Given the climate of tension and excitement, and the realization that for many this would be the last Fourth of July celebration on U.S. soil, the announcement of a picnic at Sandy River Beach was received eagerly and noisily.

Sandy River Beach was not far north of Jonesport on the Chandler Bay side, a rare half-mile curve of sand between Wash Out Point and Hall's Dike Marsh. Protected by a covey of large and small islands, its sheltered shoreline was not devastated by large breakers. The Atlantic reached in with moderate waves that dumped and thrushed rhythmically and persistently, fringing the shore with ever-changing patterns of whitelace.

In times of storm the waters raged into the rocks at Wash Out Point, tearing away the clay and peat bank. But on hot summer days, when the temperature reached ninety or a hundred from Boston to Bangor, the sea breeze at Sandy River Beach provided a breath of life. It kept skin cool under a broiling sun. The combination of cool breeze and hot sun did make for burnt noses, cheeks, and ankles (nothing more was showing in those days of modesty).

Coming by the shore road, the picnickers arrived by carriage and by foot, early enough in the morning to stake out a claim at the north end of the beach. More sand waited there, lifted high by the eddying sweep of waves. Where Sandy River and high tide met, water was deep enough for swimming. A pleasant grove called The Greenwood shaded the beach in late afternoon. By July fourth a spectacular clustering of lupine and wild iris edged the stand of spruce and fir.

An explosion of youngsters burst onto the beach with aimless gyrations, much sliding to rump-dropping stops in the sand, and a winter's supply of shouts stored up from patterned behavior in home and school. There was bristling activity along the shore as fathers and older brothers brought boards and saw-horses for tables. Mothers and teen-aged daughters followed with hearty food—homemade bread, cakes, pies, strawberries, and rich cream whipped to perfection.

A voice used to commanding against the sound of the sea required attention and obedience. "All you Norton, Leighton, and Rogers boys fan out and gather firewood—mind, the dry stuff at the edge of the grass." At the fringe of the saltwater grass and wild sweet peas, driftwood had been tossed by the high tides of winter storms. It was ready for burning, and small boys came dragging more than they could carry while larger ones proved their independence by carrying less. A stalwart lad of six puffed his way to the chosen spot, piled to his eyebrows. "You lazy thing," Ackley chided good-naturedly. "Whadda ya mean, lazy? Look how much I carried." "Right, too lazy to make two trips!"

The Adams and McKenzies arrived together, Clarence hitting the ground before the carriage stopped. The ladies headed for the table, carrying substantials and delicacies. Abe went straight for the high tide line marked by sea weed and called for help to hoist the "broad stripes and bright stars." A tall slender pole, washed up on the shore, was found, and a hole dug. A dozen rocks were added to firm up the base. With the flag unfurling, G. J. walked onto the beach as if it were a stage—the only man at the picnic dressed in Sunday clothes.

"Edwin, Orrin, and any others of a mind to, over you go to Bar Island and dig clams." Rolla Floyd held clam hoes and rollers, proffering them to the willing. "Come on, I'll race you to the fish weir," Edwin McKenzie, Jr., 19, challenged his brother, Orrin, 17. Velma, their beautiful fifteen-year-old sister joined them. "I'll beat you both!" They gave her fifty feet and were off.

Rolla then made ready for steaming the clams that would not take long to dig. He placed stones in a circle high enough to allow a fire under the flat metal fish flake he put on top to hold the kettle. Water scarcely more than covered the bottom of the kettle. The clams would steam from the water they held tight in their shells. When they were done, the shells would open wide. At other fires, fish chowder and vegetables were simmering.

Theodocia, Rolla's wife and older than he by many years, tended their baby, Everett, not yet one year old. She and the others with infants had gathered with the bond that draws mothers together. For "Docia," Everett was an only child. For the others—Phoebe Tabbutt, Abitha Leighton, Mary Gray, and Anna Watts—the babies they cuddled or nursed were the latest of several.

With boards bending under platters and bowls, and the clams already at hand, Abe McKenzie, the area's favorite master of ceremonies, called everyone together at 11 o'clock. "Welcome to our Fourth of July picnic. It's the ninetieth anniversary of the Declaration of Independence. Some of you will recall from last week's issue what Editor Forbush wrote in the *Republican* —that's the only good Machias paper. . . ." The remark prompted a chuckle and some applause. "He said it was good to have picnics, sailing, etc., on the Fourth but that there should be more to 'recall to mind from time to time the deep-toned notes.' So we plan to have races for young and old, a meal to remember, and we've arranged for our favorite preacher, G. J. Adams, to deliver a brief patriotic address. A bevy of little misses will sing some sweet songs, too. But now we're off to the races and the first event—a gunny sack race for the ladies."

Gram Burns was the first to volunteer. "Lucy, for goodness' sake, act your age!" chided her husband, John. "I am," she retorted. She had no idea of jumping around in one of those gunny sacks, but her gesture got the whole thing started in fine shape. Velma McKenzie was first into a bag, followed by others in their teens—Carra Wass, Esther Norton, Theresa Rogers, Mary Leighton, and Louisa Lynch. When the newly married Marcella McKenzie was finally pushed into it by her husband, Ellis, Jr., she was greeted with good-natured catcalls: "Too old to run!" somebody yelled. "Or too tired!" another said and giggled. Taunted, Marcella won the race, with Velma a close second.

Contestants of other ages tried the gunny sack. Then there were three-legged races and just plain foot races. G. J. and Shad Wass were judges. The tide was narrowing the beach, but the boys and girls worked up a game of ball, which ended abruptly when someone threw the ball too high to catch. It landed in the water and the whole crew dashed after it, clothes and all, splashing and wrestling until all were soaked.

When the steaming clams were ready the word for eats was shouted along the beach. The ball-rescuers ran awkwardly with wet clothes for the outlet of Sandy River to trade salt water for fresh.

"Hurry up," the little ones shouted. The others, coming up from the water, cupped their hands to hold and throw water at small brothers and sisters.

"If we can manage a moment of quiet . . .," Abe said with

pointed patience, "we'll have the blessing by Elder Joshua Walker."

Prayer over, the forward contingent of nine- through twelve-year-olds shouldered, elbowed, and leaned into each other competing to be first in line. As table covers were removed, fried chickens lost their legs immediately. Lobster, crab meat, fish chowder, roast beef, venison, and black duck were in abundance. From the gardens came fresh peas, canned green beans, pickles (sour, sweet, and dilled), bright green lettuce leaves (to be vinegared or sugared and rolled for finger food), relishes and chutneys; from backyard fruit trees, canned pears, peaches, and plums; cracked wheat bread, baking powder biscuits, cinnamon rolls. Pies (deep-dish apple, blueberry, cherry—all from last year's crop—and lemon meringue) and cobbler (both apple and peach) were still oven-fresh. And there were strawberries and whipped cream, plus cakes and cookies.

To whet their appetites, the men headed first for the clams. Mothers tended to the very young. The clamor of a few moments before gave way to relative silence, interrupted only by "This is *some* good!" and the reply, "It's not too nasty!"

Within minutes the tables straightened up under their lightened loads while still holding plenty for second helpings. Finally the covers were laid on against flies—to be lifted later by small hands in search of cookies.

Abe strained to his feet and called the picnickers to the top of the beach where it bent to the river. He stood between them and the gentling waves lacing the shore.

"Has anyone missed his portion?" Everyone laughed at the irreverent use of the traditional query after the sacrament was served. "Now, if they can manage to breathe deep enough that 'bevy of little misses' will sing."

With much tittering and self-conscious grinning, they shaped into line from Mary Gray and Rebecca Norton, age eight, to Sabrina Watts, age four. They merited applause, and responded with an encore. Then, a half dozen young ladies took up the strain and sang some patriotic songs.

"And now, ladies and gentlemen, boys and girls, the man who has given much, and suffered much—the man who has given us a goal to live for, and will lead the children of Ephraim to their new home—a new Joshua, George J. Adams!"

They welcomed him with loud clapping of hands and "Hear! Hear! Hear!" To have heard him so much—more than any other person in their experience—and to look forward eagerly to his next address was tribute indeed. They were not disappointed. He was thoroughly convinced that God had moved upon Christopher Columbus, the Pilgrims, and the Founding Fathers. The Declaration of Independence and the Constitution were expressions of the Divine Will for the new nation. The Revolutionary War was just and the recent war a necessity in order to continue the integrity of the nation. To give allegiance to the United States of America was to fulfill an honorable—even holy—obligation. He said it all, and he meant it all. G. J. Adams was loyal to his country.

His hearers were attentive, poignantly so, for they were thinking of their own patriotism—to be tested by separation. What would they be in Palestine, Americans in exile? Protected or neglected? And when the Jews returned, creating a new nation, what would be their status? In the meantime, what of the Turks?

Their applause was genuine but not exuberant, they were too pensive for that. G. J. had done well. They knew it and he suspected it, but their solemn applause left him feeling unfulfilled.

Following the speech they stood to sing the national hymn. Then there was a prayer of thanksgiving for the past and of hope for the future—and a solemn prayer for a community still in gestation.

Mothers of the very young found places of seclusion for feeding babies who were beginning to be fretful. Children a little older had fallen asleep during the address and were sleeping in friendly arms or stretched out on quilts or comforters. Young people were content to explore in groups or walk hand-in-hand through the greenwood or across the dike onto the point. A few brave young men, led by Edwin McKenzie, knew they had waited long enough to avoid cramps and went swimming. The adults talked earnestly in small groups, anticipating Jaffa. G. J. made his way from group to group, encouraging, asking questions, and occasionally defending. L.I.L. Adams moved from one group of ladies to another, but when she arrived the conversation became stilted. They had been willing to accept her as they had her husband and son, but she was awkward in her loneliness and made them feel she didn't really care. They were in gingham; she was in brocades and hoop skirts.

L.I.L. turned from them to watch the children playing and smiled to see Clarence in the middle of the festivities. She hoped he wouldn't get hurt.

Figuring the time it would take to get home, adults dismantled the picnic. Families began to disband, exchanging happy goodbyes and reflections on a marvelous Fourth of July. It was a celebration to remember.

FINAL PREPARATIONS

It was Shad Wass who brought G. J. Adams to Addison, Indian River, and Jonesport. The Wass home was the first to welcome and shelter the preacher, gratis, and when they travelled together it was Shad who received the offering, paid the bills, and turned over what was left to G. J. Soon ordained a bishop, Shad was the chief financial officer of the Church of the Messiah. At first, there were few expenses except for the Adams family and these were met by generous members and friends as Adams made his rounds.

There were no books to balance, only notations which Shad Wass could keep in his coat pocket, except for the *Sword of Truth* with its list of paid and unpaid subscriptions to keep sorted and up to date. He was proud to be bishop of the church, and when the emigration project began to mature he became the purchasing agent and keeper of accounts.

It was a responsible position. Thousands of dollars were being entrusted to Adams and Wass. Families were selling all but the barest necessities to get ready for the great venture. Sometimes they sold at a loss, sacrificially, because they felt that they were on the Lord's mission, or like Shad Wass, himself, because it would prove profitable in time. After all, they were going to where rich Jews would shortly be investing life and money in a renewed Holy Land.

Motives were mixed among the members of Adams' church. There were thinly veiled opportunists who talked loudest about conviction and pioneering. Some were tentative in their commitment, like Levi Mace who was going in the hope of improving his position. At the first hint of trouble he could be depended on to remind the whole company of the wisdom of Tim Drisko and Morey Wass. Zebediah Alley and John Watts were only partially convinced, but their womenfolks, two Norton sisters, were adamant. To keep peace in the family they were going along . . . with reservations . . . too stoic to grumble.

There were others who were weighing the costs and doing a minimum of talking. These were thoroughly convinced of their divine calling to rebuild the waste places of Zion and to pave the way for the coming of Messiah. Rolla Floyd, Joshua Walker, Ben Rogers, John Burns, and George Clark were among them. They said little but quickly sold their belongings, like Abigail Alley who gave up her home at the west end of

Jonesport and her summer camp on Slate Island just off Great Wass Island. No one was more committed.

The young people reflected family attitudes, whether full or partial in support, until the delegation from Surry, Lebanon, and Rochester began to arrive, readying for departure. From then on, palpable excitement banished doubts and reluctance.

Jonesport was a hubbub. Anticipating an earlier departure, those from far away arrived in the last days of July. They crowded into Norton's Inn and the Jonesport Hotel, cottage hostelries. Others stayed with friends, relatives, or strangers. Steamboat Wharf was already stacked high, waiting for the *Nellie Chapin* to arrive from Machiasport where it was being loaded with lumber and other building supplies. The lumber, both rough and finish, was pulled from Whitneyville by the steam engine, *Lion*. The operation in Machiasport was under the direction of Shad Wass, while the bustle at Steamboat Wharf was superintended by G. J. himself. His shock of black hair, collar-long and whipping in the wind, signalled his presence and the nervous energy which was infecting everyone.

When the *Nellie Chapin* hove into sight, a team of carpenters and helpers converged on the ship to start transforming lumber into temporary bulkheads and partitions. These would divide 'tween decks into temporary cabins, later to be transformed into housing units at Jaffa.

A few of the emigrants, favored financially, would occupy first class cabins on main deck. Most, however, would make the journey in the temporary cubicles to port and starboard of a companionway. The clean smell of fresh lumber gave no clue to the pungence they would experience later from air which had little encouragement to circulate. Sea-sickness would add its share to chamber pot fragrance which would hang on after the daily first-light-of-dawn spilling of contents into the sea.

By block and tackle hogsheads of potable water, brined meat, and coal oil were lowered into the hold and lashed securely. That this was no communitarian venture pure and simple became quickly apparent. Adams had encouraged two, without either knowing of the other, to take supplies of coal oil. Each had been promised a monopoly. Colonists and Jaffans alike would depend on the supply. To Adams' surprise and consternation, each man showed up loaded with coal oil. One was Mayo Smith of Boston who, although not a member of the church, had yielded to the persuasive powers of Adams. The other was Levi Mace, quick to anger and not a rousing supporter of the President. Tempers flared, and Adams took the brunt of it, accused by each of betrayal. Neither had the good sense to propose a partnership. Each was after a quick profit.

Smith, a spiritualist, claimed some knowledge of medicine. Also from Boston were three women, more anxious for the adventure of going than building a community. Their fares would help pay expenses for the chartered ship, and one of them, Miss Jane Flagg, a piano teacher, was bringing her piano with her. It was a touch of culture for which both G. J. and L.I.L. were glad. They would welcome her and her piano into their home. Perhaps Clarence would take lessons.

Trunks and boxes loaded with household supplies and clothing not needed on the voyage were lowered into the hold. Trim for gables and soffits, slim pickets for porch rails and wider ones for fences were stacked adjacent to a variety of building timbers for framing. Flooring, a full inch thick, was quarter sawn and of first grade. Doors for the houses were hung in the 'tween decks cabins. They carried the typical Christian cross panel design. Dozens of blinds (shutters), typical of New England houses, were stacked alongside glassless window sash that looked too frail to withstand the voyage. Drums of paint included customary dark green for the blinds. Glass for window lights was on order from Loewenthal and presumably already on hand for their arrival. There was gutta-percha for roofing, nail kegs, and boxes of butts and screws. Cement to plaster the lath and bricks for foundation and chimneys were stacked high in the hold.

Gunny sacks bulged with seed potatoes. Farming implements, including a newfangled threshing machine, were securely stowed. Bridles, single and double-trees, saddles and other trappings awaited the Loewenthal purchase of Arabians which were to be broken and trained to harness.

Abe McKenzie's skilled hand was apparent in the thoroughness of equipping the company. He and Adams had finalized their decision. He definitely would stay in Indian River. There were plenty of reasons why. Somebody capable and credible would have to remain to ready the next contingent for Jaffa, and it would have to be one of them—either "Caleb" or "Joshua," who had seen the land and could bear firsthand testimony of its promise.

They would duplicate the present effort with an equivalent number to board the *Nellie Chapin* or another vessel no later than July 1867. In addition they would contract for a smaller vessel to be built which would carry lumber and other supplies for the colony. It would also be available for coastal traffic in the Mediterranean and to facilitate import-export for members of the Palestine Emigration Society in Jaffa and their counterparts back home in Maine.

Abe would have to edit the *Sword of Truth*. It was important for recruiting, soliciting funds, keeping the message moving, and building solidarity of support. G. J. would submit copy from Jaffa, and the sheer appeal of it would add power to their press. No one was better equipped to manage the whole enterprise than Abe. This, of course, also recommended him for the Jaffa end, but, given their assumed identities, there was biblical precedent and that weighed heavy in the balances. It was Joshua, not Caleb, who led the children of Israel (Ephraim and all) into the Promised Land. And so it was decided: management would stay behind—for a year.

It should work. Everything was well planned. There was enough to do to occupy everyone at Jaffa. There were houses and a community to be built there. Loewenthal should have everything in readiness. Livestock and seed waited. The agent of the Sublime Porte had already agreed to land them, duty free. It was their confidence that any day now they would hear he had agreed to the remainder of their request, to permit purchase of the plot and sufficient land to farm. It had to be. To rent would put them in the grip of an unbearable oppression—no better off than the fellaheen who were required to give up a minimum of 50 percent to rent and taxes. That was out of the question. They had Loewenthal, and he had been appointed U.S. Vice Consul for Jaffa by the New Jerusalem Consul, Beauboucher. But at the time of departure word had not arrived. They would have to proceed on faith.

By noon of August 10 it became clear that the company could depart the next morning. The news spread quickly. Only the tiny children slept soundly that night.

The "Lion", steam engine which brought the lumber from the Whitneyville sawmill to Machiasport.

CHAPTER 7

VOYAGE OF THE *NELLIE CHAPIN*

They converged from every direction like filings to a magnet, townsfolk as well as those bound for Jaffa. All the gear except for last-night necessities was already on board. The farewells ranged from quiet heart-pounding hugs to near hysteria. Relatives clung to relatives as long as possible. Friends chatted hastily, knowing they might never see each other again. Young lovers, unfulfilled, spoke hesitant words, pressing hard against each other, hands locked against separation. Mothers and older daughters herded and carried little ones up the gangplank. Small boys and girls, baffled and excited, scrambled aboard as if they were pirates.

"All ashore that's goin' ashore!" began a last minute, reluctant shuffling of feet down the gangplank. George Adams, on the wharf, was the last to board. He and Abe had things to talk about. Then the time had come! They clasped hands, and George said, "Next year, Jerusalem, Abe!" Abe nodded, knowing that was little enough time to build one ship, hire another, and ready at least one hundred more pilgrims for the Holy Land.

As the bark eased from the wharf, someone noticed a rocking chair left behind by order of George Adams. He wanted no excess and awkward cargo—and no symbols of idleness on board. Someone in the cluster of those against the venture gave it a heave toward the ship, threatening those aft along the rail. They caught it just as Tim Drisko yelled, "Give it to her ladyship so she can ride across in style!"

Adams grabbed the chair, mustered all his strength, and flung it toward the wharf. "Keep it, Tim Drisko, you lazy croaker—we've got no idlers here." The chair fell short but with that mighty toss he was not only rid of the offending chair but also Tim Drisko, Morey Wass, and all the rest of his enemies. It was a gesture of defiant victory. He turned and broke the silence with "Hip-Hip-" and the passengers thundered, "Hooray!" He called again, "Hip-Hip—" "Hooray!" they yelled. And then once more, "Hip-Hip—" and the third time "Hooray!"

Like an echo the crowd on shore answered "Hooray" three times. Hands were raised high to wave goodbye, and then, as yards multiplied between them, kerchiefs and hats waved to signal loving farewells and kept on waving until people merged into memory.

Some relatives and friends were permitted to remain on board, or were on the tug, *Delta*, which drew them out past Great Wass Island into Western Bay. The *Delta* could tell its own story, so recent from scenes of battle in the Civil War. Wounded, it found its way to Maine and was overhauled for coastal traffic and for taking holiday crowds on excursions. Captain Hall of Jonesport knew the waters well.

They passed headlands, to starboard, near Indian River, too far away to distinguish family and townsfolk who had their eyes peeled for the graceful silhouette of the three-masted bark.

Near Spoon Island Captain Hall slowed, slacking the tow line between the two vessels. He maneuvered the steamer near to the *Nellie Chapin*. The time for final separation had come.

A young lawyer, Archibald McNichol, stepped forward to give a farewell address. Only a week before, he had defended Adams against the last attempt of Tim Drisko and Morey Wass to abort the venture. They remembered and pounced upon Adams' unwitting failure to meet the stringent requirement of Maine law to register before performing a wedding. On December 10, 1864, he had married Arthur Leighton and Louise M. Donavan in Addison. Learning his error, he had refused to marry any others. No one had pressed the issue until the *Nellie Chapin* was nearly ready for departure. Then Tim Drisko filed charges, forcing the arrest of Adams by Deputy Sheriff H. T. Smith and the nuisance of a hearing in Machias. He deposited $2,000.00 in gold, pled guilty, and was ordered to appear before the October term of the Supreme Court. He had to leave $1200.00 of the deposit as bond. The money was crucial. Time was crucial too, but beyond that Tim and Morey had succeeded once more in holding him up to ridicule.

Adams reported McNichols' speech appreciatively in *The Sword of Truth* as "a most thrilling and appropriate address, which touched the hearts of all present, as he spoke of the persecutions and sufferings of President Adams, and the triumphant success with which his indomitable perseverence had been crowned. In concluding his remarks he predicted for us a glorious future." George quoted the descriptive phrase "indomitable perseverence" with satisfaction. It was nice to be appreciated. He continued. "The steamer dropped alongside, the parting time came, tears, prayers, good wishes and 'God bless you,' and 'Peace be with you,' closed the parting scene. . . . All who were homeward bound having passed from the barque to the steamer, the steamer was loosed from the barque [which] stood for our new home in the far off East. Thus we parted. May that parting be but short. May we soon meet in the land of Zion, and enjoy peace on earth, and practice good will to men."

With the last flurry of shouts and vigorous waving of hands and kerchiefs, the master of the *Nellie Chapin*, Captain Warren Wass, spoke to the chief mate, "Set your sails, Mr. Hinkley." James Hinkley was an old hand with sailing ships, fully qualified at twenty-eight years to transform the Captain's wishes into action. A Jonesporter himself, he knew many of the passengers. Now he called out the command which would change the gently rolling vessel into a thing of beauty before the wind.

The *Nellie Chapin* plunged into the sea as if restless for the voyage. Then, as its stern settled down its bows rose up to show new and still-bright copper.

With the deck no longer parallel to the horizon and moving to the shape of the water and the action of the wind, those unfamiliar to the sea discovered that they hadn't got their sea legs on and one by one found something to hold to or sit on. A few, especially those of middle years, began to feel queasy. Most of the older ones and the young would make the voyage without the torment of seasickness. Gram Burns, especially, and Josh Walker's mother, Mary, took to the sea like veterans. They were disgustingly hearty—or so it seemed to those whose usually ruddy complexions paled.

Anticipating strong winds in crossing the Bay of Fundy and the banks of Newfoundland they turned to securing their belongings. The wind, however, was light and the sea smooth from Saturday until Wednesday. On the Lord's day they "assembled on deck and devoutly worshipped the God of our fathers, thanking him for mercies and favors past, and invoking his blessing, peace, guidance and protecting care for the future."

On Wednesday, August 15, they entered the Gulf Stream, its warm waters signaled by a bank of clouds stretching for hundreds of miles. As expected, the wind commenced blowing from the Southeast and intensified into a gale. During the storm some of the lashings holding household goods broke, endangering stacks of furniture. Thursday, at midnight, the storm abated. Adams reported:

During the storm the barque worked nobly under the judicious management of Capt. Wass. The great body of the passengers stood the storm nobly, and manifested no fear. The officers and men did their duty manfully and cheerfully.

Thus we have the pleasure to record the fact that the *Nellie Chapin* and all on board passed safely and triumphantly through its first storm at sea. To the God of our fathers be everlasting praise for his mercy.

From Thursday evening, midnight, until Friday, August 24, some eight days, the wind continued fair and strong; and we now found ourselves in the parallel of the Western islands, less than one thousand miles from Gibraltar, and a good strong fair wind still blowing. A number have been sea-sick, but none have been dangerous, not in the least. All are now getting well and smart. . . . Very few of our children have been sick, and all are in better health than when we started, and we may say that health, peace and union prevails, and every other spirit gives way before peace, union and brotherhood.

According to the memory of Herbert Clark, who was ten years old at the time of the voyage and later served as U.S. Vice Consul in Jerusalem, "Life on board was not monotonous for us children . . . our only troubles were getting enough to eat. The food for so large a party was naturally a sea-faring diet, salt beef and fish, stewed beans, boiled potatoes and plum duff, all indifferently cooked in a small galley by two men." Michael O'Lothlin, the steward, apparently was able to commandeer one of the seamen to stand duty part time in the galley because of the large number of people on board.

A list of passengers was prepared by G. J. Adams "as a matter of future history." By oversight he did not include his wife and son except in the total count of 167 passengers and crew.

NAMES	AGE
G. J. Adams, President of the Palestine Emigration Association, and President of the Church of the Messiah	53
S. L. Wass, Bishop of the Church at Addison and Jonesport	49
Mrs. S. A. Wass	39
Miss Carra O. Wass	14
Miss Hattie A. Wass	6
John A. Drisko, Elder	32
Mrs. Charlotte Drisko	26
Andrew Tabbutt, Elder	36
Mrs. Phoebe W. Tabbutt	32

NAMES	AGE
Ernest A. Tabbutt	10
Norman W. Tabbutt	8
Miss Genevra Tabbutt	6
Miss Anna Tabbutt	4
Leon A. Tabbutt	1
Capt. Ackley Norton	38
Mrs. A. Norton	37
Miss Alice B. Norton	18
Miss Esther C. Norton	14
E. Eugene Norton	8
Loveatus P. Norton	5
Miss Lewella Norton	3
Oliver A. Ward	46
Melville B. Ward	17
Drusille S. Ward	20
George A. Drisko	35
Lizzie C. Drisko	32
Julia E. Drisko	11
John Burns	66
Lucy W. Burns	66
James E. Burns	29
Charles E. Burns	18
B. B. Leighton	54
Mary W. Leighton	49
Ell A. Leighton	25
Frances M. Leighton	20
Mary S. Leighton	18
Uriah W. Leighton	36
Abitha A. Leighton	36
Idella W. Leighton	12
Ralph I. Leighton	7
Flora L. Leighton	1
E. K. Emerson	38
Mrs. Rosa K. Emerson	30
Elmer E. Emerson	5
Samuel P. Kelley	61
Mrs. Belinda N. Kelley	56
Moses W. Leighton	49
Nancy S. Leighton	30
Melville B. Leighton	14

NAMES	AGE
Seward W. Gray	33
Mrs. Mary M. Gray	36
Mary L. Gray	8
Frank J. Gray	1
Eugene W. Gray	13
Daniel W. Emerson	29
Robert F. Emerson	23
Josiah M. Gray	16
Rolla Floyd	29
Theodocia Floyd	39
Everett M. Floyd	1
William H. Lynch	40
Charlotte B. Lynch	33
Varanes C. Lynch	18
M. Louisa Lynch	16
Joshua S. Walker, Elder	38
Mrs. Mary Walker, his mother	63
Ellis B. McKenzie	55
Mrs. Margaret E. McKenzie	51
Miss Ruth E. McKenzie	27
Edwin B. McKenzie	19
Orrin W. McKenzie	17
Velma McKenzie	15
Ellis B. McKenzie, Jr., Elder	22
Mrs. Marcella F. McKenzie	20
Benjamin K. Rogers, Elder	37
Lucy D. Rogers	33
Miss V. P. Rogers	14
Theresa L. Rogers	13
Bradford Rogers	8
Arthur Rogers	6
George Rogers	2
Mrs. Elizabeth A. Batson	39
Everett W. Batson	16
F. C. Batson	11
A. L. Norton	43
Phoebe P. Norton	39
George E. Norton	16
Lucy A. Norton	14
John L. Norton	11

NAMES	AGE
Rebecca Norton	8
Daniel J. Norton	6
Daniel J. Watts	36
Anna T. Watts	28
John N. Watts	6
Elvira K. Watts	2
Sabrina H. Watts	4
Ida May Watts	mos. 5
Zebediah Alley	33
Abigail R. Alley	36
Willie Alley	6
Capt. A. H. Wass	42
Mrs. E. S. Wass	42
Clifton A. Wass	6
Mrs. Eliza Dyer	65
Mrs. Eliza Corson	60
Mrs. A. E. Williams	33
Orland H. Tibbetts	43
Mrs. Lydia A. Tibbetts	43
Charles W. Tibbetts	20
Arvilla A. Tibbetts	3
Levi Mace	46
Caroline Mace	44
Caroline E. Mace	16
Mary A. Mace	14
Levi E. Mace	12
Sarah A. Mace	10
Ezekiel Mace	7
Isaiah B. Ames	30
Martha S. Ames	42
George W. Ames	28
Zimri Corson	50
Dorothy Corson	46
Miss Eveline Corson	15
Lydia A. Corson	11
Leonard Z. Corson	14
Charles M. Corson	9
George W. Clark	36
Ellen Clark	34
Herbert E. Clark	10

NAMES	AGE
George B. Clark	8
Mary J. Clark	7
Frank C. Clark	5
Eugene A. Clark	1
W. F. Clark	22
Capt. F. W. Witham	31
Mrs. C. H. Witham	28
F. M. Witham	7
Mark T. Wentworth	34
Mrs. A. R. Wentworth	30
Fanny E. Wentworth	5
Clinton Wentworth	4
Mark DeWitt Wentworth	3
Lilli Wentworth	mos. 4
C. K. Higgins, M.D.	47
Mrs. Helen E. Higgins	34
George W. Higgins	9
Lizzie B. Higgins	7
J. B. Moulton	36
Mrs. A. M. Moulton	30
Lauraetta Moulton	4
Leon A. Moulton	2
Mayo G. Smith	50
William B. Stevens	23
Mrs. Matilda M. Richardson	50
Miss Jane A. Flagg, Music Teacher	36

As a matter of history, we also add the names and ages of officers and men of the *Nellie Chapin:*

Warren Wass, Master	46
James W. Hinkley, First Mate	28
Michael O'Lothlin, Steward	20

The seamen's names and ages are as follows:

Henry L. Belmont	27
Thomas Chesterton	30
Reuben Hall	17
William Whitney	23

NAMES	AGE
Sewell Hopkins	23
Thomas Knnuteson	18
James Woolfall	20

From the storm at entering the Gulf Stream to the Straits of Gibraltar on September 4 the company enjoyed fair winds and good sailing. It was a time for marveling at the size of the Atlantic, day after day the same vista and the vast quietness, broken only by the creaking of blocks, the occasional shifting of ropes and sails, the sea beating against the bow, and the wind whistling through the rigging. When the wind beat more heavily against the sails they filled out and backed against the masts, sounding as if a storm were brewing.

Sunrise at sea had no song of birds or first light on trees, spires, and housetops, but it had its own stark beauty as the blackness gave way to streaks of grey along the eastern horizon. The ebony of the sea with its awesome masking of depths deeper than imagination transformed to an indistinct touching of light on the surface. The melancholy loneliness was relieved by horizons made visible all around. In the half-light luminescent drops of water turned from the bow as the sea was split and tumbled. Flying fish lifted from just ahead of the bow and scurried off to port and starboard from the monster which had disturbed them.

"Forward there, rig the head pump!" The larboard watch turned to at daybreak, washing down, scrubbing and swabbing the decks, filling the "scuttlebutt" with fresh water, and casting up the rigging until half after seven when all hands got breakfast. At eight the day's work really began.

Every crew member was kept at work as he stood watch—four hours on and four hours off until noon—then all hands for eight hours.

Idleness was a pleasure enjoyed only by the passengers, especially the young, who watched it all with eyes of wonder. Fair days meant freedom to be on deck for sun and make-believe. Twenty teen-agers had no difficulty finding ways to pass the hours, remembering, anticipating, exploring the vessel, and sitting by the hour forward or aft to watch the action of ship against the sea. When all else failed they turned to euchre and dominoes. Rolla Floyd, sociable and always keen, watched the young folks for a while and then, walking the deck, encountered James Hinkley.

"It's a pleasure to shake the hand of a man who knows his business as you know yours," he said with an admiring smile to the chief mate.

"Thank you, sir. We've got a good crew."

"A crew's as good as its mate."

"And vice versa. Tell me, what do you plan to do for a living in Palestine?"

Rolla was thoughtful. He was not given to rash answers. "Well, I figure that people will always be going to the Holy Land, some to live and some to visit. Nearly everyone who goes must see the sights. Every Jew who lands at Jaffa heads for the wall at Jerusalem. Every Christian wants to walk where Jesus walked. I plan to be the one who gets them where they're going and tells them about it on the way."

"It must be you that's taking a carriage. Don't they have them in Palestine?"

"Apparently not. At least that's what Abe McKenzie told me when he and Brother Adams came back a year ago. You know they've got a new asphalt road in mind; that means more people and less need for camels."

"Camels. Where do you sit on those things?

"On the hump, I guess."

"That'd be all right on level ground but climbing a hill, look out. I can feel myself slipping already!"

"Can you imagine any of these ladies on a camel?"

"Gram Burns."

"How about her ladyship?"

"Well, that's a different matter!"

For the adults it was a time to reminisce or to dream, to spin yarns or quietly to share their mixture of dread and anticipation. In Adams' journal it all translated into peace and happiness, which wasn't quite true; what George Adams wanted to believe *was* believed in his own mind. He conveniently dismissed from his reports the untoward confrontations which threatened tranquility. The most persistent complainer was Levi Mace.

Mace was not at ease aboard ship. In fact he was miserable with seasickness. He would have hailed any ship heading back toward home. Conviction regarding the return of the Jews and the coming of Messiah was submerged. He attacked Adams verbally, "What's the idea of permitting that outsider, Mayo Smith, to bring along all that coal oil? You promised that I would be the one to supply coal oil!"

"Levi, you were one of the first to think about coming—and one of the last to make up your mind! We needed coal oil, and it's a great opportunity for some one to make a go of it—no, to flourish. Do you realize what a commercial center that is going to be, beginning with our colony just north of Jaffa? You have a chance to be the first coal oil merchant. You could expand right up to Jerusalem when we get the ships running from Maine to Jaffa."

"G. J., your eyes turn wild every time you open your mouth. All right—I want to believe you, but why did you cheat me by letting Smith bring coal oil?"

"Because you couldn't make up your mind. I thought you weren't coming so I offered it to Mr. Smith. Why don't you two get together?"

"I'm not about to be linked with an unbeliever!" Levi shot back.

It angered Adams to be challenged by Mace. He was embarrassed by having two dealers show up with oil when he had anticipated only one. He spoke too hastily and with too much feeling. "Well, Mayo Smith may not want to be linked to a croaker and a bigot." It was a foolish thing to say and cut the sensitive Mace. A battle line was drawn in that moment which could have been avoided by tact and compassion. Levi Mace went from mumbling to croaking aloud.

The ship was to put in at Gibraltar so mail could be posted, but as it neared the coast the waters were becalmed. When a breeze finally came the mate decided to use it and sailed by Gibraltar. To Adams the disappointment was lessened by recollection of English port authorities overcharging and handling his mail and money with tongs one year before.

Later, as the *Nellie Chapin* was becalmed near Tangier, a small craft loaded with green figs and grapes came alongside. The youngsters were delighted by strange sights and sounds, and being weary of food on board gorged themselves with fruit.

In an exciting race with a steamship the *Nellie Chapin* pulled far ahead of her rival during a strong wind, but when the wind died down the steamboat pushed far ahead.

The ship was making good speed, all in all, blessed by fair winds and clear days most of the time. There was no severe weather from the Gulf Stream on until between Tangier and Malta. Then near tragedy struck in a sudden and violent storm.

Passengers dashed for cabins; hatches were shut; and the ship began to tear through the water like a mad horse, throwing foam from its head, yards to leeward. Then, with the waters of the Mediterranean gone mad the ship pitched as if it were shaking the masts loose.

The sea was rolling in great surges one of which put the bark on her beam ends, her deck at forty-five degrees, and her fore yardarm under water. The sudden lurch threw the two men at the wheel across the deck. Captain Alexander Wass, one of the colonists, was standing by and seized the whirling spokes, holding the ship steady until it righted.

It was close, too close, to tragedy. Everything loose, human and otherwise, was thrown into bulkheads and to the decks. As if by a miracle, all were spared major injury except one—Levi Mace. He would suffer for weeks and be handicapped at a most crucial time by a broken leg.

Hatches and lashings had held. All was secure, even the coal oil, water, and seeds stored below.

When it was over, Adams raised his voice publicly in praise of God who had saved them from disaster, but Levi Mace did not say "Amen." He blamed the incident on Adams and Captain Warren Wass for not having competent helmsmen—"too young," he said, "and the ship is flawed."

Adams was quick to reply that the *Nellie Chapin* was a mighty vessel and not the first to go onto its beam ends. It was in fact a tribute to her builder, Leander Knowles, that she recovered without broaching.

There was also mounting tension between Adams and the very man he was protecting from Mace, Mayo Smith, the spiritualist. They spent hours in debate, first because they enjoyed debating and then in abusive argument.

Adams simply could not have his leadership jeopardized, and both Mace and Smith were beginning to worry him. Added to these was a complaining, seasick wife; the journey which was more blessed by good fortune than cursed by bad was beginning to turn sour.

Adams came upon Mace, grouching to one of the McKenzies, and lashed out, "Levi, stop your bellyaching—it's enough to drive a sober man to drink!"

"Even a prophet?" Levi taunted.

"Especially a prophet!" G. J. retorted.

Levi was getting to George. So was Mayo. So was L.I.L. So was the journey. Maybe Joshua should have preferred Caleb; Abe McKenzie could probably have shaped up the whole company.

The vessel that had looked so large at departure was now

too small to offer escape. If he could only get away for a little while. Perhaps L.I.L. . . .

Too queasy throughout the journey for any show of affection, let alone intimacy, her support had been minimal and her complaints maximal. But George had need, and sometimes, when awakened from slumber, she had welcomed him.

In that night's darkness he stood for a long time, holding to the royal halliard and listening to the rushing of water beneath the rail. Suddenly he turned and walked resolutely toward his cabin. Moments later he eased his naked heaviness over the protecting sideboard into a bunk already crowded with L.I.L.'s voluptuousness. Mace and Smith were already giving way to anticipation. He touched warm yielding flesh only to have it stiffen. Her hand pushed his away. "Don't!" she said.

His frustration became anger and then degenerated into self-pity, and that prompted recall of other moments when escape was necessary. He caught a fleeting glimpse of downtown Boston and a place of rendezvous in New Bedford. He could have neither, but there was a way. It might take longer with communion wine, but he had no mind to stop short of oblivion.

American Colony on the beach of Jaffa September 1866

Jaffa and the ledges
Courtesy Harvard Semitic Museum

CHAPTER 8

AT JAFFA

"George—wake up, wake up, you fool!"

He had slept the clock around and more—sweet, blessed relief. Now L.I.L. was in a dither of dismay and consternation. "Mayo Smith is talking to your flock, telling them your Church of the Messiah is a delusion. If that's not enough, your son Clarence just came in to tell you about it. Now he's hiding somewhere. Can you imagine what he thought when he laid eyes on this mess of bottles and you passed out, half in and half out of bed? Five years I've kept you sober! Now. . . now, with the Holy Land close to view, our leader, our Joshua, with the blood of Ephraim flowing in his veins, is stinking drunk!"

Like some islanders who are deathly seasick until they sight land and then are miraculously well, L.I.L. lost her malaise—not to the sight of land but to the return of shame. She was back on long and better lost ground, his folly and her chagrin, and she was rising to the occasion. When George was not in charge, she was.

"Clean up your puke and get yourself decent. Then get out there and protect your kingdom!"

When George left his stateroom he moved directly to the rail and held on, walking a little too casually toward the group clustered around Mayo Smith. There was just enough pitch and roll to mask his hesitant steps. He moved alongside L.I.L. as she stood, listening, and leaned against her for support. She stiffened just enough to provide security and had enough vested interest to stay put.

Whether casually, or as an opportunist, Mayo Smith was filling the void, sensing incapacity in a leader too easily piqued by challenged authority. Smith was, himself, becoming puzzled if not disenchanted by Adams who had seized his admiration when they first met. Coming from Boston and likely privy to Adams' fame turned to notoriety in earlier years, Smith had been drawn to the charisma of one who effectively claimed to act in response to divine calling and approbation. He wouldn't have come on the journey, with intent to participate fully, had it not been for confidence in the ability of George Jones Adams. If there was weakness and even folly in George's past there certainly had been no trace of evidence in the present. Smith was also scripturally knowledgeable enough for the prophecies of return to have a familiar and compelling ring.

Now, somewhat objectively and somewhat playfully, he was probing and exploring. George heard him speak of a likely point of beginning of the Church of the Messiah between the Restoration doctrine of Joseph Smith and the advent concepts of William Miller. Given time to consolidate church and colony George Adams (as he would confess to T. W. Smith years later) was planning not only to admit his Mormon background but his intent to link his church with the followers of the son of Joseph Smith. But having hidden his background so long, and fearful of the crumbling of his authority, he could not tolerate the present threatening exploration by Mayo Smith. That he was thick-tongued escaped his notice.

The explosion of his words startled the whole company: "I was called by a voice from heaven, a voice heard in my youth. I speak by authority of the priesthood of Melchisedek. Our cause is just and is, in fact, a great and marvelous work destined to bring heaven and earth together, reestablishing the cause of Zion and calling the sons of Jacob to the land of their fathers. It is written in the Holy Bible—and we move to fulfill the prophecies spoken on the mountains of Olivet and Bethel. You, sir, do not know whereof you speak."

George let go his hold on the rail to gesture his point and

lost his balance. L.I.L. caught him, short of falling, but he was awkward and suddenly embarrassed. Control of himself meant control of the situation. Steady on his feet, he could parry and thrust verbally as if he were a swordsman or pugilist. Now a rolling ship, a throbbing head, and an unfair situation conspired against him. Rising to the occasion he had spoken his conviction, only to appear silly. L.I.L.'s expression in that moment betrayed something other than loving concern.

George turned abusive, flinging accusations at Mayo Smith as if he were an editor from Machias or Springfield. The more he lashed out, seeking to win points, the more he lost. It was a bad show. Even Smith was embarrassed and anxious to draw it to a close.

George heard some of the young people giggling nervously. L.I.L. took him firmly by the arm and said, "Come, George, it's time for dinner."

As they passed two of the sailors, one said, soft-voiced to the other, "The old man is drunk." L.I.L. felt George bristle as if to speak and pushed him toward the dining salon.

From there to Jaffa remorse and constant vigil by L.I.L. kept George away from the other spirits he had stowed for purposes of communion, water purification, and emergencies. The pressures of drawing things together before arrival also lent their weight toward keeping him sober.

George turned from being morose and argumentative to something close to congeniality and confidence. The colonists, awed and worried by the unknown before them, closed ranks.

Since it was a charter voyage, the *Nellie Chapin* had no pressing need to call at other ports, and when the wind proved strong near Malta Captain Wass set his course for Jaffa. On the morning of September 22 the headland of Carmel was visible on the horizon before them. The first mate called for change of course to starboard, and the bark made for the small cape which marked the colony's destination.

They were still too far from shore to see the lay of the land, but they were aware of well-wooded Carmel fading into the distance and giving way to the Hills of Ephraim. They were conscious, too, of a plain that was too much grayish tan infrequently broken by splotches of hazy green. It looked forbidding.

The expanse of sand gave way at last to a point surrounded by groves of trees and by bushes vying with houses rising tier above tier from tidemark to the crest of Jaffa's hill. They dropped anchor at 2:00 p.m., September 22, forty-two days out of Jonesport.

Adams was the first and only passenger over the side and into a Turkish version of the yawl boat. There were ledges of rock to navigate and time enough later to coax their own yawl from ship to shore after the ledges became known.

Keeping excitement under control and looking very much the president, George Adams faced toward the uneven pyramid of structures that was Jaffa. Never really at home any place else, he was coming home to the land he had felt was his own since accompanying Orson Hyde as far as England twenty-five years before. And he would be welcomed by Loewenthal, good friend, agent of the colony, and now vice-consul of the United States in Jaffa by appointment of the new U.S. Consul in Jerusalem, Victor Beauboucher.

Through the ledges the small boat turned toward the city quay. As expected, Loewenthal hastened to meet him, and the two of them went directly to the place of customs near the Gate of the City and close by the constabulary of the Turkish police.

Greetings were warm, and the two men turned immediately to the paper work. Adams had prepared his passenger manifest with care, correcting an oversight by including

Mrs. L.I.L. Adams, age 39 years, born in Maine
Clarence Agustine Adams, age 11 years, born in Maine

He did forget to include one seaman, Sewell Hopkins, by name, but the total count of passengers and crew included him.

With a flourish Adams wrote his own name first, changing it to George Washington Joshua Adams, President of the Palestine Emigration Association and President of the Church of the Messiah, age 53 years, born in New Jersey. It was a combination he could not resist. He was the president, thus George Washington. He was divinely called to lead into the promised land, thus Joshua. He was quite content with the rest of the name—Adams. It was not a playful embellishment, this addition of names. He was each character, and he would play each part on this vital stage. George W. J. Adams was well aware of the drama.

Duly registered, he was ready to get started with unloading members of the colony, getting them into temporary quarters within the walls or improvising shelter for the eager ones at the site he and Abe had chosen one year before. That they could unload duty free was confirmed by the Turkish officials.

Loewenthal seemed reluctant to get under way. Then he handed Adams a letter from Joy Morris, U.S. Minister Resident at Constantinople. Adams opened it with enough confidence to cover his nervousness. Morris repeated almost exactly the message he had received from the office of the Sultan:

"The Supreme Porte declines to grant the firman for the proposed American settlement near Jaffa. The Sultan has no domain at his disposition there for those who are not Ottoman subjects. . . ." He went on to say that "the promoter of the scheme should not have encouraged families to embark from America until the result of their application to the Porte was known." Morris had learned of the decision in early July and wrote on July 13 to Victor Beauboucher, Consul at Jerusalem, advising him. Morris had also communicated the information immediately to Senator Morrill of Maine, but it was of course futile. By the time that message had arrived it was too late to intercept the colonists. For them the die was cast. The *Nellie Chapin* was already at sea, and all on board were oblivious to the decision which might have delayed their departure or at least diminished the company to its most hardy and determined.

Adams staggered under the blow of refusal and equally under the humiliating criticism. An unsuspecting boatload of people waited, with all their possessions, intent on living out their years on land he had assured them would be their own. Now permission to purchase that land was denied. In the moments before frantic anger would take over, Adams uttered a desperate prayer: "Oh, God, why hast thou forsaken me?"

He turned to Loewenthal, the one who had always, as merchant, given assurances that anything could be worked out, one way or another. "I thought you had already purchased the land. You said it could be done. We even gave you the money to do it! Furthermore, you know me well enough to know that we would come, permission or no." Loewenthal had anticipated the rashness and had said as much to Beauboucher, who had repeated it in a letter to Joy Morris.

"I thought it could be done and I still think it can, but we will have to be careful, and it will take time. . . ."

"Time?" George exploded, lashing out at the only one he could hold responsible. "We haven't got time. See that bark—it's loaded with men, women, and children anxious to set foot on shore. Where am I going to put them while you take time?"

"I have permission for you to land on the beach north of town and near to the land you have your heart set on."

"On the beach? You can't be serious!"

"I'm serious enough. You have been denied the right to take possession of any land. You must either land on the beach which the Turkish government does not want, or you must reprovision and return home, which the Turkish government does want. What will it be?"

Angry, dejected, and despairing of a way to break the news to the folks on board ship, Adams longed for the steady hand of Abe McKenzie. The honest way to go was to lay it out fact by fact to the people on board, but his judgment and authority were in jeopardy. He was curt with Loewenthal and declared his intention to stay. Then he headed back to the ship. As he came aboard he called out, "Glory enough for one day—everything we asked for is granted."

Everybody cheered lustily, breaking the tension and signaling together the victory for which they had hoped and never really doubted. Adams had his faults, but the Lord had indeed laid his hands on him. "We'll stay on board 'til morning. It's too late to risk the ledges, but with the sunrise coming over those Judean hills, we'll set to with yawl and rafts toward the beach just over there a quarter mile north of Jaffa. The plot is roughly the same distance straight in from the beach. See that rise with the dark green of the trees—that's our land! We'll have to clear the tangle of brush and cactus, lay out the streets and building sites. It will take about the same amount of time as it takes to set our gear on the beach, maybe two to three weeks. It would be less if we could land this bark at the wharf but we cannot. We have got to stay at anchor out here two miles from shore. When ashore, we'll stay together except for those who wish to take lodging in the town. For temporary shelter on shore we will use sail cloth. We have prefabricated units to use for walls plus doors galore. Our friend, Herman Loewenthal, has been appointed vice-consul for the United States and even now is completing arrangements. By the time we are ready to build it will be full speed ahead. Now, let's thank God for a safe journey and safe arrival. 'O gracious God of Israel . . '"

Deception or no, there was no turning back. At this juncture Adams sensed that there was only one who would be anxious to reprovision and head back home. That was Levi Mace. He could lift his hand for one thing only, to keep himself steadied against falling with that painful game leg. He wanted pity and got it—from himself.

The others bent their backs and started the long duty of shifting cargo from bark to shore and setting up a temporary camp. It had to be high enough to stay above the tide, and higher still to protect against any storm. The uneven ledge of rocks that kept the *Nellie Chapin* two miles out to sea would give them scant protection from high seas breaking against the beach and the wind sending saturating spray into their makeshift camp

Their temporary camp was near enough to the city to offer some deterrent to marauders and far enough away from the mouth of a small stream in case it should overflow with any rainfall. What they did not know was that they were in too close proximity to the mass burial site in the upper portion of the beach occasioned by the cholera epidemic a year before, nor were they aware of the custom of the town to empty sacks of rubbish into the sea.

Some of the colonists found quarters in the town, especially at the Greek convent. The Adamses responded to the invitation of the Loewenthals. Except for their quarters, the others were rustic to say the least—being primarily outbuildings of the German consulate. Most of the settlers, however, busied themselves with building tents, shelters, and shacks, from whatever cloth and lumber could be used to provide protection against the sun. The rain had not come yet, and they planned to be on the plot by then. Barrels and hogsheads were formed into a perimeter wall. Doors, intended for new houses, were used for shelter walls. In the center a sandy courtyard offered a place for small children to play under watchful eyes; it also served as a place of meeting.

Sturdy McKenzie-built-and-owned yawl boats went back and forth from ship to shore. It was back-breaking work for those who loaded and unloaded, day after day, for three weeks. Lumber had to be rafted to shore, the roll of surf and determined action of the waves threatening to break and strew the prefabricated sections over the ledges and along the shore.

With tendency toward exaggeration in order to promote optimism—or perhaps it was his hearers' tendency to grasp at small wonders and play them out of proportion—Adams had held out a promise he may not have intended. This time it almost worked to his advantage, however, as the colonists recalled his promise that the aged would renew their youth in the Holy Land. Herbert Clark was to recall in later years that "the men and boys joined the ship's crew in rafting the lumber shoreward. Of the party was one, whose locks bleached by the snows of sixty winters, displayed the first signs of the return of youthful vim and vivacity. Now he runs far out in shallow water and, seizing a stick of timber, hastens toward the shore. Again and again he outstrips many younger until his associates, recalling the words of their great leader, suggest the renewal of youth. On the shore the women and children repeat the suggestion and the whole colony unite in spontaneous joy believing they have discovered the fountain of life."

Dismay turned to hope, an emotion which was strengthened by the welcome received from all officials and by milling crowds of Arabs, Jews, and Turks. Even the pasha was pleasant and friendly.

"Never," said Adams, "was a people more universally received with kindness and love or treated with more respect and distinction." The colonists, wandering from the shore to investigate the desired site of the colony and scanning the great groves of fruit trees growing in the fertile plain of Sharon began to believe that their new home could be made into the paradise which Adams had painted for them.

The teen-agers, not seriously impressed by the gravity of the colony's situation, found Jaffa with its narrow streets and crowded bazaars to be an exciting place for exploration. Some of the adults, however, were concerned for the safety of their children. They were ill at ease in strange surroundings and found, as Robert Emerson said, that "the streets which are very narrow seem to be literally swarming with people, camels, donkeys and mules, all mixed into one homogeneous mass, each one apparently endeavoring to make all the noise he is capable of. . . . A more dirty, filthy and lazy set of people do not exist on the earth. . . ."

Loewenthal, as promised, worked hard to complete the purchase of the plot of ground they had selected for their village. Why he had not already purchased the building site by ruse of using a Turkish citizen remained a mystery. The process offered no great problem once he determined to act. Perhaps he wanted to avoid the appearance of going contrary to Turkish officialdom. Having already spoken for the land, he knew it was in no danger of purchase by another, not even Aharon Chelouche who was to be so prominent in founding a new city on the sands north of Jaffa.

Horses were plentiful, although not broken to harness, and could be purchased after buildings were up and the time for plowing had come. Water, though scarce, would be no problem, although it had to be carried in skins. That encountered unexpected resistance from pure water folk from the coast of Maine. What Loewenthal did not know, and no others suspected, was that the Arabs hired for the job were drawing water from polluted sources rather than the city well as ordered.

By the time parents of small children began to complain the damage had been done. They neither boiled the water nor followed Adams' advice. When they came to him, suspecting that stomach sickness and diarrhea came from the water, he gave sound advice which was taken as evidence of his weakness and duplicity. He instructed, "Put your faith in God and use a little wine or rum." Affronted, they limited themselves to prayer and refused to follow the custom of the centuries—water and wine roughly mixed ten to one, or even more diluted for little ones.

Exposure and lack of adequate sanitation led to dysentery; first the children and then the adults began to be sick. Mayo Smith, anxious to make dramatic reading, gave graphic description in correspondence to the Boston *Traveler:* "In our rear was a graveyard. Nearly 200 had died of cholera and their bodies, many or most of them, I believe, being buried there. The exhalations through the porous sand from such a vast body of decomposition was very bad. We were flanked by two dirty villages of Arabs. The shore was the world's privy. Anyway, the butchers put their offal there which always gave off no heavenly smell. Decaying seaweed in the front was not always a pleasant perfume."

On October 25 Adams described the events of the first month and three days on the beach:

> We were two weeks and four days in unloading, or discharging our vessel. Since our arrival we have been honored by two American war-steamers, viz: the *Ticonderoga*, commanded by Commodore Stedman, and the *Canandaigua*. We were treated with great consideration and respect by both these noble vessels; that is by their officers and men.
>
> For two weeks after we arrived all went on well. But soon the hand of sickness and death reached us. First, Brother Rogers lost his youngest child, George, who was sick before he left America. Next, our dear Brother Andrew Tabbutt, lost his youngest, and dear child, little Leon, who died from teething and erysipelas. Then followed the death of Brother Seward Gray's infant child, who had long been sick of the Summer complaint, and died finally from the effects of teething. But now comes the saddest tale of all. Brother John Burns,—the good,—the pure,—the just,—the kind hearted old man, (who had suffered much before he left America,) was stricken down by the fell destroyer of our race. He died peacefully at the age of sixty-six years. He died without a groan or struggle. Yes, he fell asleep in Jesus, there to await until the trump of God shall sound and awake the dead.

Brother Burns was a man whose life and conduct had ever been pure, upright, and good. He died in the full faith of the dispensation of the fulness of times; yes, he fell asleep in full hope of a glorious resurrection from the dead. There was a large attendance at the funeral of Brother Burns. The procession was headed by the English, Prussian, and American Consuls, and their attendant officers. The funeral was a perfect triumph. No man could be more honored in a foreign land, than was Brother Burns.

Soon after the death of Brother Burns, Brother George W. Clark was stricken down in the prime of life, and the vigor of manhood. He fell a victim to maltreatment, under the practice of a man named Mayo G. Smith, a self-styled doctor; and I here say there was no necessity for the death of Brother Clark, he might and could have lived, if he had obeyed council, but he died a repentant man in the full faith of the Gospel. Two of Brother Clark's children have also died; so has brother Rolla Floyd's infant child; brother Uriah Leighton's child, also Sister Polly Leighton died; she having thrown her life away by her own imprudence and foolishness. Thus, of our Colony of one hundred and fifty-six persons, nine now sleep in peace and quiet in the beautiful Protestant grave yard, near the upper gate of Jaffa. Of these nine, six were children.

The Colony is now in a most prosperous condition. Our prospects are good,—we may say first-rate. We already have ten houses up, and as many more in preparation. The sound of the hammer, the saw, the plane, the trowel, and other implements of mechanism, now greet our ears on every side. The first rains are now upon us; they come thick and fast. The people here have never known so early a season

November 9.—We have just got through with moving from the beach to our favorite location. We commence ploughing and planting tomorrow. Our friends may ask have none found fault, or murmured? We answer, yes! they have murmured, that is some six or eight traitors have murmured and found fault. Some of them have sickened and died, and others soon will, unless they repent.

Some have folded their arms and done nothing; but all agree that it is a glorious land, a land of wheat, and barley, and corn, and fruit, and vines, and a heavenly climate.

We say to our friends, far and near, if you believe in the Dispensation of the fulness of times, get ready and come; if you believe it is now the set time to favor Zion, come; if you are willing to work in the great restitution, come. But don't come to murmur and complain without a cause.

It is now the 14th of November, only three months and five days since we started from Jonesport. We have come five thousand miles, landed safely on the beach without accident or mishaps; built some eight two-story houses, and have as many more in course of erection; and this day we are ploughing with five teams, and with blessings of Israel's God, we shall soon have an immense amount of wheat and barley in the ground.

Palestine will soon shake herself from the dust of ages, and arise in glory and grandeur, as in the days of old. The great Restitution, as foretold by the Prophets and Apostles, has now commenced. The sons of Ephraim are now gathering home; and all things show the glory of the latter day to be near; yea, at the very doors. May the Lord prepare us for the great things that are coming upon the earth. I remain, dear brethren, yours most truly and sincerely, in hope of peace on earth.

G. J. Adams

FARM AND HOME

With all due respect to scattered Israel there were more immediate demands which had to be met. Children had to be housed and fed. That necessity had been driven home the hard way, with too many families feeling the wretched gnawing of grief. Yet even that had to be submerged by the frenzied transfer of possessions from shore to shanties contrived of building materials consigned to later construction projects.

Herman Loewenthal, vice-consul and entrepreneur, had finally completed the transaction for purchase of the plot from Sheikh Muhamad Sherkowi. Adams immediately began laying out streets and platting lots according to a long-determined plan dreamed of at Indian River. Now the dream had to be cut to the available cloth. He was decisive, modifying plots where necessary, staking them out, and getting the crews onto building sites as quickly as possible.

Construction was, of course, speeded by the prefabricated units. There was a standard design, with some modifications. The houses were two-storied, complete with green shuttered windows. The windows were four over four—a variation of the standard six over six back home. Gables, eaves and soffits were trimmed in a manner reminiscent of Maine houses. Recognizing the different climate and also with a nod toward the beauty of their surroundings—orange groves, a storied city nearby, and the blue Mediterranean—many of the colonists added porches, especially to the second story. Upright bearing timbers were 3 x 6 or 4 x 4. Porch decking—each board rounded at the end for style—was fully one inch thick and frequently, as in the Leighton house, ten inches in width. Railings were made of slender rungs with the hand railing itself of excellent quality quarter-sawn lumber. Finish work showed class and certainly intention to remain in livable quarters of which one could be proud. Picket fences were added to define lot boundaries in proper style.

Two of Gram Burns' sons, John and George Drisko, began their three-story hotel. It was to prove a disappointment to them because they would not be ready for the normal tourist season of 1866-1867. Their business would languish during the hot summer of 1867 when tourists stayed away, and they would be gone before the next tour season. That it would be the first of the hotels to be built in the tourist center—this very American colony—they had no way of discerning through their disappointment, except in the wild imaginings of G. J. Adams whom they had begun to mistrust.

They were not alone. Adams was occupying the first building up—not as a resident but as storekeeper. He decided to be in charge of the storehouse, both for disbursement of goods brought and belonging to the colony and as resident merchant. He saw the necessity of close supervision of supplies, but how he fancied himself as storekeeper defies imagination. He had ship captains who had been their own supercargoes. He had storekeepers on board. Mrs. A. H. Wass had been a highly successful one. She and her husband began their journey to Jaffa with more resources than any others, with the possible exception of G. J. Adams and wife. Listed as colonists from California, they were actually from Rockland,

Maine—by way of California. In Rockland Mrs. Wass had been proprietor of a fancy millinery store and as a specialty created grave clothes.

The store was the point of control within the colony, like Joseph Smith's Red Brick Store in Nauvoo. It served as liaison between the colony and the community. Since Adams did not trust anyone as much as he trusted himself, he had appointed and unwittingly placed himself in the line of fire, front and rear.

The first hassle came when lots proved smaller than Adams had promised. The plot was 25 percent smaller than anticipated, which required a scaling down of each lot. Next, when they asked for clear title, Adams' deception on arrival was starkly uncovered. It would have been enough to hear them grumble about size of lot and lack of title, but these only illustrated the disillusion of Levi Mace who was getting desperate about the support of his large family, of Shad Wass who resented being pushed aside as an incompetent, and of Ellis McKenzie, Jr., who was turning his keenness to nit-picking and audible complaint.

The second hassle turned on a combination of Adams' recently uncovered penchant for intoxicating spirits and his appalling lack of discretion in stocking his (their) storehouse with a generous supply of brandy (201 bottles), wine, English pale ale, and some casks of Arrack. He spent in excess of 250 dollars of their limited resources, expecting to make a profit for them (again from their own resources) by encouraging them to drink wine as a health measure. "A little wine for the stomach's sake," he was fond of saying. That was scriptural, written by Apostle Paul.

They were shocked by his brazen defense of his own weakness and his open invitation to join him. They dismissed as a weakly-veiled excuse his insistence that there was antiseptic and therapeutic value in alcohol. Back home in Maine he had preached on its evils and was known for his sobriety and support of the temperance movement. He publicly abhorred intoxication in anyone. Now he—their minister—was the offender, and they resented it bitterly. They responded with a temperance crusade, each adult signing a pledge of sobriety in the colony. That cut off the sale of spirits but not necessarily the consumption of it. Given time, G. J. could dispose of it personally.

They could have helped, but didn't. They were incensed, and their rebuke drove him to drink all the more. The last thing he needed was separation from the colonists, but they wanted nothing to do with him.

The Adamses remained in the Loewenthal home. It was an uneasy arrangement. L.I.L. was distant in any environment but in these strange surroundings—where only hesitant English was spoken—she found it easier to be aloof than to run the risk of misunderstanding. George was preoccupied with building a village, running a store, and greeting a constant stream of curious visitors, especially from America. Loewenthal commented to Victor Beauboucher that it was sometimes a trial having Adams in their home, especially since he came home late and all too frequently a bit unsteady on his feet.

After the store, the next public building to go up was the meetinghouse. A few temporary partitions were added so the Adamses could move in. Their own house—to be the most elaborate of all, befitting their station and appropriate for the welcoming of important visitors anticipated through the years—would be built later. They invited one of the four non-member adults, Mrs. Matilda Richardson, to join them. A sensitive person, long protected from the ways of the world and easily offended by loudness and profanity, she was also easily scandalized by evidences of domestic strife. While living with them, she collected memories of the volatile Adams family.

In mid-November all who intended to farm began to ready

fields for planting. Except for one small plot, negotiated by Loewenthal and Adams, all lands were rented. Close by the Jaffa wall were farm lands of the Greek convent, and those of the "rich Greek." Beyond the colony, out Nablus Road, was the Model Farm. The McKenzies made arrangements to cultivate that acreage.

Back in Indian River, Maine, the McKenzies had been boat builders and merchants. In Palestine they were to make their way as farmers. While Ellis, Sr. and Jr., continued building, Edwin, 19, and Orrin, 17, "started plowing with a new span of horses on good land belonging to the Greek convent north of Jaffa." In the two weeks following November 16, 1866, the two of them plowed, harrowed, and sowed six acres. During the same period twelve others of the colony planted another sixty acres with barley.

In the adjacent fields Arabs were plowing, and Edwin was struck by their primitive methods and equipment. His diary includes a description of the small steers and the plow "which consists of a peculiar crooked tree [that grew] up a little way and then makes a kind of a cane crook . . . with a kind of a spear head or anchor hook thing stuck on the point of the crook. . . . They tore up the ground about three inches deep and generally sow their grain on the unplowed ground and plow it in." Here was visible evidence of the superiority of his own equipment, and he was not surprised when shortly after landowners came to hire him for plowing.

On Tuesday, December 4, Edwin went with G. A. Drisko and G. J. Adams to look at some land called the forty acre lot. It was about a mile through the orange gardens out the Jerusalem road on the edge of the plain. According to Edwin, "It is a plot that Loewenthal bought and cheated us." It was to become a tragic bone of contention.

While relations between Loewenthal and the colony were deteriorating, Consul Victor Beauboucher was striving to secure the right of the colonists to stay. The Turkish

Governor of Jerusalem was being politely difficult by pursuing the official line of the Supreme Porte. He misunderstood the number involved, counting each member of the colony as a head of family. "The emigrants," he wrote on November 19, "amounting to the number of one hundred and fifty persons, come to settle with their families in Turkey cannot be considered as foreign individuals...but as forming a colony...[and] the American emigrants cannot but submit to this category." Beauboucher tried to relieve the tension in his answer of November 24:

> The number of these persons [is] men 40, women 43, children 69. The interests of each are individual and several of them have an intention of applying themselves to agriculture upon lands belonging to different persons formerly established in the Turkish Empire and rented to these American families....These American families have come to Palestine with a design of enterprise and to try the fertility of the soil. It is probable that the results being favorable they will definitely establish themselves and be followed by other families. "Then and only then" they would form a colony but at present being but farmers or holders *of land belonging to persons subject to the laws and regulations of the Sublime Porte*, they will preserve all the rights to the protection of the United States Government as well as all the Europeans who being established in the Empire upon the same conditions have a right to that of their own government. Of these 40 persons arrived with their families the greatest part are handicrafts such as carpenters, joiners, shoemakers, tailors, etc., and each one of them intends to settle in the country as all European workmen and nothing else for the present.

For a new consul Beauboucher was doing very well. Furthermore, he was anxious to do an impressive job on his first assignment. An idealist, writing for liberal journals in Belgium, he had identified with Abraham Lincoln's stand on slavery. He went to the United States, he said, "having resolved to fight for the principles I uphold...immediately after my arrival was presented to General Stevenson, through whom I made the acquaintance of Colonel Byrne, commanding the 28th Massachusetts Volunteers, who induced me to enter his Regiment, at the head of which he died with honor on the 4th June [1864] at Coal Harbor. On the same day I had a foot shattered [in charging a rebel battery] which was in consequence amputated."

In less than two years he had left Belgium, became a Union war hero, was appointed U.S. Consul (August 1865), found himself in Jerusalem threatened with a second amputation, and now was consumed by an aggravation that would probably require him to take painful journeys to Jaffa.

Adams would have been well-advised to cultivate Beauboucher. Instead, he blamed him as a party in interest for every misdeed, real or fancied, committed by Loewenthal. Added to that he was one more noncitizen, representing the U.S. government in halting English. He had assumed that his tour of duty, subsequent disability, and appointment as consul carried with it the citizenship he yearned for. Discovering otherwise to his embarrassment, he submitted to the Secretary of State Seward a request for citizenship. "I now come. . . to address myself to you, Mr. Secretary, to beg you will be so kind as to give the orders necessary to put an end to the false position in which, at this moment, I find myself placed."

The mills of government like those of the gods grind slowly, and Beauboucher was still in his "false position" when the colonists arrived. Sensing a chink in official armor, Adams chose to reserve that knowledge for possible exploitation. He calculated that Herman Loewenthal had "swindled and cheated" them out of approximately seven hundred pounds sterling. There was enough evidence to make a convincing argument of it, and so he and nearly the full roster of males in the colony presented a "Bill of Charges" against Herman Loewenthal to Beauboucher at Jerusalem. They also sent a copy to Secretary of State Seward.

In the bill they asked for the removal of Loewenthal from office as vice-consul for these reasons:

1. For having received money of us to purchase a certain favorite plot of

land and having used said money for other purposes.
2. For having purchased lands for us that are no benefit to us at present.
3. After having purchased our favorite lot he charged us nearly double the price which he paid and has never given an account of what he did pay but we have had to learn it from other sources.
4. For having purchased for us a lot of old horses and an old mule at very low prices and charging us in his bill an exorbitant price with the addition of ten percent commission on the entire sums which he charged in the bill for horses and mules.
5. For having hired houses for us at a low rate and charging us 25 percent advance in addition to 10 percent commission on the whole account.
6. For having sent us a poor quality of goods and charging us a much higher price than he did other people.
7. For having been impudent, tyrannical and insulting to a number of American citizens and having charged us unjust fees and oppressed and cheated us in various ways.
For these and many other reasons and from the fact that he is not an American and does not use his influence to promote the welfare of the American colony recently established here, we therefore earnestly pray for his removal at the earliest moment and the appointment of Mark T. Wentworth, Esquire, as a suitable person to fill this office. . . .

Beauboucher, the U.S. Consul, had no choice but to respond to the serious petition, and he traveled from Jerusalem to Jaffa reluctantly, every mile a torment of pain from a stump of leg that would not heal properly.

He met with his appointee on Monday evening, December 17, and according to *The Sword of Truth* account, "With only themselves present, examined the whole subject and acquitted Mr. Loewenthal." At any rate, when the hearing began the next day the consul infuriated the colonists by permitting Loewenthal to read his defense before the charges and case for the prosecution were presented.

"There, you see I am not guilty!" Loewenthal declared when he had finished.

Mr. Adams. . . arose and showed [Loewenthal's] utter ignorance of American law and for over one hour astonished and electrified the entire court and audience. . . . As [he] laid before them, in great plainness, American laws and customs they fairly quailed under the truthful and withering sarcasm, as it rolled from the lips of Mr. Adams

G. J. was back in form.

The consul adjourned for dinner. Afterward Adams took up the case of the colony. Loewenthal had charged $35.00 for stone that was never delivered. One thousand eggs were charged for twice—once to J. E. Burns and once to R. T. Emerson. Adams enumerated every offense. The trial continued for three days with Beauboucher acting as "a commanding officer" according to Edwin McKenzie, and adamant in excusing Loewenthal.

As a last resort Adams left the courtroom and went to the Turkish Governor of Jaffa who, after listening to Adams' account of what was going on, ordered his Cadi, or judge, to secure the copy of a transaction from the Land Record. It was most convincing and condemning. Loewenthal had charged Mr. Adams 480 pounds after paying the owner only 175 pounds on the one purchase, clearing 305 pounds for himself. In the proceedings it also became clear that Loewenthal had charged 750 pounds for another plot for which he had paid out only 365 pounds.

Instead of punishing Loewenthal, however, Beauboucher awarded him 40 pounds "for his trouble as Commissioner," kept him as vice-consul, and then stipulated that he was relieved of any responsibility for dealing with Adams and the colony. Instead of appointing Mark Wentworth, as requested by the petitioners, he appointed Shad Wass.

For the colonists it was a worm-eaten victory. They felt betrayed by a government that had appointed two noncitizens to represent the United States—and then only to be treated shabbily. As for Adams, he added Beauboucher to his list.

Edwin McKenzie, with his horses working well, managed to plow about an acre a day. Usually he was accompanied by his younger brother, Orrin. On the way to and from the plot, if they and the horses were not too weary, the boys would race. The McKenzies had brought a two-wheeled cart for hauling grain and implements. As plowing continued they hauled bags of barley, later peas, wheat, corn, cessin (sesame), and potatoes (cut for planting) to the various plots.

A week before the hearing, toward the end of plowing, a whiffletree came off, frightening the horses. They ran through the gardens and down the Jerusalem Road to the fountain near the gate where someone stopped them. Having lost sight of them, Edwin and Orrin had no idea which way they had gone, and once found, had to go searching for whiffletree and chains through gardens and Arab village until, in the dark, Edwin got thoroughly lost. It was a stormy time in Palestine with hard rains, wind at gale velocity, thunder and lightning. Edwin called December 16 the most wintry day they had experienced.

There is no reason to doubt the accuracy of Edwin's account of the events and mood of the final days of 1866. It reveals continuous productive activity, including a full day's work on Christmas. His entry of December 23, the day after the trial ended, contrasts with the tension which seemed to prevail:

> It was a beautiful day until evening. Then there was quite a thundershower came up. Velma and I went out to look at the grain. . . went over on top of the hills where we could see all around. The River Ogee, the plains of Sharon which was nearly all cultivated as far as you could see, it was a beautiful sight. We came home and got ready as soon as we could and went to meeting. We had a good meeting after which I went in to see Alice Norton who is sick but is now getting better. Came home with Velma after dark. Got home just before it began to rain.

December 24 was another busy day of sowing and harrowing barley. Then—

> Tuesday, December 25, 1866.
>
> Christmas in Palestine. I got up late, was awakened this morning by hearing the girls wish somebody a Merry Christmas. After breakfast we went down to the plot with the horses and got two bushels of potatoes. Went out and furrowed off a piece then turned the horses loose and went to

planting potatoes. We got the last hill covered just as the sun sank behind the hill. We caught our horses and hauled in the cart and things to the old Greeks, took our horses out and jumped onto them and came home a good jog. When we got home Mother went to work and warmed over a dinner for us that they saved which consisted of stuffed chicken, turnip sauce, squash, gravy, potatoes and bread. A good Yankee dinner. Thus goes Christmas in Palestine.

Wednesday, December 26, 1866.

We went out early, took a bushel of potatoes and a few peas, got the potatoes and peas in in the forenoon, ate dinner and then went to plowing. Done a big afternoon's work and got home early. Finished plowing on the forty acre lot.

Thursday, December 27, 1866.

We went out early. Took five bushels barley with us and put in three and a half of it before dinner which finished up our work on the Jerusalem road. We have twenty bushels of barley in on the Jerusalem road and twenty-nine here and on the convent land. After dinner we packed up and started home, went on to the plot and got a bag of barley and straw and was coming home but Captain Ackley wanted me to haul three loads of sand and I did after which Mr. Walker wanted me to haul some lumber. I could not very well refuse so I hauled it up. The last load was large and one of the horses bucked me, threw off some of it, went along all right. I started for home about sundown, had a good load of one thing and another, got home all right, ate supper, fed the horses and went to bed.

Friday, December 28, 1866.

We went out to look for land on the model farm to see where to begin to plow for we are going to cultivate this land. We harnessed up and began down on one of the largest fields in front of the house. We plowed over half an acre in the full moon and pampered our horses and let them go. When we wanted them mine was gone. I took Orrin's and went and found him and we went to work. Worked until four o'clock, then went down to the plot and got four bushels of wheat to sow on the model farm.

Saturday, December 29, 1866.

We did not get to work so early as we ought but we done quite a day's work. We carried out four bushels of wheat and sowed seven pecks. Finished plowing what we marked off yesterday, sowed and harrowed it in, marked off eight paces, sowed and plowed it in. In the afternoon had about two acres in when we got done. Finished just at sundown and went down to the plot and got some straw before supper, bono.

Sunday, December 30, 1866.

It rained nearly all night and still continues. I have not done much today but read. There was a meeting but I did not go down to the plot at all.

Monday, December 31, last day, 1866.

We went to work quite early, down where we left off but it was too muddy and sticky so we did not plow there but came up on the side of the hill where it was not so damp. We cut away the bushes, sowed the seed, and plowed it in, put in about three-fourths of an acre and marked off a New Year's stent. Our horses worked well.

Tuesday, January 1, 1867.

We worked clearing off bushes before breakfast and until about 10:00 then we went to plowing and plowed all we marked off for a stent, which was nearly four-fifths of an acre. Got done just at sundown. When I came to the house they had no flour so I took a pail and went down and got a pailful out of a sack we have got down there. Thus I cannot say that I spent the first day of 1867 very pleasantly, neither can I say that I spent it at all unpleasantly, but. . . I think it gives perfect satisfaction at least on my part.

JANUARY IN JAFFA

Mayo Smith was after George Adams' hide. Since he had no intention of staying in Palestine, he was under no obligation to build or to plant. He had time to move about and talk. . . and his words gained authenticity. He was gaining a reputation as a newspaper correspondent. People in the United States from New York to Maine were fascinated by the courageous, if foolhardy, venture of the colony. Mayo was a major source of news, sending off reports to the *Boston Traveler*—and slanting them to his own purpose.

A few weeks later those reports from the Jaffa correspondent came back to Palestine. The colonists, anxious for news from home, found themselves mirrored and exposed.

Some were infuriated; others were impressed and listened to Mayo with more respect.

Smith, once so obviously pro-Adams in accepting the invitation to make the journey, drew a sizable collection of the old anti-Adams letters and articles from his trunk and began to work on Levi Mace, Shad Wass, Seward Gray, William Lynch, Orland Tibbetts, and others. His most telling effect may have been on Ellis B. McKenzie, Jr., whose ailing and homesick wife, Marcella, was daily and tearfully pleading with Ellis to return to Maine.

Families that had been drawn together by faith, near shipwreck, and shared grief began to drift apart and to treat each other as strangers. Greetings that once had come so easily at the intersection of the two streets of their small village turned cool. Eyes betrayed suspicion and anger.

Two letters written on the same day from Jaffa illustrate the mounting tensions. On January 2, 1867, Isaiah B. Ames wrote to members of his family:

> This is the pleasantest country on earth, and the most fruitful when properly cultivated. The land is smooth and undulating, not flat, and you can sow your grain, and plow it in, without fencing or meeting rocks or stumps. . . . The natives, Turks and all, great and small, high and low, treat us with the greatest respect, and will do everything for our comfort. I speak of this because I suppose you have heard awful stories about us, written to the *Boston Traveler*, by Mr. M. G. Smith, a very bad man who came out with us on the bark. He brought with him all the old slanderous letters against Mr. Adams, that he could find, and has commenced circulating them in this place and at Jerusalem. . . . But we have all the inhabitants of the country on our side. Those that have fallen from the faith have given us the most trouble. They are those whom Bro. Adams lugged or helped out here, through kindness, which makes it the harder to bear.

Carried on the same ship was the letter from E. B. McKenzie:

> I take this late hour to inform you in relation to [the] great humbug. You have had particulars by my sister in regard to G. J. Adams' wild character in keeping a rum shop and getting drunk and undertaking to cheat the colonists out of all their money. I take pleasure in announcing that I have returned to my former faith and shall soon return to my native country,

although rather chagrined at such a ridiculous mistake. My wife has been sick for three months and is quite discouraged. She cries almost every day when she thinks how useless her coming out here was and says, "Oh, if I was only home again."

The business of the colony grows more and more complicated every day. The colony you understand is divided, part for getting back, part for staying. The part that are for Mr. Adams are fanatically mad. Those that wish to return have the U.S. Consulate on their side. Hence there is a warring between the two parties. . . .

My pleasure is to come home in the Spring so here I close.

That the first letter was printed in Drisko's *Machias Union*, and the second in Forbush's *Machias Republican* was in itself a strange switch.

Adams had anticipated the yearning to return to Maine. After landing he had proclaimed in public meeting that any who were dissatisfied could return on the same vessel, free of charge. The offer was repeated at least three times publicly before the *Nellie Chapin* pulled away. No one expressed a desire to return.

Much was made of the colonists' sale of property back home and turning the proceeds over to Adams. He did take their greenbacks with him to Boston where they were converted into gold, the international medium of exchange. The gold was then held for safekeeping, until sometime prior to their arrival in Jaffa when it was paid to the families. Not all the greenbacks had been turned over to him. In a consular survey of resources in mid-1867 John Drisko and Shad Wass showed $1,000.00 each in greenbacks, while Mrs. E. S. Wass listed $935.00 in paper money. The tragedy lay in the fact that cash reserves on leaving America averaged much less than $1,000.00 per family, except for the G. J. Adams, J. Moulton, Ackley Norton, E. S. Wass, Shad Wass, Fred Witham, George Drisko, John Drisko, and Rolla Floyd families plus Mayo Smith. Only four had resources exceeding $2,500.00—G. J. Adams ($5,000.00), Fred Witham ($4,500.00), Ackley Norton ($2,500.00), and Mrs. E. S. Wass

($2,890.00). B. K. Rogers was typical, beginning the venture with only $400.00. By the time of the survey Adams had invested his money in property, planted twenty acres, borrowed $2,800.00, and loaned $3,000.00 to members of the colony. Contrary to popular supposition, Adams had more invested in the enterprise than anyone else.

Building, planting, and living costs were eating away their limited resources. Prices went up (meat by three cents per pound) in response to their arrival. Mutton was eight cents per pound, flour $14.00 per barrel, and milk, 30 cents per quart. There was little work available for the skills the colonists possessed, and their strange language limited their ability to search out employment and to communicate once employed.

The foodstuffs purchased by Loewenthal as their agent were uniformly bad. Bread, rice, and flour were infested. Oil was rancid. They finally went on their own into the market, inspected and purchased the vegetables and small quantities of meat they could afford. Meat was hung for easy inspection and was brushed by garments passing by. Grain was sifted and vegetables handled by soiled fingers.

Shad Wass was running short of funds and publicly clamored for a settling of accounts with G. J. Adams. Wass had bought provisions for the ship and was in charge of loading the vessel at Machiasport. He had held and dispensed the funds of the Association plus more than $400.00 belonging to Adams. When the accounts were reckoned Wass, not Adams, was found to be in arrears. Whereupon, to settle accounts, Wass demanded $40.00 for helping to load the vessel at Machiasport (for which he had already received free passage for himself and family) and then charged Adams $63.00 board and room for when he was, at their invitation, a guest in their home four years earlier.

As storekeeper Adams was also holding the bag for doors, windowsash, and bricks for which he had paid personally in cash and which were now being refused by some who had ordered them.

A detailed account of the difficulties, with a favorable report on the integrity of Adams, was mailed to the *Sword of Truth* in February. Thirty-two men of the colony signed the letter which declared "our faith in Bro. Adams as a faithful minister of the Gospel, as an upright and just man in all his dealings, and as a man strictly honest, is now stronger than ever." They also indicated possible areas of development and employment with special reference to the mills on the Ogee (now Yarkon) River—cotton, woolen, sugar cane, oil, and grist. Coasting vessels "of from one hundred fifty to two hundred and fifty tons burthen, a good butcher, . . . a nice, neat hotel at the foot of the mountains of Judea." They said it would make a fortune in a few years, especially with a line of stages, since "travel in this country is on the increase beyond all precedence." The area they had in mind for the hotel was not far from Ramla and Lod.

During the time he was not farming, Edwin McKenzie hauled supplies for others and helped his father build a stable and place of storage. On January 8 he roofed the stable and calked the windows against leaking, and on the next day fitted it with pegs, nails, and shelves. Then the stuff that was stacked outside was moved in and by evening of the tenth the yard was "all fixed up in good style . . . and the stable in good order."

On January 11 Edwin started to make his bedstead, hand cutting the legs. In two days it was almost completed, but since the thirteenth was Sunday he waited until Monday to finish it. He corded it up, ropes making a grid of support beneath a straw tick. Then he made the bed "already to sleep on." It was just in time. The next day he was sick and piled on the bed clothes to "sweat it out."

He hadn't felt up to par on Sunday, and it took all morning "to clean up and get ready for action." Sunday dinner was a delight, with fresh meat, fresh fish, cabbages and onions. In the afternoon he and Elizabeth Batson rode out to look at the crops, "some good and some bad." On the way back they encountered eleven men and one woman from the colony on their way to Jerusalem. Nine of the men had decided to solve the problem of land ownership by becoming Turkish subjects. Adams was one of them.

The day Edwin was finishing up his bedstead, his brother Ellis, Jr., went to visit Loewenthal. He found a good saddle, and whatever their conversation may have been Ellis headed immediately for Jerusalem to visit with a merchant friend named Nassir C. Gargour—the U.S. deputy consul in Jerusalem responsible for all business transacted with the Turkish government.

Acting on authority of Beauboucher, Gargour went to Hornstein's Mediterranean Hotel where G. J. Adams and company were staying and informed Adams that he was his prisoner and could choose whether he would go peaceably or by force. Adams went peaceably and, in the words of Ellis McKenzie, "was put in prison and the key turned." The change of national loyalty to Turkey had been scotched, but a new fury burned in Adams' heart.

Back in Jaffa Edwin bought some silk to make violin strings and, still feeling sick, stayed home and "practiced on the fiddle for amusement."

On January 17 all returned from Jerusalem except Ellis and Adams (who was still locked up). Edwin said, "They lay the trouble to Ellis."

On hearing of the release of Adams a large company rode out to meet him on Sunday, the twentieth. When they arrived back at the colony with Adams, they were greeted with three cheers and, since it was Sunday, they held a short meeting. According to Edwin, they were "all in good humor and fine spirits."

Sunday was followed by turnip and potato week, with the

workers manuring the land for the potatoes and stooping to put in hill after hill of turnips. The January rains came fitfully in heavy showers accompanied by thunder and lightning. Edwin ended the week lame from riding his horse and not being able to stop him short of the stable. He had to jump and wrenched his back. Saturday's ball game found him tallying score, and "well nigh fagged out."

That same week a *New York Tribune* correspondent wrote with mild rebuke about the Yankee emigration from Down East in Maine to Down East in Palestine, scoffed at their pretensions of being identified as the "tribe of Ephraim," and their insistence that the curse was being taken off the land of Palestine. After all, he declared, "There are still thorns and thistles and weeds growing on every side."

Comment in the *Machias Union* for the week was "When will the world learn that the kingdom of Christ is a spiritual kingdom, and that the Jerusalem where he is to reign is a spiritual Jerusalem, and not the old, dirty Jewish city?"

G. J. Adams was already written off by the press as a visionary, a deluded deceiver of the innocent. At Jaffa, Mayo Smith's angry scowl covered a smile of satisfaction.

On January 27 Edwin went to hear a Baptist preacher Luther Stone of Chicago, Illinois, but wasn't much impressed. It proved to be a very full Sunday. G. J. preached afternoon and evening and was on the mark with "good old Indian River sermons."

Edwin chose on the twenty-eighth to comment on a new farm area being opened up farther out and then remarked that there were "built or nearly built fifteen houses, three board tents, a shop, and a skill house presently used for a dwelling."

A sad note followed, eased by the fact that "none have died for some time." The dead totalled thirteen as given in the consular report from Jersualem:

1. October 8, George Rogers
2. October 17, Leon A. Talbot
3. October 23, John Burns
4. October 24, Francis J. Gray
5. October 27, Eugene Clark
6. October 27, George W. Clark
7. October 30, Mary W. Leighton
8. October 30, George B. Clark
9. November 5, Flora L. Leighton
10. November 7, Everett M. Floyd
11. November 17, Elvira A. Watts
12. November 28, Mark D. W. Wentworth
13. November 29, Phoebe P. Norton

Of these, nine were children.

Edwin rounded out the month of January by planting potatoes and peas, stopping cracks, whitewashing, and playing a game of euchre in the vault.

First residence built by American Colony in Jaffa, 1866
Leighton House

German Templers took over much of the American Colony in 1868

CHAPTER 9

THE HAMSEEN AND THE LATTER RAIN

On March 8, 1867, Edwin and Orrin McKenzie and their young friend Everett Batson lay flat on their backs "and talked to the top of [the] sitting room." The McKenzie two-story home was nearing completion, and the boys had been lathing the walls and ceilings to ready them for plaster. Like the others, this house showed signs of craftsmanship. To the observer landing at Jaffa, the village looked very prosperous. Twenty buildings, white-washed and trimmed with dark green shutters, clustered together. Picket fences marked off the lot each family called its own.

The day before, the most elaborate house of all, just completed, was opened for a grand house-warming and reception. It was the home of President and Mrs. Adams. Two hundred and fifteen people from outside the colony came to visit, including the consuls of Britain, France, Prussia, Russia, Greece, Persia, and Italy. The Governor and all the local civil and military authorities plus the dignitaries of the Latin, Greek, and Armenian convents were there. Three U.S. flags were flying. Although it was a few days late special honor was paid to George Washington.

Jaffa oranges were in abundance plus a great table of goodies. In the evening, with E. K. Emerson on the violin, the crowd danced until twelve o'clock. G. J. called the reception "a grand triumph."

The boys agreed that everyone had a good time. In fact, for the young folks especially, it had been a banner month.

"Do you realize what our eyes have seen in the last month? It's been some different from Indian River." Edwin declared. "Oh, I know, we could have been hoein', paintin', and lathin' in Maine, but . . ."

"Yeah," said Orrin, "I reckon that Turkish jubilee was about the most interestin' thing I ever did see. Remember all those tents in the graveyard? You wouldn't catch me sleepin' that close to the dead."

"Me neither," chimed in Everett. "But how about those guys on horseback chasin' and throwin' sticks at each other? Crazy!"

The Turkish "jubilee" was Ramadan, the fast required of every Muslim in remembrance of the giving of the Koran (Qur'an), the word of God for Muslims—to them the final revelation, given through the prophet Muhammad.

Thirty days of fasting were scrupulously observed, each day beginning when dawn's light was sufficient to distinguish between white and dark thread. The rules were strict regarding the taking of food or any substance into the body—no eating, no injection, no coitus until the sun's last arc of flame has vanished behind the horizon. The nights were free for food and love, but the festivities were focused in three days of feasting and sports at the end of Ramadan. Then, in Jaffa, it was like a county fair with everybody in costume. Arab youths, normally in the garb of poverty, surprised the boys of the colony with their finest clothing. The colony girls moved among the Muslim families in the marketplace and played with the babies, fascinated by their large black eyes. There were swings, set up specially for the feast. Edwin and the others headed for them, swooping and swinging to their hearts' content. Horses could be ridden for a penny. Vendors had sweets and other edibles. Clothing and trinkets were spread out in the open and under black goats' wool tents. Here and there soiled hands reached out pleading for coins. The boys would remember one young mother on her haunches dressed in tattered black with a grey shawl held by her lips to cover all but her eyes and nose. With one arm she nestled a nursing child and with the other reached for alms.

It was all clustered about and beyond the bazaar near the North Gate and the great fountain of Abu-Nabbut. At the edges of the market, sheep and goats were offered for sale or barter. Beyond, toward the flat reserved for sport, one-humped camels waited, reclining or standing and looking quite aloof. No, it was not Maine.

Except for putting in vegetable crops that needed to be staggered and stretched out to prolong harvest—such as peas, turnips, potatoes and beans—the planting was done and now the harvest was awaited. The former rains dwindled in early February with one final storm that caused a near flood. The crops were well watered for the period of waiting for the latter rains. In between would come the wind, called Hamseen in Arabic and Sharav in Jewish. It was a good time for boys and girls to go for long walks to see how the crops were doing or to go on horseback rides farther afield.

Everett was curious about Edwin's disappearance a few days before. "Where'd you go anyhow after we got through playing cards that morning?"

"Oh, I took the horse and went for a ride. I didn't know where to go when I started but kept on the Jerusalem road. An Arab asked me if I was going to Ramley and I told him yes so that's where I went. I went to see the old tower. It must have been magnificent at one time. I climbed to the top, 122 steps, and then climbed up another five stones higher. Each step is about a foot rise, so I figure it is a 125 feet high. Some tower. I expected to see the Ogee and the Mediterranean but didn't."

"What else of interest is out there?"

"Well, I went to an old cave—or rather an underground vault. It's big. One room would be about 50 by 100 feet with bearing pillars about 15 feet apart. I got so interested that I didn't notice the time and had to high-tail it for home. They were some worried about me. I didn't get there until about eight o'clock."

Ramadan, ruins, and visits to the Greek and Latin convents—the boys were not accustomed to the rituals and stations of the cross and drank it all in.

Back in the colony the lull in planting and building prompted G. J. to get the long-promised school started. It was a night school at the beginning with emphasis on spelling and elocution, to be followed later by debating, and classes in Arabic to be taught by Serapion Murad, the Arab secretary chosen by G. J.

Spelling bees were open to all ages with L.I.L. "giving out the spellings." Edwin reported on considerable mischief among the spellers and some personal pique for being spelled down on simple words like "seton." "Whoever heard of a seton except her ladyship? She must have grabbed words out of the dictionary for sheer meanness. Imagine, phthisic . . . and seton."

Ellis, Jr., anxious to have his parents see Jerusalem, left with them and eight other "secessionists" to see the Wall of Wailing, the Mount of Olives, and the pools of Bethesda and Siloam.

While they were away, Edwin and Drusilla Ward spent some time walking. One day, when they neared the home of Antonioni, the "rich Greek," they were invited in and offered cigars, which they refused; they did accept some jelly and drinks including Turkish coffee—thick and powerful. Back at the village, they got together with the other young people at Ben Rogers' to play Authors and dominoes and to dance. It was tight quarters in the Rogers' small parlor, but they had fun.

It was not all sight-seeing that took the elder McKenzies to Jerusalem. While there they intended to talk with Consul Beauboucher to register complaints against Adams who had "silenced" Bishop Shad Wass and young Ellis and also excommunicated Levi Mace. That was admittedly an internal issue, but they were infuriated by the high and mighty ways of both Mr. and Mrs. Adams, the latter having drawn a line across her front yard and excluded every "secesh" from her property. Things were going from bad to worse, and the McKenzies wanted the consul to be aware of conditions and the necessity of aid to some who were talking about going back home.

On March 10, while they were gone, the Reverend W. H. Bidwell arrived at Jaffa and came directly to the colony, accompanied by fifteen American travelers. He presented his credentials "as commissioner and special agent of the United States to enquire into and examine the situation of the American colony at Jaffa."

In a private letter Reverend Bidwell wrote: "I walked out to the colony in an anxious state of mind, intending at once to order a hundred loaves of bread to be sent to them on my own responsibility. In this state of mind I entered the colony grounds, and it would not at all have surprised me if I had met two funerals. But, strange to tell, I met with the cheerful, happy, and contented faces of strong men, just out of their meeting-house from the morning service!"

According to Adams, Bidwell was welcomed with gladness by "the true and faithful." It is likely. They had much to show for their labors. A model village on a shore far distant from America. Diverse crops of lush green. The taste of the new crop of Jaffa oranges in their mouths, and the fragrance of orange blossoms in their nostrils. Bidwell was impressed, and G.J. did everything in his power to keep him that way. Adams knew what he was doing with the agent of Seward who was venerated as the editor of the *Eclectic* magazine of New York City. It was a golden opportunity to reverse the untoward publicity fanning out from the *Boston Traveler*. In private conversation and then in public meeting with all the American tourists present, Bidwell heard the story told by the old spell-binder; then he put three questions to the congregation: (1) "Are you happy and satisfied with the country, climate, and people?" The united response was, "We are." (2) "Have you full faith and confidence in your pastor and president, and is his statement just made in your hearing true?" The united vote was affirmative. (3) "Are you happy, contented, and determined to remain in this country?" The answer: "We are."

One woman said she was homesick, but that was the only negative expression voiced. Why was the vote unanimous when division was so apparent and reported so extensively? The top "croakers and apostates" were in Jerusalem.

Bidwell associated primarily with Adams and avoided Loewenthal, who later complained bitterly about this to Beauboucher. He rode out to the fields and gardens, talked with whomever he chose, and visited the spelling school. Edwin reported with a playful twist of phrase that the old gentleman "looked the likes of things very much indeed." Bidwell then went to Egypt for a few days.

On March 15 all the seceders were suspended from the Church of the Messiah. The next day Edwin plowed and Webster planted beans. On Sunday, March 17, many of the colony walked into the old city of Jaffa and visited the legendary house of Simon the Tanner, the place of Peter's vision.

On the morning of March 18 Consul Beauboucher was in town, alerted by the seceders that things were coming to a head. Edwin's entry for that day was serene,

> The orange trees are blooming and the air is heavy with the odor that arises from the groves of oranges loaded with blossoms and fruit at the same time. The air seems very much like Indian Summer at home. It is the most delightful time I have seen and I guess it is the best time in the year for everything is in the height of its blossoming. Wild flowers are plenty and travelers are coming in fast, sometimes 25 in a steamer of Americans.

His entry for the next day:

> They are trying to settle up the business of the colony. They find it hard work.

The rains began the twenty-third and continued for four days.

> It rained last night as hard as I ever heard it, and I think if I could have seen it I could have said it rained as hard as I ever saw it rain, and there was considerable thunder and lightning with it..

In his diary entry for the twenty-third G. J. Adams wrote:

> We this day have had the full commencement of the latter rain in all its beauty, glory and grandeur. It has commenced two weeks earlier than common. The colony are in high spirits and the apostates are chop-fallen. The rain has come just in time for our wheat, barley, potatoes, corn, beans and all other garden vegetables. We know that our friends have heard many lies about us and our colony and we know that there is disposition in thousands to believe a lie sooner than the truth. The apostates will soon leave for America. Will they all reach that land in peace and safety? Time and history will answer.
>
> In our settlement with the apostates we have been most fortunate. Mr. Beauboucher has acted all on one side. He is a man devoid of justice, truth, reason or common sense. The apostates are low, vulgar and insulting. Today one of them struck a brother for indicating the truth. The horse-shearers and carriage-cutters of Indian River are gentlemen to the apostates of this church.

The rain did indeed seem a portent of prosperity for those with conviction and courage to stay. What they did not realize was that the Hamseen, or Sharav wind, with its minimum humidity and relatively high temperature had opened the flowers for pollenizing. Coming too soon, the two weeks early Adams had taken as a good omen, the latter rain had washed away much of the pollen. The crop was gone before it really began, and they didn't know it.

THE ACCENT OF REPROOF

The examination and final report of W. H. Bidwell was a triumph according to Adams and his supporters. The report carried glowing reports of the American colony to William

Seward in Washington. It was written in spite of the wrath of Loewenthal and Beauboucher who saw things differently and felt that both they and the colony would be inaccurately portrayed to Seward by Bidwell.

In anticipation that Bidwell would report favorably, Beauboucher sent word to J. Augustus Johnson, U.S. Consul at Beirut, to come immediately. Things had gotten out of hand and he wanted a transfer, preferably to Italy. With the excruciating pain of a leg in danger of a third amputation, aggravated by grueling horseback to and from Jaffa, he had had his fill. The colony had long since gone from challenge to nuisance, absorbing too much of his time and most of his correspondence.

In the meantime Consul Johnson had already received word from Washington that he should proceed to Jaffa to investigate charges against Beauboucher and Loewenthal in petitions by the colonists to the State Department under date of January 17 and February 4, 1867.

While Johnson made his way to Jaffa, Reverend Bidwell was the honored guest of the colonists on a journey through southern Palestine, the land of the Philistines. He was accompanied by G.J., L.I.L., and Clarence Adams, Ackley Norton, A. L. Norton, James Burns, S. J. Murad, and Ab de Neb de (Ned), the Adams' servant. They enjoyed eleven thrilling days of emotion-packed experiences among ruins of ancient cities and in valleys and hills known by Samson and David.

Captain Ackley Norton, the seasoned traveler, was in awe of the arrangements made by their two dragomen who were more tour directors than guides. Three cooks and waiters, three muleteers, two footmen, nine horses, and six mules were involved. Tents and luggage were carried, of course, but there were also bedsteads, bedding, tables, chairs, china dishes, silverware, cooking utensils, an iron range (stove), charcoal, and provisions. He said that the accommodations and food were "as good as those of a tavern."

Ackley reveled in riding on horseback along the Mediterranean shore and watching the natives. He even looked for the hand prints of Samson on large pillars among the ruins at Gaza. Under the shade of a sycamore tree he was incredulously appreciative of a lunch consisting of baked chicken, bread, boiled eggs, mutton, oranges, figs and nuts. Every newcomer to the land would, of course, experience boiled eggs sooner or later—and often.

Solomon's Pools to the south of Jerusalem reminded him of the dry dock in the Charlestown Navy Yard at Boston. The Dead Sea was "as salt as pickle," and he was quite convinced that Lot's wife had simply dissolved into the intensely bitter brine of the Dead Sea. At Jerusalem he had his heart set on drinking from the Pool of Siloam but changed his mind after descending the steps where he discovered "an Arab down there bathing," and women washing clothes.

Bidwell and Adams were impressed by the antiquities on every hand but also by the tens of thousands of acres in the vicinity of Jericho waiting to be cultivated—"some of the richest land in the world." It was further confirmation that "the great age of restitution had commenced." While at the Jordan River near Jericho and at the very spot traditionally thought to be the place of the baptism of Jesus, G. J. Adams baptized his son Clarence. Then after going up to Jerusalem and spending some time there in sight-seeing, Bidwell said fond farewells to the party of travelers before their return to Jaffa and his journey north into Lebanon.

When G. J. and the others arrived home they discovered that Consul Johnson was there and already investigating the colony. The hearings were held "in the true style of the Roman inquisition" according to G. J., at Blatner's Hotel inside the city walls. Doors were closed, and only one person was admitted at a time—not to give testimony but to answer questions. Those favorable to Adams felt themselves to be "insulted, threatened and abused in a most shameful manner" and that partiality toward Loewenthal was reflected in Johnson's remarks.

Johnson was thorough, probing the story from their arrival. In his report to E. Joy Morris, U.S. Minister Resident, Constantinople, he gave evidence of pressing all parties for a clear picture of the arrest of G. J. Adams in Jerusalem and of the resolution of misunderstandings between Beauboucher and Adams at that point. In his account of the December investigation by Beauboucher in Jaffa, Johnson spelled out in clearer detail the terms of the land purchase in which the colonists felt they had been swindled by Loewenthal. Somebody was swindled, but whether it was the owner, Sheikh Muhamad, Loewenthal, or Adams was never spelled out for certain. £480 were paid by Adams representing the colonists. Loewenthal kept £40 as his fee and reportedly gave the remainder to Sheikh Muhamad, but when it was reported by Muhamad to the authorities he listed his proceeds as £170.

When Beauboucher annulled the purchase, he required Loewenthal to pay back £440. The colonists wanted the full £480 returned, and when it was refused by Beauboucher they cried, "Swindle!" Beauboucher insisted that it was fair reward for work done.

As for Loewenthal, Muhamad refused to take the land back. As far as he was concerned it was final and he was protected by a different set of laws. Loewenthal was left holding property he did not want and still had to pay out of his pocket £440 to Adams. To top it all, Beauboucher left him neither jurisdiction over the colony as vice-consul nor any relationship as agent. And by appointing Shad Wass as his official point of contact with the colony, Beauboucher had further infuriated Adams.

Consul Beauboucher was catching abuse from all sides except the secessionists in the colony. They were delighted. They had status with the Wass appointment. There was division between the colony and Loewenthal. Most of all, Adams was embarrassed and angry.

Between the December investigation by Beauboucher and the April investigation by Johnson, real financial needs had developed in the colony. Some of the families had exhausted their resources. Beauboucher responded, digging into his own pocket to provide $260 in gold. He hoped to collect it from the Department of State.

In his report, Consul Johnson cleared Loewenthal of all charges and asked for official vindication for any guilt. The vice-consul, Johnson said, was already punished by "withdrawal of the business of the colony from his hands." Johnson felt it only fair therefore to provide him with "such an expression on the part of superiors as will free his name from the accusations which are ruining his credit as a merchant, blasting his reputation as a man and creating a prejudice against him which must prove his destruction unless warded off by an official vindication."

Johnson recognized the problem of communication aggravated by inability with the English language on the part of Loewenthal and Beauboucher. "It may be conceived therefore that with the best intentions on all sides mistakes and misunderstanding [were] inevitable."

In a situation that could not help worsening without immediate corrective action, Johnson recommended the transfer of Beauboucher, preferably to Italy, and that "a man of prudence, firmness and legal knowledge be appointed consul at Jerusalem with instruction to spend six months of each year at Jaffa during the existence of the Jaffa colony." If that were not possible he recommended that "a full consulate be temporarily established at Jaffa with special reference to the 'colony'. . . he should be [salaried] and not be allowed to trade." He further advised that no one from the colony should be chosen to consular office in Jerusalem or Jaffa.

At the same time that he wrote to U.S. Minister Morris,

Consul Johnson wrote to Secretary of State Seward very briefly reporting on the investigation, clearing Loewenthal but indicating that it was "highly expedient that an American citizen should be appointed consul at Jaffa . . . during the continued existence of the American settlement at that place."

One incident came to light in Johnson's investigation which had further strained relationships. One morning the colonists discovered that the American flag flown by Loewenthal as vice-consul was at half mast. Worse than that, it was upside down. "What disaster? Who's dead?" Adams hastened to ask. During the night the vice-consul's daughter had died. A grieving father had declared his sorrow by a lowered flag. It had remained aloft through death after death among the children of the colonists. In G. J.'s anger a moment of empathy was forfeited. G. J. knew the child and yet, busy with his own thoughts, he remained untouched.

Preoccupied and defensive, he had been aloof from the heartaches of his own people as well. No gentle touch of empathy, no tears. A lonely people, made lonelier by death and separation, longed for a shepherd and a father. Even the gentle ones whose admiration for Adams had excused one fault after another, began to think of returning. Ben Rogers was among them. His limited resources exhausted and the work of building slowing to a stop, he had time to see the concern in Lucy's eyes, especially as she held the baby "Kip" to her breast. She had lost one and gained one on the beach. And there was little Bradford, how would he ever manage in this world of strangers? Better off in Maine, even with the cruelty of thoughtless children taunting the child who is different. She knew that the other children would manage. Theresa was almost too independent—too trusting of the natives and too eager to play with them. Already receiving gifts from Arab neighbors, her dark-eyed and beautiful child showed a preference for other dark-eyed people in strange garb. Her eldest, V.P.—well, who could tell? In midteens she had already started looking. Her hair had never been so often brushed. Maybe like the other parents they ought to get back before a Maine winter had time to set in. The McKenzies were obviously anxious to get their vivacious fifteen-year-old Velma home. Her acquaintance with a local resident, George Teracy, was fast ripening to a danger point.

As Lucy thought of six-year-old Arthur her concern increased. He was hard to keep track of, even running into the old city with the Clark boys. A favorite point of rendezvous was the roof of the house of Simon the Tanner. They did not go for reasons of biblical association but, with pockets filled, they did what small boys have always done—threw stones into the water to hear them splash.

Harvesting began while Consul Johnson was still in Jaffa. The reaping machine was put to good use. The threshing machine was, too, but only after repairs were made on the winnowing part of it. At first it simply would not winnow fast enough to keep up with the rest of the machine.

On May 8 some of the undeveloped barley was cut for grass and reported by Webster Emerson as stolen by the Arabs. In his diary the next day Edwin wrote, "Webster's grain isn't stolen so much as it was an unaccountable mistake."

On some days they were planting sessin (sesame) and on other days they cut and threshed barley and wheat or dug potatoes. The potatoes were "small business," Edwin reported, but there were enough to require several days of plowing and picking them up. In fact, the harvest had to be speeded up because the observant Arabs would go into the fields when the colonists weren't looking and steal bushels of potatoes.

The crops were smaller than hoped and that was traceable—though they didn't realize it—to the hamseen. In spite of it, the McKenzies harvested enough that Edwin wrote on

May 25, "We have got everything full now. I do not know what we shall do with our other produce." Another problem was their undoing as far as the harvest was concerned. They were required to pay toll or tax to the government at a rate up to 20 percent of their harvest and another 25 percent to the landowner from whom they had rented. Fulton and Webster Emerson harvested 96 bushels of barley. Nearly half would go for toll and rent, leaving only about fifty bushels for feed and seed. McKenzies planted twenty bushels and harvested only fifty-three bushels. They were on the contested property now held by Loewenthal and did not know whether he would be generous or vengeful.

The Floyds and Tibbetts dug about ten bushels of potatoes, hardly more than they had planted. Zimri Corson threw up his hands in despair and announced to his wife Dorothy that they were going back to Rochester, New Hampshire.

Consul Johnson left Jaffa in time to catch ship May 17 at Beirut to go on leave to the United States and while there to report the truth of the Jaffa colony to the Department of State, hopefully before Bidwell could get to the ear of Seward. Bidwell's decision to travel into Galilee and on into Lebanon gave sufficient delay. Also he was discredited by traveling with Serapion Murad, the young colony secretary who, as it turned out, was the son and nephew of two Murads who had had run-ins with Loewenthal and Beauboucher. Young Murad was even then under threat of possible arrest for presumed theft and for indiscretion relating to his handling of colony business in Jaffa.

Another consular official, Charles Hale, had been summoned to Jaffa to assist Johnson and Beauboucher. Consul general in Alexandria, Egypt, he was there specifically to help settle colony affairs with particular reference to accompanying the colonists scheduled to return to the United States on May 31. While there he apparently participated in a trial of G. J. Adams for nonpayment of debts owed to Mrs.

A. H. Wass ($40 gold), Mayo Smith ($155.50 gold), and Mrs. E. B. McKenzie ($173.60 gold). They were preparing to leave on May 31 and wanted their money.

The consular court demanded payment immediately and if there was a delay Adams would be required to pay 12 percent interest. The complainants were given authority to seize Adams' property and, if contested, Adams would be subject to arrest. The order was signed by Victor Beauboucher two days before Johnson left. Beauboucher, with his leg aching unbearably, headed back to Jerusalem and required Loewenthal to complete the action.

Denied authority with the colony for months and waiting to resign only as long as it took to get vindication from his superiors, Loewenthal proceeded to act against Adams, demanding payment and threatening seizure. He reaped the whirlwind. Adams replied by a letter, "I give you notice that if you come into our private enclosure to carry out your shameful and abusive threats I will not be accountable for your safety. . . . If you continue this outrage and abuse us any further you will do so at your own risk. . . ."

Loewenthal immediately sent word to Beauboucher in Jerusalem. Beauboucher then telegraphed Morris in Constantinople; "Adams threatens to attack Loewenthal's life if executing consular orders. Please send a warship to Jaffa to enforce law and hinder bloodshed." In spite of his anger, Adams smiled with some satisfaction at that overreaction. Imagine—a gunboat to silence him!

If Levi Mace ever had cause to get out of Palestine it was now, and he had the means. Consul Johnson had left over $1000 for the Mace, Lynch, and Batson families to return to the U.S. Elizabeth Batson would be returning to her husband, William, who was "home in America" according to the Johnson report. Johnson had also provided for Helen, the widow of Dr. Higgins, who died in early May, her two small children, George and Lizzie, and 22-year-old Woodbury Clark.

Linc Norton and his large family also decided to go, along with Shad Wass. The Misses Flagg and Richardson took advantage of the opportunity, the latter being relieved to be away from the violence and obscene language of the Adams' home. In all, 32 left for the United States May 31 on a Lloyd steamer.

It was a bad day for the colony. The steamer had hardly moved out of sight when grief devastated two families. Anna Tabbutt and Sabrina (Sibby) Watts, both five years old, died. It was a prophecy of continuing tragedy. Sibby's father D.J. had come against his better judgment and only at his wife's insistence. Once committed, however, he was one of the staunchest and most durable of Adams' supporters. Now he was done with it. "I'm going home!" he announced to his wife Anna.

She was there by conviction, her own and that of her older sister, Abigail Alley. Both of them were determined to stay, no matter what, and even though they recognized with disappointment the frailty of G. J. Adams they were still loyal. D. J. would have to choose between home in Maine and home with Anna in Palestine. He chose Maine. They agreed that he should take their six-year-old son, John, leaving Elvira and Ida May with Anna. By public subscription in Maine, D. J. was provided with 1,020 francs for passage. Anna was left to make her living in Jaffa by gathering and drying small wild flowers for Holy Land souvenirs and by domestic labor.

Zebediah Alley decided to stick it out for a while. There was rumor that work would be forthcoming on the macadamized road, long rumored but now soon to be built between Jaffa and Jerusalem.

On June 9 Edwin followed his summer Sunday morning custom in Palestine and rode to the shore to swim and then wash down the horses. Later he went to the meeting at Captain Norton's home. The text of George Adams' sermon was, "Be not discouraged in well doing for if you faint not you shall reap." Edwin commented on the mood of discouragement: "Quite a number have come to the conclusion that there is not much of a living to be made in Palestine."

Through the months of daily entries in his diary Edwin McKenzie made only brief and infrequent comments about the intracolony battle. He was either aloof or playing it down. The diary was a running account of hard labor, building, plowing, planting, and harvesting, eased by personal pastimes and frequent good times with the other young people at Captain Norton's, old Ben Rogers, or walking and riding to farm plots and the Ogee River. One day in a comment, slipped in almost casually, Edwin reflected on those who had fallen in battle a year before alongside him. It was a recent memory and quite likely conditioned the months of undisturbed composure. The verbal battles and disturbances around him were minor in contrast to the confusion and death of the battlefield. Now, however, with the disappointing crops, unrewarded labor, the departure of many colonists for Maine—especially his brother Ellis and family and his sister Ruth—the three deaths in May, and an increase in illness in the colony, his mood changed from persistent good humor to disenchantment. He wrote, "I do not think there is a half dozen that can say they are well."

He even worked at not working. "It's hard work to loaf," he wrote. Instead of fleeting and uninformative comments about avoided public meetings in which there was dissent, he turned suddenly to spelling out the ever present hassles, "E.K. [Emerson] got up and spoke of the abusive language he, Mr. A., had used against him . . . and expressed the disgust with which he looked upon Mrs. A. Mrs. A. twiddled him of learning elocution of them and then using it against them." Ed reasoned his elocution ". . . done him as much good as her French she learned 28 years ago." Regarding another meeting Edwin said, "Mr. Adams arose and occupied about an hour trying to give encouragement and strengthen the faith of those concerned. After talking this long he said he would let anyone make any remarks they wished and sat down but kept right on talking. Sat a few seconds, then got up and said if there was no one going to make any remarks he would keep on but mind he had not stopped to give them a chance. By this we saw he did not want any one to speak."

Disillusion with Adams and his wife was becoming an epidemic. With everything awry in the colony and at home, he turned more and more to the only thing that wouldn't talk back—alcohol—in increasing quantities and potency.

His drunkenness was no longer a private matter for the family to rue and hide. G. J. began to frequent grog shops along the quay. Then he would stumble into the city. There, where walking through the streets was like climbing stairs, he could not manage without losing his balance. Falling, and finding it ever more difficult to navigate, he would have to be guided home. There he found no sympathy from his disgusted and strident wife, while Clarence, at age eleven, could not cope with adults gone mad. He shrank from encountering either of them.

The Adams house was more battleground than home. Clarence stayed away much of the time to avoid the noise and the cross-fire. Fretting became fuming. Needling and baiting each other, George and L.I.L. built to a crescendo of violent accusations. It happened nearly every day and ran into the night.

"I wish you were dead!" L.I.L.'s voice was shrill.

"I'd welcome it!" G. J. snapped back.

"You'd welcome what? Death?"

"Yes. . . and oblivion."

"You should be so lucky! You can't get away from me. I'll be right there to make you miserable through eternity—and enjoy every minute of it!"

"Never fear, my love," George said softly, "I'll be where

you would never consent to go—and where I probably belong. Anyway, God has been waiting for you—to sit on his throne, take charge, and let him rest for a while."

L.I.L. started to explode, but sputtered into silence.

In her teens she had been attractive—large-boned with ample, reasonably well-proportiond flesh. But she abhorred anything physical except eating and rearranging things. In mature years, as her flesh pushed against her clothing, she turned imperious, and thought of herself as full-bodied and regal. She tried to reign on every occasion. Because of her attitude George experienced a bitter tyranny that he didn't need, and that the colony could have done without. In verbal combat—a life-style she cultivated—she was savage.

George longed for refuge, a place he could feel at home. For years he withdrew in silence, holding his tongue. Eventually he threw caution to the wind and fought back, matching blow for blow. He only traded frustration for futility.

The latter part of June and the first part of July found the colonists selling houses and implements to the highest bidders. The threshing machine was to go to the Montefiore farm, more for hire than for working that property. According to Bidwell it was used, to the astonishment of all. The rich Greek, Antonioni, bought nearly all the implements of the McKenzies who were still planting sesame seed and roofing their house. When Ellis, Sr., went to get his roofing tar from the Adams store, G. J. was gone and L.I.L. refused to give it to him, holding on for dear life until she was smeared with tar from head to foot, to no one's regret.

On July 4, 1867, one year from the Sandy River picnic, Edwin commented on "dull times," betraying heartache that the rest of his diary entries denied. The previous evening "we had a little amusement in the hotel in the form of shaking a shin." Then on the Fourth "we dragged out the day until near evening by eating watermelons, damsons and other fruit. Had some hens and roosters for dinner. The Consul gave some from the plot, a Fourth of July dinner. Toward evening we went below the city to a grape vineyard that George Taracy had rented. He took us out there and gave us as many grapes as we could eat. Had a good time and it was quite late when we all got home for it was over a mile out there. We danced in the evening until all the fiddlestrings gave out. Mr. Adams had a grand reception but not much company. I signed some documents that are to be sent away."

The arrival of a ship with mail brought a letter from Abe McKenzie to Adams containing news of the certain departure from Jonesport of the next contingent of colonists for Jaffa. There would be "two ship loads of wooden and living cargo" under Abe's management. Adams rallied to near sobriety to read the letter to the colonists and waved aloft a draft in the amount of $800 from Abe. He also announced that a company of Germans would come shortly to occupy the plot with them, and that they had a capital of $2 million.

To everyone but Adams it was a fantasy, except the $800—and they needed that to get home. They also needed to stop Abe from bringing others into desolation. That Abe could add the saving element of leadership and bring order out of chaos aided by the stability of Rolla Floyd, Ben Rogers, and Joshua Walker and bolstered by the German Templars who were indeed planning to arrive, they never gave a thought. They were desperate.

On June 28 Captain Fred Witham, Captain Ackley Norton, and Ellis B. McKenzie, Sr., went to Loewenthal representing three-fourths of the colonists. Their message was three-fold: to enlist the help of the U.S. Government in dissuading Abe McKenzie from coming; to beg pardon for the wrong they had done to Loewenthal and to offer a letter of vindication for him; and to gain approval for Captain Witham to proceed to Paris and London with certificates attesting to need in order to raise funds for the colonists' livelihood until spring, and then their return to America when severe weather at home would be over. Fred Witham declared to Loewenthal that he was "as hot an antagonist of Mr. Adams as he had formerly been his hot friend."

On July 11 Victor Beauboucher reported at length on various deputations and petitions, one of them being signed by almost all heads of families in the colony. Even those who were still loyal to Adams were so concerned for the welfare of the other families that they joined the petition.

Beauboucher in his letter to Seward recommended that Abe McKenzie be summoned to Washington "and be informed of what regards the colony. This honest person who visited Palestine with Adams in 1865 has up to this period only seen through the eyes of Mr. Adams. It is he who prints the vile reports which Adams sends from here. . . . If Mr. Abraham McKenzie arrived here today after having heard the unfortunate ones who are forcibly obliged to stay here he would lift the anchor and return to where he came from, too happy to escape from numerous and inevitable calamities. . . ."

Edwin McKenzie was party to the actions, signing a preliminary document of petition on July 4, endorsing Loewenthal and Beauboucher while condemning Adams "and him only who has so cruelly wronged, deceived and ruined us and our families." The petition also contained a request for Loewenthal's retention as vice-consul in Jaffa.

The colonists were no longer waiting for Adams to call meetings and to order their affairs. They had taken charge of their own destiny. An extract of their "An Appeal to Humanity, Charity and Benevolence" written on July 4, among other things, sorted out those in support of Adams: the Uriah Leighton family of five, Joshua Walker and his mother; Rolla and Docia Floyd, the Zebediah Alley family of three, and Mrs. A. Williams. Others would eventually stay, but these thirteen refused to be party to the account of the colony's decline and fall. The rest of the eighty-six remaining (excluding the three Adamses) declared:

Farming had been praised up to us as the most lucrative business here, and among many other like things, we were solemnly assured that we should reap three rich crops in one year from the same piece of land. So all our hopes were centerd upon our crops, and in spite of increasing sickness and disappointments and want from which we had to suffer, we still went on working and hoping rich harvests would make up for it all. . . . Before harvesting our crops looked well, and it was estimated by us at that time that we should get a yield of about 8,000 bushel of wheat and barley and 2,800 bushel of potatoes.

But also this our last hope failed and failed most miserably. On harvesting we found that our crops were so bad that we did not get our seed back again. The reason of this most disastrous failure is, that we had cultivated bad land, sown imported seed not adapted to this country, and did not understand how to work the ground as the natives do, and as the climate required. And further, because influenced by Mr. Adams we refused to listen to the proffered advice of experienced residents.

Our machines are valueless here especially because also not adapted for this land. Thus are we left in this strange land utterly ruined, sick of fever and ague, without means, our clothes worn out, our children *without school or teaching whatever*, and in distressing ignorance, suffering from the climate, with starvation staring us in the face and not the slightest prospects of any kind of work or way to earn our living, for if our health was not broken down, even we could not compete with the natives here, who work at a very low rate from *10 to 25 cents per day*, and whose constitutions are of course such as to bear well the heat of the glowing sun, while we people from a cold northern climate feeding on entirely different food to what we had always been accustomed, vexed with disappointments and cares, sicken and die.

Mr. Adams denies all assistance to those who will not submit longer to his tyrannical sovereign sway, and bear a slow course of starvation. And as our doctor died some time ago, we are also left destitute of medical aid and advice in our continual sickness.

Out of 156 souls that sailed with us from America 54 have returned, 17 have died. The remaining 86—16 (Mr. Adams family and 13 others) excepted, are all longing to return to America.

But forty (40) of these are so entirely dependent on Mr. Adams at present for the means of subsistence, that they fear to act openly, and according to their desires and convictions and therefore do not sign this appeal, but we add their names and number of the members of their families. As we know that they will be in the same need as ourselves in a few weeks hence.

Words cannot express the bitter sorrow and humiliation that weigh us down, heightened by the mortifying consciousness of being duped by the machinations of an *inhuman deceiver.* We have blindly followed his advice, believed his word, obeyed his counsel and remained his most ardent supporters in everything, even against *the true and innocent,* as we now know to our deep regret.

In this our desperate situation our only hope and desire is, to go back to the United States, where if we are pennyless now, we at least can begin life again, and by honest work can earn the bread for ourselves and children.

It was impossible to keep their proceedings a secret and upon hearing of the various communications in process Adams took action to hinder the departure of all mail from the colony except his own. He offered gold pieces to the assistant of Mr. Santelli, the French postmaster in Jaffa. The boy not only refused but reported that Adams had tried to bribe him. The wrath of the colonists was quick in coming. They sought his arrest, but since Santelli had not personally been a party to the reported attempt at bribery, the charges were dropped.

Adams was thwarted on every hand. His imperious demands to "obey counsel" were no longer effective. He was discredited in the colony and in Jaffa.

On July 18 Beauboucher reported to William Seward that Adams had been found in a state of "most degrading drunkenness" on two days running, requiring him to be carried to his home. Beauboucher complained bitterly about his own leg and said that all his time was being taken up with the affairs of the colony. He went on to say that he would like to be sent to "Palermo, Messina, Genoa, Torino, Brindisi or Naples,"—any place out of reach of George Jones Adams, alias George Washington Joshua Adams!

On August 1 Beauboucher sent off another letter to Seward, documenting that Adams' "language for which he no longer takes the trouble of veiling is of a revolting obscenity." Nine more persons have gone home, he said. They were, of course, the McKenzies, Tabbutts, and Emersons, enabled by the "advances of Mr. Loewenthal so kindly made to them." The McKenzies left in new clothes tailored to their measurements in Jaffa. The night before leaving on July 28, after packing, Edwin, Orrin and Velma went for a last swim in the Mediterranean.

On August 17 Herman Loewenthal was officially relieved of his duties as vice-consul with honor for "the rare and noble qualities constantly showed in the discharge of official functions."

One of the last to go on record with his feelings of disenchantment was Edward Emerson. He had made his speech in meeting and had experienced his confrontation with Mrs. Adams, but now he put it down in black and white to Consul Beauboucher on August 18.

> After having lived for two years with Mr. Adams in America and having seen his public and private life and having never seen anything condemnable but on the other hand he preached high morals and such noble elevating principles that I think it not at all strange that I had almost learned to think him incapable of wrong. However . . . to my great surprise and sorrow I found that I had been following one of the most heartless imposters of the 19th century . . .

On August 24 Adams was placed under arrest by Beauboucher, in response to charges made by the colonists. They ranged from fraud to immorality and habitual drunkenness. Beauboucher then telegraphed Consul General Hale asking him to return to assist in settling the colony problems. The action took Adams by surprise and, though drunk when arrested, he sobered up, momentarily forsook abusive language, and wrote a note confessing wrong-doing and begging pardon from Consul Beauboucher. His sudden change of attitude brought a ray of hope to Beauboucher for the first time since the early arrest of Adams in Jerusalem.

Adams' letter was handed to Charles Hale who had come posthaste to Jaffa. Hale swore that the note was prepared by Adams "entirely on his own accord, and not by any prompting or coercion of others."

Immediately following this incident a tourist party arrived whose adventures were being recorded by Mark Twain (later to be printed as *Innocents Abroad*). The tourists were forced to remain without continuing their travels because fourteen horses they had contracted for were preempted by the Turkish governor of Jerusalem. During the delay, Twain had time to learn the story of the American colonists. His interviews, strangely, were minimal. He dismissed the colony as "a complete fiasco." In the meantime Moses Beach of the *New York Sun*, already recognized as a generous philanthropist, engaged Consul Beauboucher in conversation regarding the colony. "This very kind gentleman" wrote Beauboucher, "moved with compassion, spontaneously offered to me to advance $1500 in gold which I believe will suffice for taking them back and a little more if necessary . . . it is well understood that if the subscription (per Captain F. Witham and others) will amount to the sums which will be dispersed by the Honorable Mr. Beach, this money will be . . . reimbursed to him. If otherwise he agrees to bear the difference. . . ."

Consul General Goodenow, from Constantinople, arrived on board the *Quaker City* with the sole intent of assisting the colonists to close up their affairs and get them on their way home. The presence of so many consular officials with uniform intent had its effect on Adams, prompting unusual sobriety and cooperation. On September 9 and 10, in his typical flourish-stroked penmanship he wrote two documents agreeing to settle debts and difficulties and to refrain from invoking the assistance of the United States authorities. Both of the documents carried his bold signature. One of them also carries the signature of L.I.L. Adams.

I will not invoke the aid of the United States Consuls, or agents in any such case whatever. I remain Gentlemen Yours Most Truly and Sincerely
Jaffa Sept 9th, 1867 G. J. Adams.

For Victor Beauboucher the end of trouble was in sight, and he could hardly wait for the *Quaker City* to leave the roadstead of Jaffa before writing to the Secretary of State.

Sir: Thanks to God, our unfortunate Colonists are now on their way for the States.

Thanks also to the generous intervention of the Hon. Mr. Beach, these poor people have been able to embark at Jaffa under the direction of Consul General Goodenow who will accompany them as far as Alexandria, where Mr. Hale will provide for them their passage home with the money already received by the Relief-Fund, about six hundred dollars in gold obtained from Europe, and the sum advanced by Mr. Beach as I have already explained in my preceeding dispatch.

Here beneath are the names of the Colonists who left on the 1st of October by the Quaker City.

The following without means got their expenses provided for by the Relief Fund:

Mr. Corson, wife, two grown up children and two minor ones		6 persons
________Rodgers, do, two do	two do	6
Miss Drusille Ward		1
Mr. E. K. Emerson		1
Mrs. Witham, one minor child and one baby		3 persons
Mrs. Tabbut one minor child and one baby		3
Mr. and Mrs. Moses Leighton and one grown up child		3
Mrs. Ames and child		2
	Total	25

The following paid their own fare:

Mr. Ames	1 person
________Drisco	6
________Ackley Norton	6
________R. W. Emerson	1
Mr. Wentworth, wife and three children start the 4th of October by Lloyd's steamer, having alone received 22 Napoleons contribution from the U.S. ship *Lwatara*.	5
Total	44 persons having left

The following persons remain still at Jaffa:

Adams and household	6 persons
J. Walker and his mother	2
Floyd and wife	2
Moulton and family	4
Z. Alley and family	3
Mrs. Clark and family	4
Mrs. Uriah Leighton and family	3
Watts and family	3
Ward and son	2
Total	29

These unfortunate people completely fanaticized by Adams, have obstinately refused to listen to the counsel of Messrs. Johnson, Hale and my own. They have freely and voluntarily taken the engagement never to have recourse to the Consular Authority for themselves and families, as they are satisfied to settle their present and future affairs with the *Local* Government. They have declared that they are happier here than they had ever been in America, and profess never to quit the country whatever may be the position they will find themselves in. . . . These unfortunate persons are without any resources, they count upon Adams as being sent by God!

His next paragraph signaled an event which would pave the way for a new era in Palestine. His painful leg and eagerness to be finished with both Jerusalem and Jaffa, obscured the realization with pessimism:

On the 3rd of October the first stroke of the pickaxe was given for the establishment of a carriage road between Jaffa and Jerusalem. The

Governor of Jerusalem says it will be completed in five months; I think however. . . in a few years.

LETTER FROM CALEB

At Indian River, Maine, Abe McKenzie refused to believe what he was reading in the newspapers. He discounted letters from Jaffa and didn't want to credit his nephew Ellis B. McKenzie, Jr., when he arrived home and laid it all out with angry accusations about a fallen G. J. Adams and that "embodiment of evil spirits in the form of a woman," L.I.L. The questions Abe was beginning to ask, however, were becoming more acute and, reported back to George Adams, drove G. J. deeper into depression. They threatened to dissolve the strongest bonds G. J. had with any person, his dearly beloved friend, his "Caleb."

Abe had laid his life, reputation, possessions, everything, on the line. Since the colony had left Jonesport he had secured 150 more people to join the venture at Jaffa. A ship was chartered for families, furnishings, and supplies. A schooner of 130 tons was ready for launching, to transport lumber for dwellings, and then to enter into coastal traffic in the Mediterranean. Contracts were ready for import-export across the Atlantic, especially with one Jonesport packer, eager to supplement his already flourishing business of $150,000.00 per year in canned lobsters and sardines.

In spite of those who wanted to erode confidence, Abe had managed to keep that mood alive by personal testimony and by keeping the *Sword of Truth* affirmative. If ever there was hope for the colony's survival and success it was in the ability and conviction of Abe McKenzie and the potential of his managerial expertise at Jaffa.

Then Ellis B. McKenzie, Sr., arrived in Indian River on September 25, 1867. When he and his brother Abe met, Ellis' eyes betrayed what his lips would confirm. A few days later,

Abe McKenzie offered to Forbush, the friendly editor of the *Machias Republican*, an open letter. Abe was more devastated than angry but felt that the people of Washington County should know that he and others had been betrayed—not by an unworthy dream but by an unworthy dreamer:

Indian River, Oct. 6th, 1867.

To G. J. Adams, President of the remaining fragment, of the once Noble, Proud and world renowned American Colony to Palestine;. . . alas! what has been the result of this great enterprise, and where are the noble sons and daughters of Maine, with their families, which composed that Colony, full of faith and hope in the fulfilment of scriptural prophesy as explained by you in relation to the gathering of Israel at this time, and who had proved their faith by their works almost beyond a precedent; and what are their conditions today? Oh! the sad tale; many through exposure and the want of proper nourishment have fallen victims to disease and death. Some who were advanced in years; others who were in the prime of life and vigor of manhood and womanhood; while the larger portion of the decreased were swept away in childhood and infancy. Then, again, something over one third have left them in disgust and returned to their Native Land, houseless, homeless and penniless, to make the best shift they can to obtain a livelihood, amid the derision of many who are ready to point the finger of scorn at them, as having been duped, sold and deceived. And then, again, for a moment, imagine our feelings for the rest of our friends that are yet left without any means of obtaining the most common necessaries of life, or to get themselves out of their miserable condition, but have been driven to the necessity of asking for the charities of their friends, and the public for funds to rescue them from suffering, sickness, starvation and death.

What, we ask, has caused all this disaffection, division, and dissatisfaction, which has broken up this Church and Colony and brought so much suffering, misery, and shame on this people? You must allow me to be plain, for I am going to lay before you in an unvarnished style some of the causes which have led to the foregoing results, as I understand them.

And first I will commence with the beginning of your labors with us. You came among us a stranger, and as you would have us believe a Messenger from God, to make proclamation of the Everlasting Gospel and take the lead in the Dispensation of the Fulness of Times, which time you labored to show was at hand, by arguments from the Scriptures that such a

Dispensation was still in the future and inseperably connected with the restoration of Israel to their Nationality, I admit was unanswerable. . . . That yourself was the messenger is another and quite a different question, and has proved a fallacy, as the sequel will show. Allbeit, at that time, we received you as that messenger and continued to treat you as such, giving you our most implicit confidence, pouring out what little of money and means we had for the advancement and success of the work like water, stood by you closer than a brother at all times, through evil as well as through good report, until a ship was got in readiness to take a portion of the Church as a Colony to the Land of Promise, with anticipations of another to start the following season; when some one hundred and fifty or more stepped forward with willing hearts and ready hands to labor and sacrifice their houses, kindred, friends and homes for your sake and the cause in which they had engaged, and casting the most of their treasures into your hands with all the confidence imaginable of your integrity, uprightness, and honesty of purpose, and looking to you for council and instruction, for precept and example in all that is good and great, just and true, noble and high-minded and intelligent band of brothers, united under the power and spirit of Christ and his Gospel.

But according to undenyable proof and evidence, your course and conduct has been distinctly the opposite. Instead of setting forth, by precept and example, principles of morality in your own course of life and proceedings, it appears that you had resource to the bottle, which contains a spirit the influence of which has overthrown its thousands of the best intellects and talents of the world and brought disgrace and degredation on themselves and all who were so unfortunate as to be in anywise connected with them. This spirit of the bottle, connected with that embodiment of evil spirits in the form of a woman, it appears has ruled or rather misruled one of the most honest-hearted, noble-minded, enterprising and industrious company of emigrants that ever embarked to Colonize in a far off country—in "tyranny," "broils," and "confusion," berating and scandalizing in the most shameful manner all who saw fit to differ with you in the least and to discountenance your low, intemperate and unjust proceedings—even with your best and most staunch friends—until many of them had become heart-sick and disgusted with the sight of their head and leader who was to commence the restoration of God's elect Ancient covenant people, the "Jews," wallowing in drunkenness and debauchery. No wonder their hearts bled, and that their confidence was lost. No wonder that we have had days and weeks of heart-rendings, on receipt of the sad intelligence from our friends and relatives. But we were kept along in the belief that the state of things there was not as stated by the apostates as you called them but by those that were overlooking the real state of things and hoping for a change for the better, they being all the while led by the before stated "influences," which makes the oft-repeated adage, you have so many times quoted to us, that "like Priest, like people," until starvation and sickness brought them to their senses and lifted the "scales from their eyes"—when they too constituting the larger portion of your adherents at the time became disgusted, heart-sickened, discouraged, and ashamed even of their preceding course of conduct to uphold and sustain you in your debased conduct, even to perjuring their honor and honesty as men. When lo and behold the report comes from you that another set of apostates have left the faith, ten times meaner and worse than the first.

The question now comes, what have they apostatized from? Was it a belief in Christ's obedience to his precepts and commands—on the fulfilment of his prophecies—on those that spoke in his name before and after? No; but it was from the iron rule of their now two leaders among them, that had so successfully played their game of deception and fraud, with an apparent design of leading an honest, well-meaning and virtuous class of people (on the whole) into the same low, drunken, and degraded position, into which yourselves had fallen after landing at Jaffa, and which commenced to show itself after leaving the shores of America on shipboard.

The foregoing statements are proceedings connected with the Church and Colony at Jaffa, I acknowledge are put forth in plain outspoken language such as I never dreamed in the past of having occasion to address to you—you whom I once loved, honored and respected as a brother and spiritual guide and teacher, with all the honesty and sincerity of a child to a father. But on learning the true state of things there during the past year, and not quite ready to put myself under the leadership of a man who has become an inebriate through excessive drinking and governed mostly by that embodyment of evil spirits in the form of a woman before spoken of, I have come to the conclusion to become one of the apostates from the rule and reign of tyranny and confusion which it appears has been predominant with our Leaders, who had stolen the livery of Heaven to serve the devil in, with anticipations, no doubt, of becoming the Lords and Rulers over God's Heritage, and a large company of duped and deceived people, who would be unable to extricate themselves from under your iron heels.

But your first company had too much manhood about them and were a little too smart. The bubble has burst, and the project must fall. Your cards have been badly played in the cash part of the game. And what are the consequences that must follow? Yourselves denounced as deceivers, your names become a hiss and a byeword throughout the world, and some thirty or forty families, the most of them who were in comfortable circumstances, stripped of all the earthly possessions which they had earned through a life of hard labor and toil, to commence anew the struggle of life in their old age, to obtain a living and a home for themselves and their families. And this is not all; we, both of the Church and Colony must continue to wear, in the eyes of many, the stigma of having been duped, humbugged, sold. Was it by having been deceived in relation to the doctrines taught in the Bible? No, that we can meet at any time or place, and contend for successfully if we wish to take up the challenge, with a bold face. But when our teacher and instructor is alluded to as an unprincipled man and a drunkard, our mouths are closed in his defence.

The time was when we were not ashamed to advocate the character and course of our Leader in connection with the doctrines which he preached as the doctrines of "Moses and the Prophets," "Christ and the Apostles." Those doctrines will ever stand the same as they are written in the Bible, and if there is any reliability to be placed in the truths of the Bible as being the word of God, as it has been handed down to us, your conduct or mine cannot alter those truths or that word.

It has often occurred to me of late the great contrast there is between the tenor of your letters and journeyings to the Church here during the past year and those which Paul wrote in his absence to the different churches which he had raised up. I apprehend that your success with the Church and Colony there, and the tone of your addresses to us, would have been very different had it not been for the influence of that spirit which when put to a man s mouth will steal away his brains. Had you not been governed by such influences, in connection with the other before spoken of; but had you pursued that temperate and manly course that you did in your labors with your Church and people here, there would not have been hardly a person in that Colony but would have stood by you through any amount of privations, even to death's door.

Oh! how sad it is to look back over the past and contemplate the many beautiful and powerful discourses on the prophecies of the Scriptures, and the order of the Gospel, and the many solemn and sublime scenes in the administration of that order. To know that he who had officiated so successfully in the capacity of God's Servant, should so soon give himself up to the cravings of an appetite, which he must have known would sooner or later have brought loss of confidence, disrespect, disorganization, suffering, and shame on his followers. Now you are not ignorant of human nature and the power of an inherent appetite in man, over his better feelings. I therefore look upon this move with a Colony to Palestine as extremely hazardous in you, knowing as you must have known, whether or not you were able to control that appetite; which, without that power in you to control, the result and failure of the Colony must inevitably follow. The foregoing statements and charges which I have gathered from observation, your letters and journeyings, and the testimony of a very large majority of the Colony, are what I consider some of the main causes of the downfall of this Church and Colony. From the experience of the Colony in their farming operations for the past year, and what knowledge they have gained by an acquaintance with the natives as to the average yield of their crops, I have come to the conclusion that the land is still lying under the curse and will not reward the husbandman for his labors and toils, although I was led to believe that it would produce abundantly, getting my information that such was the case from others who I considered at the time reliable. On the whole everything connected with the Colony seems to have proved a failure. The land has failed to produce successfully; all the improved implements of Agriculture taken out by the Colony, failed; the fishing operation failed, and G. J. Adams has failed to meet the expectations and anticipations of the Colony, and his people here.

Now if any of the foregoing statements, charges, or assertions which I have made are not correct, I humbly ask your pardon for such. I have not written this lengthy epistle to you out of any feelings of hatred or revenge, and I am ready to take back and make ample restitution for all that I have said which is not true and cannot be sustained. I have written to you thus because I felt it to be my duty, standing in the place which I do and having been connected with this affair, not that I feel myself righteous or perfect above others. I know that my faults are many as a finite being. But had this enterprise been conducted on principles of justice, temperance and morality, which would have given it union and harmony, it would have been a success. . . for it would have received the good wishes and help from many of the so-called christian world, and especially of the Jews; and your name would have stood among the latter, and with many of the former, as the leader of one of the best enterprises of the age. I have ever, until of late, had high hopes and expectations of being one of the numbers to help forward and carry on this enterprise to a successful completion, preparatory to calling home the scattered sons and daughters of Israel, to reclaim and build up their Nationality for the reception of their Messiah, who has promised the Jews, and through them the gentile world, that he would return and restore the Kingdom to Israel, [to] rule over the house of Jacob, [and] bring peace on earth, and good will to man. . . .

. . . I feel very unwilling to believe that God would call a man to take the lead of so great a work as the gathering of Israel and his people in the last days on the Dispensation of the Fullness of Times and not give that man power over his appetite and thirst for strong drink, and to rid himself from under the control of such an influence as you have been continually surrounded with. Taking all things into consideration since the landing of the Colony at Jaffa, that God has not blessed one single effort of yourself on them, either spiritually or temporally; that instead of union, peace and harmony in the Church and Colony there, it has been only strife, discord, and wranglings, I have come to the conclusion that this work is of man, and not of God, for the "word" says, "by their work shall ye know them," . as I said before, so say I again, that if I have made any statements or charges which is not correct, I will take them back and ask your forgiveness, as I ever wish to cherish and extend to all that spirit of forgiveness with which I hope to be forgiven. Yours in hope of a new and glorious age and an interest in a Ruling Kingdom, wherein shall dwell only the elements of peace, harmony and love.

A. K. McKenzie

New England doorway at Jaffa

Rolla Floyd

Docia Floyd

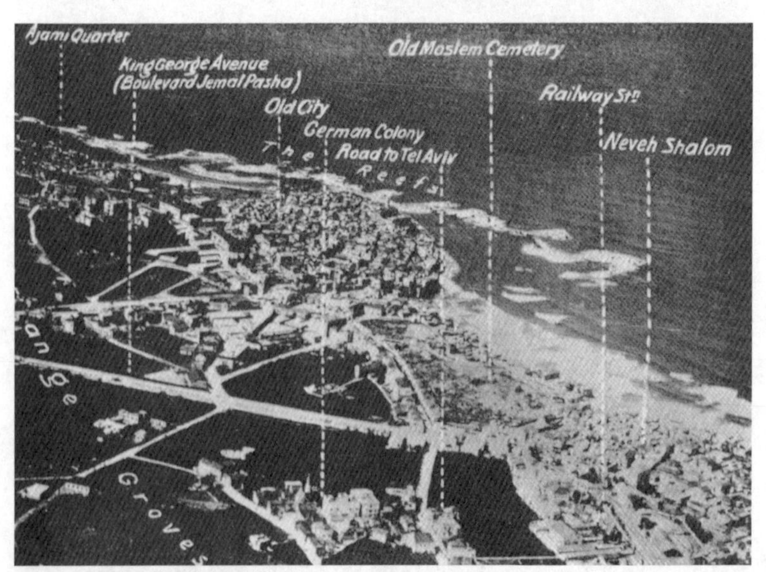

Location of German Colony
(Read, American Colony)

CHAPTER 10

THE PHOENIX

During these months of the Colony's digression from prophecy's fulfillment, Secretary of State Seward had been minimally responsive. To him, the small tempest in Palestine hardly warranted all the attention his consular appointees and the press were giving it. Post-Civil War reconstruction took priority, and a prophecy of his own required a bit of self-fulfilling. The months of the colony's agony were the months of his own dream's painful gestation.

As a senator in 1860 Seward looked with longing to the far northwest where the Russians were building seaports and fortifications. "Go on," he said, "build up your outposts. . . they will yet become the outposts of my own country. . . the United States in the northwest."

March 1867 was a crucial time for the dream which many would call "Seward's Folly." Word came that Russia wished to sell its North American Colony. Seward and the Russian Minister, Edouard de Stoeckl, hurried to draft a treaty of cession before Congress would adjourn. The job was done at 4:00 a.m., March 30, and rushed to Congress. The debate was heated and frequently sarcastic. "Seward's Icebox" was scoffed at, and a lot of ignorance was aired. "It was described as a land with no animal life except for a few fish." Nevertheless the measure was approved early in the summer of 1867, and plans were laid for a ceremonial transfer of ownership at Sitka, the capital of Russian America, on October 18, 1867.

In addition to this preoccupation, Seward was anxious in regard to Turkey. The Sultan was uneasy about the possible designs of France and England toward Palestine. Another item of major consequence in the Middle East was the Suez Canal, 90 miles long, 300 feet wide, and due to be completed by July, 1868. Already it was altering international trade and perhaps relations. The Jaffa Colony was a mere flea bite by comparison.

Seward had met G. J. Adams. . . reluctantly. . . at the behest of Senator Lot Myrick Morrill of Maine. He remembered the meeting more because of the unpleasant sequence of events that followed than by any inherent value of the meeting. Adams, although short, stocky, shrill, and grating, had a strange magnetism about him. That could be expected of one who had succeeded in rallying a group of respectable people bent on a brave venture of faith. . . or folly.

Seward had even asked for the Sultan's favor in behalf of Adams, and then was embarrassed and irritated when the colony sailed for Palestine before an answer was forthcoming. When the Sultan withheld approval there was the devil to pay, and Seward's staff was projected into too much unnecessary but polite haggling with the local authorities in Palestine.

Later, Seward's emissary, Bidwell, had been outmaneuvered by the consuls. The Secretary of State bought their assessment and their criticism of Bidwell as a meddling old man, outsmarted by L.I.L. Adams.

Now, a thousand aggravations later, he was little disposed to commit the whole government of the United States to a rescue operation in Palestine. Besides, his budget was too small to permit it. What help the unfortunates received would have to be by public subscription or by the sacrifice of their own families at home.

On the scene Seward's men may have been mutually overprotective, but they were generous to the needy colonists. Among them they gave nearly $2,000.00. Beauboucher, considered the culprit by many of the colonists, dipped into his own limited resources, hoping to be reimbursed eventually by his new nation. He won the gratitude of those he helped rescue, but twenty years later he was still trying to collect from the United States.

With the "croakers" gone, and a document attesting a kind of independence from the representatives of the United States government, G. J. and the colonists began to regroup. It became clear immediately that Rolla Floyd and the others staying on would no longer be responsive to his arbitrary control. That they were supportive was evidenced by their staying, but their major reason for staying was the persistence of their conviction about the return of the Jews. They were also staying because they could cope; they were strong enough to stand on their own . . . and to stand up to Adams if need be.

Zebediah Alley had come reluctantly but with some conviction and a sense of purpose. He weathered the winter and spring of confusion and stayed on with his gentle but strong-willed wife Abigail and their son Willie. At the suggestion of Adams they had accepted a building site one mile away from the colony's plot, putting them close to the Isaac's "Model Farm" and the Clarinda Minor colony farm lands. Their association was not limited to the colonists. When the new road was commenced, Zeb was one of the first to be hired. When the Netter Agricultural School was founded in 1867 the Alleys felt at home and lived at the school for at least one period of four months.

On completion of the road to Jerusalem, Abigail and Zebediah were proud when Rolla Floyd was chosen to drive the first vehicle (loaded with a millstone) from Jaffa to Jerusalem. It was a Maine spring wagon, and it was the beginning of a line of stages to be operated by their friend as Rolla Floyd took the first steps toward a legendary career as dragoman, tour agent, and innkeeper in Jaffa and Jerusalem.

The pull of Maine was too much of a magnet though for Zeb Alley. Once the road was finished and no other job was immediately at hand, he became restless and broached the idea of return to Abigail. She flatly refused to go with him. She was completely committed to the purposes which had brought them all in the first place. Zeb could not jar her loose. "I've made my bed and will lie in it," she said. Six-year-old Willie would stay with her, even though her nephew, John, had returned with his father, D. J. Watts.

The two sisters would tough it out, sustaining each other. Abigail joined Anna in washing, ironing, paperhanging, and making dried wild-flower cards for Holy Land souvenirs. Of Anna's four children, Johnnie had gone home; her two oldest daughters died and were buried in the Jaffa Protestant Cemetery, leaving her with the youngest, Ida May, only five months old when the colonists arrived in September 1866.

Anna Watts was not only committed to the purposes of the colony, she was intensely loyal to G. J. Adams—so loyal, in fact, that her husband was jealous of Adams' influence. Anna and D. J. quarreled, mildly and then bitterly. D. J. finally railed against her to L.I.L. and also to Docia Floyd. L.I.L. and Docia repeated to her what he had said. From that moment Anna flatly refused to go with him back to Maine.

On his arrival home with a young son to care for, and lonely for Anna, D. J. wrote to her saying he would come back to her if she wanted him. The extent of her hurt is revealed in the reply she sent to him by Ackley Norton on September 30, 1867:

> You say you would come back if I would send for you I ask you would you live with such a bad woman as you have said that I was I should be pleased to have you come back but as sure as there is a god in heaven I will never live with you againe untill you go to Mr & Mrs Adams and Mrs Floyed and retract all the lies you have told about me and then give it to me in writing that you will never slander me any more or abuse me with all of your jelouses I never dreamed that you could be so hardhearted as to talk about me as you have but I dont hold any hardness against you but if ever we live together againe the world must know that I am not the dirty wretch that you say I am . . . I live to Zebs and have ever since you left

there is not much news to write the apostates leves here tomoro morning in the quaker Sity

When she wrote again, January 8, 1868, she was lonely but still determined:

I hope that you will be happy and I do not want you to greave any about me for you have to take your road and I have taken mine and so you must make up your mind that come what may I shall not give up my faith in the gospel for anyone or any thing, God being my helper. So forget me in all things but to write as you would to a friend. Don't be angry at what I say for you know when you turned from the faith and went back that you turned from me. Perhaps you would like to know where I live. I will tell you. Brother Adams has had the house that we lived in finished and Zebediah and family live in it and I live with them. It is a very comfortable house now. Brother A_______ thanks you kindly for standing up for the truth and he has ever been your friend. . . . The colony looks prosperous and things are going nicely. . . . This grease spot here is where Ida put her bread and butter on here. She has just kissed me for you and Johnie. Kiss him for me. I must close now. Tell all the friends to write.

When little Ida May became ill, Anna got her on board ship to the United States. She travelled alone, tagged for identification, as if she were baggage, finally arriving in Machias.

Anna became ill, as much from loneliness as anything else, and died in Jaffa at the age of 39.

Abigail Alley kept in trust her sister's few personal effects of value and sent them, in 1892, to Johnie and Ida May as keepsakes of their mother.

Willie Alley was only five years old on arrival in Jaffa and grew up more as a native of Palestine than a child of Maine. Like the man he admired, Rolla Floyd, he mastered Arabic, became skilled in folklore and historic sites, and could handle horses and the native yawl boats with the best of them. He was the "Iron Man" in the tourist trade because of his tireless energy. Willie fell in love with a young Catholic woman and married her, February 14, 1888. A little girl was born to them February 3, 1889. Abigail, fussing over the baby, did her level best to convert young Mrs. Alley to what she had decided was the truth Adams had failed to honor. She succeeded in readying both Willie and his wife for baptism. From her sister, Susan Norton in Jonesport, she learned of the visit of T. W. Smith, a follower of Young Joseph Smith III who had, with his mother, refused to follow Brigham Young. Young Joseph was now leading a rival faction as the true successor to his father. T. W. Smith and his leader had followed the Jaffa venture eagerly. When it collapsed they agreed that T. W. should go to Jonesport to pick up the pieces. He did, preaching a familiar gospel, and succeeded in baptizing and ordaining Elders Ben Rogers and Joshua Walker after their return. Those two were the presiding officers and stalwarts of the Olive Branch of the Reorganized Church of Jesus Christ of Latter Day Saints. It became the largest and strongest branch of that church on the East Coast.

When Susan Norton wrote to Abigail about the phenomenon, Abigail recognized a familiar spirit and doctrine. She could hardly wait to get some of those "Reorganized" elders to Jaffa. Nearly every letter contained a plea, and finally she became a correspondent for the church's magazine, *Autumn Leaves*, providing its readers with contemporary news and first-hand descriptions and impressions of the Holy Land.

Editorial comments by Marietta Walker were a contrast to the prevailing criticism of Adams and the Colony:

> They styled themselves the "Church of the Messiah," and were then making preparations for starting to Palestine. We remember what an impression this made upon our mind at the time, and reasoning from effect to cause, we were convinced that this church must be an offshoot of Mormonism; and so the result proved, for George J. Adams had been an elder in good standing in the old church, and the doctrine taught by him was the same everlasting gospel preached by Christ and his apostles. As the readers of the *Herald* are aware, this colony went to Palestine, and although the movement was reported as an unfortunate one, and generally looked upon as a failure, the letter of Sr. Alley proves that it was not. It

may be that so far as the intention which was in the mind of its leader was concerned, it was a failure. "Man proposes, God disposes," and though what may have been proposed by man was not brought to pass, who is prepared to say that the purposes of God were or ever have been in any wise frustrated?.

Shades of Orson Hyde! No wonder Abigail and later Rolla Floyd were to feel themselves to be legitimate members of the church led by Young Joseph on the authority of their baptism by G. J. Adams.

Abigail's comments twenty-two years after arrival at Jaffa bear witness of mature allegiance to an authentic dream:

> It is nice weather here at the present time, just temperate. I think a little of the cold has got here from other parts of the world, as it remains different from what it was last year at this time. It is just lovely here at present. Every day there is a nice breeze to make it healthy. So far the grain is not hurt, but will be a fair crop as usual—thanks be to God for all his kindness to the children of men.
>
> In fifteen days more, I am told, the people are to begin to reap the grain of the land, the wheat and the barley crop. I can not describe the land, nor half its beauties to you. I am lost in astonishment to see its resources, which are greater year by year. It can plainly be seen that the land is being restored; and this whole land shall become like the garden of Eden. It is already a land of gardens, fenced in by cactus walls, to keep out the thieves. The thorns of this plant pierce and burn like fire. The fruit of it is sweet, and the Arabs make molasses from it; but the best molasses is made from grapes, and the next best from figs. The Arabs call it dibs, instead of molasses. They dry the fruit of the apricots in thin sheets after taking out the pits, so it can be had at any time one wants it, and quickly made into sauce. The cherries of this country are as large as Damsons. They date since our colony came here; and the corn of the present time I brought the seed of myself, and planted it, but as soon as the corn was ripe it was stolen. Abigail Y. Alley.

Rolla Floyd was among the first to lose a child at Jaffa. He and Docia were no less grieved than any others, but mourning ran its course more quickly. They reached out to the young people of the colony, sharing their work and play.

They were from Surry, Maine—not from the tight little peninsula on which Jonesport, Indian River, and Addison were located. Family ties were lacking in the colony, and Rolla was not one to shelter inside himself. Sturdy in build though slender, he stood head above most of his neighbors whether natives of America or Palestine.

Rolla was thoroughly committed to the biblical prophecies regarding Israel and the promises of Jehovah. If Ben Rogers had stayed, the two of them would have made a mighty pair—Ben with the black unruly thatch of hair, flashing eyes, and a gentle touch. Each of them was firm in his beliefs, but Ben had a large family to be mindful of and Lucy who was pining for home and wanted never to mention the Jaffa colony so long as she lived. Nor did she. When the name of Adams was mentioned her lips drew into a thin line, and usually she disappeared into another room. But Rolla and Docia had only each other. While they felt agony over the breaking up of the corporate venture, they were slow to condemn. While others looked toward home in Maine, Rolla looked longingly in the direction of Jerusalem and the hills of Ephraim and picked up his Bible to figure out what happened, where and when.

By December, 1869, Rolla had, by hard labor, gained a surplus of $12.00. But in a letter to his sister, Aurilla Tabbutt, he wrote:

> On the 14th day of December I hired with the Turkish Government to drive a stage from Jaffa to Jerusalem, and the first of May . . . a contract to oversee all the stages and horses . . . [for] $60 a month in gold. I have one young man from the Colony. His name is Mellville Ward . . . He is better than all the rest I have.

Rolla was initiated into the dangers of travel on the lonely highways:

> A little while ago I went to Jerusalem to see about having a stage repaired that got broken coming over the mountains. There I had a telegram from a French princess to come and take her to Jerusalem the next day. So I started on horseback and alone as I had done many times before. I never have taken any arms with me for all the natives like me very much. But this night I had a large whip, and just after I passed the mountains I saw

several wild Bedowins who are very dangerous. When I saw them I was a little afraid for there were six of them. I had no time to think then for one of them caught hold of the bridle and said in his language, "Get down and give us your money." I struck him across the head with the big end of the whip so that he fell to the ground and before the others could get to the horse. . . I got away.

April to July, 1870, a slack season for tourists journeying to and from Jerusalem, Rolla spent a good deal of his time reading the history of this country and preparing to travel throughout Palestine as a guide. He wrote:

> I went with some Americans from Jaffa to Beyrout. I was gone 29 days and gained $50 and got a very nice recommendation from them that I knew the language and country well. . . . I had thought of going to America. . . [but] the American Consuls have advised me by all means to be a guide and I think I can make money faster that way than any [other]. The traveling season is only from December to the last of March, so I think I shall try it this season. . .

It was the beginning of an exciting career. Rolla Floyd became the best tour agent and dragoman in the Middle East. Hundreds of prominent personalities and thousands of others depended on him to make all arrangements for their journeys.

> The Public is informed that all steamers touching at Jaffa are met by Mr. Rolla Floyd or one of his agents with boats in readiness to land passengers.
>
> First-class carriages, landaus and saddle horses always ready to convey passengers from Jaffa to Jerusalem and elsewhere at fixed prices.
>
> Mr. Floyd has also complete arrangements to carry passengers from Beyrout to Baalbec and Damascus and back, by train or special carriages or saddle horses, also at fixed prices.
>
> First-class hotel accommodations provided at Jaffa, Jerusalem, Damascus, Baalbec and Beyrout.

In January 1878 Rolla was honored to be chosen by General Ulysses S. Grant to conduct his party and to act as interpreter for "official calls on the Pashas, Patriarchs and Bishops, etc." General Grant expressed his appreciation in a letter of February 17, 1878.

Mr. Rolla Floyd,
Dear Sir.

Before leaving Jerusalem allow me to thank you for myself and entire party with me for the great assistance you have rendered us in our visit to all points of interest in and about the Holy City. Your thorough knowledge of Bible references, History & Tradition of all points of interest in the Holy Land and your clear and concise explanation of the same has very much added to the interest and pleasure of our visit.

Very truly yours,

[signed] U. S. Grant.

General "Chinese" Gordon, whose investigation of an alternative location to the crucifixion and resurrection led to the designation of "Gordon's Calvary" north of the Damascus Gate, traveled with Rolla who was not bashful about expressing his own doubts concerning the authenticity of the site known as the Holy Sepulchre.

When Kaiser Wilhelm made his triumphal entry into Jerusalem through a breach in the wall adjacent to the Jaffa Gate, Rolla was on hand and then drove the Kaiser in one of the Floyd carriages to inaugurate the new macadamized road from Jerusalem to Bethlehem.

Rolla was the prime agent of the London travel company, Thomas Cook & Son, for many years and traveled for it to Cairo, London (for five months at the Crystal Palace building good will), Paris, and to Philadelphia for the Centennial Exposition. On that occasion he and Docia visited their relatives and friends in Jonesport. The Machias newspapers made much of his success and the mementoes and artifacts he left with members of the Floyd and Tabbutt families.

On July 31, 1878 in a letter written to Abijah Tabbutt from Paris, Rolla said, "In your letter dated the 30th of June you spoke of meeting a man who said that all of our Colony returned to the States beggars. I should like very much to know his name!" Eventually there was a falling out between the Cooks and Rolla, but his reputation was so well-established that it hurt them more than it did him.

Rolla had his problems with the U.S. Consulate, too, especially with Rev. Selah Merrill, to whom he often referred as "an old cow." He was not alone in his estimate of the consul. Merrill's preference for Cook & Son and his constant endeavor to steer business away from Floyd only made matters worse.

The founders of the American Colony in Jerusalem became close friends of Rolla and Docia Floyd. It was a natural relationship. There was an affinity of views and mutual respect. When the Spaffords arrived from Chicago it was Rolla who took them by carriage to Jerusalem.

Horatio Spafford was a lawyer and realtor on Chicago's North Shore, whose business was devastated by the Chicago fire of October 8, 1871. In the years that followed he was associated closely with the great revivalist, Dwight L. Moody. Eventually they came to a parting of the ways because Moody's method of "shaking people over hell to make them good" was a natural consequence of his belief in the "swift and everlasting punishment of God meted out as the wrath of God against sinners." Spafford believed that people were never so wicked that they couldn't be saved and that God was indeed a God of love.

That faith was sorely tried but managed to sustain Horatio and his young wife when she was rescued from the wreck of the *Ville du Havre*, November 21, 1873. Her four children were torn from her as she went under with the ship. In those days harsh Puritan thought of sickness or sorrow as the result of sin and as a just retribution conditioned the reactions of many of their friends. When the Spaffords lost another child, Horatio, from scarlet fever, it was a final blow. "What have the Spaffords done to be so afflicted?" was a common query, reflecting the judgmental attitude of many regarding the suffering of the Jaffa colony too.

The Spaffords chose to leave Chicago. They latched onto a previously vague but often mentioned idea that they might someday go to Jerusalem "to watch the fulfillment of prophecy on the spot." Their need for refreshment of body and spirit made their determination resolute. Before they left, Horatio Spafford was expelled from his church for believing that there were no infants in hell and that people would be punished only for their own sins.

When the Spaffords arrived at Jaffa they found in Rolla Floyd one who not only could arrange their journey to Jerusalem but was a good friend of similar faith. Young Bertha (remembering in later years) wrote:

> The American-made spring wagons that were carrying us to Jerusalem had been brought to Palestine by a group of "Latter-Day Saints" who had come from Maine, I believe, about twenty years before, bringing prefabricated farmhouses in sections that they set up near Jaffa, where some are still standing. They introduced modern—for that time—farming implements, including wagons, to the Holy Land.
>
> Among remaining members of this colony at Jaffa, occupying their original houses, were Mr. and Mrs. Rolla Floyd, who proved such wonderful friends, and Mr. Herbert Clark, representative of Thomas Cook and Son, and who was in charge of our transportation, as we were traveling on Cook's tickets. Because the high wagon seat terrified me, Mr. Clark held me on his knee all the way to Jerusalem.

Their fascinating story was recorded by Bertha Spafford in *Our Jerusalem*. Their care of the poor and wounded, especially their care of the children for many generations, is one of the finest chapters in the history of Palestine. One incident, trifling at the time, symbolized the impact of both American colonies—the Jerusalem one of more dramatic influence, the Jaffa one less noticeable but nevertheless significant. One day in January 1883 Horatio received from John B. Cotton of Tasmania in Australia a package of seeds from the ubiquitous blue gum tree. After talking it over with friends he decided to give the seeds to Mr. Netter at the agricultural school outside Jaffa which came to be known as the Mikveh Israel Agricultural School. Netter planted them and they multiplied into millions throughout the country, supplying firewood and lumber. They were also planted in the swamplands to absorb water. In his diary, Horatio wrote, "May a mighty blessing come through these seeds to Palestine." It did, indeed.

Late in 1888 Horatio Spafford died. His widow came down immediately with a high fever which would not respond to medication. Bertha's record of the occasion adds insight to the relationship of the Spaffords and the Floyds:

> After several weeks Mother felt she was not making the progress she hoped, and a bed was made in a large carriage and she was taken to Jaffa. Mr. and Mrs. Rolla Floyd made her a welcome guest. Mrs. Gould went with her and faithfully nursed her. Later she was invited to stay at the home of Baron and Baroness Ustinov in Jaffa, where she could sit in their beautiful garden and regain her strength.
>
> Never shall I forget the ecstasy of joy when Mother returned to us, weak but recovered.

Baron and Baroness Ustinov occupied the mansion house at the main intersection of the American colony in Jaffa. It would later, at his suggestion, be turned into the Park Hotel, given that name because of the beautiful gardens containing plants and animals native to the Holy Land. The Baron contributed two large palm trees, one of which (according to his grandson, Peter Ustinov) is still growing at the rear of the building once used as British headquarters at the intersection of Bir Hofman, half way between Eilat Street and Rabbi Mibachrach.

The Spaffords and Floyds were friends, pioneers, and forerunners, detested by the U.S. Consul, Selah Merrill, for their unorthodox religious views and their strong individuality and refusal to give in to his control.

Herbert Clark, who carried Bertha Spafford on his lap on the high spring wagon at the time of their first trip to Jerusalem, became a prominent business leader in Jerusalem and served as U.S. vice-consul during the crucial periods of the first and second Aliyah. In the YMCA across from the King David Hotel in Jerusalem, the Herbert Clark collection of Holy Land antiquities remains one of the finest museum collections in Israel.

Herbert and his brother, Frank, began their relationship to the tour industry very early. Reverend Richard Newton, D.D., visited the Holy Land in 1870. On his arrival in Jaffa from Alexandria he reported in his book, *Rambles in Bible Lands:*

> We found two bright intelligent-looking American boys, about nine or ten years old, at the door of our hotel, and ascertained, on inquiry, that they belonged to one of the families remaining of the colony. They were eager to offer their services as guides to take us through the town, and especially to show us the house of Simon the tanner, which is by the seaside. . . . We called. . . our young American guides to take us into town.

Their hotel was the American, run by Rolla Floyd as a pension and inn. Their dragoman, Ali Solomon, was an associate of Mr. Floyd. Years before, he had guided Abe McKenzie and G. J. Adams on their journey to Jerusalem and Beth-el.

Mary Jane Clark, Herbert and Frank's sister, grew to womanhood as a short, rather petite woman of quiet, warm personality. She married Ralph, the son of Abitha and Uriah Leighton. Uriah had returned home to Maine where, with legal counsel, he placed notices in the *Machias Union* requiring Abitha to appear to give reason why they should not be separated. She never did and died on June 3, 1889, two months after Ralph, her son, and Mary Jane had a son whom they named Albert Wentworth Leighton. The Leightons moved to Jerusalem, and with their properties on Agrippas Street and the Clarks on Mamilla, the two families became well-to-do. The Leightons established the first theatre in Jerusalem, the Eden, which is still in operation. They also maintained colony properties at Jaffa as rentals.

Following Ralph Leighton's death in 1891 and the death of

Docia Floyd (between July 1898 and November 1899) Rolla married Mary Jane. Young Albert's affection for Rolla grew until he determined to be known by the name of both his fathers. He was henceforth Albert Leighton-Floyd.

Rolla and Mary Jane went to the Jordan, the Dead Sea, and Jericho on their honeymoon. His beard and hair were by the time of their marriage in 1900 "as white as snow." He had suffered from a lame leg "nearly as large as two legs" almost to the point of amputation, but, he wrote to Aurilla Tabbutt, "I am glad to say that since I got married I have had no more trouble with my leg. As a natural consequence it got well at once."

On their honeymoon, however, Mary Jane got the "Jericho buttons," a boil type infection "that is red blotches which after a while become dry and look like a wart, not quite so large as a hen's egg each." They result from an insect bite. Mary Jane's appearance discouraged them from having photographs taken to send back to America. By January, 1902, Rolla, Mary Jane, and Albert had moved into their new home on Agrippas Street in Jerusalem, one block away from the intersection of Jaffa Road and King George.

In November 1910 the long-awaited elders of the Reorganized Church of Jesus Christ of Latter Day Saints, Gomer T. Griffiths and F. G. Pitt, arrived in Jerusalem. The Floyds and Clarks had kept Abigail Alley's dream alive since her death sixteen years before. The Floyd home was open. They made two trips to the Jordan with Griffiths and Pitt, once to baptize an entire family by the name of Carr, and the second time to baptize Mary Jane Clark (Leighton) Floyd, and a man named Whelan. Rolla Floyd had refused rebaptism saying that he had been baptized by G. J. Adams and that was authority enough. He was entered on the church rolls in Independence, Missouri, on the basis of that baptism by G. J. This said much for both Rolla and G.J. . . . and for the church, too.

Through the influence and devotion of Mary Jane Floyd

and the Clarks, a property was secured in 1921 at what is now the intersection of Ussishkin and Bezalel streets. Dimensions of the plot of ground in what was a desolate area outside Jerusalem were 100 feet by 400 feet. They worked together to establish a school and mission home there which was sold in 1934. It was remembered in 1977, by a long time resident, as "the flower of the neighborhood" because of the beauty of the building and its landscaping. It has since been converted into apartments.

In 1911 Rolla Floyd died, and when World War I broke out in 1914 Mary Jane left for America to homestead in Montana. Her interest in Palestine remained, however. She returned to be buried in the Protestant cemetery on Mt. Zion near the graves of her mother and her brother, Herbert. She was the last of the colony to die in Palestine.

Adams remained a lively mixture of good and evil. With his primary targets gone and a reservoir still half full of spleen, he poured it on L.I.L. at the least provocation. She responded in kind. To Abigail Alley, L.I.L. confided (if a bold pronouncement can be called confiding) that she would see him dead and only then could she be happy. They were enemies with their brawls spilling out into the street, yet they were inseparable, depending on each other's violence in a desperate distorted mutuality.

G.J. was lonely . . . had been for years . . . and in those first months after the removal of so many from the colony he was growing closer to his son Clarence. The boy who had walked alone now stretched his legs to his father's stride and, being with him, kept him from turning into the grog shops along the quay.

Providentially, Adams had further cause to rally his resources of persuasion and to curb his drinking. Questions from colony-watchers in Lyk, East Prussia, were coming in. These were readers of *Hamagid*, the Hebrew weekly. A. L. Silverman was the paper's editor and, in those pre-Herzl days, an ardent believer in Jewish colonization in Palestine. The correspondent of *Hamagid* in Jaffa, Meyer Hamburger, called upon the Jews of Europe to settle in Palestine. He shared with them the "important news" of the American colony and spoke appreciatively of the colony's "noble purpose," which was "to pave the way for the children of Israel to make possible their return to the land of their fathers." This echoed the sentiments expressed in the *Jewish Chronicle* in Britain: "if the settlers really discard all conversionist 'proclivities' and thus gain the confidence of the Jews, their arrival will be hailed as a blessing to the Holy Land."

The Jaffa Jews saw in the American colony an example for their own objective to establish a Jewish agricultural colony at Jaffa. Hamburger put it on the line in a letter published in *Hamagid* in 1867:

> How long shall we regress, and stand aside, and not learn from the non-Jews? . . . Why shall we be a byword and a laughing stock to the American colonists who always ask us, "Why don't you buy yourselves some land?" And when we answer them that our brethren, the children of Israel live abroad in want, they tell us: "If each person would give only ten francs annually, a sum which is spent on cigarettes every month, they would succeed in buying at least enough land to sustain sixty families." What answer do you have for them?

Then rumors of the colony's problems of dysentery, dissension, and drunkenness reached Europe as well as America. Worst of all, in light of Jewish hopes of return to the land of promise, was the news of difficulty with crops. Hamburger immediately moved to scotch the rumor. He wrote to *Hamagid*:

> Our dear readers know well of the colonists who came from America to our town and are occupying themselves with agriculture and are ready with all their hearts to help our brethren the Children of Israel who will want to work the land. . . . But a rumor has recently been spread in the newspapers declaring that these colonists are not succeeding and that the land does not give forth its fruit . . . [which has] caused many of our

brethren of Israel, who desired to work the land, to lose heart, and recently Zelig Hausendorf of Jerusalem passed through the town and asked us whether we could get a document from the President of the colony. . . scotching the above-mentioned rumors. The purpose of their malevolent author was to cause damage, for he is a Jew by the name of Lowenthal who forsook his religion. My brother-in-law, R. Blattner, immediately went to the President of the colony and reported the matter to him. The President was deeply aggrieved at this slander and he immediately wrote a letter in English. . . and my brother-in-law sent the letter to Rabbi Zvi Kalisher, who is the Gabbai of the Hevrat Yishuv Eretz Israel (Palestine Settlement Association). . . for all to see and know that this was a time of grace, the time to rebuild the ruins of our Holy Land.

In the same issue of *Hamagid* Adams' letter to Blattner, denying all the accusations, was also published.

A letter also written by Adams in August, 1867, to Hamburger attests his cordial attitude to the Jews and his desire that the Jews come to Palestine and join the colony, where "they would be able to live according to the precepts of their religion."

Hamburger and, one suspects, Aharon Chelouche and others were more than casual partisans toward Adams. He represented hope. They had a vested interest in the success of the colony. His avowal of nonproselyting and obvious sense of mission *with* them rather than *to* them was a sharp contrast to Loewenthal's zeal as a recent convert from Judaism to Christianity. To Loewenthal, Adams was, among other faults, a traitor to the truth espoused by the vice-consul.

The warmest support for the colony and for G. J. Adams in particular came from the Jewish community. When in December 1867, Moshe Zachs of Jerusalem reported through *Hamagid* the end of the American colony as such he stated the cause simply as lack of experience and money, and then declared, "They left one by one and all their efforts were in vain. . . . The courageous man, great among giants, the head of the group, borrowed more money than he could repay and in this way the creditors took over the land and the possessions."

Meyer Hamburger wrote in reply that it was true many had left but others had come to replace them, "and the place is lovely to behold. They succeeded and brought forth fruit." From the point of view of the Jewish community, then, and more recently in the testimony of Ben Gurion and Shlomo Eidelberg the consuls, especially Loewenthal and Beauboucher, exaggerated their accusations against Adams and were grossly unfair to a man with a magnificent obsession. They not only prophesied the demise of the colony, they guaranteed it.

To the Jews the disappointment of the colonists was a major factor in the deterioration of the settlement. Their standard of living in the United States, by contrast to Palestine, was very high. Adam's enthusiasm for the Holy Land and his anticipations for the future had led him to paint glowing pictures. It was to him a land flowing with milk and honey, and his confidence justified use of superlatives in winning recruits. He neglected to say that it was also a land which "eateth up its inhabitants." Both reports were important to potential residents. It is quite likely that he did not even see the negative. The colonists looked for an easier, healthier, and certainly more prosperous life. It was a legitimate dream as potential, but the stark demanding reality shocked them. Their expectation of an easier livelihood had given them too much confidence in minimal resources and led them to risk small children to exposure in ways they would have considered ridiculous in the conservative clime of Maine.

Fighting for his life and reputation, Adams turned his attention to recruiting others in the vicinity of Jaffa to guarantee continuity of the colony. He was still convinced of the dream and, by January 1868, had succeeded in baptizing seven male converts. True to his word, he had not stolen sheep from the Jews, nor did he proselyte among the Arabs. He baptized other expatriates, especially the English among whom he had had notable success a quarter of a century before. The successful conversions started him to thinking seriously of returning to England, apparently not realizing that in that country all derivations of Mormonism had become unwelcome because of polygamy and other beliefs of Brigham Young.

G. J. was also busily engaged in negotiations with the German Templars, a group committed to the return of the Jews but especially avid in their anticipation of the imminent coming of the Messiah. They came, with money and several hundred committed adults, settling in the American colony houses and also near Haifa. They committed their resources to the development of vineyards in contrast to the cultivation of grain.

Adams turned his attention to the son he had so long neglected. He would become "Noble" Clarence—G. J. would see to that personally, and he started by subtle as well as direct ways to develop a minister of the gospel who would combine the old Adams fire with the gentle strength of a shepherd with his sheep.

Clarence responded, and before long chagrin and awe changed to respect and affection. By the time they packed their bags in June, 1868, Clarence was ready to enjoy the tutelage of his father, especially in England where they would linger for a while.

On their return to the United States the Adamses settled in Philadelphia, not far from the places George knew as a boy and where he had played Shakespeare.

With uncommon resilience he reestablished his Church of the Messiah in Philadelphia, tying closely to the Baptists whose congregational autonomy gave him just enough latitude. By the time Clarence was nineteen he was ready to assume the pastorate. He grew in the esteem of his own congregation and eventually stood tall as a religious leader in the city of Philadelphia.

His father, so characterized by sobriety in later years that his grandchildren have never found it possible to equate the G. J. Adams of Jaffa with the G. J. Adams of Philadelphia, preached from time to time. The older he got the more his doctrine resembled that of the man who had captured his allegiance in Nauvoo. In 1879 he declared to T. W. Smith, an apostle of the Reorganized Church of Jesus Christ of Latter Day Saints of which Young Joseph had become leader in 1860, that it had been his intention all along to bring his Church of the Messiah under Little Joseph's leadership when it was ready. G. J. had been expelled by Brigham Young and had no intentions in that direction, but he felt an affinity with the teachings and the personality of the boy he had seen set apart beneath the prophetic hands of his father in the Old Red Brick Store in Nauvoo. His eyes were misty when he told T. W. Smith about sharing the honor of that occasion by holding the bottle of oil which was used to anoint the prophet to be.

Smith tried to set in motion the return of G. J. Adams to the Latter Day Saint movement and proposed that he be admitted to membership and priesthood. Joseph Smith III, with friendly recollection of the man who had been so close to his martyred father, sought the more objective counsel of his associates. Whether that counsel was either objective or redemptive must be judged. W. W. Blair wrote to the one who would be called "Young Joseph" until his death at age 82:

Sandwich, Ill.
December 9th./78

Bro. Joseph Smith:

Bro. I. L. Rogers gave me this a.m., the letter of T. W. Smith, of the 7th inst.

In reply, I can only say, I would have nothing to do with G. J. Adams for the present. His accession to the church would be a source of weakness and scandal to the church, and a hindrance to the work generally.

His career in respect to the church when connected with J. J. Strang, was and is regarded as very corrupt—wilfully & intentionally corrupt. Also his career in respect to the Jaffa Colony was very bad indeed.

For us to pick up and place in the ministry such *proven* bad men, is, to my mind, to defile the church.

The Books teach, what wisdom likewise teaches, that no man should be suffered to rule or teach in the church, except they are *good men*.

T. W. Smith did not leave the matter alone, and as late as 1888 said of G. J. Adams:

I heard him preach, and he came as near showing the angelic visit to Joseph as he could without mentioning names, and spoke of the falling away in the former age, and the necessity of the restoration of the gospel. He heard me on the following Sunday night in the hall at the corner of 9th and Callow Hill streets, on the same subject, with Joseph Smith and the Book of Mormon added, and after the discourse shook hands heartily with me and said, "I endorse every word of that." He has a son, an able preacher in the Baptist church who preaches more truth than his co-laborers, from the reason that he learned of the gospel in its fulness from his father.

George Jones Adams died in Philadelphia, May 11, 1880, at the age of sixty-nine years and was buried in the Cedar Hill Cemetery. He had commanded thousands of column inches during his life. In death, his obituary was brief.

In 1904, Young Joseph as editor of the *Saints Herald*, responded to a need for a statement of his own and his church's beliefs. He wrote:

Being impressed the other day to write a gospel sketch, and thinking about the subject, a whisper of the Spirit said, "Examine the *Times and Seasons* which lies on your desk." Opening the book without premeditation the two following articles, written in 1843 and published from the Boston, Massachusetts, *Bee*, were presented to our attention. The first was written by Elder George J. Adams, one of the most able elders of the later period of the presidency of the Martyr and Patriarch. He was at work in the missionary field at the time of writing of the article and took up the pen in defense of the faith as he was duly entitled and accredited to do by the church, for which task he was amply able. We produce it in its entirety as being as good an article for the purpose as we feel qualified at the time to present. It is a voice from the past, the early portion of the year 1843. . . .

"What Do the Mormons Believe?

"This is a question often asked, and the following sketch from the pen of

Elder Adams, the big gun of Mormonism in these parts, will throw some light upon the subject:

"'A Short Sketch of the Rise, Progress, and Faith of the Latter Day Saints, or Mormons.

"'The Church of Jesus Christ of Latter Day Saints was first organized in the state of New York, in the year of our Lord one thousand eight hundred and thirty, on the sixth day of April. At its first organization, it consisted of six members. The first instruments of its organization were Joseph Smith, Jr., and Oliver Cowdery, who received their authority and priesthood, or apostleship, by direct revelation from God—by the voice of God—by the ministering of angels—and by the Holy Ghost. They claim no authority whatever from antiquity, they never received baptism nor ordination from any religious system which had previously existed; but being commissioned from on high, they first baptized each other, and then commenced to minister its ordinances to others. The first principle of theology as held by this church, is faith in God the Eternal Father, and in his Son Jesus Christ, who verily was crucified for the sins of the world, and who rose from the dead on the third day, and is now seated on the right hand of God as a mediator, and in the Holy Ghost who bears record of them the same to-day as yesterday, and for ever. The second principle is repentance towards God; that is, all men who believe in the Father, Son, and Holy Ghost, are required to turn away from their sins, to cease from their *evil deeds*, and to come humble before the throne of grace with a broken heart and a contrite spirit. . . .'"

Joseph Smith, in his 70's, was remembering the voice of the man who was his friend in the year the article was written. His views were conservative, soundly based on the scriptures, and stated succinctly, with polish. Toward the end of the statement of belief, George Adams reflected the faith which was to give purpose to his life and take him on his greatest and most heartbreaking venture:

We wish well to the individuals of all societies; we believe that many of them are sincere, and that they have the right to enjoy their religious opinions in peace. We wish to instruct them in those principles which we consider to be right, as far as they are willing to receive instruction, but no farther. We also believe that the scriptures of the Old and New Testament are true: and that they are designed for our profit and learning. . . . We further believe that the restoration of Israel and Judah, and the second advent of Messiah are near at hand, and that the generation now lives who will witness the fulfillment of these great events, and that the Lord has raised up the Church of Latter Day Saints, and has set the truth in order among them as a commencement of the great restoration.

Out of the dust, Joshua's voice was still speaking.

He still speaks, quietly and unnoticed, from the largest city of Israel, Tel Aviv, the Hill of Spring. He did not build it, but he dreamed it as the commercial center of a nation that was to be reestablished. He still speaks from several hundred small agricultural communities, kibbutzim and moshavim. He did not build them, but he knew that they must come and tried to establish the first of such on the fertile soil of Sharon. He speaks from plants and implements introduced. He speaks from mistakes by which others were helped to avoid mistakes. And he speaks from the families whose dimensions of life were broadened by his strengths and even by his weakness. He speaks from the contributions made by Rolla Floyd, the Leighton-Floyds, the Clarks, Abigail Alley and others, in the formative years of a new nation which they helped to bring into existence. Perhaps theirs was a minimal contribution—but beginnings are always small. Their venture has been always thought of in terms of fiasco and failure, but who can say that a pilot project from which others have learned is a failure? It was perhaps an impossible dream, a magnificent obsession, in which one man seemed to fail but who in failure helped many to succeed.

Mr. Rolla Floyd of Jerusalem, Palestine

Rolla Floyd and Docia Floyd hosting Anna Spafford (seated on right of Docia), Mrs. Whiting (seated on left of Rolla), and other members of the Jerusalem American Colony. c. 1898.

THE SEARCH FOR JOSHUA—

A Bibliographical Essay

George Jones Adams was so frequently and roundly condemned during his lifetime that his reputation as pariah has obscured his genius and the good he did or at least wanted to do. Long before I realized that my own people—church and family—were involved in the story, I assumed the standard assessment of Adams' character to be correct. Since then I have discovered it was only partly warranted. He was both saint and sinner, mixing prophetic vision and feet of clay which crumbled disastrously for all.

My search for the real G. J. Adams, interrupted for thirty years, received a sharp stimulus from Ralph Leighton-Floyd whose article in *The Bangor Daily News*, December 29-30, 1973, put things into new perspective by telling of his forebears (my own kinfolk I was to discover) who remained at Jaffa when everyone else retreated to Maine or elsewhere. My frequent visits to Israel have confirmed the impact, modest but nevertheless real, of the sturdy ones who stayed there to tough it out, and of the influence of those others who were sufficiently sold on the dream to go to Jaffa even though they returned to their native land without realizing the fulfillment of their dream.

I have returned to Maine time and again in the last six years and have had the generous support of colony families. They want the story's full facts set down for all to see and are relieved to discover the splendor of their forefathers' vision and motives. Some of them have provided original letters, photographs, and diaries or have offered clues alluding to rich resources in private collections, public libraries, and newspaper morgues.

The most thorough and reliable of the researchers who

have written for magazines or who have prepared larger manuscripts are George Walter Chamberlain, Shlomo Eidelberg, Clarence Day, and Peter Amann. Finding an Amann footnote to the prominent Mormon historian, T. Edgar Lyon, led to a major windfall, the complete file of Amann's extensive correspondence and voluminous research findings. Amann was on the track of Adams' Mormon connection, dovetailing largely with my own growing convictions about motivations for the Jaffa venture. Professor Amann had left the file behind, apparently forfeiting a book project on Adams when an opportunity in his scholarly field of nineteenth century French history became available to him in Europe.

To discover that the bulk of diplomatic correspondence from 1865 to 1868 between William H. Seward and his consular staff in the Middle East was related to the Adams' colony was a researcher's delight. The tensions between Adams, the colonists, and the consuls, especially Victor Beauboucher and Herman Loewenthal, are aired, and I suspect rationalized a little too much in favor of the establishment. Adams was not easy to deal with, and one can feel the hackles rising among the consuls and vice-consuls. (See National Archives microfilm 453.1-5).

Both the historian's office of the Church of Jesus Christ of Latter-day Saints in Salt Lake City and the History Department of the Reorganized Church of Jesus Christ of Latter Day Saints in Independence, Missouri, were cooperative with original sources and microfilm. The *Journal of the Mormon Church* which consists of diverse materials brought together in a day-to-day account of early church history was most revealing. It tipped history's hand to hitherto unsuspected close relationships between the prophet Joseph Smith and G. J. Adams during the last six months before Smith's assassination in June 1844. That Adams had been a major apologist for Mormonism from New York to Boston and in

England betwen 1840 and 1844 had largely escaped notice.

Since the Mormons and the Saints had both dismissed Adams as a charlatan, each of these major churches of the Restoration movement neglected to assess his remarkable skills as an orator and catalyst. In fact, they had buried him to cover embarrassment. Through the years he has refused to stay buried, a bit of him surfacing to capture passing and usually superficial attention. To me, the process of researching Adams has been like reaching down to dislodge a small promising malekite stone in the earth of King Solomon's mines only to discover it to be a much larger stone of tantalizing color as the earth was removed from around it. Cross sections and polishing reveal insights only dimly perceived at that first glance.

A partial itinerary of the search, with a listing of major sources uncovered, may suggest both the plodding tediousness and the thrill of discovery. I was hooked first of all by Newman Wilson. He was one of the best storytellers Maine has produced. He captured my attention with an array of yarns but kept coming back to the man whose "eyes were set so close together he could look down the neck of a Johnson's liniment bottle without squinting." The character, G. J. Adams, always painted with wry humor and caustic comment, had altered the history of the Jonesport area. Three of the colonists, all of them of the Benjamin Rogers family, were living in Jonesport in their seventies and eighties in the winter of 1942-43. They had been at Jaffa—Theresa as a twelve-year-old, Arthur a mere tad, and Alton (Kip) born on the beach to even up the colony's first loss by death. Kip would say little. Arthur was voluble and was recorded extensively in newspapers and magazines. I chose to interview Theresa Rogers Kelley whose personal recollections I felt would be most reliable. The interview was a winner, and I came away with notes, a photograph of a beautiful sixteen-year-old Theresa, and memories of a charming lady. Someday I would write it up. Then came the sharing of a grief-filled tragedy and a transfer away from Jonesport. The Jaffa Colony story would have to wait.

Thirty years slipped by, each new year more quickly than the last. Then in Maine in late 1973, fresh from Israel in that Yom Kippur war year, I read Ralph Leighton-Floyd's article, little suspecting him to be a remote relative who lived in my hometown of Independence, Missouri. It was time to get moving on the story. I contacted an old friend, Geneva Rogers Church, daughter of Arthur Rogers, the boy who had been in Jaffa. Trusting that I would deal fairly and write with love, Geneva shared information, beseeched the offspring of other families for anything that would shed light, and gave me the priceless picture of the colony on the beach at Jaffa in 1866. Its images were indistinct but unmistakably authentic. The same line of the beach can be discerned today as one looks north from Jaffa toward the hotels that line Hayarkon.

Denny Pinkus, a Jaffa antiquarian, gave first clues as to the general vicinity of the colony, the "Malikan" section, but no one in that vicinity seemed to have the slightest idea as to origins. Frustrated, I stood in the midst of the colony without even enough knowledge to make certain identification. In February 1977, on clues leading from Yair Magen at Ben Gurion University, Beer Sheva, to Aharon Chelouche at Tel Aviv University and Anina Kaplan, Director of the Museum of the History of Tel Aviv-Yafo, I found immediate identification was possible. The great-grandfather of these, Chelouche and Kaplan, was a contemporary of G. J. Adams in Jaffa. After visiting the Isaacs and Minor colony locations, Chelouche took me to the front door of the first house built in the Jaffa colony, the Leighton home. A little later he pointed me in the direction of Pinchas Ben Shahar, a Tel Aviv history buff, and among the three of these, plus the archives of the Museum, I had found a treasure trove of information. Also welling up in me was a new sense of appreciation for those early pioneers who came with strong motivation and paved the way for others who would be better equipped and wiser because of the very ineptitude of their forerunners.

Back in Maine, Lawrence Norton, the prime folklorist of Jonesport and vicinity, who dwells in the midst of his own private museum, came to my assistance with unexpected congeniality and generosity. I had found rather frequently that many offspring of the colony were inclined to shut up like a clam. Their forebears had been so frequently presumed to be witless that there was a natural feeling that anyone prowling around the corridors of Jonesport history was to be considered suspect. Lawrence Norton opened his home and his heart and led me into a wealth of letters, especially from Abigail (Norton) Alley and Anna (Norton) Watts. He also pointed to source materials I should have known—the Abigail Alley correspondence and articles printed in *Autumn Leaves*, edited in Lamoni, Iowa, by Marietta Walker (now available in the Saints Archives, Independence, Missouri).

For newspaper sources Susie Zuhorst, librarian at the Porter Memorial Library in Machias, introduced me to the *Machias Union* and made me acquainted with Lyman Holmes, a young Machias attorney and probable relative who not only led me into the archives of Washington County but has kept me in mind during his own extensive research efforts into Maine coast history.

There is serendipity involved in research, with doors opening which were previously hidden to view. Interlibrary access through Mrs. Zuhorst took me eventually to the Bangor Public Library, the State Library at Augusta, and the Library of Congress. The best copy of *The Sword of Truth and Harbinger of Peace* was located at the Library of Congress. Major newspaper coverage was to be found there, especially the *New York Times* for 1866 and 1867. Then tracking down the Abraham McKenzie diary led me to the Maine Historical Society at Portland, Maine. The next step was to Springfield, Massachusetts, to view the microfilm of the *Springfield Republican* with the vitriolic comments of its editor, Sam Bowles. Reading that the crowds of listeners had grown so large as to require Adams to use the newly constructed Rice Hall and then glancing up to see "Rice Hall" over the Library door caused goose bumps and a tingling of the spine.

Clarence Drisko of Columbia Falls, Maine, contributed vivid recollections from his own research into the families of the neighborhood as well as an opportunity to hold in hand the Rolla Floyd correspondence. The Leighton-Floyds had already furnished copies of the letters plus other memorabilia of their heroic ancestor. Arnold Davis, a wilderness dweller and educator, added folklore, while Alton Norton's widow generously shared hospitality and photographs of the shipbuilder's model of the hull of the *Nellie Chapin*, found in a rubbish barrel at Addison Point, Maine. Her husband's "Moosebec Manavelins" lent family flavor to the Gram Burns and Norton tribes which outnumbered all others on the trip to Jaffa.

I have mentioned Clarence Day from time to time. He has just died in his nineties in Orono, Maine. He has been fascinated for years by the Jaffa colony and researched it diligently. He and Lawrence Norton became fast friends. Day's unpublished manuscript, "Journey to Jaffa," is the most complete drawing together of source material that I have encountered. His narrative, based on sound scholarship, provided many insights.

Of the dozens of magazine and newspaper articles written about Adams and the colony during the last seventy-five years, the only ones really worthy of attention in my opinion are "A New England Crusade" by George Walter Chamberlain (*New England* magazine, April 1907); "The Adams Colony in Jaffa" by Shlomo Eidelberg (*Midstream, a Quarterly Jewish review*, Summer 1957) and "Prophet in

Zion, The Saga of George J. Adams," by Peter Amann (*New England Quarterly*, December, 1964.)

Eidelberg's lecture given at the Museum of the History of Tel Aviv-Yafo was published in *Hadoar*, a Hebrew magazine in the United States. His lecture is a reliable source to which I would add my own lectures at the Museum of the History of Tel Aviv-Yafo in January, 1979, and at the Mormon History Association annual meeting of 1978 at Logan, Utah. David Ben Gurion and Zev Vilnay, in their writings, contributed reliable information regarding the Adams colony.

Among the most fascinating evidences of the existence and impact of the colony are casual references by various persons to experiencing the colony as they traveled through Jaffa and then published their recollections in book form. One of the first of these was written by John Franklin Swift, *Going to Jericho or Sketches of Travel in Spain and the East* (1868). Another, written in consequence of a journey to the Holy Land, is *Rambles in Bible Lands* by Reverend Richard Newton (c. 1870), and a third reflecting the situation at the turn of the century—*Palestine Depicted and Described* by G. E. Franklin, published in 1911. Not firsthand but helpful is *The Gateway of Palestine—A History of Jaffa* by S. Talkowsky (1925). It includes aerial photographs from 1917 and 1923 identifying the location of the colony.

While the Spafford family which founded the American colony in Jerusalem came a few years after the return home of most of the American colonists at Jaffa, their close association with the Rolla Floyd family is reflected in the book *Our Jerusalem* by Bertha Spafford Vester (1950). For basic descriptions of the condition of the land at mid-nineteenth century, *The Jewish Presence in Palestine* by Samuel Katz, a pamphlet of the Israel Academic Committee on the Middle East, is very helpful. For firsthand observation of the condition of the land and of the people just prior to the arrival of the colonists from Jonesport in 1866 the

Journal of a Visit to Europe and the Levant by Herman Melville is very helpful indeed.

I found background information on the Mormon period in Nauvoo, Illinois, most adequately given in the book by Robert Bruce Flanders, *Nauvoo, Kingdom on the Mississippi.* Milo Quaife's *Kingdom of St. James* provided fascinating information concerning the Strang period of G. J. Adams' life. Primary source materials included the *Times and Seasons* and *Millenial Star* (available in the Saints Archives, Independence). The Chicago Historical Society provided the December 9, 1878, letter from W. W. Blair to Joseph Smith regarding G. J. Adams.

The most recent acquisitions to my own resources have come from Leonard Tibbetts of South Yarmouth, Massachusetts, and Dr. Ruth Kark of Hebrew University, the Department of Geography, Jerusalem. Dr. Kark has led me to correspondence in the Israel National Library located on the Hebrew University Campus and has also provided invaluable photographs. One letter from Commissioner Bidwell giving information as to the productive use of harvesting equipment left by departing colonists has been especially helpful. Other materials in that collection are adequately covered in the microfilm of consular correspondence in the national archives of the United States.

Leonard Tibbetts has a life-long research project into the ancestry and posterity of the persons listed on the passenger list of the *Nellie Chapin.* He is a descendant, and I greatly appreciated his generosity in sharing information. Various persons whose forebears were involved in the colony will find him to be a most helpful source of information.

The last comment regarding source material is one of gratitude for a person whose name I cannot share. Preferring to remain anonymous, this person made the Edwin McKenzie diary available to me to use as I deemed appropriate. The confidence thus indicated is deeply appreciated. That diary did more than anything else to open up the human side of the story lived out so long ago that its reality seemed impossible to recapture. To that person and to Geneva Church who brought us together in mutual trust and helpfulness I say thank you very much.

My personal motivations for writing the story of the Jonesport to Jaffa venture have been strong and have intensified with the search for information. Beyond this, however, the story demands telling as completely as possible and has been waiting over a hundred years for such candid and comprehensive treatment. There's more yet to be discovered. I have not exhausted the family sources, for instance. Somewhere, yet, someone will turn up letters, photographs, and—hopefully—a diary or even the *Nellie Chapin*'s manifest. These may alter details and clear up some questions which may change a surmise here and there. Was it really Levi Mace who took coal oil. . . or was it another?

I have relied strongly on a wealth of primary source materials. At the time I started to dig I had no inkling that they would be available in such quantity. Personal interviews with participants or their offspring have yielded the stuff of human interest—recollections of shame, anger, pride, personal quirks, habits, etc. Folklore abounds in Maine generally and in regard to G. J. Adams particularly. I have checked this against the primary material, keeping conjecture to a minimum while trying at the same time to flesh out the story. It is, after all, a very human parable. Primary materials have had to be primary. Too many people have been hurt by suppositions and easy conclusions, even snidery through the years. Some, no doubt, may be offended by what I have written.

Various ones have helped me to sort out, integrate, and comprehend the multitude of facts and fancies. The very competent historian, Dr. F. Mark McKiernan, has patiently encouraged me to hew to the scholarly line. His technical assistance has been invaluable and his support during the dry seasons of writing beyond price. Dr. Philmore Wass, long with the University of Connecticut at Storrs and one of the Colony Wass's posterity, gave competent counsel in the late stages by tucking in some loose strands. Dr. S. J. Soper, psychiatrist, has helped to probe areas of motivation in Adams and the colonists and has been especially helpful in exploring G. J.'s alcoholism. I must, however, accept responsibility for the ways in which I have used the insights and encouragement of these professionals. The writing, the conclusions, and the exercise of judgment in what went into the story and how it was put together is my doing.

This seems to me to be an appropriate place to comment on the debt writers owe to long-suffering and competent secretaries. Jean Reiff is such a one. She has my profound respect and sincere gratitude.

A final comment of appreciation is due to G. J. Adams himself and especially to the people who followed him, deserted him, loved him, hated him. The comment brings us full circle to our point of beginning, the search for motivations. Two major aspects of the "Restoration" process are intimately related, neither being thought of as separate from the other. One was the restoration of the primitive gospel of Christ. The other was the restoration of the Jews to the land promised to their fathers. These were linked with the imminent coming of the Messiah.

In common with his peers in Mormonism Adams interpreted the scriptures literally and could conceive of nothing more significant than to be a prime mover within this process. Those who responded to him and shared the dream and the hazards were of the same literalist mind-set. They are not to be chided but understood. And they are to be appreciated because they proved to be, after all, "the forerunners."

Epilog 2003

To the second printing of The Forerunners

By
Jean L. Holmes

A Dream in the Making

Dawn, May 2002, I awaken to the sound of soft cooing through my open bedroom window. A soft breeze stirs through the garden. Doves fly from palm tree to red tile rooftop and back again. Where am I? Ah, my first morning in the Jaffa American Colony. I am in the restored home of Rolla Floyd. The garden just below connects this house to the exotic trees and birds of an era long past. My mind fills with stories from the many years Rolla Floyd lived here and I enjoy a few peaceful moments before a busy day. I am not on vacation, no, I am here to restore another American house, and the days are never long enough.

What brought me here? That story begins over twenty years ago. My thoughts turn to my first visit to this American Colony in Jaffa, just south of Tel Aviv. It was January 1981. Rain had made mud holes of the roads and painted the wooden beams almost black in the wooden houses from Maine. Falling red clay roof tiles and loose chunks of stucco and plaster revealed American origins. Wood from the pine forests of Whitneyville still held strong in spite of evidence of rot from years of neglect and exposure to winter rains.

A half dozen houses remained in Jaffa, witness to a story from long ago. What would become of them? Now abandoned, after a few more rainy seasons, they would be food for the hungry bulldozer looking for new land for modern high-rise development. However, my years of experience in restoring New England houses from neglect to their former beauty, spoke to me. I knew that this area could once more be a lovely neighborhood. Not just one house, but a host of houses could be renewed and tell the story of the people from Maine. It was time for these diamonds to be polished.

Upon my return to Massachusetts, I thought a great deal about my first trip to Israel. My heart had found a home in this feisty land. I longed to return and find a way to share this land with others from around the world. I began to explore Jewish history and heritage and the Hebrew language. In 1982, I joined with Reed Holmes in leading ViewPax Mondiale, a non-profit organization that would help us bring many visitors to Israel on "Friendship Journeys". Our vision was to encourage world-wide peace through friendship. The brave Mainers who established the Jaffa Colony linked our histories. We would establish a "Friendship House" in Jaffa to tell their story and welcome visitors from many countries. This house would be a meeting place for all people, a symbol of international friendship.

Steps Along the Way

If the Jaffa American Colony was to be saved, a plan of action was needed and should be implemented as soon as possible. Before my next trip to Israel, I developed a detailed plan to restore the Colony. The first step would be to check zoning and protective laws. Second step would be to obtain a building and restore it as a model for the neighborhood. Third step would be to open the building as a visitor's center to tell the story and show the American heritage of modern Tel Aviv-Yafo (Jaffa). This was not to be, or at least, not easily.

Step One: zoning laws and protection. Problem one. Industrial zoning surrounded the area and a wide new road was planned to streak across the Colony. Several houses were to be demolished. In addition, there were no laws to protect historic properties. If a property was not at least 500 years old, it had no historic value and could be destroyed. Prime example was the Herzlia Gymnasium, the first Jewish high school in Israel. On its site now stands proudly the Shalom Meir Tower. This is an achievement, but sends the wrong message to those who value history.

An Israeli grassroots preservation movement was in the making. As the homes and old synagogues from the early years of Tel Aviv were threatened, the public rose up against their destruction. Eventually a program of revitalization of Jaffa and early neighborhoods of Tel Aviv was put in place. The American Colony was included in this plan. A network of walking paths would connect the historic neighborhoods. The publication of a shortened edition of The Forerunners in Hebrew translation was arranged by invitation of the director of Museum Ha'aretz, Rehavam Zeevy. The Hebrew book was called HaNachshonim, after the Biblical Nachshon, known for his bravery in jumping into the water before Moses parted it. So, too, were the Americans honored for their courage as pioneers. Radio programs and magazine articles appeared, giving the American story a home in Jaffa.

Reed's contacts from many years in Israel began to help us. Contacts within the municipality of Tel Aviv-Yafo, especially Anina Chelouche Kaplan, brought us to Mayor Shlomo Lahat's attention. The American Colony was pointed out for its historic role in developing international relations and tourism long before the state of Israel was founded. Chief engineer, Shamai Assif, was instrumental in developing an alternative route for the new road. It was diverted. United States Ambassador Bill Brown was invited to tour the Colony. Tourist guides, schools, and preservation groups began to bring their groups to the area. Plans for protective laws began to jell.

However, simultaneously we proceeded with step two, the purchase of a building. We focused on obtaining a large building at the central intersection of the Colony. Its address was Auerbach Street 10. We had identified it as one of only five remaining American-built structures. We entered the site and explored its layout. Ample space was available. The building had a basement in one part, two full floors and an attic that could be finished with several rooms. The street level would provide for display rooms furnished with period pieces and photos of the families from New England. A manager's apartment, audio-visual room, library/archives, conference room, several guest rooms, and office space for Keshet haShalom would fill the "Friendship House".

Negotiations began with the Israel Land Authority, but continued at the pace of cold molasses. Meeting followed meeting. An attorney was hired to help form an Israeli non-profit organization. The name Keshet haShalom was designated. Its hopeful meaning was "Peace Rainbow". We celebrated the potential. According to Israeli law, the sale of land and properties under Israeli ownership is restricted to Israeli citizens or entities. We had now met that criterion. Finally a price of $90,000 was agreed upon. Although it seemed high to us, we were told that it was very reasonable for Tel Aviv. One obstacle remained. The sole resident in a three-room section of the house was to be offered a new location by the Land Authority. We would need to provide "key money" as inducement for this couple to move. The sum of $75,000 was mentioned. Before we could officially object, this sum increased to $300,000! The sole resident had mysteriously become three families, all entitled to "key money" of $100,000 each. We were not amused, but we were defeated in this round. A change in official party control then took over at the helm. All our contacts were disarmed. We abandoned hope of purchasing the building at Auerbach 10. Step two was yet to be accomplished, along with step three, the Friendship House.

Nevertheless, at that time we asked to switch our application to another, smaller American building. But we did not pursue it with vigor. When it came up for public auction years later, a notice to inform us was improperly handled, and we never knew it was sold. Perhaps it was our good fortune, for that is the house I am now visiting. This Rolla Floyd house was purchased and lovingly restored by Sophie Jungreis, an Israeli sculptor. Her garden is graced with her works. Her home is furnished with antiques in the spirit of the Floyd family. Their handprints are to be felt, if not seen, on retained wooden windows, shutters and doorjambs. Their footprints wore down the floorboards around the knots.

As preparation for our future restoration project, ViewPax Mondiale had studied the buildings in detail. We had contracted with Yaacov Schaffer, an Israeli student of preservation architecture in Boston, to do architectural surveys of four of the remaining five American buildings. These drawings were shared with the director of the Maine State Preservation Commission, Earle G. Shettleworth Jr. The Maine buildings in Israel arc of special interest to Maine historians, as they are among the few very rare examples of a great pre-cut housing industry when sails ruled the waves and captains of ships from Maine traded throughout the world. This story was also presented at the International Workshop on Heritage and Conservation, Jerusalem as Laboratory in 1986. Yaacov, Reed and I did a joint presentation on the Jaffa American Colony with emphasis on the house at Auerbach 10 and our future plans. At that time we discovered that this building was actually only half wood, the half at the corner. The remainder was a stone addition built around 1892 when the new railroad connecting Jaffa to Jerusalem was opened. The owners, the German family Frank, expanded their house to accommodate tourists. The house became known as the Frank Gasthaus.

When another large American building was sold at the entrance of Auerbach Street, just off Eilat Street, Yaacov Schaffer was in charge of historic properties in Tel Aviv-Yafo, as officer of the Preservation Council. An urgent telephone call from him gave me 24 hours to find a good builder experienced in restoring19th century buildings. Fortunately Mark Haines was available. He was highly qualified and was ready and willing to experience Israel. Indeed, he worked miracles on the dilapidated house at Auerbach 4. After his initial shock at its bad condition, and a later confession that he "could have killed me" when he saw the true extent of the damage, he carefully assessed the job and took the building under his care. While replacing and restoring doors, walls, floors, sheathing boards, and windows, Mark discovered a strange pattern written on joists and studs throughout the house. When he showed it to Reed & me, we discovered that the writing was authentic and original to the house. Read upside down, it spelled out the name of "Ackley Norton". At one place it said "A.N. 2 frames".

This indicated the owner of the house. Captain Ackley Norton arrived with the group from Jonesport, Maine, on September 22, 1866. His family included two teenage daughters and three little ones. To accommodate family and guests, he had ordered a double house to be joined as one. This gave room for parties and teas. And for the first time we knew the original family of a Jaffa house.

Another discovery made during the restoration of the Capt. Ackley Norton house was that the original roof was flat. A covered stairway led to the rooftop. Remains of posts were found at the corners, and a puzzle was solved. A sketch by Andrew Tabbutt, a leader of the colony, was drawn in his later years. It showed a fence around the roof and a chimney-like structure. Now we knew what it was, the stairs, covered with a shed to keep the weather out, a fenced in roof for play and enjoying the evening sunset over the nearby sea, and a roof with a slight slope from its center allowing just enough runoff to keep from puddling. The rooftop was covered in a tarry substance called gutta-percha. Sand and shells were strewn over the surface to keep your feet clean. As it turned out, four of the remaining five houses had flat roofs such as this one.

The restored Ackley Norton house was a hit. It became home to a French restaurant, the Keren, which maintains its popularity today with notables and guests. Mark completed his work in 1990. This project was recognized for its excellence by Israel's head of preservation, Yossi Feldman, and honored by the President's Award for Preservation on May 1, 1991. Quite an accomplishment for a New Englander willing to learn a new language and work in a strange environment where tools and supplies often needed to be brought from home.

1991 - A Banner Year for the Jaffa Colony

The year 1991 was a banner year for the Jaffa American Colony. The Presidential Award in May was followed by a community celebration in Jonesport, Maine, on the weekend of August 9 and 10. This marked the 125th anniversary of the sailing of the ship the "Nellie Chapin" with the Colony people and their houses on board. Mark's careful records of his project in Jaffa were put to good use. The first event was Mark's evening slide talk showing the complete restoration of the Capt. Ackley Norton house. Another talk included remarks on the history of religion in Maine in the early and mid 1800's, where faith ran deep and the Bible was read at every table. The Feinberg Duo, a couple who taught us a little Hebrew, Yiddish, and folk dancing, topped off the evening with a joyful song show. For the first time in Jonesport, we all joined in dancing the Hora in a chain around the hall.

The next morning was sunny and bright, a perfect setting for the outdoor celebration. The location was authentic. The old wharf, which is now the U.S. Coast Guard station, had been made available to the community for our gathering. Director of the Maine State Preservation Commission Earle Shettleworth from Augusta, author Dr. Reed Holmes, and historian Dr. Yael Katzir greeted descendants and friends of the Jaffa Colony. Passages from the diary of Edwin McKenzie were read to give the flavor of life in Jaffa. Their bravery was pointed out; their actions seen as a pioneer model to be applauded. In appreciation, descendants unveiled a granite stone monument. A new composition, "Ballad of the Nellie Chapin" was performed on the site of her departure. Lobster stew, hot rolls and blueberry pie brought us together, while Yael Katzir interviewed and filmed descendants for a documentary.

As an extension to the 125th anniversary of the departure from Jonesport, we decided to ask for a special event in Tel Aviv-Yafo to mark the arrival on the beaches of Jaffa. Many of our Israeli friends helped organize events around the date of arrival, September 22. One year after the Jonesport event, we gathered on the beach where the Americans landed. Mayor Lahat, Dr. Reed Holmes, and a US embassy representative applauded the model set by the pioneering Americans. A monument was unveiled noting the American venture of 1866. A gracious lawn party was held at the Keren restaurant, hosted by the mayor. The next evening Katzir's film, "To Brave a Dream". celebrating the Jaffa Colony premiered in Tel Aviv. An audience of over four hundred historians, community and political leaders, preservationists, and friends of the Colony were present. Flowers and smiles showed the acceptance of the American story as a vital part of local history.

The Jerusalem Connection

Having abandoned hope of purchasing a building for the Friendship House in Jaffa, Reed & I turned our attention to other activities in Israel. In January 1992 I studied at Yad vaShem under their Teachers and Leaders program. Later that year I studied Hebrew at Ulpan Akiva under the direction of Shulamith Katznelson. One of my fellow students was director of a unique study program at Ratisbonne Center in Jerusalem. I was invited to join her program of Jewish studies and given a grant. For three years I participated in the study of Talmud, Midrash, Psalms, and Bible. Reed and I had married and enjoyed our apartment living in Jerusalem with our summers in Maine. Our photography leasing business grew and we traveled the length and breadth of Israel capturing new images to share in publications worldwide. It was another way of showing the beauty of the land of Israel. Even though an active peace process was ongoing, news of tension in the region had a negative effect on group travel. Our "Friendship Journeys" had become few and far between. We expanded our Friendship Journeys to include Turkey, Greece, Malta, Sicily, and Rome. At home in Jerusalem we learned of many inter-religious activities hosted in the capital, and began to participate.

What about ViewPax Mondiale, Keshet haShalom and our longed-for Maine Friendship House? In researching the Colony history, two family names stood out, the Floyds and the Clarks. Both came to Jerusalem. We began looking for their buildings. Rolla Floyd had landed in Jaffa in 1866 with vigor and carved out a career in tourism. He studied the Bible, the Land and languages. Rolla Floyd pioneered modern group travel. He met people on the shores of Jaffa and escorted them around the countryside and to all sites. His Jaffa home became a guest-house. In addition, he had a home in Jerusalem on Agrippas Street. It was near our apartment. We often walked to the place where the house once stood. We even took olive shoots from one of the trees and tried, unsuccessfully, to root it in our garden. The land is now a parking lot in the heart of Jerusalem. A small stone building still stood to the side of the lot. It was probably part of the storage buildings where, long after Rolla's tenting days were over, he rented out space to budding artists studying at the nearby Bezalel Art School. Still standing on this land is the former theatre building, called the Eden Cinema. This was a mother-son project built and run by Mary Jane and son Albert Leighton-Floyd. The Eden is now a parking garage. Even nearer to our Jerusalem home is a building that Rolla's wife, Mary Jane had built. It became the schoolhouse for her program begun in the Floyd home, where Arab and Jewish children learned to speak English together. It is now an apartment house. Two other large buildings have been built in the gardens. Exactly in the front of the garden on Bezalel Street is a small grocery store where we buy our fresh cookies and milk.

Rolla Floyd trained Mary Jane's brothers, Herbert and Frank Clark, in the tourist trade. Their careers included political appointments. At the turn of the century, Herbert Clark was U.S. Vice-Consul. His office was just inside the busy Jaffa Gate area, which was full of hotels and bazaar shops. To receive guests and provide appropriate living space, he built a mansion just outside the Old City. This building still stands, thanks to our concerted efforts at the International Workshop on Heritage and Conservation held in Jerusalem in 1986. As noted above, a grassroots movement to save historic properties had just begun in Israel in the 1980's. The Mamilla neighborhood, where the Clark house stood, was targeted for demolition. Public protests seemed to have no effect. We were worried, to say the least.

Frantic to make a significant move, we decided to approach the Mayor at the conference. Mayor Teddy Kollek, host of the Conference, greeted the entire group at the main evening gathering. As customary, at the end of his brief remarks of welcome, he briskly walked down the center aisle toward the exit. I had my weapon in my hand. It was a photograph of U.S. Vice Consul Herbert Clark and his family seated in the Marble Hall of the Clark House on Mamilla Street. "Mr. Kollek..." I began. I showed him the picture and impressed upon him that the building must be saved. It was built by Herbert Clark, an American Vice Consul, and must be preserved as part of our combined history. The Mayor agreed with me, saying that the plan was to preserve the facade. I was shocked and it showed. I insisted that saving the facade was not enough, saying that it would fall. The entire building must be saved. Mayor Kollek is a wise man. He agreed that the entire building must be saved, but instructed me to get the approval of architect Moshe Safdie as well and call him at 7 o'clock the next morning to tell him what Mr. Safdie said. I knew that Mr. Safdie was still in the room, but I did not know Mr. Kollek's telephone number. As Teddy Kollek exited, I turned immediately to the conference organizers office. "Tell me Teddy Kollek's phone number. I have to call him at 7 in the morning". I asked. It was no problem. With the number in one hand and the photograph in the other, I tracked down Mr. Safdie and told him of my discussion with the mayor. Mr. Safdie said, "OK, we will save the whole building." Did I sleep that night? Not much. But I made the call as promised at 7 am, and the Clark House still stands.

The New Millennium-2000

Our Jerusalem search had turned up three important links to the Jaffa Colony, the Floyd home site, the Bezalel school building, and the Clark House. Other sites were located as well, including the gravesite of Rolla Floyd on Emek Refa'im. We looked for a way to tell the American story in Jerusalem. We focused on the Clark House. By the year 2000 it was the only building left of the old Mamilla neighborhood. Now surrounded by partially finished cement office buildings and shopping areas, the Clark House stood proudly displaying its beautiful stone details with keyhole shaped windows. It could be readied for occupancy. We contacted the contractor's office and got permission to tour the building. We found it in good shape and took documentary photos inside and out. It is connected to the Jaffa Gate area by a short walk between the shops on the rooftop of a new underground parking garage. The location would be ideal for the American story. Perhaps a museum of the history of modern tourism? After all, the Floyd and Clark families brought people to Jaffa & Jerusalem by the hundreds.

Our interest piqued, we decided to check on progress at the Jaffa Colony. One fine day we drove to the Colony and, to our great delight and surprise, one of the major American houses had been restored. It looked charming. The balcony and doorway were inviting, but we found no one home. We asked another friend in the colony about the house and discovered that an artist had bought it and lived there now. By chance, Reed had been preparing a talk on the Floyd letters and had found another important link with a photograph. This showed a group of Jerusalem Colony friends surrounding Rolla Floyd and his first wife, Docia (died in 1898). The letter said that a photographer had been in the area and they had a group picture taken in front of his house. That is where we were standing. This house was the Floyd home. When we met the new owner, Sophie Jungreis, she knew of its origins and indeed, honored the history by appropriate furnishings. Our occasional guests are often invited in to see this home. The Jewish congregation from Bangor, Maine, and the executive officers of the NCLCI (National Christian Leaders Conference for Israel) are two of the groups who have seen the restored Floyd home in Jaffa.

The Maine Friendship House Revisited

Sophie's experience encouraged us to ask again about a building in the Colony. To our amazement, the corner house at Auerbach 10 was up for sale. But only the original American wooden half. Unknown to us, it had been sold and re-sold and was now for sale, a dilapidated derelict. When we called the number painted on the metal fence, we were told that a demolition order had been given for the house to be destroyed on February 14, 2002. By coincidence, this was also the date for the U. S. Embassy staff to tour the Colony with us. We responded to this news with a flurry of letters, faxes and phone calls, some to and from Mr. Shettleworth in Maine, some to Mayor Huldai's offices, some to the chief engineer of Tel Aviv. By fast action, and some help from our preservation friend, Yossi Feldman, and his diligent assistant, Tamar Tuchler, we entered an agreement to purchase the building personally, and prevailed on those in charge to cancel the order to demolish. On February 14 we toured the Colony and celebrated the saved house with a delightful lunch at the Keren. Our work had just begun. With the cancellation of the order to demolish came a requirement to make the building safe by stabilization. We were pleased to have the American part of the house in our hands. The space would accommodate a limited display, archives, and a director's apartment. Small can be very beautiful. We began to plan for excellence.

Within days Reed and I were leaving for the States. A quick search of possibilities turned up our friend Yaacov Schaffer, now in a prominent position with the Israel Antiquities Authority. He could organize a crew to stabilize and clean out the house, fix the roof and exterior walls, and close up the windows and doors for security and safety. We left it in his hands.

A quick trip to Israel in May and June brought me face to face with a shell of a house. Yaacov's crew had successfully cleaned out the basement, and removed all the roof tiles as well as stripped off all remaining exterior stucco. Some new beams and joists were in place, helping to keep the house in place. However, the extent of the damage was now exposed. What would be the next step? I was told to hire an architect. I interviewed five, each of whom had their strengths and limitations, but none had experience with wooden houses. I received three written proposals and chose to work with the one architect who had prior experience in the Colony, who arranged for a new survey and began measuring and drawing. Her work laid the foundation for the architectural file, which is still now in progress. An engineering firm and a building contractor were also hired. The three parties were introduced to the municipal preservation department and a second "tik kahol" (blue file) was signed. This gave permission to continue working. With a new team in place, I asked for the work to begin immediately.

Within weeks Reed and I returned to Israel. We planned to stay in Jerusalem as I had done in May, but that was not necessary. A neighbor in Jaffa just next to our project moved out and we rented her furnished apartment and moved in. What had happened since June 6? Well, we had held a sweet, new little great-grandbaby, Sylvia Louise Nicol, born in Boston almost on Reed's June 17 birthday. And we planted a big garden at the farm in Pepperell, Massachusetts. We visited family in Washington DC, Maryland, and Missouri, and then flew back to our project in Jaffa, leaving the birds to the birders, the garden to our friends and family, and our pond to the beavers.

As anyone who works on restoration projects can tell you, nothing went as planned. Our crew did a monumental job with the municipal authorities, but the Tel Aviv preservation department had no experience dealing with wooden houses. Our first real problem came when we suggested that the exterior plaster (stucco) should stay off and a new wooden siding be installed on the building. Our master builder, Yonatan, made a sample of lap siding to show the authorities. They were not pleased. Their preconceptions based on photos from later periods blinded them to the witness of the house itself. Its studs and board sheathing had rotted out wherever water entered between the stucco and the boards. Interior stone and sand mortar walls had also helped trap the moisture, so that a stone sandwich was made of the wooden walls. As our friends in the neighborhood say, "hem lo haverim". wood and plaster "are not friends". They are "like electricity and water". In other words, the neighbors and other visitors to the Colony agree, the house should have wood siding, for its own sake.

One priority in working with the Tel Aviv preservation department had been to complete the historic documentation file. We had been given a green light to stabilize the house while working on the file and doing other interior work due to the urgent need for stabilization. We also spent many hours researching appropriate U.S. Standards and Guidelines for Preservation and Rehabilitation. We contacted numerous experts for specific advice. Yet we favored reading the house itself and letting it tell its story. One day it did. As noted, the Ackley Norton house had been signed by its owner. The Rolla Floyd house had a photo linked to a letter designating ownership. We had also located a map of the Colony that showed the founding family names on most of the American houses. What was missing? Our own house at Auerbach Street 10 was designated with a question mark. No clues were given as to its original owners. That did not deter Reed. He carefully examined every piece of lumber still in place. One mid-morning, he came over to Yonatan and me and said, "Come take a look". Upside down, in the middle of our salon on the joist that used to support the roof were initials written in red carpenters pencil. What were they? M or W? Both? We finally deciphered the initials: M T W. And who would that be? A quick search down the passenger list of the Nellie Chapin revealed only one possible name: Mark T. Wentworth. This name is the ancestral connection of Reed Holmes to this Colony history. Reed went to college with his cousin, Mark Wentworth Holmes. Their mutual great grandfather was Wentworth Holmes, grandfather to Reed's father. And now we have roots in Jaffa.

This work continued for several months. Yonatan, our master carpenter, pulled us through due to his creativity, skills and knowledge gained from his own Amish carpentry experience. But a threatened stop order finally arrived at the engineer's office. By this time, our new apartment was ready for occupancy, although still unfinished. The historic file was also complete, as were the architectural drawings. Not surprisingly, historical documents said that the Americans lived in "unfinished" houses. Where most houses were stone, any wooden building would probably be considered "unfinished". Several photographs and examples show wood siding on some of the buildings. We were very hopeful that this evidence would help settle matters with the Tel Aviv authorities. Numerous calls were made. No response. Other preservationists and friends were called in to help re-establish connection with the authorities. Finally a date was set to evaluate how to proceed after the winter. The meeting was rained out!!!! While we sat at home in our unfinished apartment, Tel Aviv flooded. We sopped up a few errant drops and sipped our hot soup supper.

The end of this story is still to be written. You are invited to visit the Jaffa American Colony when you come to Israel. We plan to open this "Maine Friendship House" very soon. The book you are holding demonstrates our high hopes. A display is planned to illustrate the story of those courageous 157 Americans, including the Wentworth family, whose home we are pleased to call our own and now live in. You can be sure that at least two and a half American buildings are still standing proudly, a witness to the brave Mainers whose motto was, as it still is, "Dirigo, "we lead".

Thressa Rogers Kelley is my link to this story. After all, Reed interviewed her in my birth year, 1943. In honor of these past sixty years of research and discovery, we invite you to step into the story. Come visit the Maine Friendship House in Jaffa.

May we be a blessing.
Tu B'Shevat 5763
January 2003

Rolla Floyd house restored by Sophie Jungreis

Auerbach 10 in 1982

Mark Haines, master carpenter from New England

Captain Ackley Norton house in 1981

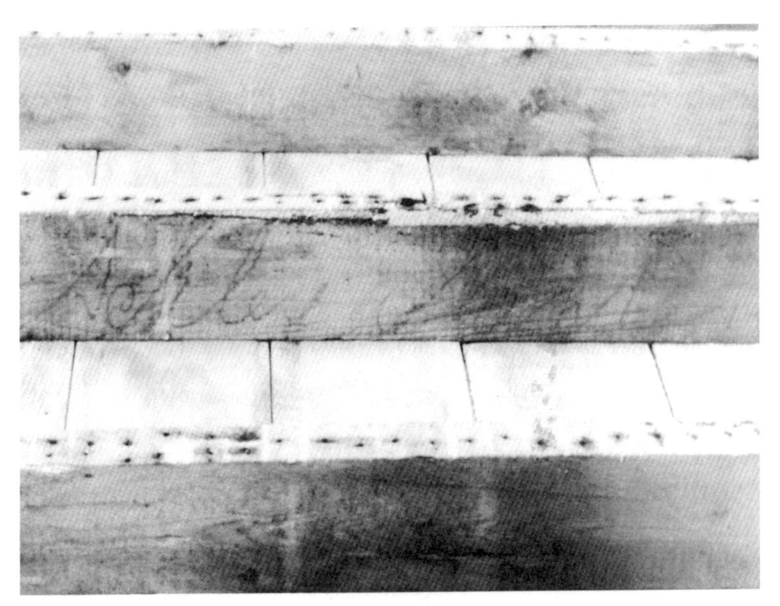

Each precut house carried the owners name

Captain Ackley Norton house renewed in 1991

Sketch by Andrew Tabbutt showing flat roof on his house

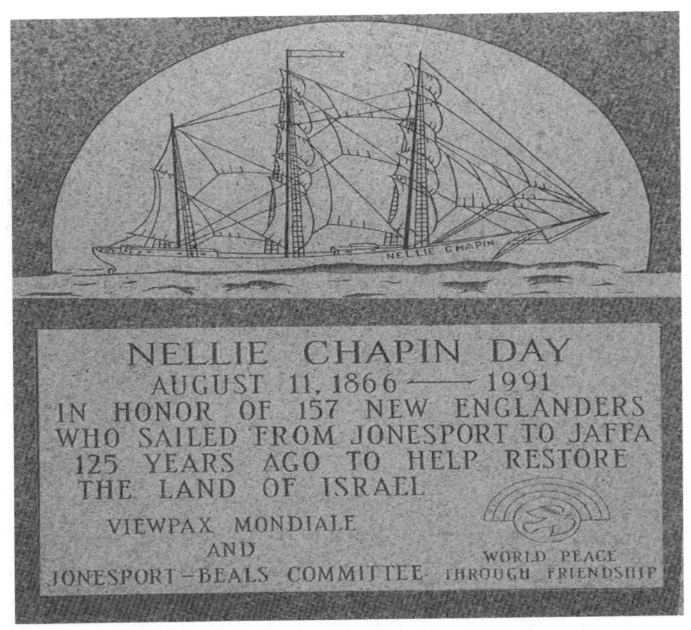

"Nellie Chapin Day" Monument at Jonesport, Maine

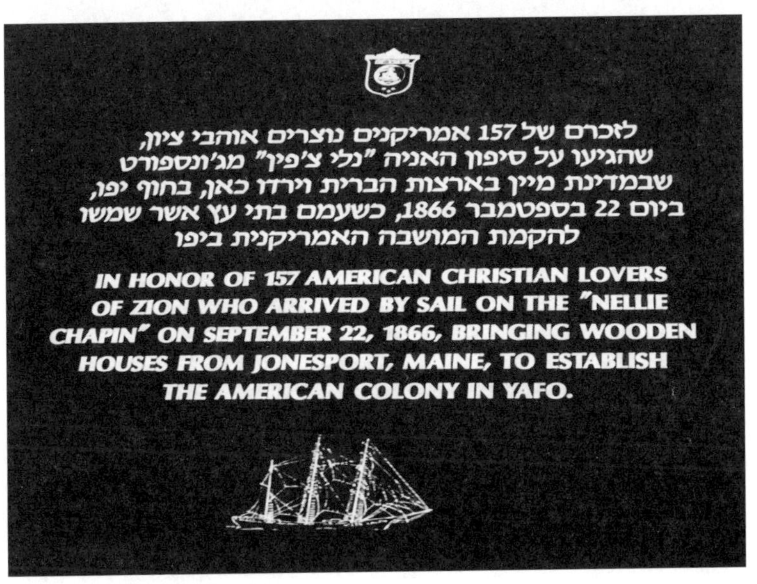

Monument at Jaffa (Yafo)

Rolla Floyd's boat, ready to take passengers from ship to shore in Jaffa

The Clark House with Reed Holmes

Jean and flag of Maine on Auerbach 10, heralding the future Maine Friendship House

Wentworth house at Auerbach 10 being restored by the Holmes couple

Theresa (Thressa) Rogers Kelley soon after her return from Jaffa

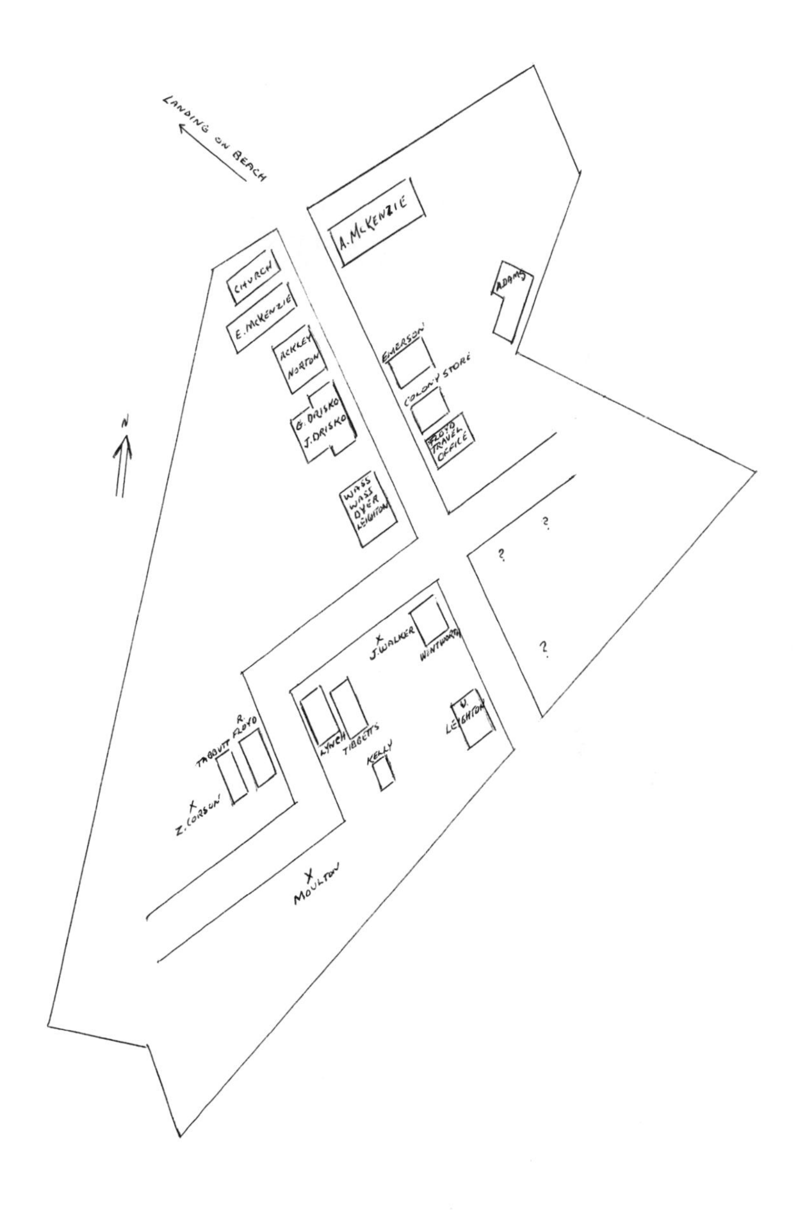

American owners identified with their house locations